DEAD END STREET

Also by Trevor Wood

The Man on the Street
One Way Street

TREVOR WOOD

DEAD END STREET

QUERCUS

First published in Great Britain in 2022 by

Quercus Editions Ltd
Carmelite House
50 Victoria Embankment
London EC4Y 0DZ

An Hachette UK company

Copyright © 2022 Trevor Wood

The moral right of Trevor Wood to be identified as the author of this work has been asserted in accordance with the Copyright, Designs and Patents Act, 1988.

All rights reserved. No part of this publication may be reproduced or transmitted in any form or by any means, electronic or mechanical, including photocopy, recording, or any information storage and retrieval system, without permission in writing from the publisher.

A CIP catalogue record for this book is available from the British Library

HB ISBN 978 1 52941 478 3
TPB ISBN 978 1 52941 477 6

This book is a work of fiction. Names, characters, businesses, organizations, places and events are either the product of the author's imagination or used fictitiously. Any resemblance to actual persons, living or dead, events or locales is entirely coincidental.

10 9 8 7 6 5 4 3 2 1

Typeset by CC Book Production
Printed and bound in Great Britain by Clays Ltd, Elcograf S.p.A.

Papers used by Quercus are from well-managed forests and other responsible sources.

For all the wonderful volunteers at
The People's Kitchen, Newcastle.
The very definition of good people.

’Cos that’s what we need now to make the place neat
Take the homeless man’s rags, no sleeping bags no
place to sleep
Because we’re far too civilised around here to see
An unkempt human being, a broken human being

Louisa Roach, from ‘Poem’ by She Drew The Gun

1

He liked sleeping with the dead.

Some people might think it weird but sod them and the horse they rode in on. There was a reason they talked about laying people to rest. Graveyards were an oasis of calm, a place to think about where it all went wrong – or, as in his case, how others had screwed it up for you and how you were going to make them pay.

But this wasn't really a graveyard. It used to be, according to the sign by the road, on the other side of the grassy expanse where he was lying down. Ballast Hills Burial Ground was the place they buried non-conformists in the eighteenth century.

These days it was practically invisible, unless you looked very closely. On the surface it was just a small park with a winding footpath around it; a footpath made up almost entirely of old gravestones. How many people had even noticed that they were literally walking over people's graves? The one beneath his feet read:

Burial place of Richard Dunn Cabinet Maker.
Henry, his son, died August the 8th 1753.
Aged 2 years.

It was one of several kids' graves scattered along the path. What a miserable fucking era to be born in. Two was no age to die. At least these days most people managed to make their three score years and ten. Most people.

He reached into his rucksack, searching for another can of lager to take the edge off but he was out of luck – could have sworn there was one left. Instead he pulled out a steak pie that someone had dropped in his lap earlier that day when he'd been sitting in a doorway on Dean Street, studying the passers-by, hiding from some but mainly hoping to see *his* face. He hadn't been hungry then and it was stone cold now, obviously, but, in his current circumstances, when life gave you a meat pie you ate the bastard and enjoyed every last morsel of it.

Voices carried to him on the wind, moving closer, he reckoned, and then footsteps, coming up the stairway from the riverside. A few moments later two men appeared by the entrance to the park, stopping as they caught sight of him sitting on the grass. Though it was getting pretty gloomy he saw them put their heads together, as if they were having some kind of quiet chat, before they started moving towards him again. He was pretty new to all this but there was a bad vibe about them, like the guys who'd chased him the other week – how he wished he'd stayed in that shed, ignored the screams, minded his own business like usual. He wolfed down the rest of the pie and started to get up. He was way too late, his reactions dulled by one beer too many. They were almost on top of him now.

A camera flashed in his face, momentarily blinding him.

'What are you doing?' he cried, turning his head away and blinking furiously as he tried to clear his vision.

'D'you think it's him?' one of the men said.

'Fucked if I know, they all look the same to me.'

'You look familiar. Have we seen you before?' The first guy again.

Maybe they really were the same ones who'd chased him? He looked back up at the taller of the two men, who he thought had asked the question.

'Well?' Lanky said. The man's voice was muffled by a scarf wound tightly around his mouth but it was obvious he was a local.

'Don't remember.'

Lanky laughed.

'Trust me, you'd remember us. Where you from?'

'Round and about.'

'You don't sound like you're from round here,' the second, shorter, man said, edging around his mate, closing off any possible escape route. If there were any doubts in his mind about the threat level, they'd disappeared. He glanced around, looking for help. There was no one in sight.

'Well?' Shorty said, adjusting his old-fashioned balaclava. Both men were clearly attempting to hide their faces. There was never a good reason for that. He needed to get out of there.

'I've been away.'

'That right? How about you go away again?'

'No problem,' he said, struggling to his feet. If he was upright he might be able to outrun them.

'Let me help you,' Lanky said, holding out his hand.

The man instinctively reached out to take it and was yanked up, too quickly to keep his balance, his rucksack slipping from his shoulder and falling to the ground. Lanky picked it up for him.

'Got your car keys in here, have you?'

'I don't drive.'

'Aye, right.'

The tall man looked across at an old Nissan parked just across the road.

'Whose is that then?'

'Not mine.'

Lanky felt around inside the rucksack then checked the pockets on the outside.

If he was going to run, now was the time, but all his worldly possessions were in that bag. He watched in horror as the contents were tipped onto the ground.

'Pack it in!' he cried, reaching out to grab the bag. His hand was slapped away which stung like a bastard in the bitter cold. 'What d'you do that for?'

'Sorry, but my mam always taught me snatching was rude. Here you go.'

Lanky held the rucksack out but pulled it away again as he tried to grab it. Then the bastard did it again.

'Try saying please,' his mate said, sniggering.

'Please,' he muttered, ashamed of himself but wanting this over before it got out of hand.

'That's better,' the tall prick said, holding out the bag.

He reached out for it again but once more it was pulled away.

'Stop messing about, you twat,' he said, immediately regretting it.

'Twat, am I?' The tall man looked over to his friend. 'If you think I'm a twat you haven't met my pal,' he added.

The kidney punch sent him to his knees where his head collided with Lanky's knee, which was no accident. Neither was the kick in the balls from behind which had him rolling around on the floor.

The kicks came fast and furious from then on, any pretence at this being anything other than a planned beating long gone, each kick punctuated by a word.

'Fuck. Off. Back. To. Manchester. Or. Whatever. Shithole. You. Crawled. From. You. Benefit. Scrounging. Freeloading. Twat.'

He covered his head with his hands but glimpsed one of the men's steel toecaps through his fingers as it thudded into his face, several teeth snapping, broken chunks falling into his mouth. Half-choking on the bits of enamel and old fillings floating about in his throat, he tried to sit up. That only made him more open and the kicks rained in again.

A rib cracked, then another. He moved his arms to his side to protect them but got another boot in the face for his troubles. Through the blood he saw one of the men – he'd lost track of which was which – slip a pair of knuckledusters onto his hand. The first punch broke his nose. The second crashed into the side of his head, making his ears ring. It would have knocked him out cold if he hadn't turned his head at the last minute.

When he looked up and saw the blade of the Stanley knife glinting in the light of the nearby lamp-post, he almost wished it had.

2

April 2015

Jimmy paced around the waiting room as if it was a prison cell. Why wouldn't anyone tell him what was going on?

A door behind the reception area opened and a woman in scrubs that he'd never seen before came through to the counter and picked up some notes.

'Any news?' he said, anxiously, as she turned to leave again.

She looked back at him, clearly not having a clue who he was or what news she might give him.

'Mr Green will come and talk to you as soon as he's finished with his patient,' she said, eventually. 'You may as well sit down instead of wearing a hole in the carpet.' And with that she left.

As usual, when someone in authority spoke to him, he did as he was told, happy to move away from the counter – the opening of the door at the back had let those sickly smells that always linger around medics into the room, a combination of illness and disinfectant that you didn't find anywhere else.

Jimmy stared at his feet. How much longer? If the worst had happened he'd . . . He shook his head. What would he do? It would leave a hole the size of a planet in his life just when he was finally getting things back on track.

He got up and walked over to the noticeboard, desperately needing a distraction. Staff vacancies, appeals for donations and information on parking charges didn't provide one so he sat down again, staring at the backroom door, willing the doc to come through it with a smile on his face. Anything else was unimaginable.

Jimmy could feel his anger building. He made a vow on his pal's life. Whoever was responsible for this would have no hiding place in this city. A dead man walking. It had been a while, but he'd tracked down psychopaths before and could do it again.

Suddenly a door at the back of the room opened and Mr Green came out. He was talking to someone behind him so Jimmy couldn't see the man's face. He sounded sombre.

'He's dead, isn't he?' Jimmy said, far louder than it needed to be in the small waiting room.

Green turned. A puzzled look on his face that quickly turned into a smile.

'Calm down, Jimmy, man. Dog's fine.'

Dog was curled up on a chair fast asleep. The last time Jimmy had seen him he'd been struggling to breathe, unable to stand by himself and had blood pouring from his mouth.

'Poor thing's exhausted,' Green said. 'I had to get him to vomit up everything he'd eaten and it's really taken it out of him. He's sturdier than he looks, mind.'

The vet glanced back at Jimmy.

'You're the one I'd be worried about, you seem stressed to hell; you'll have a heart attack if you're not careful.'

'I was just worried, that's all.'

'Aye, fair enough, I suppose, he looked pretty rough when you brought him in.'

Jimmy sat on the edge of the chair and put his hand on Dog's chest. His breathing was much more regular now, thank Christ.

'Was it rat poison, like you thought?'

'All the symptoms point to it. It's the fourth time I've seen something similar this year. Some sadistic arsehole is leaving poisoned meat lying around in the parks, apparently. One of my other customers actually brought a bag of tainted meat in with them that they found lying under a rubbish bin. I passed it on to the police but it's pretty hard to stop unless you catch them in the act.'

'Why would anyone do that?'

'Don't ask me. I'd cut their balls off if I got hold of them.'

Dog twitched under Jimmy's hand. He always had something going on in his dreams. Jimmy would bet that rabbits were involved somehow. Or seagulls. Dog hated seagulls.

'Is he gonna be OK?'

'Aye, don't worry. There might be a bit of internal bleeding but I've given him a big dose of vitamin K which will stop that in its tracks. I'll give you some more to take away with you. One tablet a day.'

Jimmy nodded, reaching into his pocket. Money was no object where Dog was concerned but he had no idea whether he'd be able to cover it. He wasn't exactly flush.

'Thanks. How much do I owe you?'

'Put your wallet away, Jimmy, your money's no good here. I don't charge the homeless to look after their pets, you know that.'

'I'm not homeless any more, Bill, I've gone up in the world.'

3

The flat was small but self-contained with a kitchen area set off from the living space and a separate bedroom. Compared to the hostel rooms Jimmy had dossed down in it was like a penthouse suite in the Malmaison. Obviously he'd never been to that particular hotel, only slept in the pavilion across the road from it, so he didn't even know if it had a penthouse suite. The point was, for the first time since his life had imploded after the Falklands War, it finally felt like he had a home.

He'd started working for the House and Home charity as a volunteer, at a hostel for kids aged 18–25, offering advice to the youngsters in their care about how to survive and stay safe, where to go for help, that kind of thing. Using his 'lived experience' they called it. Once he'd got settled, they let him do some of the admin, nothing complicated, just checking that people were signing in and out, not using, and keeping their rooms tidy, baby steps to get him back into the working routine.

Jimmy was as shocked as anyone when Caroline, the boss

there, suggested making it official. At first he'd thought she was winding him up and he actually checked the calendar to make sure it wasn't April Fool's Day but she wasn't that kind of woman. He'd had to get references, but Andy Burns had stepped up. Saving the cop's life a few years back was still paying dividends, even though Burns had more than paid him back for that in favours. He was the gift that kept on giving.

After that it was just a matter of keeping his nerve at the interview and he was in. When they told him that the job came with on-site accommodation he nearly cried.

Which was what he felt like doing now as Dog spat the vitamin K pill out for the third time.

Jimmy sighed with frustration. He didn't have time for this. The vet had given him several tips and none of them had worked. He'd hidden it in his normal food; Dog cleaned out the bowl leaving just the pill behind.

Next up he'd carefully placed it into the mutt's mouth and blown up his nose, which seemed really stupid but he'd been assured was foolproof. Not for this fool.

In desperation, he'd stuffed it into a bit of bread like a sarnie and dropped it on the floor. Again, the food was gobbled up but, somehow, the tablet had been ejected. The bloody dog would normally eat anything, including his own shit, but not a little white pill apparently.

Jimmy glanced at the small radio alarm clock by the side of his bed. He had to get going. Gadge reckoned he had something important to tell him and he didn't want to be late. The man had grown increasingly cranky recently – his heavy drinking really starting to take its toll – and he didn't want to do anything to make things worse.

'One last chance,' he muttered as Dog settled down in his basket again.

He looked into the fridge. Another bonus to his new accommodation – it had been a long time since he'd been able to store his own food. Not that he did a lot of that, he thought, seeing just a couple of tomatoes, a small bottle of milk and some crunchy peanut butter on the shelves. He went for the latter, scooping out a spoonful and pressing the pill into the middle, keeping his back to Dog just in case the crafty mutt was watching. Once he was done, he turned and knelt down by the basket, holding the spoon out towards the cautious animal. Dog sniffed at the peanut butter for a moment, then to Jimmy's relief he swallowed the lot.

Jimmy waited, watching carefully, but this time no pill appeared.

'Eu-fucking-reka,' he said, grabbing his rucksack and heading for the door. Since the poisoning Dog had been very happy to be left in the flat during the day. The rest was doing him good and one of the other staff would take him for a walk at lunchtime if Jimmy wasn't back. He remembered to switch the radio on – Dog seemed to like the sort-of company.

Jimmy left the flat and tapped on Deano's door. Another bonus of getting the job was that he'd managed to get the kid a place in the hostel. It was great to have a friendly face around and Deano had responded brilliantly. Coming up to six months later he'd stayed off the gear and generally kept his nose clean, in every sense. The kid had been trying hard to clean himself up ever since the untimely death of his brother, Ash, a couple of years earlier but had, inevitably, suffered the odd relapse along the way. This time it seemed to have stuck. He was even holding down a part-time job at the local greyhound track.

Deano bounded out of his room, raring to go. He loved their Saturday morning trips out to the city library. And today they both had an appointment: Jimmy with Gadge in a nearby pub and Deano for his adult literacy class. The kid was finally learning to read.

As they walked down the corridor another door opened and Aaron, a recent arrival at the hostel, walked out. Jimmy frowned, he had a number of questions about the baby-faced youngster that he hadn't yet got satisfactory answers for and was beginning to suspect he was younger than he was claiming – too young to be staying at the hostel even. He seemed almost incapable of looking after himself. He never used any of the equipment they provided for him, even the microwave went untouched. And he was barely able to dress himself. Jimmy glanced down. The kid's shoes were on the wrong feet.

'How you getting on?' Jimmy said.

'What's it to you?' Aaron muttered, turning to walk off.

'Just trying to do my job.'

The kid didn't bother looking back.

'Just because you get paid doesn't mean you really care

though, does it?' he shouted as he headed out the door. 'If you did, you'd try harder.'

The kid was proving a difficult nut to crack. Stubborn as fuck. Fortunately for him he wasn't the only one.

4

Gadge was pissed off. Given that he was sitting in the pub at eleven in the morning, this was unusual. Normally that would be enough to make him very happy indeed.

Fair play, he was pissed as well, but there was nothing unusual there. Being pissed off though, that was different. He just didn't like being the odd one out. He, Deano and Jimmy had always been the three street musketeers, all for one and one for all, but now, with the pair of them practically shacked up together, he was often on his own. Like now. Jimmy was already ten minutes late. The last time they'd arranged to meet he hadn't shown up at all, not even a bloody text.

And the number of times he'd come into the Pit Stop lately to find the pair of them chatting about someone he didn't know, or laughing about something he hadn't seen, didn't bear counting. It was getting to him. All members of a team had a role and if that got messed up the team fell apart. He was the story-teller, the gagsmith, the funny one. Jimmy was the worrier, always thinking someone was out to get him, and Deano was the fuck-up, the one they had to save. Now the roles were changing. Now he was the outsider, often on the back foot, playing catch-up, and he didn't like it. Not one bit. He couldn't complain though because that was even worse. Once you had a whinger in your team your days were numbered. And he wasn't going to be that guy, no siree, team-player was Gadge's double-barrelled middle name.

But being the outsider wasn't why he was pissed off – well, maybe a bit but it wasn't the whole reason. He was angry because he was sure someone had been following him. He'd spent years taking the piss out of Jimmy because of his paranoia and now he was even worse. Time after time he'd had the sensation that he was being watched but he'd never managed to catch anyone in the act. He'd whipped his head round to get a glimpse of his follower so many times that he was getting a stiff neck – but still he'd seen nothing. It had got so bad that he'd done some research on the internet and discovered the existence of Persecutory Delusion Disorder. Sufferers from it were convinced that they were being hunted or threatened and often self-medicated with alcohol to help them deal with it.

That wasn't him though. No chance.

He necked the rest of his pint and ordered another one. With a whisky chaser. If Jimmy didn't hurry up, he wouldn't be in any fit state to show him the other thing he'd discovered.

*

The Facebook page was packed with photos of homeless men and women in various locations in the city. Each one was captioned with 'Do you know them? Do they live near you? If so, contact us immediately with their name and address.'

Jimmy stared at Gadge in disbelief.

'So this knobhead reckons there are only six genuinely homeless people in the whole city?' he said.

Gadge nodded. 'It would seem so.' He yawned and leant back on his chair, nearly going arse over tit, but correcting himself at the last second. Jimmy pretended not to notice, though he could see the man's eyes were starting to close. At least he wasn't continually looking over his shoulder as he had been in the pub.

Jimmy had dragged him to the library as soon as they'd eaten to stop him drinking, though it hadn't been as hard as expected because Gadge was desperate to show him this site on the computers there. Now Jimmy could see why.

'And he thinks all the others are just pretending to live on the streets?' he asked Gadge, to try and keep the man focused. It seemed to work as he sat up straight and turned his full attention to Jimmy.

'Aye. That's why he calls his page *Fake Homeless*.'

Jimmy shook his head. They'd started talking about the recent spate of attacks on the homeless in Newcastle over breakfast – which in Gadge's case, as was always the way recently, was mainly made up of liquid. At least half a dozen people they knew had been harassed in one way or another, and one or two of them badly beaten, including Gandalf, a regular at the Pit Stop who, though being tall and having a long beard like the guy from the *Lord of the Rings* movie, had actually got his name from the card tricks that he occasionally entertained people with when they were eating their scran.

Jimmy glanced across the room to make sure Deano was still in his class. He could see him through the glass walls, sitting near the front, rapt with attention as Aoife, the librarian, spoke to the small group. The kid had managed to shelve his ADHD for the time being, though maybe he was just terrified of incurring Aoife's wrath; she was a friendly but formidable woman. Even Gadge had been known to button his lip around her.

'Am I boring you?' Gadge said, grumpily.

'No, man, just checking on Deano.' Jimmy returned his attention to the screen. 'I don't get it,' he went on. 'Why are they doing this?'

'The prick who runs the site thinks the homeless figures are part of some scam to get more funding,' Gadge explained. 'He reckons the council get funded per head which means it's in their interest to overstate the numbers. So they don't care whether people are genuinely homeless or not and don't do anything to clear them off the street.'

Gadge waved a hand at the photos, clipping the edge of the screen as he did. His perspective was clearly all over the place.

'And another thing,' he rambled on. 'He also believes that most of these people live in a comfortable semi outside the city and can't be arsed to get a proper job cos they can get two hundred quid a day begging. Apparently they just pop into town every day, drop themselves down in a doorway somewhere, stick a cap on the ground with a sign and Bob's your uncle.'

'So he thinks they're commuters?'

'Aye. Man's a nutcase.'

Jimmy laughed. That was pretty rich coming from Gadge, the man normally saw conspiracies everywhere. Aliens built Stonehenge. Tick. The Queen was descended from lizards. Obviously. A particular favourite of his was that Paul McCartney had died in 1966 and had been replaced by a lookalike who took over his role in the Beatles and had been pretending to be him ever since. So if Gadge thought this was crazy then it was really fucking crazy.

'Who did you say he was?'

'He's called Archie Simons; he owns a bar in the centre of town. Reckons the numbers of people on the streets are driving the punters away. If you saw the price he charges for beer you'd know that's bollocks. It's mostly shite lager as well. He even wants the Pit Stop closed down because he thinks that offering free food attracts the homeless to the city.'

'That's a bit arse about face, isn't it?'

'You'd think so, wouldn't you? But it's all about the bottom line for Simons.'

'He's just doing it because he thinks it's costing him money?'

'Obviously. You always have to follow the money, man. That's why they killed McCartney.'

Jimmy laughed.

'Same with Elvis, I suppose?'

Gadge gave him a sympathetic look. 'You think Elvis is dead?'

Jimmy didn't bite. He knew when he was having the piss taken out of him, he'd had plenty of practice where Gadge was concerned. The man may have been shit-faced but he still had his wits about him.

'Seriously though, you think this site is why our lads are getting beaten up in the street?' Jimmy asked.

'No doubt. This gives all the nutters a licence to kill. It's like porn for psychopaths.'

'Can't the police get it taken down? It's incitement to violence.'

'I doubt it. Divvn't you read the news, bonny lad?'

It wasn't a genuine question; he knew fine well that Jimmy didn't.

'Facebook claim to believe in free expression and it's hard to get them to take anything down. If it had existed back in the 1940s Hitler would have a page. And a hell of a lot of followers.'

Jimmy sighed. He didn't really understand what had happened to the world. One day he took his eye off the ball and the next it had changed completely; people's lives were an open book and everyone was talking to themselves in the street. Technology had a lot to answer for. Gadge poked him in the chest.

'Ya knaa what we should do, right, rather than ganning to

the polis?' Gadge continued. He often became more Geordie when he'd had a few.

'No, but I'm sure you're going to tell me.'

'You and I should pay this wanker Simons a visit and kick the living shite out of him.'

5

'What's wrong with this picture?'

Jimmy kept his gob shut. It was almost certainly a trick question. Sandy smiled and pressed on.

'You haven't cocked up in months, that's what's wrong. You're giving me nothing to work with here, Jimmy. I could take the week off and drag a work experience kid in to hold meetings with you and no one would notice. If I hadn't lost my sense of smell, I think the strong stench of rat would be coming at me from somewhere.'

She flicked through the papers in front of her, shaking her head and tutting.

Normally Jimmy would have been worried but he had been as good as gold recently so the sense of doom he usually had when his probation officer called him in was way to the back of his mind. Even so, it was best to keep things simple.

'Job's going well, flat's great. All good,' he said.

She raised an eyebrow.

'Not been arrested recently?'

He shook his head.

'Investigated any more murders?'

She knew the answer to that. It had been a couple of years since the last one – a series of bizarre drug-related deaths had come a little too close to home and he'd been sucked in. Those days were gone. He was settled now.

'Nope.'

She sighed. Truth be told, Sandy was well off her game. She was normally as sharp as a paper cut but today she was distracted. Even Dog's presence under her desk had gone unnoticed – she was usually all over him.

'I've just been keeping my head down,' he said but he was talking to himself.

Sandy was gazing out of the window. He glanced at his watch. He'd only been there for fifteen minutes but she seemed to have run out of questions. He wondered if she was ill but pushed the thought aside. The woman was indestructible.

'Are we done then?' he asked.

She glared at him. That was more like it.

'I say when we're done. Just because you've been a good boy lately don't get cocky.'

'I wasn't—'

Her sudden loud coughing fit was enough to make Dog shoot out from under her desk.

'Water,' she croaked, pointing at a jug and some glasses on a table in the corner of the room. He jumped up and filled a glass for her.

'Ta,' she said as he handed it over.

'You OK?'

'Do I look OK?' She dared him to answer that. He kept his gob shut this time.

'Not quite that brave, eh?'

He smiled. She was absolutely right, he wasn't. Another couple of coughs. She took a second slurp of water.

'I'm fine, just got this horrible dry throat, been hanging around for weeks, can't seem to shift it.'

She put the water down, picked up his file and dived straight back in.

'The hostel manager's given you a very good reference. Reliable and trustworthy, it says here. Get you to write it yourself, did she?'

Jimmy didn't say anything. It was one of her traps.

'Scrub that. There aren't any spelling mistakes.'

He could sense her slowly moving through the gears.

'Maybe all my hard work on you is finally paying off. You could be my poster boy when they put me up for social worker of the year.'

'Is that a thing?'

She raised her other eyebrow, returning to form.

'Here's the thing though,' she said, pausing for impact. 'I've been reading about these attacks on your homeless compadres.'

Jimmy closed his eyes, cursed her psychic abilities. He tried to push Gadge's plan to pay Archie Simons a visit to the back of his mind, where she couldn't possibly read it. He'd put the man off but, a bit like Sandy, his friend didn't usually take no for an answer.

'And I'm thinking it's exactly the kind of thing you get yourself caught up in. Fits right into your saviour complex,' she continued.

He nearly snapped. His ex-girlfriend, Julie, had once accused him of thinking he had to save everyone, but it just wasn't true. He just felt compelled to support his friends. Or at least he used to. Maybe these days he had too much to lose. He opened his eyes again, looked Sandy straight in the face and took a deep breath.

'I'm not getting involved in that,' he said. 'I promise.'

His friend was on his own.

6

Gadge was in serious bother.

His plans to 'have a word' with Archie Simons had got off to a terrible start earlier on that evening. He'd intended to find a quiet corner in Simons' shitty bar and nurse a beer or six until kicking out time when he'd corner the man himself and put him in the picture. It was a quiet Tuesday night so he didn't think there'd be many punters around to get in his way.

It had been a good plan right up until the time the bouncer stopped him going in. He'd tried to turn the old charm on but he'd already had a few pints earlier that day so he wasn't exactly on top form. The man had been polite but firm – despite which Gadge had been raging; he really needed to work on his anger management.

He'd grabbed a few tinnies and a small bottle of own-brand vodka from a nearby offy and found a convenient bench just across the road from the bar where he could see everyone coming and going.

Then, what must have been hours later given how dark

it had become, he was woken up by a flash and some loud laughter in his ear.

It had taken him a moment to regain his vision but when he did he realised there was a tall man, wearing a scarf around his face, sitting next to him on the bench and a second, shorter, man, wearing a balaclava, standing right in front of him holding a camera.

'Say cheese,' the man said, and took another photo.

Gadge started to get up but his arm was pinned down by the tall man.

The smaller man grabbed Gadge's other arm and they pulled him up and marched him into a nearby alley. That was the last thing he remembered. Until now.

The light was shining in his face again but it was different this time, a harsher beam and more prolonged. He tried to put his hand up to shield his eyes but a fierce pain shot through his shoulder so he just closed his eyes instead. His whole body ached and he tried to remember what had happened after he'd been dragged into the alley. He put his other hand to his face and flinched – it was swollen and sore as hell.

'Keep your hands by your side,' a woman's voice said.

Gadge felt the light move away from his face and opened his eyes again. Two young policewomen were standing in front of him. The one holding the torch moved the light down to his body. He followed its beam. He was covered in blood.

Jimmy woke up to a buzzing sound.

He rolled over and saw his cheap mobile rattling on the

bedside cabinet. The travel alarm clock next to it said it was 5 a.m. He sat up and grabbed the phone. A call at this kind of time normally meant one of the kids was in bother. Or they'd lost their keys. He hoped it was the latter.

Jimmy glanced at the screen. It was Andy Burns. That couldn't be good. He accepted the call.

'D'you know what time it is?' he said.

'Shut up and listen,' Burns said. 'Your mate's been arrested.'

'Deano?' Jimmy said. 'What's the stupid sod done now?'

'No, not him, the other one . . . Gadge.'

That threw Jimmy for a moment. Gadge could be a gobshite when he was in his cups but he'd only once been arrested for being drunk and disorderly and even then they just kicked him out in the morning when he'd sobered up. He must have been really hammered this time if Andy Burns thought he needed a heads up. Jimmy sighed and rolled his legs out of bed, keeping his phone to his ear.

'I'll be down there in twenty mins,' he said, yawning.

'There's no point in that, Jimmy, he's not going anywhere soon.'

'What d'you ring me for then? I thought you wanted me to pick him up.'

'No. But you might want to get him a decent solicitor. The duty guy's shite.'

'A solicitor! What does he need a solicitor for?'

'He's being held on suspicion of murder.'

7

An early morning east coast train whistled through Central Station as Jimmy waited for Burns to show his face.

He was sitting in front of a small coffee shop on the platform, nursing a cup of tea, wondering what the hell had happened last night.

Gadge was being held in custody in Newcastle's brand spanking new police HQ, which was tucked just behind the train station, both near enough for the two men to meet up and far enough away to make sure that prying eyes didn't see them.

Jimmy knew that Burns was taking yet another risk. The cop clearly couldn't be seen briefing the best mate of a murder suspect before all the evidence had been gathered, but Jimmy also knew he would help him – pulling someone out of a burning building built up a lot of credit.

He'd just about finished his tea when Burns came through the open turnstiles, checking around to make sure he wasn't being watched. He sat down on a separate table just in case. Jimmy knew the drill by now and didn't look at him once.

'What's going on, Andy?' Jimmy said. 'You know Gadge wouldn't hurt a fly.'

'No, I don't. And neither do you. I know what you guys are like – you barely tell each other anything about your past. I remember how hard it was to get any details of young Deano from you last time I got dragged into one of your "investigations".'

He had a point. There was an unspoken code between him and his friends that there was no past, only the future. It was clear they'd all screwed things up big time so it was best to be judged on what happened from then on.

'Fair enough,' Jimmy said. 'I don't even know Gadge's real name,'

'It's Keith Kane. I checked the arrest sheet after they'd put him in the cells.'

Jimmy laughed. He couldn't imagine anyone who seemed less like a 'Keith'.

Burns glanced at his watch. 'Look, I haven't got long. Did you get him a proper brief?'

Jimmy shook his head.

'Not yet.'

'I can recommend someone if you like.'

'That would be great. I've already put a call in to Bob Pearson, to see if he can help. He'll know the local scene and I'm sure he'll front up some dosh if we need it for an investigator or something.'

Pearson was another man in Jimmy's debt. The former councillor's daughter had nearly died after taking some dodgy spice and Jimmy had been instrumental in bringing her dealers to justice.

'OK, scores on the doors, and you didn't hear this from me, right?'

Jimmy nodded.

'Your man was found unconscious, by two policewomen, in an alley down the side of Archie's, the bar near the Bigg Market. He was covered in blood and had clearly been on the wrong end of a fight.'

Jimmy nearly said something about the bar – it was the one owned by Archie Simons, the guy who'd been behind the Facebook page Gadge had shown him – but, until he knew more details, he didn't want to provide Burns with a motive for whatever his friend had done. Burns often accused him of operating a 'one-way street' policy where information was concerned and he was right. Better safe than sorry.

'So why is he the one getting arrested?'

Burns held up his hand.

'At first they thought he was the victim. They even phoned it in as an assault. Then they found the body a few yards further down the alley. A tall male, approximately six-five, mid-thirties, they think. Ring any bells?'

Jimmy shook his head, still trying to take it all in. Burns carried on.

'Name as yet unknown – he had no ID on him at all, which is unusual in itself. Someone had thrown a large sleeping bag over him to hide the body from sight. Looks like it was Gadge's sleeping bag.'

'Hardly fucking conclusive, is it?'

'Not on its own, no. But from the man's head wounds it was clear he'd been badly beaten with a blunt instrument.'

'Jesus. But what's that got to do with Gadge?'

'He was covered in blood, too much for the injuries he'd sustained, apparently.'

'Is that it?'

'No.' Burns took a deep breath. Bad news was incoming. 'Gadge had a baseball bat in his hand.'

8

Jimmy didn't like lawyers. He'd only met a couple but both times he'd ended up with a prison sentence so he wasn't much looking forward to meeting a third.

On top of that, the waiting room felt like a doctor's and he didn't have very good memories of those either so it was no wonder he was nervous. The receptionist had told him that the brief was running late. The woman seemed nice at first but she kept glancing over at him, as if she expected him to nick the second-hand car magazines the moment she stopped paying attention.

Finally, a door in the corner of the room opened and a young woman's head peered round it.

'Mr Mullen?' she asked. Given that he was the only one waiting it was a strange question but he nodded and got to his feet.

'Come through,' she said, disappearing back into the room.

Jimmy followed her and was surprised when she moved behind the desk and sat down.

'I was expecting to see Mr Gascoigne,' he said.

'I prefer Ms,' the woman said, half-smiling.

'Oh,' he said, kicking himself. 'I was expecting someone . . . older.'

'I'll take that as a compliment. I'm old enough.'

She was sharp. It was obvious that he'd been expecting a man – Andy Burns had just texted him the name 'Charlie Gascoigne' and a phone number and Bob Pearson had concurred with his suggestion – but actually this would work much better. Gadge could be surly but he liked to turn on the charm with women so he'd probably be much more cooperative.

The inner office was neat and tidy but not intimidating. There were no framed certificates on the wall, no photos of famous clients and no bookshelves full of learned, lawyerly publications that he'd bet no one ever read. Instead there were some kids' drawings Blu-Tacked to the wall and an exercise bike in the corner.

Seeing him glance at the bike, the solicitor laughed.

'I don't get much time to stay fit, what with work and two kids at home,' she said. 'So I quite often sit on there, pedalling away, when I'm reading case details, kill two birds with one stone, like.'

Jimmy nearly made a shit 'chain of evidence' crack but that was more Gadge's thing so instead he just nodded.

She stood up, leant over her desk and held out her hand. 'Anyway, nice to meet you, I'm Charlie.'

'Jimmy,' he said, gently shaking hands.

'Mr Kane speaks very highly of you.'

For a moment he was lost but then remembered it was Gadge's surname.

'You've already seen him then?'

'Yes, we had a chat this morning. He's doing OK, all things considered.'

'Did he tell you what happened?'

'He has no real idea. He says two men dragged him into an alley and that's it. No memory of anything else.'

'Not even the bat?'

'He claims never to have seen it before. Trouble is, it looks very much like the murder weapon and I'm sure his prints are going to be all over it. I'd be amazed if the dead man's hair isn't on it too. And then there's the blood evidence. Your friend's clothes were covered in it.'

'But wasn't he injured too?'

'Aye, but nowhere near enough for the amount of blood. They haven't got the tests back yet, but the police are very confident that some of it will have come from the victim.'

'Shit.'

'Indeed. It's not looking great for him.'

'And do they know who the victim is . . . was . . . yet?'

'No. Or at least if they do they haven't told me. But I'm sure it's only a matter of time and when they do I want to know everything I can about him. My working theory is that he's one of the two men your friend remembers grabbing him.'

'Nothing on the other man either?'

The lawyer shook her head.

'So what do you want from me?'

She sighed.

'Full disclosure: this is a very weird situation which I'm not entirely comfortable with. But my boss and Bob Pearson are old friends and to a large extent I've been railroaded into it.'

Jimmy knew all about weird situations, people were surprisingly good at adapting to them, even lawyers, so he just nodded and waited.

'I told Mr Kane that I wanted to hire an investigator to help look into his background and that of the two men he saw but he told me there was no need, that he already knew the best one in town.'

She looked at him questioningly but again he waited. It was pretty clear where this was going.

'That being you, apparently. I checked with Mr Pearson and he supported the idea, very enthusiastically, in fact.'

Jimmy smiled. Bob Pearson had once tried to persuade him to set up as a private investigator and though he'd considered it, he'd eventually declined. It was too much of a risk in his situation.

'I'm not sure that this is a good idea,' he said.

'I could probably persuade him to pay expenses if that's what's worrying you?'

'It's not about the money.'

'Then what?'

Jimmy sighed. It wasn't something he liked to talk about but there wasn't much choice.

'I'm on a life licence. It's a long story but I ended up in prison and while I was there, I killed a man in a fight. As

I'm sure you know, if I commit any kind of crime or even go anywhere near something dodgy, I can be returned to prison immediately. And you know what they say about making omelettes; well investigating's the same, only, instead of eggs, it's laws that tend to get a bit broken.'

Charlie Gascoigne's upbeat front faded as he gave her more details and she scribbled notes on a pad in front of her. She was obviously weighing up the risks, both for him and for her reputation.

'This puts a different complexion on things. Can you give me a moment?' she said. 'I need to get a second opinion.'

Jimmy sighed. It looked like he was going to have to let Gadge down again. He already blamed himself for what had happened. If he'd just agreed to do what his friend wanted, and pay Mr Simons a visit, then Gadge wouldn't have got himself in such a mess. He was too busy watching his own back to help his mate. And now Gadge needed him once more and he was hesitating again. What kind of friend was he? But Sandy would kill him. And so would Julie.

At one time he'd thought he and Julie might make it work long-term but they'd never got their relationship back to the same level after he let her down big time, putting her son in danger. She'd moved on and found someone a bit more reliable but they'd managed to stay friends and he knew she'd read him the riot act if he got involved in something else. Maybe he did have that Messiah complex after all.

He was solidly wedged between a rock and a hard place; whatever he did someone would get hurt.

Charlie Gascoigne came back into the office. She looked a little happier, though still tentative as she sat back down.

'I appreciate that it's a risk for you, as it is for us,' she said. 'But Bob Pearson has vouched for you, and my boss has given it the OK, with certain provisos, so if you're up for it then so are we.'

'What are the provisos?'

'That everything you do is strictly legal. If you get caught breaking the law you're on your own.'

Jimmy sighed. He knew how that was likely to end up.

'I understand if you don't want to take the risk. We do have other investigators we can call upon.'

Other investigators who wouldn't care half as much what happened to his friend.

'What do you need me to do?' he said.

9

Gadge looked like shit. His skin was grey, aside from the yellowing bruises running along his jaw, and it sagged away from his skull, forming pouches under his cheeks. His hair was lank and his beard was a bag of shite. And he looked about a stone lighter than the last time Jimmy had seen him – which was less than a week ago. Plus he hadn't once looked up in the last two minutes.

Jimmy was staring at him through a glass panel in the door of the interview room, waiting for permission to go in. The two guards he'd spoken to so far clearly weren't going to make life easy for him but he knew that they'd have to let him in to speak to his friend eventually.

It had taken a couple of days for Charlie Gascoigne to make arrangements so that Jimmy could be her official investigator. The police had resisted at first, citing Jimmy's criminal record, but she'd played hardball, pointing out that they had the apparatus of the state behind them whereas she was just one person and a mere woman at that. He knew that this approach had stuck in her throat but she knew how to play the game – no judge would look kindly on their refusal to allow an investigator to talk to her client.

By the time they folded, Gadge had been charged with murder and placed on remand in Durham prison. Despite being warned by Charlie that this was likely, Jimmy had still been shocked by the speed at which things were moving. The police had fast-tracked the tests. The blood Gadge had been covered in came from the dead man, as did some of the hairs on the bat, which was more than enough for the CPS.

Jimmy finally got the nod from his escort and entered the room. Gadge still didn't look up. As he got closer Jimmy could see a bald patch on the top of his friend's head that he was sure hadn't been there before. He'd bet that Gadge had been pulling it out from sheer anxiety. Been there, done that. It was one of the reasons Jimmy had always had his head shaved when he'd been locked up – less hair to pull out.

Gadge's left hand was tapping out a rhythm on the desk but as Jimmy approached he realised that it wasn't intentional, the man had the shakes, and he had them bad. Gadge looked up and saw Jimmy staring at his hand. He pulled it under the table, his arm trembling from the effort of keeping it still.

Close up, Gadge looked even worse. Bloodshot eyes and one broken tooth were the most obvious things, but there was also a look in those eyes that Jimmy had seen on prisoners before. Despair.

'You agreed to help then?' Gadge muttered, looking away again.

'Of course.'

'I wasn't sure you would. I thought probably but I wasn't certain.'

A shudder of shame rippled through Jimmy. He was supposed to be the man's best friend yet he'd doubted that Jimmy would come through for him when he was in real trouble.

'How you holding up?' he asked.

Gadge finally looked at him properly.

'How d'you fucking think?'

Jimmy nodded. He remembered being on remand, knowing that you were almost certainly going to get convicted. And it was worse for Gadge. With his age and heart problems he must know that once he was in prison, he was unlikely to leave on his feet.

'It gets easier.'

'Maybe for you. But you weren't a raging alky. I can't stop shaking. I don't suppose . . .' He glanced over to the door and back at Jimmy, probably looking for a bag or a bulge in his pocket.

'I can't bring alcohol in. They practically strip-searched me.'

Jimmy knew from experience that it was much easier to be a druggie inside than an alky. The former could nearly always get their hands on something to help them get through the day. It was pretty easy to smuggle in pills or powder. Most prisons were dry though; he'd known some inmates who tried to brew their own, but the smell nearly always gave the game away.

Gadge hung his head, whether through disappointment or shame, Jimmy wasn't quite sure.

'We'll get you out of here.'

A small smile passed quickly over Gadge's lips and he looked back up again.

'I admire the positivity, Jimmy, man, but we both know it's a long shot. I know I didn't do it but even I'd find me guilty on the evidence they've got.'

'What do you think happened?'

'Like I told the lovely Ms Gascoigne, I haven't a clue. I was shit-faced. I remember them waking me up and taking a picture but after that nothing.'

'Taking a picture? I didn't know about that.'

'Aye, they had a camera. The flash woke me up.' Gadge gave him a knowing look.

'You think they were something to do with that Facebook site you showed me, don't you?' Jimmy said.

'Aye, given I was outside Simons' bar at the time I think it's a racing certainty.'

'Did you tell the police about that?'

'Course, they said they'd check it out but I could tell they weren't that convinced it was relevant. They seem pretty sure they've already got their man.'

'Charlie Gascoigne thinks the dead guy was one of the two men who dragged you into the alley.'

'Makes sense.'

'Which means we need to find the second man,' Jimmy said.

'Fuck me, you should be an investigator,' Gadge said, his sarcasm maxing out.

'Don't push your luck, *Keith*.'

Gadge laughed for the first time.

'You can pack that in for starters.'

'Fine, then don't take the piss. I need to talk to you about any enemies you might have.'

'Enemies? Are you the conspiracy nut now? I always thought that was my job.'

'Look, I know that neither of us have been an open book, let sleeping dogs lie and all that, but shit's getting real now and I need you to be honest with me. Maybe you were just a convenient scapegoat – wrong place, wrong time. But it could also be deliberate, someone out to get you.'

Gadge laughed bitterly.

'Everyone loves me, you know that.'

'I need to know everything, Gadge. What about family problems? You've told me about your ex-wives often enough. Any skeletons in the closet there? Problems with divorce settlements, child maintenance? Shit, I don't even know if you've got any kids.'

Gadge's body language changed considerably. Jimmy had never seen him so rattled. He seemed to fold in on himself, as if making as small a target as possible.

'Gadge?'

His friend looked up; his eyes filled with tears.

'I don't have any kids,' he said

10

1984

Gadge walks up the drive carrying a huge bunch of roses, whistling happily. As good days go this has been a belter.

When he'd pitched his latest idea for a digital music player to a group of investors the week before it hadn't gone brilliantly. He'd knocked over a glass of water, his slides got jammed in the machine and the stress had made him sweat so much that he could actually feel the dark patches under his armpits growing larger by the second.

He'd known it was a long shot – the technology wasn't really out there to support it at the moment – band widths were way too small to transmit what he needed – but he'd confidently asserted that this would change and that by the time his player was ready the rest of the world would have caught up.

Until today it looked like he'd failed to persuade them but the offer had come in on the fax machine that morning. Fifteen grand's worth of investment. Enough to hire a couple more bodies and keep progressing the development work. Inspector Gadget strikes again – he didn't much like his nickname when one of his schoolmates first coined it but now he revels in it. Lucy's just about the only one who still calls him Keith.

He hasn't told her about the investment yet, wants to surprise her, knows fine well she's been worried about how tight money has been, but now the sky's the limit for the Kane family. Onwards and upwards.

He opens the front door and hears absolutely nothing. That's weird. Lucy is a noise fiend. She hates silence, always has to fill it. When he's around it's with conversation, she could talk for England, but when she's in the house on her own she turns to the radio. You name it, she listens to it; lately she's even started enjoying *The Archers*, despite the fact that she's barely set foot in the country in her life and is scared of cows.

Today is different though, it's very quiet. Puzzled, he slips his shoes off – she's also a real neatness freak, nothing is allowed to mess up her white carpets – and calls out.

'Lucy?'

No response.

Gadge heads towards the kitchen. Normally, at this time of day, she's busy conjuring up some bait from one of the latest celebrity chefs. She loves that Keith Floyd guy, the only man she knows that makes Gadge's drinking habits look mild. He knows there's something up as he edges closer to the door, no tell-tale banging of pots, no smells at all. Complete silence.

He wonders about leaving the flowers on the kitchen counter while he looks for Lucy but still wants to surprise her with them, to catch that smile on her face, the one that had captured his heart the first time he'd met her, when she served him a pint of foaming ale in the Ship Inn, under Byker Bridge. How he'd persuaded her to first go out on a date, and then to marry him, was still a mystery to him – his mad inventor persona had always put women off before her.

He's beginning to get a little worried. Maybe she's had a migraine, it happened once when they'd first moved in together which he'd assumed was just from the excitement of creating their first home. He realises that he doesn't know much about the causes and makes a mental note to find out; he likes to know how stuff works, even people.

Gadge moves towards the stairs and, just as he hits the bottom step, he finally hears something, a quiet moan coming from the bedroom. That's odd. In the two years they've been together, aside from that one migraine, he's never known her to be ill at all. She keeps herself super-fit. The only thing she likes more than noise is exercise – and the combination of the two is her dream ticket. She'd jump around to that Green Goddess on the telly every day of the week if she could.

As he climbs the stairs the quiet, but insistent moaning becomes clearer. What is going on? It can't be what it sounds like. She would never do that to him.

Gadge pushes gently on the bedroom door, nudging it open slowly. He drops the flowers on the floor in shock.

Lucy is lying on her back on the bed in a pool of blood,

quietly sobbing. She doesn't even seem to notice he's there. He runs over to her, grabs her hand. She opens her eyes and the sobbing grows louder.

'I'm sorry,' she mumbles. 'I'm sorry.'

'Sorry for what?' he says, unable to take his eyes off the growing red patch underneath her.

'I've lost our baby,' she says.

11

Dog didn't have any problems wandering around Heaton Park, despite what happened the last time he'd been there. Maybe the mutt's memory was going along with everything else. Just to be sure, Jimmy was keeping him on a tight rein.

'He seems to have recovered pretty well from that poison crap,' Kate said.

Jimmy's daughter had been ready to kill someone when she heard about Dog's poisoning. She'd threatened to send the entire Anti-Social Behaviour Unit into the park every day until the culprit was found. Fortunately, Jimmy had managed to talk her down before she actually told the staff. She'd only been the boss there for a couple of months and something like that would surely cause ructions – especially as she was still one of the youngest people on the team.

'He's indestructible, man,' Jimmy said. 'Take more than a bit of rat poison to take Dog out.'

'Even so,' she said, giving a young kid who walked past them with a carrier bag in hand an evil glance. The kid saw her face and sped up considerably to get away.

Dog was pulling Jimmy towards an overflowing rubbish bin, but he was still quite weak from his treatment so it was easy enough to keep him away.

They headed towards one of the benches that lined the old bowling green – it had been abandoned to the weeds and dog walkers a few years before, another victim of the vindictive austerity measures that had reduced the country to a shit-tip.

'What are you going to do about Gadge?' Kate asked, as she slumped on to a bench.

'I'm going to check out Archie's bar first, see if anyone saw something. Maybe someone there will know who these two men are.'

'That place is a den of snakes. It's where some of our most problematic residents hang out. They reckon half the drugs in the city pass through there at some stage. You be careful.'

'Careful's my middle name.'

'You don't have a middle name, do you?'

'Actually, it's Ian.'

'No wonder you keep it quiet. Has Gadge got someone else to visit him? Any children?'

Jimmy shook his head.

'His first wife had a miscarriage,' Jimmy said. 'He only told me on my last visit. The kid would have been about the same age as you.'

'It's more common than you think,' Kate said.

'Is it?'

'Sadly, yes, at least two of my friends have had one.'

It was always a shock to Jimmy that he was old enough

to be a grandad. He still imagined he was in his thirties rather than his fifties even though the mirror told him a different story.

'Any other plans – other than trawling the drug dens?'

He hesitated, knowing she'd like this one even less than the first but he tried very hard to be honest with Kate, so he took a breath and put it out there.

'I'm thinking about going back on to the streets, to get a clearer idea of what's actually happening out there.'

'You're going to use yourself as bait!'

'Well not exactly bait, but—'

'Promise me you won't do that, Dad.' She looked genuinely scared this time. 'People are getting hospitalised out there. And you're no fighter.'

'I used to box.'

'Before I was born.'

She grabbed his hands.

'Promise me, please, I need you in one piece. Find another way. For me.'

How could he resist?

'I promise.'

She nodded and let go of his hands. They settled into a companionable silence broken only by Dog's snores as he rested under the bench. Jimmy guessed they were probably both thinking about how little they really knew about each other. He popped a piece of chewing gum into his mouth and offered one to Kate but she pulled a face.

Kate had done most of her growing up while he'd been in prison so he still had to pinch himself sometimes that his daughter was a grown woman now. He wished he could have taken some of the credit for it but it was all down to his ex-wife, Bev, and Graham, her new bloke – though 'new' was a bit of a stretch as they'd been together for about twenty years.

There was a sudden noise behind them. Jimmy turned to see a young kid trying to climb the huge oak tree that overshadowed the bench. A young woman, his mum presumably, was standing under the lowest branch, shaking her head. She saw Jimmy watching.

'Bloody kids, eh! Send you to an early grave with the worrying.'

'Tell me about it,' he said, earning a slap from Kate. He rubbed his arm as if he hadn't enjoyed the contact.

'I'll not tell you my news if you're going to be like that,' she said. 'Well, two bits of news really.'

'If you're doing good news/bad news, I'll take the good first.'

'Actually, they're both good, sort of.'

'Go on then, hit me.'

'I'm getting married.'

Jimmy spat out his gum, almost hitting a passing cyclist.

'To Carrie?'

Kate play-punched him on the arm.

'Of course. Who else would it be?'

Jimmy smiled. In a way he'd been responsible for the pair of them getting together. Carrie's dad had disappeared and Jimmy had, somewhat reluctantly at first, helped her find out what had happened to him. She, in return, had put him back in touch with Kate and the relationship had started then.

'Congratulations,' he said, reaching over and enveloping his daughter in a hug. 'I'm thrilled for you. She's a cracking lass.'

'She is that.'

'Who proposed?'

'She did.'

'On bended knee?'

'Nah, we were in bed.'

Kate took great joy in embarrassing him and he knew this was another attempt so he pretended not to have noticed.

'Straight after we'd had sex,' she added, forcing him to put his hands over his ears.

'Too much information,' he growled, as she convulsed with laughter next to him.

A scream ripped through the air behind them. They both turned to see the young mum, pulling her sobbing son into her arms.

'Oh, Christ, that's disgusting,' she said, nodding towards something behind the tree.

Jimmy and Kate leapt off the bench to take a look. There was a dead rabbit lying on the ground a few feet away from the base of the tree. It had clearly been foaming at the mouth before it died.

It looked like the mystery poisoner had struck again but there was no sign of any dodgy-looking food lying around this time. It could be anywhere, he supposed. He grabbed a pile of nearby leaves to cover up the body.

'We should get Dog away just in case,' he said, moving back towards the bench, to untie his lead.

'I'd better be heading back to work,' Kate said, as they walked away. 'You should maybe stop walking through here until it's sorted.'

'Aye, you're probably right.'

She gave him a quick hug and turned to leave.

'Wait a minute,' he said. 'You said you had two bits of news. What else have you got in store for me?'

'It's not me,' Kate said. 'It's Mum. She's thrown Graham out. They're getting a divorce.'

12

Archie Simons' place was exactly what Jimmy had expected. Big-screen TVs on all the walls, shiny stuff everywhere, including a pole in the middle of a small stage and lots of mirrors to make the place look bigger than it was.

Jimmy sat at the bar, staring at his reflection in the biggest of them. It ran along the entire wall, its lower half covered by bottles of cheap spirits, which had no doubt been watered down in preparation for their nightly three-trebles-for-a-fiver promotion. He smiled back at himself – he was looking relatively respectable these days, having replaced his Pit Stop hand-outs with a cheap and not very cheerful wardrobe from TK Maxx, consisting mainly of T-shirts and cargo pants.

'You looking for me?' a voice said from behind him.

Jimmy swivelled on his bar stool and found himself face to face with a toad in human form. Or maybe a human in toad form, it was difficult to be sure, what with the way the man's bulging tongue poked out from between his fat lips. The olive-green suit didn't help either. The rest of him was short and squat with a face on top that looked like it needed a good iron running over it.

'You Simons?'

'Mr Simons to you.'

Jimmy nodded slightly but didn't correct himself. Instead he handed the man his card. Charlie Gascoigne had got them printed out for him to add a bit of weight to his new guise.

'I'm looking into the murder in the alley next door.'

As Simons glanced at the card, Jimmy noticed they weren't alone. A large, long-haired baboon in a grey shell suit was hovering next to a games machine which was clearly turned off. Almost certainly a handy bit of protection for the bar owner, who didn't look like he'd be much of a fighter.

Simons glanced at the card and handed it back.

'Keep it,' Jimmy said. 'My number's on there. You might remember something later.'

'No need. I'm not talking to you.'

'Seems like you already are.'

'Don't be a smart-arse.'

'I wasn't. I'm normally the dumbest guy in the room.'

Simons smirked and glanced behind at his protection who was looking at his phone. He shook his head.

'Aye, not today though. It's true what they say about paying peanuts. Why should I speak to you?'

'I just thought you'd prefer I asked you about it rather than stand around out front bothering your customers. Knowing someone was killed a yard away might put people off coming in.'

For a moment he thought Simons might send him packing or set his tracksuited minder onto him but instead the man shrugged, like he was used to dealing with chancers and Jimmy was just the latest in a long line.

'Make it quick. How can I help?'

'What do you know about what happened?'

'I heard about it, obviously. That's all, though.'

'Only heard? Didn't see anything?'

'I was away. One of my staff has already given a statement to the police. He reckons the bloke who did it had been trying to get in here earlier. My doormen are always on the ball, they can spot a nutter a mile away.'

'Can I talk to him afterwards?'

'No problem, though he's not on till six. And don't get in his way. He's a busy lad. We get all sorts trying and failing to get in here. You must have got lucky.'

There'd been no one on the door when Jimmy came in. He glanced around at the empty bar. The barman was sitting on a stool doing a crossword. They weren't exactly packing the punters in. He turned his attention back to Simons.

'What about CCTV? I saw the camera outside.'

'My bar manager's given the police full access. Nothing to hide here.'

'D'you have any idea who the dead man was?'

'Not a clue. What's his name?'

'They haven't released it yet.'

Simons shrugged and looked at his watch.

'I think we're done here. I've got an appointment.' He started to head towards the door.

'D'you think it's got anything to do with your Facebook page?'

Simons stopped in his tracks and turned around. The tongue was out again.

'What Facebook page?'

'The "Fake Homeless" one.'

Simons glanced at his minder again. He was chatting to one of the cleaners. The bar owner sighed.

'You don't want a job, do you?'

'I've got one thanks.'

'Look, this murder's nothing to do with me or my campaign.'

'Campaign?'

'To clean up the area.'

'Is that what you're doing?'

'Course. Being a good citizen and that. D'you think it's right that these chancers should be allowed to con good-hearted people into parting with their hard-earned when they're not really homeless? I've seen them trouser a couple of hundred quid, then after sitting in a doorway for a couple of hours, they climb into their Merc to head home to their two-up, two-down out in the sticks. It's not right.'

'You've *seen* them?'

'I've been told about it. And it's not fair on the proper homeless, the ones who genuinely need the help, is it?'

'And you help them, do you?'

'Course. I pay my taxes and employ loads of people who pay theirs too so the council can build more houses. The sooner we get them off the streets the better.'

'And does that include putting them into hospital? Beating them up?'

'Beating them up? Who said anything about that?'

'The man who's been charged with the murder, for one, though he's not the only one. You post photos of the supposedly fake homeless on your page. He reckons that two men took his photo before they beat him up in the alley.'

Simons laughed.

'Hey, don't get me wrong, sunshine, but he's the one who's been arrested for killing some poor sod, isn't he? Why would anyone believe what a homeless murderer tells them?'

13

Deano wasn't eating. That was a very bad sign. Normally the kid wolfed down anything within arm's reach. He was worse than Dog in that respect. You saw it a lot in people who'd served any kind of time. They learned to finish their food quickly before someone tried to take it away from them.

Jimmy didn't think the kid was using again, if anything he went the other way when he was on something, eating even faster than normal. Something else was bothering him. His eyes were darting here and there, one minute checking out the people in the Pit Stop's dining area, the next the front door and, sometimes, even the staff beavering away behind the food counter.

Jimmy glanced around but couldn't see anything out of the ordinary. A few of the regulars were scattered about, mostly in groups, one or two loners but nothing that looked out of place. There were a couple of people he didn't recognise, one sour-looking woman sitting with her back to the wall in the corner of the room, sipping tea from a mug, the other a very short, pasty-faced man who appeared to be fast asleep even though he was sitting up. He was definitely on something – spice would be Jimmy's guess. He'd seen people literally asleep on their feet after a heavy dose of that shit.

'What's wrong?' he asked Deano.

'Nothing.'

'You seem a bit wired.'

'I haven't taken anything if that's what you reckon,' Deano said snappily. 'I'm not doing that any more.'

Jimmy had heard that before. Normally just before the kid disappeared for three days and came back looking like he'd been wrung out by a giant. But he knew how hard Deano was working to keep his shit together so gave him the benefit of the doubt this time.

'What then?'

'That woman keeps looking at us.' Deano nodded to the tea-drinker in the corner. 'It's freaking me out.'

'You're a good-looking lad.'

Deano put his fingers in his mouth and made a retching sound.

'She's old enough to be me nan,' he said, once he'd finished with the fake vomming.

Jimmy took another look at the woman, who didn't seem to be watching anyone, just staring at the notices on the wall. The lad was being a bit harsh, he reckoned. She was maybe in her late thirties, early forties max, though it did look like she'd had a hard paper round. To be fair, the same could apply to most of the people in the room, including the volunteers. There was something off about her though and it took him a moment to work out what it was – her trainers. Her grey fleece and black leggings were standard uniform for the Pit Stop regulars, but the trainers looked box-fresh and expensive.

The woman got up and examined one of the lists pinned to the board. The Pit Stop ran a variety of group sessions to entertain the 'friends' who used the place. They ranged from the gentle – a book club – to the more adventurous, like the hiking group that disappeared into the wilds once a month. The woman seemed particularly interested in the hiking group and after a few minutes she grabbed the pen that was tied to the board and wrote her name on the list.

As she turned to leave, she caught Jimmy watching her and held his stare for a moment. There was something slightly cold in her eyes and he could see why Deano had been thrown by her. She looked like she might be coming over to talk to him but eventually she nodded, turned around and headed for the exit. Deano sighed with relief and pushed his chair away from the table.

'Thank fuck for that.' The kid got up.

'What you doing?' Jimmy asked.

'Homework,' Deano said. The kid had a quick glance at the front door to make sure the woman had left before he went over to check what she'd written. Jimmy smiled. A year ago, Deano wouldn't have gone anywhere near the board, too embarrassed to tell people he couldn't read, but this was a clear sign that his confidence was growing; Aoife's lessons were really doing the trick.

Deano froze for a moment or two but then turned back

to look at Jimmy. All the colour had disappeared from his face and his hands were shaking as he pointed at the board.

'C-can you ch-check this for us, Jimmy?' he said, quietly.

Jimmy got up and joined his friend.

'D-does that say what I think it says?' Deano asked.

The woman had written in block capitals to make it easier to read and Jimmy immediately understood what Deano's problem was. Scrawled across the bottom line of the sign-up sheet was the name SUSAN BECKET.

14

Jimmy ran out of the Pit Stop and just caught sight of Susan Becket heading towards Chinatown. He legged it after her and got lucky. The lights changed just as he hit the busy main road. She was walking pretty slowly, checking her phone as she went, as if she was following a map on it.

He kept his distance, crossing to the other side of the road to make sure he couldn't be seen. It was just like the old days – in the navy he regularly led the shore patrol, keeping an eye on the ships' company to make sure they got back on board safely, and without upsetting the locals.

She cut up Stowell Street, past a couple of Chinese restaurants, before turning right into an alley that led around the side of The Gate, a large indoor bar and food complex. Jimmy had never been in there – not his kind of thing, all bright lights and noisy teenagers. He let her get a bit further ahead as the alley was narrow and he didn't want her to see him. The alley joined up with a small back street and when she turned right again at the end of that street he started to get a bad feeling – she was heading towards Archie Simons' bar.

Jimmy had been hoping that her name was a coincidence but that looked less likely now. A few years back, before Jimmy's time, a loathsome prick called Becket had made Deano's life a living hell, pimping the kid out to anyone with a few quid to spare. Gadge had got wind of this and rescued the lad from the bastard's clutches, injuring the pimp and making an enemy for life in the process. More recently the guy had showed up on the scene again but then disappeared almost as quickly – Jimmy was pretty sure that Gadge had a hand in that as well. If this woman was a relative of *that* Becket, then framing Gadge for murder might not be beyond her.

He was relieved when she walked past Simons' bar, maybe it was just a coincidence and he could reassure Deano that all was well. He carried on following her just in case but had to pull up abruptly when she ambled into Motel One, a classy-looking hotel just around the corner. Not a good sign. If she was staying in a swanky place like that, what was she doing at the Pit Stop?

The bouncer at Archie's was far from the usual type; he had the universal shaved head but was only about an inch taller than Jimmy, well short of the regulation six-footer. He also had a ready smile which he turned on as Jimmy approached the door.

'Help you?' he said.

'Your boss said I could talk to you about the murder in the alley?'

'My boss?'

'Archie Simons.'

'Oh, right. You the investigator?'

Jimmy nodded.

'Got any ID? Can never be too careful.' If anything, the smile went a little wider. Maybe he was one of those guys who kept the peace with charm rather than muscle.

Jimmy handed him his card and watched as the man examined it.

'Looks kosher to me,' he said, slipping it into his pocket. 'I'm Che Kennedy.'

He shook hands with a surprised Jimmy.

'Che? As in Guevara?'

'Aye, don't you think I look like him?' He thrust his arm in the air and shouted 'Viva La Revolucion!'

Jimmy hesitated and the man burst out laughing.

'Just pulling your plonker, man. My dad was an old school Marxist, thought it was a cool name, which it obviously is. Now what can I do for you?'

'Were you on duty that night?'

'Aye. All night. Started at six stayed on until midnight.'

Jimmy pulled out a picture of Gadge that he'd taken at the prison. It wasn't exactly ideal, what with the facial bruises, but needs must – Gadge reckoned he hadn't had his photo taken in at least ten years so it was the best he could do.

'D'you remember this guy?'

'Course. He's the murderer, isn't he?'

Jimmy held his hand up.

'Easy, man, innocent till proven guilty, remember.'

'Aye, s'pose. It was deffo him I saw earlier that night, though.'

'Just earlier? You didn't see him being dragged into the alley next door by two men?'

The bouncer shook his head.

'Nope, sorry, not going to forget something like that, am I? The only reason I remember him at all is because he was such a stroppy twat.'

'How d'you mean?'

'Felt like he was spoiling for a fight. There's always one or two of them types and you get to spot the signs. I'm pretty free and easy, me, but lairy gits like that rub me up the wrong way.'

'Wasn't he just a bit pissed?'

'Nah. Not many would get in if that was the criteria. He didn't seem that bad anyway. Just bad-tempered.'

Jimmy made a mental note to quiz his friend again on what he'd been up to earlier that day. After she'd spoken to Gadge, Charlie Gascoigne had been hoping to show he was practically comatose that night as it would have been hard for anyone to kill the victim in that state. It was odd that the bouncer didn't remember it that way, but memory could be a funny thing. He wondered if the police doc had breathalysed Gadge, or whatever it was they did to measure alcohol levels, if anything? That might help them clarify things.

'Are we done?' the bouncer said, glancing at his watch. Jimmy decided to press his buttons to see if there was another side to the seemingly affable guy. And maybe to see if he knew about the Facebook page his boss had set up.

'So not letting him in had nothing to do with him being homeless then?'

The bouncer's smile fell for the first time.

'You calling me a Tory twat, like?'

Jimmy stepped out of range, which wasn't too far as the man had pretty short arms too.

'No, course not, but I've been there, you know. Most doormen aren't as friendly as you. And your boss, Simons, definitely doesn't like them or he wouldn't have started up that campaign.'

For the first time the man looked uncomfortable, glancing over his shoulder to see who was listening.

'We can't all pick and choose who we work for, can we? I've done a bit of sofa-surfing myself in the past so I know what it's like. And if I had a problem with the homeless lads, I wouldn't have let his mate in, would I?'

'Mate? What mate?'

'Lad with a nasty scar on his chin, fairly recent I'd say, bit of a limp too. Pretty sure I saw the two of them chatting on the bench outside the bar earlier that night. Muscular lad, like he'd done some hard graft in his time. Looked like he could take care of himself as well. Maybe he's the one you should be talking to.'

15

The common room at the hostel was buzzing. A speaker in the corner was blasting out some catchy dance music that Deano reckoned was called 'Uptown Funk'. Four lads were playing pool in one corner while a couple of the lasses looked on and another group was playing Monopoly and arguing loudly about who owned the Angel of the North.

Jimmy was sitting to one side with Deano, who was still up a height about Susan Becket's sudden appearance at the Pit Stop. He'd tried to get him to focus on the mysterious homeless man with the fresh scar along his jawline that the doorman claimed to have seen with Gadge but it was pointless. The kid was stuck in a one-track groove.

'Maybe she's a relly? Could be his missus?' Deano said.

'It's possible but I doubt Becket had a wife,' Jimmy said. 'A sister perhaps.'

'What d'you think she wants?'

'No idea.'

'D'you think she knows he's brown bread?' Deano put his hand to his mouth and immediately tried to take it back. 'I mean, um . . .' He pushed his chair back and started to get up. 'I need a drink.'

Had Jimmy heard right? As far as he knew Becket had been persuaded to leave town by Gadge, or at least that was the impression his friend had given him. He grabbed Deano's arm to stop him walking off.

'Why do you think he's dead?'

'I dunno, I just heard it around an' that.'

Deano was a terrible liar. And he wasn't much better at keeping secrets. The slightest bit of pressure and he caved. Jimmy just stared at him until the kid cracked.

'Gadge told us, all right, but he told us not to say owt, so you never heard it from me.' He looked around as if their friend had managed to break out of prison and was liable to be walking in at any second.

'And how did he know?' Jimmy pressed.

'No idea. I'm gonna grab a Coke.'

Before Jimmy could stop him for a second time, Deano shot up and almost ran to the drinks machine in the corner, clearly doing his best to avoid any further interrogation. Jimmy added Becket to the ever-mounting list of things he had to quiz Gadge about at their next chat. He hoped his friend had nothing to do with the man's death – if he really was dead. If that came out then Gadge would be toast when his latest case got to court. The jury wouldn't be told about it, but the judge would be all over it if it came down to sentencing.

The door swung open and he saw the new kid, Aaron, come in. Jimmy called him over but the lad didn't hear him – or pretended not to. He glanced nervously around the room before edging past the Monopoly players and heading towards Deano.

Before he got there, one of the pool players said something and Aaron stopped and turned, ripping the cue from the kid's hand and ramming the thick end into his stomach. The kid jerked back against the table as Aaron moved menacingly towards him. Jimmy got to his feet but he was too far away to make a difference.

'Hey,' he shouted but no one heard him above the music. Just as Aaron seemed about to batter the kid, Deano appeared from nowhere and managed to get his arms around Aaron and drag him away. There was a bit of a struggle as the cue fell to the floor but eventually Deano talked him down, handing him a can of Coke, and guiding him back over towards Jimmy's table.

Dog, who despite the noise had been sleeping under the table, looked up to see what all the fuss was, then went straight back to sleep again.

'What was that all about?' Jimmy said.

'Nothing,' Aaron said.

'Didn't look like nothing.'

'Prick called me a wanker.'

'Why?'

'I dunno. Thinks he's hard, probs.'

'Did you hear anything?' Jimmy asked Deano.

'Nah, the music was too loud. He nearly shat himself when Aaron grabbed the cue off him though.'

Aaron smiled and fiddled around with his can, moving

the ring pull backwards and forwards until it came off in his hand. He looked around for a bin but couldn't see anything so put it in his pocket and started to fiddle with his chair instead.

'You need to control yourself. You'll be out on your ear if you make a habit of that.'

'He started it.'

'I'll have a word with him later.' The kid was still on edge. Jimmy tried to lower the temperature. 'Apart from that, how you settling in?'

'It's fine,' Aaron muttered.

'You spoken to your mum about moving back in yet?'

Apparently, they'd had a falling-out over her new boyfriend. Sometimes these problems ended quickly – when the boyfriend did a runner with the woman's savings normally.

'She ain't called me,' the kid said, glancing back across to the pool table, where one of the lads was celebrating a win. Aaron looked like he'd rather be anywhere else in the world at that moment.

Jimmy let it go. You couldn't force these things. Another game of pool started immediately. 'Maybe they'll let you play next,' he said, laughing.

'Don't care. They're shite anyway. I took all their cash last time I played them.'

That probably explained the fight. The kids weren't supposed to play for money but it was almost impossible to stop them.

'Maybe play for fun next time,' Jimmy said.

'Maybe.'

'Deano'll give you a game later, won't you, son?'

Deano gave him a look but Jimmy knew he'd go along with it, the lad knew exactly what it was like to be on your own at that age. His mother had abandoned him when he got thrown in a youth detention centre when he was barely a teenager.

Aaron looked at Deano, who nodded. Jimmy smiled; his work done – maybe he could win the kid over after all. He was about to head over to talk to the pool players when his phone buzzed in his pocket. He checked the number: Charlie Gascoigne.

'What's up?'

She came straight to the point.

'Did you know Gadge had killed someone? I mean, before all this.'

Shit. How did she find out? He had to buy some time to find out what really happened.

'If this is about Becket . . .' he said.

A moment of silence. She was obviously pissed off that she hadn't heard it from him.

'Who's Becket?' she said.

16

1987

Gadge's brand new, straight out of the dealer's, Jaguar XJ40 drives like a dream – it actually does purr like a big cat, he thinks, as the needle hits eighty for the first time. He's running a little late to pick Lucy up but with this horsepower under the bonnet he'll soon make up the time.

He hopes she's had a good night. She's been a mess since the miscarriage but he reckons she's on the mend now; a new job in an upmarket clothes shop on Blackett Street right in the centre of the city and her first night out with the girls for ages. And she's gonna love the new wheels.

She's waiting for him outside Jimmyz Bar when he pulls up, chatting to one of her mates, Amanda, he thinks her name is. Straight away he can see Lucy's happier than he's seen her in ages. He watches their mouths drop open as they see the gleaming black Jag pull up in front of them and he pops out to open the passenger door for her as if she's royalty, which in his mind she is.

'Oh my God, it's beautiful,' she says, wrapping her arms around him as Amanda watches on in envy. He gives the friend a cheeky wink and she laughs. He reckons she'd be up for it but he's just flirting, that's as far as it ever goes with him these days. He used to be a right player but he's never cheated on Lucy and never will.

'Can I have a drive?' Lucy asks, breathlessly.

'I don't think so,' he says. 'Not when you've been drinking.' She doesn't seem too bad but it's not worth the risk.

'Pleeeeeeaaase,' she begs, leaning closely into him. 'I'll make it worth your while when we get home,' she whispers.

He's tempted but still shakes his head.

'I've only had a couple,' she says, turning to Amanda for confirmation.

'It's true,' her friend says, 'proper lightweight these days, she is. Talking of which, I'd better get back inside. It's my round!' She gives Lucy a hug and heads back inside.

As soon as her friend has gone Lucy gives him that look, the one that he can never say no to and his resolve melts, it's been so long since they had fun together. He hands her the keys.

'Just for a couple of minutes, OK? And you go where I say.'

She squeals and hugs him again before running round to the driver's side and jumping in. He climbs into the passenger seat, adjusts it so he can get his legs in and off they go.

Lucy takes them along the Quayside, laughing as she can see people looking at the car and pointing.

'I feel like a movie star,' she says, rubbing her left hand enticingly along his thigh.

'Both hands on the wheel,' Gadge says, though he really

doesn't want her to stop. She does as she's told and pulls up perfectly at the traffic lights at the end of road.

'Told you I was fine,' she says, turning to look at him, though he can tell she's had more than a couple from the way her eyes are slightly unfocused. When the lights change again she moves off smoothly and heads up the empty stretch of road towards Walker. Her hand strays back to his thigh. His eyes close as he thinks about the 'reward' she's promised him so he doesn't see the kid step off the pavement. He does hear Lucy's scream though, and the squeal of the brakes, and the thump as the car hits the kid full on and he flies over the bonnet, across the windscreen, and back onto the road.

The Jag slews sideways and comes to a halt and for a moment they're both frozen in shock.

Then Lucy starts sobbing.

'I d-didn't s-see him,' she cries. 'He just came out of nowhere.'

Her words spark Gadge into action. He leaps out of the car and runs over to the prone body on the side of the road. The kid's not moving at all though he's on his front so all Gadge can see is his black leather jacket and the back of his head which looks OK.

He turns the kid over and it's obvious he's dead. There's a gaping wound in his skull and nothing in his eyes. Gadge puts his cheek close to the lad's mouth but can't feel any breath. There's no pulse. Fuck. A sense of guilt threatens to overwhelm him but he'll deal with that later. Lucy's his priority.

He looks around. There's no one in sight. Lucy hasn't moved, still in the same position he left her in. Why did he let her drive? She's going to get crucified for this when they breathalyse her, he knows she'll be over the limit, maybe not by much but an inch is as good as a mile. He also knows that she's not strong enough to deal with that.

He moves quickly, pulling open the driver's door and grabbing her arm. She doesn't resist, numb, in shock. He pulls her out of the car and practically carries her round to the other side. His door is still open so he bundles her into the passenger seat, catching her head on the door frame, which seems to bring her round.

'W-what are you doing?'

'Don't worry. And don't say anything, just agree with whatever I say.'

'But—'

'Just do as you're fucking told,' he screams, and she bursts into tears again.

'He's dead, isn't he?' she sobs.

Gadge nods.

'I killed him.'

He grabs her chin and makes her look at him.

'No. You didn't. I was driving, right?'

'I d-don't understand.'

'I'm going to call the police now but don't say anything to them. If you have to, tell them you were asleep and didn't see a thing. OK?'

She nods. Gadge goes round to the driver's side and adjusts the seat back to where it would have been for him.

Then he leans over Lucy, opens the glove compartment and pulls out the chunky new Nokia Cityman that had only come on the market the week before. He takes a breath to compose himself and dials 999.

When the police and ambulance arrive she actually is asleep – a combination of alcohol and shock. She doesn't see the medic confirm the kid is stone dead. Even better she doesn't see them scrape him off the road or the huge pool of blood he leaves behind.

Gadge is not sure how she would have stood up to any kind of interrogation but luckily she doesn't get one. The two young cops assume she's either fainted or banged her head in the accident. They breathalyse him and he passes easily. Unusually for him he hasn't had a drop in days, been too busy burning the candle at both ends, trying to improve the latest version of his digital software.

They get the medic to check Lucy over and accept his story without any qualms. Why would he lie? He was driving and the kid stepped right in front of the car – a story he plans to take to his grave. He just prays there weren't any witnesses.

17

'Any more bodies you want to tell me about?'

Gadge glared at Jimmy but kept his mouth shut. After he'd been confronted with what Charlie Gascoigne had read about the car accident, Mr Talkative seemed to have lost the power of speech. It wasn't the only thing he'd lost; Jimmy had never seen him so flat, like the life was slowly being sucked out of him.

'How am I supposed to help you if you keep this kind of shit from me?' Jimmy continued. 'D'you want to stay here for the rest of your days?'

Gadge looked away, gazing at the door as if hoping the guard would rescue him from any more questions. There was no chance of Jimmy letting him off the hook now though. Eventually, Gadge took a deep breath and turned back.

'Careless driving isn't the same as murder.'

'The kid died, Gadge.' Jimmy looked at his notes. 'Dennis Sweeney.'

'I know his fucking name.'

'Can you remember what happened?'

'Of course I can, I think about it every day. The kid stepped out in front of the car. There was no time to react. He was killed on impact, either with the car or the road, they weren't sure. But he died instantly.'

Gadge's recall sounded like a speech he'd given countless times. Maybe he had back then.

'And you were charged with careless driving? And just got a fine.'

'Yes. Things were different in those days.'

'Had you been drinking?'

He saw the hesitation. It was brief but definitely there. Fuck. Of course he'd been drinking.

'No,' Gadge mumbled.

Again, Jimmy let it go – for now.

'How did the kid's family react?'

'How d'you think? They were screaming and yelling in court when the verdict was read out. I didn't blame them; I'd have done the same if it had been my son. I tried to talk to them afterwards, to apologise, but they wouldn't listen. They were all over the papers for ages, complaining about the sentence.'

'D'you know what happened to them?'

'Not a clue. Why?'

'Revenge is a dish best served cold, man. What if one of them has set you up now?'

'Jesus, Jimmy, it was nearly thirty years ago. That's more than cold, it's positively ice-age.'

Gadge was probably right. But they weren't the only ones

who might have been looking to get back at him. It wasn't just Dennis Sweeney's blood his friend had on his hands.

'How about two years? Is that too long?'

'What d'you mean?'

'Tell me what happened to Becket.'

Gadge's shoulders slumped. If anything he looked even more tired than he had at the start which Jimmy wouldn't have thought possible. He seemed smaller as well, like he was slowly disappearing. Any more of this and his friend would be long gone before this ever got to court. He'd had at least two heart attacks in recent years. Maybe he should ease off a bit with the third-degree treatment?

'Fuckin' Deano,' Gadge muttered. 'I knew I should never have told the little gobshite. I just wanted him to stop worrying that the evil twat might come back one day.'

'I'm not saying he didn't deserve it, Gadge. Man was a leech. Talk me through it.'

'I did a deal with him for some of that spice we had. I offered him a few bags of the stuff to get out of town.'

'That spice was dangerous, you knew that.'

A couple of years earlier, a large supply of synthetic cannabis had fallen into Jimmy's hands. He was keeping it off the streets to try and protect some kids he knew. The normal stuff was bad enough but this was a dodgy batch – almost everyone who'd tried it had met a bizarre death. He couldn't believe Gadge had put some of it back out there again.

'Jesus, mate, you must have known that wouldn't get rid of him. That he'd keep coming back for more. And that he'd probably sell it on to other people.'

'Course. But I also knew that if I gave him a sample he wouldn't be able to resist trying it first and hoped he'd end up the same way as the rest of them. So I followed him around. If I'd seen him trying to sell any I'd have broken his arms but it never came to that. The plan worked. Twat got off his face and walked in front of a bus. I doubt anyone missed him.'

Jimmy knew at least one person who did.

18

Jimmy falls through the air, his arms windmilling like crazy as if he could fly to safety. The ground rushes towards him. His life flashes in front of his eyes and it isn't fucking pretty so he closes them to keep the shitty memories out. There's a buzzing in his ears and he feels his face compressing as the G-force squashes everything, making it hard to breathe. He senses the presence of others crowding in on him but is too scared of who he might see to open his eyes again.

He braces himself, trying to whisper apologies to all the people he's let down, even though there isn't enough time left for that. He can't help remembering the old joke: 'It's not the fall that kills you, it's the landing.'

A loud cheer woke him up. Jimmy shook his head to clear out the nightmare. It had been almost a year since the last one and he'd hoped they'd gone for good. He felt like a recovering alcoholic who'd woken up with a hangover and wasn't sure how he'd got it.

A hubbub of conversation surrounded him. He looked around the minibus, slowly remembering where he was, until his eyes met Susan Becket's. She was staring right back at him. He looked away quickly, not ready to engage with her just yet, sure there'd be a better moment to find out what she was up to once they were out in the wilds – the only reason he was there in the first place.

There were around a dozen other walkers on the bus, all clad in outdoor clothing, their small rucksacks containing water bottles and packed lunches made in the Pit Stop that morning were lying in the aisle between the seats. The combined smell of sweat and farts was rank.

Dog was on the floor by his feet, just stirring, Deano fast asleep beside him. The kid was beginning to lose his youthful looks. It was rare to see him before lunchtime and with the sun streaming through the windows onto his face Jimmy could see that the wear and tear from a life of drug addiction and sleeping rough was starting to take its toll. We're all decaying, he thought. Gadge was falling to bits; even Sandy looked like shit the last time he'd seen her.

'Fuck me, I'm getting old,' he muttered.

They'd finally arrived in the large Simonside car park, set amongst the Northumberland wilds, just the other side of Rothbury, a stark contrast to the concrete and red-brick city centre they'd set off from around an hour before. The area had become famous a few years before when a killer-on-the-run, Raoul Moat, had tried to go to ground there. Jimmy seemed to remember reading that Gazza, the ex-footballer, had got involved somehow, something to do with a fishing rod and a few cans of beer, but maybe that had just been another surreal dream. Or one of Gadge's stories.

He'd slept through most of the journey up there, as had Dog who was about to get the longest walk he'd had since his poisoning. It would do the lazy sod good, Jimmy thought, he was carrying way too much timber these days. He nudged Deano to get him moving, ignoring his grumbled plea to be left alone.

The team leader, Paul, one of the volunteers, called them all together as soon as they'd got off the bus.

'Everyone got their rucksacks?'

They all nodded.

'Make sure you tighten them up properly or they'll rub on your shoulders.'

He looked around.

'I know we've got a couple of newbies here so I'll just run through a few guidelines.'

As Paul blathered on about going at the slowest man's pace and not drinking all your water too quickly, Jimmy watched Susan Becket. She didn't appear to be giving the instructions her full attention either. Unlike Jimmy, maybe she did this kind of thing regularly and knew it all already. She didn't look the sort though and her boots were both new and high quality, as if she'd bought them specially, not like the manky ones he'd borrowed from the Pit Stop store about ten minutes before they'd set off. He wasn't looking forward to the blisters.

Once the briefing was over, they set off slowly along a wide path that climbed gently through the trees, mostly forming into pairs as they walked. Jimmy played it cool, sticking with Deano to start with. The walk was about five miles, with a stop to eat lunch on the top of the crags, so there'd be plenty of time to find out what Susan Becket's game was later. Dog, to his surprise, was like a pig in shit, stopping every few feet to sniff something new, no doubt distracted by smells that he hadn't experienced in a long time, if ever.

'This is mental,' Deano muttered as he trudged along. 'Who gans walking in the middle of nowhere?'

The kid had wanted nothing to do with the plan to join Susan Becket on the hiking trip when Jimmy first suggested it – wanting to give her as wide a berth as possible – but had been talked around when he realised that it might help Gadge. Maybe she'd been the one who'd somehow framed their friend. Though there were probably plenty of other suspects yet to be discovered, given how quickly the man's story of his past was unravelling.

As they walked, Jimmy considered what his pal had told him about the car accident. There was something a bit off about the story but he couldn't quite put his finger on it. He was pretty sure that Gadge had been lying about the drinking but how would he have got away with it? They must have breathalysed him – unless he knew one of the cops.

He was beginning to think that his friend had been lying through his teeth ever since they'd met. The miscarriage story had also been news to him – Gadge had always joked about his ex-wives being to blame for his situation, robbing him blind in divorce after divorce, whereas the picture he now painted of his first wife, Lucy, was very different. Something wasn't adding up.

'Canny dog you've got there, pal,' a voice said to his left.

A short, stocky man had loomed up alongside him from the back of the pack and was now almost shoulder to shoulder with Jimmy.

'Aye,' he said, hoping the stranger would get the message. He didn't.

'Getting on a bit, mind, looks like he's been around the block a time or two.'

'That'll be all the dead bodies he's seen,' Jimmy said.

'Do what?' the man said, edging away slightly.

'At least a dozen, I reckon.'

A lot of the Pit Stop users had criminal records, not just Jimmy, and it was highly likely that some had killed more than one person so Jimmy could tell the man thought he'd stumbled across a serial killer. He gave the guy a break – sort of.

'Dog used to be one of those cadaver dogs, you know, the ones that hunt out bodies that have been hidden or buried somewhere. Never failed, they reckoned. Could sniff a corpse from half a mile away. I'm hoping he might find one up here today.'

To his right he heard Deano sniggering. The kid knew that Jimmy was talking total bollocks.

'I thought they were mostly Labradors,' the stranger said.

'Exception that proves the rule,' Jimmy said. 'If you hear him barking any time in the next couple of hours, there'll be a body somewhere, mark my words.'

Deano couldn't keep his laughter in any longer, snorting like a good 'un, and the man finally caught on.

'Wankers,' he muttered, speeding up to get away from the wind-up merchants.

'Nice one, Jimmy,' Deano said. 'Though it would be cool if Dog could do that. I reckon he'd dig it up if he did find a body. Then there'd be a point to this wandering about shite.'

The kid was starting to breathe heavily, exercise not being one of the drugs he usually tried. Even Jimmy, who'd somehow maintained a natural level of fitness since his navy days, was struggling to keep up as they clambered up a steep hill. He'd been stabbed in the leg a couple of years earlier and had never been quite the same since.

The pair of them tailed off at the back and the rest of the group got the message that they weren't there to make friends, leaving them to their own devices until they got to the top of the crag and stopped for a much-needed lunch. Susan Becket had avoided them so far, and vice versa, though Jimmy had noticed her moving around the other groups on the way up.

Before they unpacked, Jimmy and Deano wandered over to the edge to take a good look at the breathtaking view across the green patchwork of fields to the three rising mounds of the Cheviots. Even Deano seemed lost for words, which practically never happened.

Jimmy sensed someone behind them and had a quick flashback to his dream, his body tumbling down the steep drop to the bottom of the hills. He turned quickly to find Susan Becket right on his shoulder, way too close for comfort. He stepped back from the edge, just in case. She barely noticed him though. Maybe she was one of those people with no sense of personal space.

'Beautiful, isn't it?' he said.

She just nodded. A woman of few words, but who was he to judge. When he'd come out of prison, he'd probably spoken to about four people in his first year and one of them was his probation officer. Everyone had a cross to bear and maybe hers was her brother, if that's what he was.

As they all found places to eat Jimmy made sure they were sitting close to the woman, figuring that it would look less conspicuous than sidling up to her on the walk itself. Again she didn't seem to notice. He poured Deano and himself a cup of tea from a flask that they'd made up for him at the Pit Stop that morning and noticed that she wasn't drinking.

'I've got plenty of tea if you fancy a brew,' he said, tapping her on the arm. She flinched at the unexpected contact but once she realised what he wanted relaxed a little.

'I'm fine, thanks, got my own in the rucksack.'

She had a strong accent but wasn't from the north-east; Birmingham way, he reckoned. He tried to remember how Becket had spoken but could only remember that he was a whiny twat.

'No worries. Don't think I've seen you about before?'

She looked at him curiously.

'Didn't think you wanted to talk to anybody. Your man over there' – she nodded at the guy they'd taken the piss out of – 'said that you were rude to him when he tried to talk to you.'

'Some people have no sense of humour,' Jimmy said.

She nodded. 'People say that about me. They're probably right, to be fair.'

He wondered if she was on the spectrum somewhere, she seemed a bit out of it, not really looking at him when she spoke. They sat in silence for a while, only broken by Deano's eating – he'd piled his salt and vinegar crisps into the middle of his cheese sarnie and was enjoying crunching his way through his lunch.

'He your son?' she asked Jimmy, who laughed.

'No, thank Christ, just a mate.'

He waited a moment.

'You got any family?'

She hesitated, then spoke slowly, as if she was out of practice.

'Did have. A brother.'

He'd guessed right. Jimmy saw Deano glance over. The kid had been pretending not to listen but was obviously all ears.

'He's dead,' she continued.

'Sorry to hear that,' Jimmy said, though he didn't mean it. She wasn't buying his fake sympathy anyway.

'You might not say that if you'd met him,' she said.

'You can't choose family.'

She looked away. Maybe he'd said the wrong thing but, instead of blathering on to try and make up for it, he did what he'd been trained to do back in his naval police days. He left a gap for her to fill. He was starting to wonder if that was a mistake when she finally responded.

'He wasn't a very nice man. Wasn't all his fault. We were both put into care when our dad died. Mum couldn't cope. I was fortunate, got adopted pretty quickly, lovely family. He never did. No one wanted boys back then. Luck of the draw, I guess. The only times I ever saw him after that were when he wanted something. Money for drugs mostly.'

In for a penny, Jimmy thought.

'How did he die?'

'Hit by a bus on the Tyne Bridge, year before last. Just walked right in front of it. Misadventure, according to the coroner. Two beat officers saw it happen and a witness said he was completely wasted. Which wasn't surprising for those of us who knew him.'

'Seems pretty clear-cut.'

She gave him a look – maybe he was pushing too hard? He backed off, pulled a biscuit bar out of his rucksack and took a bite out of it. Eventually she responded.

'I thought so at first. I guess I'd been expecting it for years. But something's been nagging away at me, so I came up here to see if anyone knew anything about what really happened to him. Haven't found anyone who did yet, though. I was hoping someone in this group might have known him but if they did, they don't want to talk about it. Unless you know something?'

Should he fess up? Not the full story, obviously, but maybe something close enough? He wasn't sure he was smart enough to improvise so he played for time.

'What was his name?'

'Becket. Mark Becket.'

That was the first time Jimmy had heard the man's full name. He'd always been just Becket to them.

'Doesn't ring a bell.'

'Maybe this will help.'

She reached into her pocket, pulled out a dog-eared photograph and handed it to him. It was probably at least ten years old but the man was unmistakable. Like a human ferret. Jimmy pretended to study it then shook his head.

'No, sorry, but I could ask around for you if you like – though some people don't use their real names in our world. What is it that's been bothering you?'

She hesitated and looked down at her hands. Did she know he was lying? Eventually she looked back up at him.

'He was a junkie and had all the paranoia that goes with that so it might be nothing. But last time I spoke to him on the phone he told me that he thought someone was out to get him. I'd like to find out who that was.'

19

What the hell was a langoustine?

Jimmy couldn't remember the last time he'd been out for dinner. He stared at the menu praying that something would stand out but there were so many words he'd never seen before that he was already drowning. He remembered that he liked salmon but wasn't there a special knife you had to use? He looked around at the cutlery on the table, hoping for inspiration to stop him making an arse out of himself. Kate wouldn't care but, for some reason, he did.

Carrie and Kate were sitting at opposite sides of the square table with him in between them. The other seat was empty. His daughter had been very mysterious about the occasion – just talking about another big surprise.

'How's Gadge?' Kate said.

'Not great,' he admitted. The guilt of heading out for a posh meal while his friend was still locked up was heavy, but he wasn't going to ruin their evening by dwelling on it.

Kate reached out for his hand.

'He'll be OK. He's a survivor. And he knows he's got

friends on the outside looking out for him – provided they don't go back on the street and get beaten up themselves!' She gave him one of her fiercer glares. 'You will keep your promise, won't you?'

He was saved by the waiter.

'Are you ready to order?' the man said, hovering by the table, notebook in hand.

Jimmy looked at the menu again but the whole thing was a blur. Kate saved him.

'Can you give us a moment?' she said. 'We're just waiting for one more.'

That was news to him. She'd never mentioned another guest. The restaurant door pinged open behind him.

'And here she is,' Kate said.

Jimmy turned around. It was Bev. It had been a while. She looked in much better nick than him, but that was hardly surprising given the different paths they'd taken. She seemed as shocked as he was, stopping halfway to the table.

'I didn't know this was happening,' she said.

'Me neither,' he said.

They both looked at Kate, who shrugged.

'Well now you're both here you may as well enjoy the food. We've got a lot to talk about.'

In the end Jimmy kept it simple and copied Kate. Soup and steak. He got through the starter without making a mess, though he wolfed it down too quickly, another bad habit he'd picked up in prison. Kate and Carrie didn't notice though, they were positively brimming with happiness, glowing almost. Bev, in contrast, was in a chippy mood.

'Are you OK?' he said quietly, when he thought Kate and Carrie were caught up in their own conversation.

'What do you think?' she said. 'My marriage has just broken up and now my daughter's trying to matchmake me with my ex.'

The table went silent. Then Kate's spoon clattered into her bowl.

'Are you serious? This isn't about you, Mum. I don't care who you shag next now you've finally got rid of that tool Graham.'

Bev's nostrils flared, a sign of trouble that Jimmy recognised from way back. He used to duck for cover then and almost did again.

'He wasn't that bad.'

Kate and Bev glared at each other. Like mother, like daughter. Bev blinked first.

'Look, I'm sorry. You know how much I hate surprises. You should have told me you were inviting your father.'

'I didn't think it was that big a deal, wanting my parents to celebrate my forthcoming wedding with me. I thought you could handle it. You're supposed to be the grown-ups, after all. Dad doesn't seem to mind!'

Kate looked at Jimmy for support. It was a clever move, calculated even, but there was no way he was getting in between them. Thankfully, Bev caved before he could respond.

'You're right, love, I'm sorry, it just feels a bit weird, that's all. It's been a long time since I've gone out on my own. Graham didn't like it.'

Kate looked like she was going to say something else but she bit her tongue and settled for making peace instead, reaching across to take her mum's hand.

'You'll be fine, Mum. Third time lucky eh! You can't keep picking wrong 'uns, surely?'

Jimmy made an exaggerated sad face, pretending he was upset, and picked up a napkin to dab away the non-existent tears, which broke the tension.

The rest of the meal passed without incident, Jimmy's steak disappearing in moments and none of them having any room for puddings. When the others had finished eating, he tried to say a few words, tapping the side of his glass with his spoon to get their attention.

'Here we go,' Bev said. 'Some pearls of wisdom from your father.'

'I think we're a bit past the time for the "birds and the bees" chat, Dad,' Kate said. 'I probably know more about it than you.'

Jimmy blushed. She was almost certainly right. Julie had been his only relationship since Bev and they'd taken things very slowly.

'And anyway,' Kate continued, 'I invited you, it's my turn first.'

'But—'

Carrie put her hand on his arm.

'It's always best to let Kate get what she wants, in my experience. The alternative is getting burning dog shit posted through your letter box. Not joking. Ask the neighbour who used to play his music too loud.'

Kate gave her partner a pretend frown but then the pair of them burst out laughing.

'Go on then,' Jimmy said. 'Say your piece, I'll wait.'

'I'd like you to give me away,' Kate said.

20

The library wasn't always quiet. As he approached it Jimmy could hear someone shouting at the top of the ramp. A security guard was tussling with a young kid outside the doors. It was Aaron.

'What's going on?' he shouted, as he ran towards them.

They both ignored him. The guard too busy trying to hold onto the struggling kid; Aaron occupied with loosening the man's grip, slamming his elbow repeatedly into the guard's ribcage.

The guard's footing slipped and he fell to the floor, taking the kid's jacket with him. Aaron turned and looked like he was going to get a couple of kicks in while the man lay on the ground. Jimmy grabbed him in a bear hug and received a couple of elbow digs himself.

'For fuck's sake,' he said. 'Stop fighting, Aaron.'

The kid stopped struggling at the sound of his name and when he realised it was Jimmy he calmed down. The guard scrambled to his feet.

'I know this kid,' Jimmy said. 'What's he done?' He got his

answer when a couple of DVDs fell out of the kid's jacket as the guard got up.

The guard was steaming, probably embarrassed by his fall. He grabbed Aaron by his shirtfront and looked ready to thump him. Fortunately, at the same moment, Aoife appeared on the scene, coming out of the library entrance and picking up the DVDs from the floor. As far as Jimmy was aware the kid didn't even have a DVD player in his room.

'Let go of the boy, David,' she said, addressing the security guard, who reluctantly did as he was asked.

'You know these are free if you join the library, don't you?' she said to Aaron.

The kid mumbled something, his head drooping. Aoife reminded Jimmy of an old schoolteacher he used to have. There was something about her that commanded respect.

'Is he one of your kids?' she asked Jimmy, who nodded. 'Giving you any problems?'

The pool table fight flickered through his memory but it never really turned into anything, so he put the thought to one side and shook his head.

'He's new, but no bother so far.'

'Make sure it stays that way,' she said, turning to the security guard. 'You OK with a warning this time?'

The man nodded, stepping away from Aaron and tucking his shirt back in. Aoife turned her attention back to the kid.

'You're only getting away with this because of Jimmy here, understand? If you get caught again, we'll call the police. Now get away with you.'

Aaron didn't need telling twice, legging it down the slipway towards Northumberland Street.

Aoife turned back to Jimmy with a smile on her face, order restored in an instant.

'Shall we get on?' she said. For some reason, the head librarian had always had a soft spot for him and he owed her a lot; she was the woman who'd steered him towards the Veterans' Therapy Group that had helped stem the flood of nightmares brought on by his PTSD. She had a grandson who'd served in the army and knew how much it had helped him.

'You look remarkably chipper for someone who's just been involved in a fight outside,' she said, as they approached her desk.

'I wasn't "involved". And it was hardly a fight. But, yes, I'm good, thanks.'

Aoife gave him one of those looks that made him feel about ten. You couldn't hide anything from the woman.

'My daughter's getting married,' he said.

'That's lovely news.'

'And she's asked me to give her away,' he added.

Aoife turned and gave him a huge hug.

'Oh, Jimmy, you must be thrilled.'

She was one of the few people that knew a bit about his past. She certainly knew how difficult he'd found it to get back into anything like a normal life after being released from prison and how big a deal this was for him.

'I am,' he admitted. He was amazed that Bev hadn't raised any objections to their daughter's announcement the night before but guessed that she didn't want to rock the boat after her earlier outburst. He wouldn't be surprised if she came back to it though.

'I've found what you were looking for,' Aoife said, picking up a file from behind her desk. 'Let's go into one of the reading rooms and I can talk you through it.'

Jimmy's conversation with Susan Becket on the walk had thrown him a little. She'd been one of his prime suspects for framing Gadge, as he'd assumed she'd inherited the same poisonous genes as her brother, but she'd genuinely seemed ignorant about what had really happened to Becket so he had to have a rethink. His plan B had involved doing some internet research and that definitely wasn't part of his skill set. Normally he'd have got Gadge to do it but that was a non-starter so he'd asked Aoife and it looked like she'd cracked it.

'I found some reports from the time of the accident,' she said, opening up the folder. 'Dennis Sweeney was eighteen when he died. His parents, Duncan and Marie, were in the press a lot at the time, especially after the verdict. They made a lot of noise about how lenient the sentence had been. Duncan was even found in contempt of court for claiming that he'd make sure the punishment fitted the crime "with his own bare hands".'

'Jesus!' That sounded like someone putting a marker down. But would the man have waited so long to get his revenge?

'How old was Duncan back then?' Jimmy asked.

Aoife flicked through the cuttings. She'd made notes on the edges of some of them.

'Ah, here it is. He was thirty-seven at the time of the accident, Marie was, um, thirty-five, obviously they had Dennis when they were very young.'

That would make him around sixty-five now. Was that too old to kill the man in the alley and frame Gadge? Not necessarily, he supposed. Depends how fit he'd managed to keep himself.

'Did Sweeney have any other family?' Jimmy asked.

'He had a twin sister, Leanne, and a much younger brother, Adam, who was only about four at the time.'

'And who'd be about thirty-two now, yes?'

Aoife did a quick calculation and nodded.

'Aye, there or thereabouts.'

He sounded a much more likely suspect, Jimmy thought, but Aoife hadn't finished.

'But it'll not be easy to talk to them.'

'Why not?'

'Read this.'

Aoife handed him a newspaper cutting. Jimmy checked the date at the top: 12 June 1989.

TRAGIC FAMILY SET TO LEAVE BRITAIN

A family whose teenage son was killed in a car accident are to emigrate to Australia to try and escape the constant reminders of the tragedy.

Dennis Sweeney, 18, was run down and killed in a car driven by local businessman Keith Kane, who was fined £200 for careless driving.

Sweeney's parents, Duncan and Marie, who

> were appalled by the apparent leniency of the sentence, have decided to try and make a fresh start in Perth where Duncan has been offered work as a fireman.
>
> 'It's been a tough time for the family,' he admitted. 'Every day Marie has to drive past the place where Dennis was killed. It breaks her heart, to be honest.
>
> 'Even worse is that the man responsible is just wandering around the city like he owns it while my son will never grow old, never have kids or a full life of his own.
>
> 'It's best for all concerned that we get away as I'm not sure I can control my actions if I ever see that man on the street.'
>
> Their youngest son, Adam, 5, will be going with his mum and dad but Dennis's twin sister, Leanne, is staying in the UK to take up a place studying forensic science at King's College, London.

Jimmy shook his head. It looked like a dead end, though it might be worth checking up on the sister's whereabouts – especially given her choice of degree. He wondered if she'd pursued it. How hard would it be for a forensic scientist to fake a crime scene? He added that to a long list of things he wanted to talk to Charlie Gascoigne about.

'Can I keep this?' he asked.

Aoife nodded. 'Course. I've got copies of everything. I can't promise anything but I'll see if I can find out any more information about where they all are now when I have a bit more time.'

Jimmy hesitated, he had one more request, but the words were sticking in his throat. It felt like disloyalty. Aoife seemed to sense his reluctance.

'Did you need something else?' she said.

'Aye,' he said. 'Can you see if you can find any other stories about Gadge, or Keith Kane, as he used to call himself? I'm worried that there might be other skeletons in his closet.'

21

Charlie Gascoigne sat upright on her exercise bike, pedalling away as she skimmed through the clippings that Aoife had found.

'He's a secretive one, your friend, isn't he?' she said, dropping the file onto the floor. Tidiness wasn't one of her attributes, Jimmy thought, as he scanned the other piles of discarded paperwork lying at her feet from his more comfortable spot on her sofa.

'Tell me more about this Becket character,' she added.

'He was a shipwreck of a man; a drug-dealing pimp who abused a young friend of ours for years,' Jimmy explained. 'Gadge rescued the lad from him, and battered Becket so badly that he disappeared off the scene for ages.'

'Until a couple of years ago?'

'That's right. He just showed up one day and seemed to be up to his old tricks.'

'And then he was killed in a road accident while under the influence of drugs?'

'Yes.'

'Which you think Gadge gave him?'

Honesty was the best policy if Gadge was to stand any chance of avoiding a lengthy prison sentence. Jimmy wasn't sure that his friend agreed with him on that but bollocks to him, the man was his own worst enemy at times.

'Probably,' he admitted. 'But no one else knows that and there's no way they can find out if we don't tell them.'

'So you don't think Becket's sister is involved in Gadge's latest problem?'

'No. But I'm looking into Dennis Sweeney's family as a possibility. They emigrated to Australia not long after the accident but they could have returned since. And his twin sister never left so I'll try and find out what happened to her.'

Charlie stopped pedalling for a moment, thankfully; Jimmy was starting to feel tired just watching her.

'Tell me more about this mysterious homeless man that your bouncer friend told you about.'

'After Gadge was turned away from Archie's another scruffy-looking guy had turned up at the door and been let in. The bouncer said he seemed harmless enough and unlike Gadge he was sober and lucid. He also reckoned that he'd seen the two of them sitting together on the bench that night.'

'Description?'

'Mid-thirties, well-built, bit of a limp. Oh, and a scar along his jawline that looked pretty fresh. Might be nothing but, given the limp and the scar, he could have been one of the earlier victims of the harassment looking for revenge. It's not much to go on and Gadge has no recollection of talking to him at all but I'll ask around the usual haunts, see if anyone recognises the description.'

Annoyingly, she started pedalling again. It was like it helped her to think through things clearly whereas it distracted the hell out of Jimmy.

'That leaves us with a couple more avenues to pursue,' she said. 'We need to find out more about the victim – and more importantly the other man who Gadge claims helped drag him into the alley.'

'Do we have a name on the victim yet?'

'Yes. Finally. His name is . . . was . . . Tommy Benson. The police say they've only just been able to track down the man's family, but I suspect they've been holding back the information to give themselves a head start on us. It's pretty standard practice, I'm afraid. The defence are often treated like mushrooms.'

When he didn't respond she glanced across and saw the puzzled look on Jimmy's face.

'Kept in the dark and fed shit,' she explained.

Despite her cycling fetish, he was starting to like the young lawyer.

'Have you got any other information on Benson?' he asked.

'Yes. But not much. He's single, no kids and lives alone. A couple of convictions for assault – and to no one's great surprise he was also a former member of the English Defence League.'

'What about a job?'

'He was a cab driver. Worked for a local company in Byker. Ouseburn Taxis.'

'I'll check them out. See if I can find out if he had any short friends.'

She looked a little nervous.

'OK.'

'What?'

She stopped pedalling again. This must be serious.

'Tread lightly. I hear things about them,' she said.

'What sort of things?'

'Let's just say I wouldn't book them to take you to the airport for your holidays cos you might find an empty house when you get back.'

'Noted.'

'Just be careful. Any other ideas?'

'Yes,' Jimmy said. 'But I'd rather keep them to myself at the moment.'

'I thought you were working for me.'

'I am. But I have to protect my sources.'

She gave him a cold stare. She may have been flushed and sweaty from the exercise but there was a core of steel inside her youthful appearance.

'You've seen too many TV shows, Jimmy. Spill the beans now or we're done.'

He sighed. There was no way he was giving up the full picture of his relationship with Andy Burns. He hoped she'd settle for some broad brushstrokes.

'I have a friend inside the police station. He's not on the investigation so he might help me out.'

'Ask him about Ouseburn Taxis. He'll know a lot more than me, I'm sure.'

'Already made a note. I'm hoping he'll also give me the names of some of the other victims of the harassment that's been going on. They probably wouldn't say much to the police but they might talk to me. Maybe someone can identify the other guy we're looking for.'

She looked impressed, nodding approvingly as she grabbed a towel from the nearby window sill and wiped her face. 'Not bad. And I doubt they'd talk to one of our usual investigators. I can see why Gadge wanted you on board. Anything else?'

Jimmy shook his head. There was. But he was definitely keeping that to himself.

'You want me to risk my job and give you confidential patient information?' Carrie said.

'Um, yes,' Jimmy said. Maybe he hadn't thought it through. The last thing he wanted was to get her into trouble.

She glanced at a porter passing behind them in the hospital corridor and gave Jimmy a similar glare to the one Charlie Gascoigne had given him earlier that day. But once the man had passed without seeming to notice them, she winked.

'Least I can do,' she said. 'But it'll cost you.'

'I've already offered to pay something towards the wedding.' He'd saved up a bit from his small naval pension and couldn't think of a better way to spend it.

'We don't want your money.'

'What then?'

'I want you to give me away too.'

Jimmy's mouth fell open in shock, as if he was some kind of cartoon character. Carrie actually pushed his chin up to close it.

'But . . . um, what?'

'It's very simple, Jimmy. You may not have noticed but there are going to be two brides at the wedding. Yes?'

He just nodded. This was a minefield that he wasn't about to step into voluntarily. He didn't have a clue how things worked in their world so tended to tread very carefully to avoid getting his foot blown off.

'And though I don't necessarily approve of the concept that a daughter can be "given away" as though she's some kind of possession, I know that my dad would have loved to do it. Obviously that's not possible.'

Carrie's fortitude in the face of her dad's murder had been a major factor in Jimmy finding the strength to battle his own demons. She'd become like a second daughter to him, though he didn't want to piss off the first one.

'What does, um, Kate think?'

'It was her idea. She didn't want me to feel left out and thought that it would be cool if we wandered down the aisle together with you in between.'

Bev might have a stronger reaction but that was a battle for another day.

'And that's what you want?' he said.

'Yes. Though you're going to have to scrub up better than normal. Us queers have a cool and trendy image to keep up.'

He could feel himself welling up. In the past he would have suppressed it but he was a bit different these days.

'Are you fucking crying?' Carrie said, laughing. 'You soft shite.'

'Course not.' Jimmy wiped away a tear. 'Dusty round here, isn't it?'

'So you'll do it then?' she asked.

'May as well – I'll be walking down the aisle anyway,' he said. 'Now can you get me those names?'

It took her less than half an hour. Carrie returned with a sheet of paper with eight names on it. All of them homeless men who had been beaten up in seemingly random assaults in the last six months. Only three of them had addresses next to them – not surprising but it was a start. Not all of them had reported the attack to the police – earlier that day he'd got similar help from Andy Burns – so now he had a pretty comprehensive list of potential witnesses to work with. All he had to do was track them down.

As Jimmy left the hospital, his phone buzzed in his pocket. It was a text message from Aoife: *I've found more news on Gadge. Call me.*

22

1989

The dingy boozer even looks shit when you're staring through beer goggles.

It's the kind of thought Gadge would share with one of his drinking buddies if they hadn't all buggered off home already. Fucking lightweights. Instead he necks his pint and orders another one with a dark rum chaser.

'You sure?' the barmaid asks. 'It's getting late.'

She's new. Otherwise she'd know what a stupid question that was. He bites his tongue though, no need to make another enemy when he's got so many already. Form a fucking queue, people.

'Nothing better to do,' Gadge says. 'Get one for yourself as well.'

'I don't drink,' she says.

'Body's a temple, eh?'

'No, just don't like the kind of person I am when I do,' she says.

Join the club, Gadge thinks, wondering if she's having a dig. Not that it's going to stop him. He's a drinker to his boots and it's only gotten worse since the accident. He pushes his glass towards her and, as he does, notices a red devil cartoon pinned behind the bar that he would swear he's never seen before.

'Did you know there's over a million Satanists in the United States?'

'I did not.' She's so uninterested she doesn't even turn around from pouring his shot.

He tries again.

'They're very good at hiding in amongst ordinary God-fearing people, apparently, but I guess you'd expect devil-worshippers to have a trick or two up their sleeve.'

No reaction at all this time. Lucy used to find his conversation fascinating but she was the only one who did. Used to. It's one of the reasons he's never in a hurry to head home. He can be ignored just as easily here.

Lucy's a ghostly presence in his life these days. He has no idea what she does all day since she quit her job. Apart from clean. He's tried everything he can think of to help her but suggestions of counselling, moving somewhere else, getting another job, a new healthy lifestyle maybe, have all fallen on deaf ears. She won't talk about it and their conversations have become more and more banal: 'Cup of tea?' 'Shall we watch TV?' 'Can you move your feet?' The latter being the most common as she spends every evening endlessly tidying the house, hoovering the carpets, and wiping down surfaces, like some housewifey version of King Sisyphus rolling his fucking rock up that hill. Clean house, clean soul, is her thinking, he reckons, as if it will give her some kind of redemption.

Whatever the idea behind it, it's not working as he's often woken up by her sobbing in the bathroom in the middle of the night. He doesn't know how long she spends in there as she moved into the spare room six months ago so she 'wouldn't disturb him' and won't let him in when he gently taps on the bathroom door to ask if he can do anything.

And he hasn't the foggiest what to do about any of this. So he drinks. And then he drinks some more.

His order arrives right on cue and he knocks back the rum instantly before taking a large gulp of lager to wash it down.

'Cheers,' he says to the barmaid, who nods perfunctorily and goes back to cleaning glasses. She clearly feels sorry for him. Maybe she knows he's the guy who ran a young kid down. Everyone else does. The temptation to put the record straight overwhelms him sometimes, especially when he's in his cups, but, so far, he's resisted. It would kill Lucy if people found out it was her driving. It's bad enough already but if she thought people knew what she'd done she'd disappear completely. Not in the literal sense, he doubts she'd have the energy to run away, but she'd simply fade away into nothingness. He hates it that a part of him thinks that would almost be easier.

Gadge reaches for his pint but gets it wrong and knocks the glass over, soaking his trousers and falling off his stool as he tries to avoid the beer dripping off the bar. He lands on the base of his spine which hurts like hell. He's tempted to stay down, wallowing in his own misery, but instead pulls himself up off the floor, grabs his coat from a hook on the wall and stumbles out, avoiding the barmaid's no-doubt pitiful gaze.

The house isn't far away but he's hardly walking in a straight line, so it takes a while for him to get there. He stops once, thinking he's going to throw up, but as he puts his hands on his knees the movement triggers a motion sensor on someone's front porch and a light comes on. A dog barks from inside the house and he manages to get himself going again without vomming all over the guy's garden and making yet another new enemy.

Eventually he reaches his driveway and fumbles in his pocket, dropping the keys first time round but somehow managing to get the right one in the lock before stumbling into the house. It's silent but that's par for the course these days. He thinks about making himself something to eat but knows he's too far gone for that and heads straight upstairs. The door to the spare room is wide open but there's no sign of Lucy. She's not in the bathroom either and he wonders for a moment if she's actually moved back into their own bed but the idea's so ludicrous that he knows it's a non-starter. Still, he looks, knowing for sure it's not gonna be like the last time this happened – they haven't had sex in at least a year so it's not another miscarriage. Unsurprisingly, she's not there. He heads back downstairs, somehow feeling his head clear a little. Has she finally found the courage to leave him? He checks the cupboard under the stairs, but all their suitcases are there so that's not the answer unless she's gone with just the clothes on her back.

The kitchen is his next port of call but no joy there either. It's immaculate, as usual, wiped down to within an inch of its life. If cleanliness is next to godliness, then the room's a fucking temple. Apart from the strange smell. Lucy rarely cooks now but he can definitely smell something weird. He checks the oven. She's so spaced out these days that she may well have left the gas on. Nothing.

Where is she? And what is that smell? He can't believe she would have walked anywhere so he decides to check if the car is still in the garage. They still have the Jag but neither of them has driven it since the accident – too much baggage attached.

Gadge goes out of the kitchen door and down the path to the garage which is set back behind the house. Immediately he knows. He can hear a low thrumming; the smell much stronger out here. Exhaust fumes. He runs to the garage door, tries to yank it up but it's jammed. Another go but it won't budge. There's a door round the side but it seems to be locked. He has no idea where the key is. Didn't even know you could lock it. In his half-pissed state, he thinks about checking the drawer where they keep spare keys but instead has one more go. It starts to move, and the noxious fumes pour out through the gap. Someone has hooked something heavy on the door and stuffed rags along the bottom of it. Not someone. Lucy. Even through the smoke he can see her sitting in the back seat, motionless. He runs to the car but trips over a bag of old books on the floor and cracks his head against the boot as he falls. Blood pours out of the wound, but he drags himself up and somehow gets his hand on the door handle and pulls it open. The fumes are even thicker here, she's attached a hose to the exhaust and has run it through the narrowly open car window. He doesn't stop to turn the engine off, just grabs Lucy and yanks her out of the car, falling back against the garage wall as he does. The blood in his eyes and the heavy smoke makes it impossible to see if she's breathing so he picks her up and carries her out towards the garden, her feet catching on the doorway as they hit the fresh air. He lays her on the grass, desperately feels for a pulse. There's nothing. He screams for help, tries to remember how to give the kiss of life. The lights come on next door; his neighbour looks over the fence.

'Call a fucking ambulance,' Gadge screams, pressing helplessly on Lucy's lifeless body, attempting to breathe air into her. He's still trying when the paramedic arrives but it's way, way too late.

23

'Why didn't you tell me?' Jimmy said, as Gadge stared at the table in front of him, refusing to look him in the eye.

When Aoife had shown him the story about Gadge's wife committing suicide Jimmy had to read it twice to take it in. How could he know so little about his so-called best mate?

'Didn't want your pity, did I?' Gadge muttered.

'Fuck's sake, man, it's what friends are for, isn't it?'

Jimmy knew how hypocritical he was being. He'd never told Gadge or Deano the full horror of his own backstory. Most street people wanted to put their shitty past in a box and bury it deep underground.

'All that stuff about your ex-wives was total bollocks, wasn't it?' he added. Aoife had also accessed one of the many ancestry websites out there and discovered that, contrary to what he'd always claimed, Gadge had only been married once, to Lucy.

'You never married again after she killed herself. We looked it up.'

'She was the one, man,' Gadge said. 'You know what I mean: *the one*. And I failed her completely.'

The guilt was pouring off him in waves. Jimmy couldn't think of anything to say that would help.

'I loved her but that wasn't enough.' He was speaking so quietly that Jimmy had to lean in to hear him. 'There couldn't be anyone else after that.'

Jimmy got that too. When Bev had left him, he'd felt exactly the same. And that was nowhere near as final as what Gadge had been through. He gave him a moment but knew that it was a good time to confront the massive elephant in the room.

'It wasn't you who ran that kid over, was it? It was Lucy. You took the rap.'

Gadge looked up at him for the first time since Jimmy had confronted him with what he'd discovered about Lucy's death.

'H-how did you know that?'

'Obvious, isn't it? No one commits suicide because their partner runs someone over. It's got guilt written all over it.'

Gadge was shaking his head but it was clear his heart wasn't in the denial.

'Ever since I've known you you've done everything you can to avoid getting in a car and I remember that the one time you did you were white as a sheet.'

'Makes me feel sick even thinking about it,' Gadge muttered.

'I knew you weren't telling me everything the other day – when I mentioned drinking you were twitchy as hell. Was she pissed?'

Gadge nods slowly.

'My fault though. I should have stopped her and then, afterwards, I didn't try hard enough to save her. I knew she was desperate, but I hid in a bottle and stayed there. Still am. Walking cliché, me.'

Jimmy put his hand on his friend's shoulder. He knew it was an empty gesture but what else could you do?

'You did what you could, man. You took the blame and all the flak that came with it. You were crucified in the press, you shielded her from all that.'

'Wasn't enough though, was it?'

'You have to tell people now. If you're found guilty this time it could affect your sentence. The judge might decide to take it into account.'

Gadge glared at him. 'No chance.'

'Lucy's dead, mate, she's way beyond being hurt now.'

'But her parents are still alive. I don't want them to know what happened.'

'Even if it means you going to jail for a long time?'

'Aye. Even if. Understand?'

Jimmy actually did understand. Loyalty was a fucker, but if you had it then you had it, nothing you could do about it. He nodded.

'OK. But I have to tell Charlie Gascoigne and don't be surprised if she comes back at you on it.'

'I'll not change my mind.'

'I know.'

'So how about you stop bothering me with ancient history and go and find the twat who set me up last week?'

24

Caroline Fisher was a good boss. Jimmy had pretty much nothing to compare her with, aside from a couple of fresh-out-of-the-box officers back in his navy days, but she radiated efficiency, never lost her cool and, more importantly, was the woman who'd given him the job in the first place.

'A leave of absence?' she said.

'Aye, two weeks, if poss.'

'This is a bit sudden, Jimmy,' she said, pulling a folder out of her desk drawer.

'I know, but something's come up.'

She leant her head to one side, clearly waiting for a little more. He owed her at least that.

'Circle of trust?' he suggested.

Caroline smiled. It was a phrase they used with the kids there and meant 'whatever's said in the room, stays in the room'.

'Of course.'

'My friend's been arrested. For murder.'

Even the ever-calm Caroline looked a little shocked.

'Murder?'

'He's innocent,' Jimmy added quickly.

'Well that's good.' She picked at a bobble of wool from her cardigan and, pulling it free, dropped it in the bin next to her desk. 'And what are you planning to do in these two weeks?'

'Try and clear his name.'

'Have you spoken to your probation officer about that?'

Shit. Jimmy knew that they spoke on a regular basis. Sandy liked to keep tabs on him.

Caroline nodded. 'Thought not.'

He could tell she was regretting that she'd allowed him to invoke the circle of trust.

'You'll still be using the flat, I assume.'

'Yes. Of course.' That was mostly true. Contrary to what he'd promised Kate he was still thinking about spending a couple of nights on the street to see if he could lure in the missing guy from the alley. It was a long shot but he didn't have many bullets in his armoury.

'And what about Dog? D'you expect the rest of us to look after him for two weeks?'

Jimmy smiled. He half-suspected that it was Caroline's love for Dog that had got him the job in the first place. He detected an element of hope in her voice that this was exactly what he was expecting.

'I think it'll be fine, but I might need a bit of help now and again if that's OK?'

She sighed as if looking after an animal that slept for about twenty hours a day would be an unbearable burden.

'Well it won't be easy, but I'll do my best to sort out something if you need it.'

'Thank you.'

Jimmy stood up and headed for the door. As he grabbed the handle his boss spoke again.

'I hope you know what you're doing,' Caroline said.

He turned around and shrugged. 'There's a first time for everything.'

25

If there was one thing that years of living on the street had taught Jimmy, it was how to lurk in dark corners. Which came in handy when you wanted to stake out a place before showing your hand – look before you leap.

Ouseburn Taxis' office was nowhere near the river it was named after. Instead it was hidden away on an industrial estate just behind Newcastle's ancient dog track – where Deano worked shifts at the weekends. They should have called it Greyhound Taxis, Jimmy thought, though looking at the place it was unlikely they used the services of a marketing expert when coming up with the name. It was a handy location though; most reputable taxi firms wouldn't pick up anywhere near there, so they'd probably cornered the market in local bookings.

It wasn't the only thing they'd cornered the market in according to Andy Burns. Jimmy had shared a quick coffee with the cop that morning and discovered that it was an open secret that the real boss of the firm – obviously not the name registered at Companies House – was one of the more prominent local gangsters and the business had long been considered a front for prostitution, with the cabs being used to transport working girls to and from their clients.

Jimmy had approached the place with a degree of caution, hiding in the doorway of a disused warehouse across from the cab firm but he'd seen nothing to set any alarm bells ringing. There'd been little coming and going and he suspected it was mainly a communications hub – a fancy name for a man and a telephone.

He waited until there were no cabs outside before approaching the building – which appeared to be manned by someone who was working there to supplement his pension.

When he walked in the office the old man behind the desk seemed surprised that a customer had actually turned up in person. This was going to be like shooting fish in a barrel.

'You after a cab?' the man said.

'That's right,' Jimmy confirmed.

'Where to?'

'City centre.'

'Might be a while.'

Maybe there is a God, Jimmy thought, plenty of time for a chat.

'No problem at all, happy to wait.'

He sat down on the only chair that side of the counter. The old man fiddled around with his laptop, presumably booking a cab for him.

'Sad news about Tommy,' Jimmy said.

All he got in return was a grunt. He wasn't sure the man had even heard him.

'I said, "Sad news about Tommy."'

'Heard you the first time. I'm old, not deaf.'

'You don't seem upset?'

'What's it to you? Man was a twat. I wouldn't have pissed on him if he was on fire.'

Not the response Jimmy had expected. He tried a different approach.

'Right. His mate must be upset though, you know, what's-his-name?'

'Don't know who you're on about.'

'Short guy. Hung around with Tommy in that bar in the Bigg Market. Archie's.'

'Means nowt to me. Don't get out much these days. Just Netflix and chill with the wife.'

Jimmy had no idea what the man was talking about. He tried to get the conversation back on track.

'So you don't know his friend's name then?'

'Little guy, you said?'

'That's right.'

'How about Bashful? Or Dopey?'

Everyone's a fucking comedian these days. The old fella was sharper than he looked and suddenly went in for the kill.

'How did you say you knew Tommy?'

He hadn't. But he had prepared a cover story.

'Oh, you know, used to be in the EDL with him. Went on a few protests.'

The man looked over the desk at him and laughed.

'Aye, right, "protests". The only "protests" that moron went on involved kicking ten shades of shit out of a few Asians in the West End. Racist wanker.'

This wasn't going at all the way Jimmy had expected. He was desperately trying to think on his feet and failing miserably. Charlie Gascoigne was going to wish she'd hired a proper investigator.

'It was his friend I knew better really.'

The old man gave him a knowing look.

'The friend whose name you can't quite remember.'

Jimmy could feel himself going red, he was being out-played.

'I forget stuff all the time, so I know what it's like, but I'm ancient,' the man said. 'You've got no excuse.'

A door at the back of the office opened and a young, long-haired grease monkey, who looked like he hadn't listened much to his teachers, stood there with a bicycle chain wrapped around his fist. Maybe the old guy hadn't been booking a cab at all. There was a large garage on the other side of the door. Jimmy really should have done more of a recce when he got there.

'Problem?' the mechanic asked the old fella.

'Maybe.' The old man got to his feet and produced a cricket bat that he'd been keeping under the desk. Standing up he seemed sprightlier and clearly knew how to handle the bat.

'You obviously don't want a cab. No bugger comes here to get a lift. There are buses heading into town all day long just down the road for a quarter of the price. What do you really want?'

Jimmy thought about continuing the charade, but it was pretty obvious he'd blown his cover.

'Information,' he said sheepishly. 'About Tommy's friends. I could pay you. Both of you,' he added, nodding at the younger man. Charlie Gascoigne had said that she had a small budget for 'expenses' with the emphasis on the 'small'. He put one of his new business cards down on the counter. The guy didn't even glance at it.

'D'you know who runs this firm?' the old man asked.

Jimmy nodded. Burns had given him a name, but he knew it wasn't wise to repeat it in public.

'And d'you think he'd want me to talk to you about his employees?'

Jimmy shook his head again. The man poked him in the chest with the end of the bat.

'Well, piss off then, and stop wasting my time before I knock seven bells out of you.'

26

Beasley had a face that had received a thousand punches so it wasn't surprising he couldn't remember the more recent ones.

He was one of the longest-serving regulars at the Pit Stop, there at every mealtime, but rarely spoke and always sat by himself, humming the same tune with a puzzled look on his face as if it was something he'd heard on the radio but couldn't quite remember what it was called.

In other times they'd have said he was 'special' but people knew better nowadays – even the homeless guys – and there was nothing special about Beasley at all. Damaged is what he was – whether by his original family or others along the way, no one knew. And he wasn't about to tell Jimmy about that, or about who had beaten him up last month. Not in words that anyone could understand, anyway. Jimmy hadn't been at all surprised to see him on the list, and wasn't expecting much, but he had to start somewhere.

'Ah divvn't knaa nowt,' Beasley said, before Jimmy had even sat down properly.

The Pit Stop was pretty quiet, most of the early crowd having eaten and moved off again, so it was obvious, even to someone like Beasley, that Jimmy wanted a word when he plonked himself on the same table.

'I haven't asked you anything yet,' Jimmy said.

'Ah divvn't knaa nowt,' he repeated. Jimmy tried to look him in the eye but no one had ever really managed that, the poor sod's attention span had got shot to shit somewhere down the line and his eyes darted around constantly, never settling on one spot for long enough to get any clear sight of it.

'Can I get you some more tea?' Jimmy said, noticing the man's cup was empty.

'Four sugars,' Beasley said. He perhaps wasn't quite as lost as he made out.

Jimmy wandered off to fill the man's cup. Maggie, one of the older volunteers, was watching him carefully. She was very protective of the more vulnerable 'friends' and had a particular thing about some of the bullying that went on there sometimes. Sadly, like any community, the homeless one also had its fair share of arseholes. He nodded and gave her a small smile, which he hoped might keep her off his back, before taking Beasley his tea.

'Ta,' the man said, taking a huge gulp and belching loudly. 'Sweet like me.'

'Did someone hurt you recently?' Jimmy said. 'Round the back of the station?'

Beasley looked everywhere but at Jimmy, shaking his head.

'I didn't see nothing,' he said.

'What do you mean? Is that why they attacked you? Because you saw something you shouldn't have?'

The man continued to shake his head, resolutely refusing to look Jimmy in the eye. 'I didn't see nothing,' he muttered again.

'He bothering you, pet?'

Jimmy glanced up. Maggie was clearly not going to give him an inch. She was already standing next to the table, behind Beasley, who nodded.

'I just wanted to ask him a couple of questions about some men who attacked him,' he said. 'I thought he might remember them.'

'You may as well ask him to do his times tables for all the joy you'll get,' she said. 'You be on your way, love,' she said to Beasley, tapping him on the arm. 'It'll be getting dark soon.'

Beasley did as he was told, scrambling up and heading straight for the door, rucksack in hand, leaving his tea behind and not looking back.

'Poor love's scared of the dark,' Maggie said, sitting down in his place. 'If you want to know what's been going on with these attacks, why don't you ask me?' she said. 'I'll tell you what's what.'

Maggie was one of those women who knew everyone's business. Whether that was because she was a good listener or a nosy old sod, Jimmy wasn't sure. But either way she was exactly what he needed to start his investigation off with a bang.

She grabbed his list, borrowed a pen from him and worked her way down it, crossing some names off and underlining others until there were only three or four left for him to ask about.

'These are the ones you need to talk to,' she said. 'All the others are scrappers, always getting into bother, three of them are banned from here for getting into fights. Their pictures are on the board behind the counter so the newbies recognise them if they try and come back here and send them out the door sharpish. If they got beaten up it was probably their own fault.'

Everyone knew there was a zero-tolerance rule at the Pit Stop: any violence, towards other 'friends' or the volunteers and you were out. It didn't stop some of them though.

Maggie pointed at the first name on the list. Gary Jones.

'Try and find this lad first. He was a quiet one, not the sort I'd have expected to get into any bother.'

'I don't suppose he had a scar on his face and a limp?'

'Not the last time I saw him. He was quite fit, in every sense. Nice arse.'

Jimmy laughed.

'What, man? I might be old enough to be your mother but I still know a bit of totty when I see it! Anyways, my point is he might know something. He was in here quite a few times at the start of the year but I haven't seen him since. Bit brighter than your average friend, too, so if he knows something, he'll be worth speaking to, unlike poor Beasley who couldn't tell you what he did yesterday.'

Sometimes you needed a lucky break. Gary Jones was one of the men on the list that he had an address for. And Jimmy knew exactly where it was.

27

George hadn't changed a bit since Jimmy had last seen him. Still overweight, still bolshy and still the prick who'd thrown him out of the hostel back in the day – for a minor infringement at a time when he badly needed a place to get his head down.

'Long time no see,' the hostel manager said when Jimmy knocked on his door. 'Still no room at the inn though, I'm sorry to say.'

He didn't look sorry. Just smug, like always.

'I'm sorted, thanks,' Jimmy said.

'Aye, I heard. Poacher turned gamekeeper, eh?'

'Something like that.'

'What can I do you for then?' George said, putting his feet up on the desk, just to make sure Jimmy still knew who the boss was.

'I'm looking for one of your tenants.'

'I don't allow dealing here.'

Jimmy knew that was bollocks but he let it go.

'Nothing like that, just want some info.'

'Info costs money in my experience.'

Jimmy just looked at him. He'd known how the man would react, had planned for it, in fact. There was no way he was giving this guy any cash – he gave him one last chance to help out voluntarily.

'Lad called Gary Jones.'

'Means nowt to me. I try not to fraternise with the tenants. Maybe you should do the same now you're on the payroll.'

George had always been hands-off where most tenants were concerned, turning a blind eye to all kinds of rule breaking. Which was why Jimmy had been so pissed off that he'd been punished for not using his room enough back when he had one under a 'use-it-or-lose-it' clause in the contract. He'd always suspected that a backhander had been involved – probably from Becket's tainted hands.

'I just want a room number, George.'

'I want doesn't always get, does—'

George was interrupted by the fire alarm going off.

'God's sake,' he shouted, only just making his voice heard over the loud siren.

Jimmy heard doors slamming and footsteps clattering down the concrete stairways.

'It'll be fucking kids again,' George muttered, heading out into the corridor to take charge.

Jimmy took the opportunity to lean over the guy's desk and check the register. Gary Jones was in Room 203.

He followed George out into the corridor but instead of

turning left, as the hostel manager had, he turned right and headed for the back stairs. Some of the tenants were still heading down the stairs as he headed up, one or two muttering at him that 'it wasn't safe'. Jimmy ignored them. There'd been a time when he was triggered by any thought of fire, but those days were long gone – ever since he'd pulled Andy Burns out of that burning building, in fact.

He found Room 203 and rapped on the door. No answer. No surprise. No one could sleep through the racket the alarm was making and you'd be mad to ignore the dangers unless, like Jimmy, you knew it was a false alarm. He muttered his thanks to Deano who'd followed his instructions to the letter. Well, almost. The kid knew all about creating a distraction even if he had jumped the gun a little – Jimmy had asked him to wait at least ten minutes but Deano wasn't exactly known for his time-keeping.

Jimmy took a step back and launched his size eight boot at the door just below the handle. Something gave but it stayed closed. It flew open on the second kick. He stepped into the gap and flicked the light switch on.

Nothing. Aside from the usual furniture: a bed, wardrobe and small table, the room was empty. He opened the wardrobe door. Also empty. Jones was long gone.

He was about to leave when he saw something underneath one of the table legs. He leant down and pulled it out. It was a leaflet, folded up several times, put there to stop the table wobbling – like the doors, the tables were bargain basement material, probably a job lot from a fire sale, ironically. He unfolded the leaflet.

It was advertising the services of a builder's merchant in Heaton. Jimmy tucked it away in his pocket. It was the nearest thing he'd found to a clue so far.

28

Deano was happily munching his fish and chip reward as they returned to their own hostel, laughing at the memory of George running around like a blue-arsed fly as he sat calmly on a bench across the road watching the chaos.

'It was mint, man, I tell ya. Good job it wasn't a real fire cos there's no way he knew what he was doing. He was trying to get them to stand in rows for the wossname . . . muster . . . so he could take down names, but they were just wandering off, heading for the pub across the road. He was going mental at them and they all just ignored him. By the end he was the only one left outside the building. I nearly wet meself.'

Jimmy wished his part in the plan had been as successful. It was pretty clear that Gary Jones had moved on to pastures new and his investigation was back to square one. It was a long shot at best that the builder's merchant leaflet would turn out to be useful – he'd check it out, but it was probably something a previous occupant of the room had put there years ago.

He dropped Deano off and was still mulling over his next move when he stopped in his tracks. The door to his own room was open. Maybe someone had taken Dog for a walk and forgotten to shut it? It was pretty late for that though – he hoped the poor thing hadn't had a relapse from the poisoning.

He pushed the door gently and breathed a sigh of relief. Dog was fast asleep in his basket, snoring loudly. Jimmy knelt down and gave him a pat.

''Bout fucking time,' a voice said. Jimmy nearly shat himself. He spun around on his knees to see a blond man with coke-bottle glasses sitting on the chair by his bed, cleaning his nails with a sharp knife.

'Close the door,' the man said.

Jimmy did as he was told.

'D'you know who I am?'

Jimmy nodded. Everyone knew who this guy was. Though very few of them wanted to go anywhere near him. Stevie Connors was the man behind most of the crime in the city: prostitution, drug dealing, you name it, Connors had a hand in it. There were even rumours on the street that he'd recently moved into people-trafficking. He was also the real owner of Ouseburn Taxis.

'Hear you were talking to my uncle yesterday?'

Jimmy nodded again, now fervently wishing he hadn't left his card behind at the taxi firm. He'd guessed the old guy working there must have been family. In Connors' line of work, it helped to have people you trusted running things.

'Sticking your nose in where you shouldn't, wouldn't you

say? Good way to lose it, eh?' Before Jimmy could move, Connors flicked his wrist quickly towards him, the man was like lightning. He felt a nick just at the base of his nose which stung like a bastard. He put his hand to his face, blood flowed towards his lips.

'Don't worry, son, if I wanted to really hurt you, you'd know about it,' Connors said, wiping the bloody knife on the side of Jimmy's bed. 'Just nicked your septum. It'll bleed like a menstruating haemophiliac for a bit but no permanent damage. Now, how about you take a seat on the bed while we talk turkey.'

Jimmy did as he was told, grabbing some tissues from the bedside cabinet to help stem the flow of blood, which seemed never-ending, all the time hoping that no one had seen Connors coming anywhere near the hostel. He was exactly the kind of guy that his life licence prevented him from mixing with. Sandy would have a fit if she knew he was even in the same postcode.

'I hear you're investigating my boy Tommy's murder. Does that mean that the drunken bollocks the old bill have picked up is proclaiming his innocence?'

Jimmy nodded, moving the soggy red tissue away so he could speak. 'He didn't do it.'

'Is that right? Funnily enough I've never met anyone who did anything, according to them. See, I'm old school: you get caught covered in blood with the murder weapon in your hand and you fess up, get the best deal you can and serve your time. No one takes responsibility any more, do they? It's all fucking "no comment".'

Jimmy threw the tissue in the bin and grabbed a fresh one, the bleeding finally stemmed to a trickle.

'This time it's the truth.' He expected a laugh but the gangster just smiled.

'Strangely, I think it probably is,' he said. 'Who are you working for, son?'

Jimmy knew it was a trick question because Connors had obviously seen the card that he'd left behind at the cab firm but he played it straight.

'Charlie Gascoigne.'

Connors grinned. 'Nice. I wouldn't kick her out of bed to get to you. But wrong answer. You're working for me now.' He put his finger to his lips. 'No need to say anything yet. I've got my own people trying to find out what happened in that alley – cos I don't believe for a moment that the drunken old tramp they've nicked could take my boy out. However, when I heard about you, I thought it wouldn't hurt to have a second line of investigation going on, comprende? All you have to do is report anything you find back to me. Any problem with that?'

Jimmy could think of many problems with that but now wasn't the time to mention them.

'I know I've got a bit of a reputation but if you ask around, you'll find that I'm very protective of my boys, and that includes anyone who helps me out.'

Maybe it wouldn't hurt to drop Connors' name into the conversation now and again? There was a massive downside – like being sent back to prison for life – but he wouldn't get any shit from people like George.

Connors took his hesitation for resistance.

'On the other hand, I do have a spiteful streak and tend to overreact badly to anyone not immediately doing what I ask,' he added. 'I've thought about counselling to control that but I actually quite like hurting people so, you know, win-win.'

'Can't you ask the other guy who was there? The one who ran away. Wasn't he one of yours?'

For the first time Connors looked a little unsure of himself.

'Leave him to me. He seems to have, um, gone to ground. You concentrate on whoever else was in that alley.'

'And if I find them?' Jimmy asked. 'What will happen to them if I tell you? It's no use to my friend if they just get disappeared. The police need to know who did this if he's going to get released.'

'Least of your problems, son. Let me worry about who knows what. If you need a bit of added incentive just think about what's best for your Kate and her lovely mum – bit of a MILF, if you don't mind me saying. Or your little mate Deano, who I'm told works at the dog track. Or even the manky snoring machine in the basket here, I mean I've got nothing against any of them personally, I've got a couple of dogs of my own, love them to bits, but, you know, collateral damage and all that.'

Jimmy could feel the colour draining from his face. He clenched his fists. The temptation to beat the sneering twat to a pulp was overwhelming but he'd seen the speed of the man already and knew of his reputation for brutality. He might get the first punch in, but he doubted he'd be conscious for the last. Never say never but for now, he kept his hands down by his sides.

Connors gave the knife another quick wipe on the bedspread, folded it up and tucked it away in his jacket. He stood up, dropping a white card with a single mobile number printed on it onto the bed.

'I'll take that as a "yes" then. Keep me posted.'

And with that he was gone.

29

Jimmy was convinced someone had been following him to the probation office. Or his paranoia was coming back. Neither option made him happy. He was so distracted that he almost missed Sandy's first attack.

'So where are you going on your holibobs?'

Jimmy knew that Sandy was taking the piss. He'd bet Dog's life on the fact that, like him, she hated the word 'holibobs'.

'Sicily? Marseille? Off to join the Foreign Legion? Some other underworld hotbed maybe?'

Caroline obviously hadn't been able to keep schtum completely about his leave of absence. She wouldn't break the circle of trust rule but that didn't exclude passing on broad-brush information to his probation officer and that was all Sandy needed. Her twitchy antennae would work out the rest.

'I'm not John fucking Humphrys, Jimmy, you can't "pass". I do actually require an answer.'

'Nowhere,' he muttered.

'Nowhere? Just going to spend your two weeks in the same place you work, then? Seems a bit of a waste. You may as well earn some brass while you're there, surely?'

He should have known she'd see through him; she always did. There was definitely some Romany blood in the woman, he could easily imagine her staring at tea leaves in a big caravan at the Hoppings and telling him he was going to meet a sticky end. She'd probably be right.

'Thought I needed a rest.'

'From what, exactly? You need a kick up the arse, that's what you need. Luckily that's what I'm here for. So bend over, here it comes.'

She pushed the latest edition of the *Evening Chronicle* over to him. It was open on the lead story on page 3 from two weeks earlier, the headline *Homeless man charged with Bigg Market murder.*

'Unless there's some freaky-arsed doppelgänger shit going down around these parts, I think I'm right in saying that this is your mate Gadge, aren't I?'

He nodded.

'So your pal gets charged with murder and all of a sudden you need a couple of weeks off? And you expect me to believe that you're "having a rest". Who d'you think I am? Greta Gullible of Gullible Street, Gullibleville?'

He pretended to be distracted by Dog who was resting under the table. She wasn't buying it.

'Leave the fucking dog alone, he's fast asleep as per. Look at me.'

Jimmy did as he was told. She was like one of those

old-school hypnotists with the weird glare that he used to see on *Opportunity Knocks* when he was a kid. Once they'd locked you in you couldn't take your eyes off them.

She gave him the full force of the blast, even climbing to her feet and leaning over the desk to make sure he was paying attention.

'You promised me, Jimmy. If I find out that you've gone anywhere near this shitshow,' she said, pointing at the paper, 'I'll have your balls removed, shave the little black hairs off them, paint them silver and stick them on my fucking Christmas tree. Are. We. Clear?'

As she punched the final word, her voice cracked and her whole body was wracked with coughing. She leant even further forward, her head bowed, and put her hands on the worktop just to stop herself from collapsing. Jimmy leapt round the desk and helped her back into her chair. She kept her head down while the coughing abated and, eventually, she started to breathe a little easier. Finally, she sat up again.

He stayed behind her, leaning against the window in case she needed him again.

'Well?' she said, gruffly, without turning around.

'Well what?'

'Are we clear?'

Jimmy smiled. The woman was incorrigible.

'We are.'

She took a deep breath which may have been her getting her breathing back to normal but was more likely covering up a sigh of relief.

'Excellent. Now maybe I can go on *my* break with a clear conscience.'

He thought he must have misheard her. He'd never even known her take a day off. He wouldn't have blinked if someone told him she slept on the couch in the corner of the office just to save time.

'Aren't you going to ask me where I'm going?'

It was Jimmy's turn to sense a problem. He shook his head. He somehow knew this wasn't going to be good.

'Well that's rude. I asked you.'

'Where are you going?' he asked. Though he was beginning to fear he knew the answer.

'I'm going into the Freeman for some tests.'

'Pregnancy?'

She laughed. 'A miracle birth! Chance would be a fine thing. Nah, the doctors are going to see if they can find a heart.'

Jokes out of the way, Jimmy put his serious face on.

'What's wrong with you?'

'Don't put your sad clown face on, they're just being over-cautious. You know what doctors are like.'

It was his turn to wait her out. She swung her chair around to face him and smiled, recognising her own tactics.

'Learning from the master, eh! If you must know they think I might have throat cancer. No biggie.'

'Jesus, Sandy . . .'

'Don't you go fucking soft on me,' she said, quietly. 'I'm sure it's nothing.'

'Doesn't sound like nothing.'

'Can you sit back down now? You know you're not allowed this side of the desk. Just walk back over No Man's Land and take a seat.'

He did as she asked, pretending that he didn't see her wipe away a tear from her cheek.

'I'm sorry,' he said.

'Not your problem.' She hesitated. 'Well, it is your problem in a way.' She laughed. 'Big fucking problem, actually.'

'Go on.'

'My temporary stand-in, Nick Hardass, sorry Harding – not really big on rehabilitation, more of a "commit the crime, do the time" kind of guy. So, seriously, if you were planning on doing anything to help your friend that might bring you onto his radar then don't get caught. In technical, probation-service-only terms, he'll screw you so hard you won't be able to sit down for a fortnight.'

30

Gadge had collected some more bruises since the last time Jimmy had seen him.

'Made some new friends, I see,' Jimmy said.

The old man touched the side of his face, wincing as he did. 'I'm punchbag of the month, it seems.'

'Anyone in particular? I could maybe get Charlie to have a word with the governor?'

'That would make it worse, man, no one loves a snitch.' Gadge leant in closer. 'I swear I'm not being paranoid but . . .'

He saw Jimmy's expression and pulled back again.

'Fuck right off. I'm not, not this time anyway. It's just that it's not one guy, it's like, they're all out to get me – a stray elbow in the dinner queue, a football smashed into me in the exercise yard, a shove in the back on the stairs. If I didn't know better, I'd think the dead guy in the alley was connected somehow.'

'Connected! It's not the mafia, you know.'

'Same difference.' Gadge sighed. 'Maybe I *am* getting paranoid in my old age.'

Jimmy wasn't going to mention Stevie Connors' appearance on the scene – or his new probation officer. Gadge had enough to worry about without having to carry the weight of his woes as well but didn't they say that forewarned was forearmed?

'You're not paranoid. This time. Your dead man worked for Stevie Connors.'

Gadge went pale. Everyone knew the man's reputation.

'You're pulling my pisser!' he hissed.

Jimmy shook his head.

'Shit! That explains a lot.' Gadge's shoulders started to slump but then he sat up again. 'Wait a sec, how d'you know that?'

Jimmy hesitated. He knew that Gadge would resist him taking risks that might see him sent back down.

'The man himself came to see me.'

'You can't have anything to do with him, he's a psycho,' Gadge said, shaking his head. 'Stop whatever it is you're doing. Leave the city. Change your name. Whatever. Just keep away from him. I can do the time if I have to.'

'Bollocks. You'll not last five minutes. You've only been in here a few weeks and you look a walking corpse.'

'But—'

'Discussion over. End of. Does this mean anything to you?'

Jimmy pulled out the builder's merchant leaflet he'd found in the hostel.

'Is this anything to do with Connors? Cos you shouldn't go anywhere near it if that's the case.'

'Nope, completely different line of enquiry.'

'Line of enquiry,' Gadge mimicked. 'Listen to you and your fancy words. I remember when you wouldn't say "boo" to a goose.' He grabbed the leaflet from Jimmy and screwed up his eyes to read the small print.

'Walker and Sons. Never heard of them. Why?'

'Probably nothing. I've been trying to track down some of the other guys who were beaten up, hoping it might lead me to Shorty, your missing attacker. This was in one of their hostel rooms.'

'I doubt anyone in hostel accommodation needs a builder. Just some poor unfortunate looking for occasional work, I'd guess.'

'Aye, maybe.'

'What about Sweeney's family, any joy there?'

'Not really. Looks like they emigrated to Australia.'

'Long way to come to fuck me over.'

'Probably a dead end. What about your old business dealings? Anything I should know from back then? Anyone you crossed swords with? Anyone you let down?'

'How long have you got?'

'I'm being serious.'

'Look, I was a businessman, dog eat dog and all that, but there was nothing that bad. Truth be told, if anyone wanted to kill people from back then it would probably be me doing the killing.'

31

1995

Work is all he has now.

Since Lucy's suicide Gadge has poured everything into his business and it's crunch time. He's pacing around the anteroom, knowing that the man on the other side of the door is deciding his future.

As he was hoping, the technology to support his digital music device has improved exponentially since he first had the idea. Broadband widths have increased hugely, and his wishful thinking is edging ever closer to becoming a reality. All he needs now is more money to finish the job but surely it's a no-brainer.

The development costs are growing, for sure, but the ultimate rewards are massive. He knows that some of the big tech companies are also sniffing around the idea but he's well ahead of them in the race to develop something that could get off the ground in the next couple of years. And he has the patents – all he needs now is for the money man in the next room to come to the party so he can renew them.

But. And it was a big but. A kid he'd had working for him on a placement from Northumbria University has been poached by one of the big guns in the States for their R and D team. If that little twat has stolen any of his ideas, he's going to hunt him down like a dog.

Even so, it should be a formality given the progress he's made, but finance guys can be fickle bastards so he's not counting his chickens yet. And the company in-fighting hasn't helped. Bloody cuckoos trying to take over his nest – he'd seen the conspirators off, but he knows the money men get nervous when you can't present them with a united front.

Gadge checks his watch. He should have been in there twenty minutes ago. What's taking him so long? He can feel the weight of the hip flask in his inside jacket pocket. A small snifter wouldn't hurt just to quash the nerves. It's vodka so they won't smell it. He glances at the door and pulls the flask out, turning his back just in case anyone comes out suddenly. The cap's a little stiff but he manages to unscrew it and takes a rapid gulp, rushing a little so he doesn't get caught. He can feel himself relax immediately. Everything's going to be fine. He puts the lid back on and puts the flask back in his pocket before glancing at the door again. No bother.

He hears a click and a posh voice saying 'I'll go and get him' before a young, well-groomed man wearing a smart suit and fashionably long hair sticks his head around the door. He looks a bit like that young American actor who seems to be in every film that comes out these days, weird name, something Reeves.

'He's ready for you now,' he says, holding the door open. As Gadge edges past him he sees the man's lip curl slightly at something he's seen and glances down. There's a small wet patch on his trousers. He must have spilt a drop of vodka in his hurry to hide it away again and now it looks like he's pissed himself.

A tall, balding man who is sitting behind a large desk nods at him as he comes in: Nathan Lennon, the main investor in Gadge's company. There are a couple of others but they both follow Lennon's lead. He's a cold fish but has supported Gadge in the past so he's always tried to be nice to the man, despite the lack of warmth coming in the other direction. He's always assumed that warmth and venture capitalism are mutually exclusive things.

'Take a seat,' Lennon says, nodding at a chair on the other side of his desk. It's the usual shit, both smaller and lower down than Lennon's, showing Gadge who's boss, as predictable as it is pathetic, but Gadge grants him his small victory and sits down. He glances over his shoulder and sees the smarmy young assistant perched on a chair just inside the door, holding a sheaf of paperwork on his knees like a fucking lapdog. Despite his polished appearance, Gadge suspects the kid is an intern getting paid a pittance for his efforts, probably with a trust fund to fall back on should he need another Savile Row suit. He turns back to the main man.

'Nice to see you, Nathan,' he says.

Lennon frowns and picks up a document on his desk.

'Shall we get on?' As expected, he's generating the warmth of a forty-watt light bulb.

He's reading the document as if he's never seen it before when they both know he understands what's on it inside out. Nevertheless, he studies it for a good minute or two before putting it back down on the desk.

'How would you say it's going, Keith?'

'Fantastic,' Gadge says, knowing he has to overcompensate for the lack of enthusiasm on the other side of the desk that's draining all the energy from the room. 'The prototype is coming on leaps and bounds.'

'It is?'

'Absolutely.'

'Then where's the new financial forecast? And why haven't I seen anything other than the management accounts in the last six months?'

It's always about the paperwork with these guys. As if that was the only thing that mattered.

'I thought it was better that I focused on actually developing the product rather than writing about it,' he says, trying but failing to keep the sarcasm out of his voice.

'We were due an update three months ago.'

'Like I said, I had other priorities.'

'So how far are we away from MVP?'

Minimum Viable Product. The bottom line for people with no actual imagination, some shitty version of the end product that they can show to their friends. If they didn't have something to hold, they couldn't possibly visualise it. Gadge bites his lip and gives him the polite version.

'Soon, Nathan. Like I've said before, if we put something out there too early the big tech companies will be knocking off copies of it before we can blink.'

'I thought the whole point was to get this to a stage where the big tech companies *will* come in. That's how venture capitalists like me get some return on our money. We're not a charity. You do understand that?'

Gadge nodded. Venture capitalists. Vulture capitalists more like.

'And how many of the big boys have shown an interest so far?' Lennon continues.

'None,' Gadge mumbles.

A sort-of smile crosses Lennon's lips and disappears quickly.

'It's even worse than that though, isn't it? They're actively opposing you.' He looks over Gadge's shoulder to where his underling awaits. 'How many contentions have been raised, Martin?'

The unpaid intern starts flicking through his folder until he finds what he's looking for. 'Um, fourteen.'

Lennon looks back at Gadge.

'That's one in every country you hold patents. You do know what a contention is, don't you?'

Of course he fucking does. And he also knows they are usually malicious bollocks. The big companies throwing their weight and money around claiming his player wasn't 'novel' or that there was a 'lack of invention' involved so that patents wouldn't be renewed until it was way too late. Unless you shelled out big money on lawyers which would be better spent elsewhere. It was just a bog-standard delaying tactic, hoping they could slow down the development until they were ready to put their own product out there. He knew it and Lennon knew it, but the man was using it as a convenient stick to beat him with.

'That's hardly surprising, is it? It shows they're running scared. Bastards.'

Lennon sighed and picked up another piece of paper.

'How's the drinking? Under control?'

Gadge could feel his face reddening.

'I don't know what you mean.'

'I'm told it's getting out of hand. In the pub every night until closing time, and sometimes even later.' He turns to another page. 'Late starts and early finishes. Screaming rows with the technicians and junior staff left in tears following your temper tantrums.'

Gadge is tempted to rip the paper from his hand and make him eat it.

'Do you have someone spying on me?'

'I have to protect my investment.' Lennon stands up and turns his back on Gadge, staring out of the picture window towards the Thames.

'You know my wife died, right?' Gadge says quietly.

Lennon turns around to face him.

'Yes, my condolences. Though that was four years ago, wasn't it?'

'Five,' Gadge mutters.

'Here's the deal, Keith. I will approve another round of investment on one condition: that we appoint a new chief executive officer to oversee operations, someone who will make sure that everything runs smoothly, that reports are delivered on time and that we hit all our deadlines in product development.'

In the distance Gadge can see the vapour trail of an aeroplane heading to distant climes. He would like nothing better than to be on it and not sitting here, begging for support from this oily fuck.

'It's my company,' he mutters.

Lennon turns back to look at him.

'And still will be. But this will allow you to focus on what you do best, product development. You will be the chief technical officer.'

'Reporting to your puppet? Someone you parachute in to wrap up the business in a pretty bow and sell it on?'

'Your description, not mine.'

'And if I don't agree to this, you'll withdraw your investment.'

Lennon nods.

'And the others in the consortium?'

'They will follow my lead.'

For the first time Gadge wonders if Lennon is playing both sides. Maybe one of the big tech companies has got to him. Pull your money out and we'll reward you handsomely, a place on one of our boards, share dividends, you name it.

Lennon checks his watch.

'I have another meeting to get to.'

I'll bet, Gadge thinks. Letting your new friends know that you've crippled the competition for them. Smarmy twat.

'I'll get Martin to draw up the paperwork and fax it over to your office later today.' Lennon holds out his hand to seal the deal.

Gadge stares at him. The bastard has him over a barrel. He climbs to his feet and takes the hand, pulling Lennon close and staring into his lizardy eyes. He's so close to sticking the nut on him that he can actually feel the point of impact and see the blood pouring from the man's broken nose. Somehow, he resists the impulse and instead pulls Lennon closer.

'Stick your deal up your arse,' he says.

32

It had been a long time since sleep had come easy to Jimmy and tonight was no exception.

He was sure there was a time, back when he was a teenager, when he slept like a log but it was so long ago it felt like it had been another person. Despite the obvious disadvantages he still thought that he slept better on the streets than he did elsewhere, something to do with the space around him, escape routes aplenty and the regular noises of the night, sirens, police helicopters and drunks singing happily as they wended their way home. In a small room like this there was just silence. And no escape routes.

He was thinking about Gadge's story – he knew that his friend liked to exaggerate but you couldn't make that shit up. Coming so close to success and seeing it snatched away at the last second must be a bitter pill to swallow – which was probably why Gadge had washed it down with gallons of alcohol. Maybe Jimmy was lucky to have never come near to any kind of success at all. Fewer regrets.

A sudden pounding at the door broke through his thoughts. What now?

'Wake up, Jimmy, man!'

Deano. Since the kid had been clean he'd been sleeping for England, a solid ten hours a night, so it was unusual enough to get Jimmy straight out of bed.

'Coming,' he shouted, as another volley of knocking followed. He threw a T-shirt on above his boxers and pulled the door open.

'What's up?' he said, as he saw Deano's look of concern.

'Aaron's done a runner,' the kid said.

The youngster's room was stripped bare. No sign that there'd been anyone living in there at all.

'When did you last see him?' Jimmy asked Deano.

'Earlier this evening. We had a game of pool but he was shite, seemed distracted. I tried to find out what was going on but ya knaa what he's like. Said he'd been to see his mam but that was it.'

'He didn't say anything at all about leaving?'

'Nowt. I heard a bit of noise from his room as I was dropping off but didn't think much of it, then his door slammed shut. By the time I'd got up to look he was gone.'

'You've been talking to him, any idea where he might go?'

'Not home again, that's for sure. That was about the only thing he ever let slip – his mam had a new bloke who sounded like a nightmare.'

Jimmy remembered that was the one thing the kid had told him when he first turned up. He'd made a point of it, in fact – a cry for help, maybe? Perhaps he should have taken more notice.

'Feel like I should have kept a better eye on him,' Deano added.

'Not your fault. But I'm going to have to report this in the morning.'

'I knaa.'

Jimmy could see that Deano wanted to say something else. He had a 'tell' when he wasn't sure what to do, he kind of bounced from one foot to the other – like he badly needed a piss but was trying to hold it in.

'What is it?' Jimmy said.

As always, Deano seemed surprised that he was so easy to read. One day Jimmy would tell him about his obvious body language but it often came in useful so for now he kept schtum.

'We could go after him. He's not that clever so he'll go to one of the obvious places. Make the same rookie mistakes that I made when I was young and stupid.'

Jimmy avoided the obvious joke and glanced at his clock. 12.30 a.m. He had a lot to do the next day and really needed to get some kip. This was a distraction he could do without, but it wasn't a great time for a young kid to be out there on his own – the predators would be gathering.

This time Deano seemed to read his mind.

'What if there's another Becket out there?' he said quietly.

Sod it. Jimmy nodded and Deano's face lit up.

'I'll get me coat,' the kid said.

*

It didn't take long to find him. The younger runaways always made the same mistakes, thinking it was safer to be in the centre of things when the opposite was true. Safety lay out on the edges, away from the drunks and the nightcrawlers, creepy fucks who prowled the city centre streets after dark, looking out for the weak and vulnerable. Something that Deano knew only too well.

They'd tried the area around Central Station first but then headed to the next most obvious spot, the Quayside, where they quickly hit pay dirt. Deano spotted the kid's trainers first, a distinctive pair of Adidas with an orange flash, sticking out from the bottom of a damaged cardboard box.

The stupid prat had crashed under the start of the Swing Bridge, one of the more dangerous sleep-spots in Newcastle. Jimmy knew from bitter experience that it was too close to the Quayside clubs – a walkthrough for the drunks looking for somewhere to take a piss – so you were likely to either get a kicking or a lukewarm shower. It was hard to say which was worse.

The box was no problem for one night, given it was a warmish late-April evening, and even if it rained the bridge would keep him dry, but only a real novice would try and sleep in a spot that was surrounded by bars and clubs. They wandered over to warn him but before they got close the kid's head darted out.

'Get away from me,' he screamed. The kid looked close to tears. Jimmy was even more convinced he was younger than he'd claimed. Once the night was over, he was determined to find out what his story really was.

Aaron tried to back away, the light was pretty gloomy under the bridge and the kid had obviously not recognised them, but there was a wall right behind him and he had nowhere to go.

Jimmy held his hands up and stepped under the glow from a streetlight so he could see them more clearly. 'We come in peace, kid,' he said, quietly. Dog wandered over and started sniffing the edge of the cardboard which seemed to calm the lad down a little.

'Leave us alone,' the kid muttered. 'You can't take me back if I don't want to go. They're all wankers there, anyway.' He glanced around nervously, looking for help, as if he expected them to drag him away kicking and screaming. The nearby music venue was just closing so there were plenty of bodies around and he visibly relaxed. Jimmy sat down a few feet away.

'We're not going to take you anywhere but it's not safe here,' he said.

'It's fine,' the kid muttered, not looking him in the eye.

'No, it really isn't,' Jimmy said. 'Deano here could tell you some tales that would make your head spin but, believe me, you don't want to hear them.'

Deano had sat down on the other side of the youngster, closing off his escape route but also giving him plenty of room. They didn't want to scare him any more than he already was.

'He's right, mate, it's well dodgy here. And if you're gonna sleep rough you at least need a decent sleeping bag.'

'I'll get one tomorrow.'

'Where from?' Jimmy said. 'D'you have any money?'

The kid blushed. He obviously planned to nick one. And Jimmy would bet he'd get caught doing it. Any half decent store detective would spot him coming from a mile away.

'There's no need to nick stuff,' Deano said, which made the kid go even redder. 'We'll take you to the Pit Stop in the morning. They'll give you one for nowt.'

'Really? For nowt?'

Deano nodded. 'They do a canny breakfast as well.'

'How will you find me?'

'We won't have to. We're not going anywhere,' Jimmy said, taking his own sleeping bag out of his rucksack. 'Nudge up. Can't leave you alone with this lot about,' he said, nodding towards the crowds still flooding out of the club. 'Safety in numbers and all that.'

Jimmy wasn't being entirely honest with the kid. Despite his promise to Kate he'd still been thinking about sleeping on the streets to try and lure one of the roaming thugs into a trap and now seemed as good a time as any.

All he had to do was stay awake.

33

The Pit Stop was doing a roaring trade in soup and sandwiches by the time they got there. The kid had dozed all morning – despite sleeping like a baby from the minute he put his head down. Unlike Jimmy, who'd kept his eyes peeled all night but had seen no sign of anyone looking like they wanted to give him a good kicking.

Jimmy grabbed a bowl each and some bread to dip in it and sat Aaron down on a corner table where Deano joined them. The soup worked a treat. Jimmy could see the youngster brightening up as he wolfed it down.

'You'll come back to the hostel then?'

The kid nodded. One night on the street was enough for most people.

'How old are you really, Aaron?' Jimmy asked.

'Eighteen.'

No chance, but he let it go for now. It felt like the kid was ready to open up in other ways – something Jimmy should probably have pushed earlier to prevent his sudden departure.

'How did you end up at the hostel?'

'Left home.'

The lad wasn't much of a talker but, even though it was a long time ago, Jimmy remembered how quiet he'd been at that age. And you could have multiplied that nervousness by ten if he'd been trying to survive in the wild like this kid.

'Your choice?' Deano asked.

'Sort of,' the kid mumbled.

Jimmy indicated to Deano to give the kid some space, an old trick that he'd learned in the navy. People tend to fill a vacuum. Sure enough, the kid carried on.

'I told you before, I don't get on with Ned, Mam's new boyfriend.'

'Why not?'

'He's a dick.'

'Fair play,' Deano said, taking a bite of his sandwich, crumbs dropping onto the table in front of them. 'Been there, got the T-shirt.'

'Did he give you the bruises we saw when you first turned up at the hostel?' Jimmy asked.

The kid nodded.

'We had a fight.'

'Why?'

'He killed my dog.'

'What?' Jimmy and Deano said together.

'Dizzy used to growl every time he came in the house and the twat's scared of dogs. Reckons he was bitten by one when he was a kid. One day I came home and she was unconscious on the kitchen floor. He told me she was sick, that she'd probably just eaten something she shouldn't have. Wouldn't take her to the vets though, the bastard, said it cost too much and she'd be fine in the morning. She died that night. I'd had her since she was a puppy. I think he poisoned her.'

Jimmy had a flashback to the state Dog was in just a few weeks ago. He remembered how terrified he'd been of him dying. Poor kid must have been devastated. Maybe there was a connection.

'Might not have been him. Someone's been leaving stuff in the parks.'

'She can't have eaten anything outside the house that day cos the lazy sod never took her for walks, just made her crap on the balcony. He wouldn't even clean her shite away. I always had to do it when I came home.'

The kid's voice was getting higher by the second and people were starting to earwig their conversation, but he was on a roll now.

'Prick put poor Dizzy's body in a binbag and said he'd bury her in the park. But I knew that was bollocks so I followed him. He just chucked her in a wheelie bin. That's when we had the fight.'

'Did you tell your mam?' Deano asked.

'She didn't believe us; thought I'd had a fight at school and was trying to blame him. Like he said.'

'Why isn't she looking for you?'

'I told her it was him or me. She chose him.'

34

The quickest way to explain to an alien what Newcastle is all about would be to drop them at Grey's Monument at around 2 p.m. on a Saturday afternoon. Jimmy was sitting on the steps wondering what Earl Grey, the former Prime Minister who stood atop the column at his back, would make of it all.

Gadge had once lectured him at length about the man's achievements but he'd pretty much forgotten it all. Like most people all he really remembered was that he was the bloke the tea was named after. His Lordship would probably want something stronger if he could see what was going on in front of him.

A Peruvian band was setting up in front of the steps, hoping that they would drown out the two buskers currently serenading the shoppers, one with a ukulele, the other rapping over some kind of electronic backing track that squeaked out of a small amplifier behind him. The mass of shoppers were ignoring all of them, intent on racking up their credit card bills even further in the parade of shops surrounding them.

There were two God-botherers spouting their nonsense on either side of the statue's square base – one an Old Testament eye-for-an-eye type, the other more at the peace and love end of the scale – and a group of animal welfare activists, who even by Jimmy's standards appeared to have got dressed in the dark, handing out leaflets in front of the entrance to Eldon Square. In amongst them were scattered groups of Newcastle United fans, getting bevvied up before the match kicked off later that day, and one or two brave Swansea fans, who were amusing themselves by singing 'Hymns and Arias' to drown out one of the men attempting to spread the Lord's word.

Amidst the chaos, Jimmy had spotted the man he'd come to talk to, sitting to one side of a set of cashpoints – a useful place to stick your cap on the ground in the hope of a few handouts. No one using the machines could claim they had no money on them which was what most people usually muttered as they passed by someone in need. Gandalf was one of the longest-standing homeless men in the city; he kept himself to himself but was the go-to guy for anyone who wanted to know where the best places to hang out were so everyone in the community knew who he was.

A few years before, an artist had drawn up a map of the city based on how the homeless community saw it and the word on the street was that Gandalf had provided most of that info. Jimmy didn't know him well but they were on nodding terms. And more importantly he was on Jimmy's list of potential attack victims. He'd been treated in the RVI a few weeks back. He knew the man didn't like to talk much but also that he liked animals, so Jimmy had brought Dog along to help loosen his tongue.

He waited until most of the football fans had headed off towards St James' Park before making his move, sidling over to Gandalf and giving him a short nod in greeting.

'Mind if I join you?'

The big man looked a little surprised but nodded back.

'Free country.'

'Not sure about that,' Jimmy said, settling down next to his target. Though Gandalf had been on Carrie's list, he hadn't been on the one Andy Burns had given him so he hadn't reported his attackers to the police. Jimmy was curious to find out why not – amongst other things. The man was still showing signs of his injuries, there were stitches in his ear and some swelling to the side of his face.

'Looks like you got a kicking,' Jimmy said.

The big man put his hand to his face as if he was surprised it was still noticeable.

'Ah, not really. Wasn't much of anything.'

He was also missing a couple of teeth although that might not have been as a result of a fight. People living on the streets rarely bothered with dentists, as Jimmy knew to his cost – his teeth weren't pretty either.

'Not what I heard.'

Jimmy had placed Dog in between the pair of them and the animal had behaved as if trained for the purpose, nuzzling against Gandalf's arm until he got his ears stroked, doing his job perfectly. It didn't soften the man up though.

'What's it to you?' he said.

'Have you heard about Gadge?' Jimmy asked, getting another short nod in reply.

'Bad business.'

'He reckons the guy who got killed has been going around beating up the homeless.'

Gandalf shook his head.

'Nothing to do with me.'

'Maybe you could identify him?'

'Doubt it.'

'Why not?'

The man looked a bit sheepish, which in Jimmy's experience was unusual. He was normally solid as a rock. Gandalf glanced around, as if worried that someone might overhear him before turning back to Jimmy.

'This doesn't go any further, right? And I'm not going to tell you who was behind it, understand?'

Jimmy nodded, wondering where this was going.

'I wasn't attacked.'

Jimmy waited for more but nothing came. He was going to have to work harder to get the blood out of this stone.

'What d'you mean?'

'It was a bum fight,' Gandalf muttered. Jimmy had no clue what he was on about so just stared at him until he sighed and spoke again.

'I got paid twenty quid to fight one of the other lads in the multistorey on Percy Street.'

'Do what? Why would someone pay you to do that?'

'They film it. Sell tickets on the dark web. People bet on it 'n' all.'

Jimmy shook his head. Gadge had told him about the dark web, where all kinds of perverted shit took place, but this was a new one on him.

'Who paid you?'

Gandalf laughed.

'No chance. I told you I was keeping schtum. Mean bastards, they are. Didn't pay the other lad his money after he was knocked out. Even though he'd put up one hell of a fight. Had to split my share with him when he came round.'

'That's why you didn't go to the police.'

'Course. Not stupid, am I?'

Jimmy wasn't sure about that. And if the man wasn't stupid now he soon would be if he kept getting the shit kicked out of him for a tenner a time.

'Who was the other guy?'

Gandalf muttered a name and Jimmy checked the list he'd shown Maggie at the Pit Stop. Sure enough, it was one of the lads she'd crossed off, one of the scrappers. She obviously knew what she was talking about. He sighed. Another dead end.

Gandalf was looking at his list with interest so he turned it around so the man could see it more clearly.

'Anyone on here you reckon might know something?'

He nodded and pointed at one of the names on the list.

'Try this guy. Last time I saw him he looked like a bus had run him over.'

Jimmy glanced down. Gary Jones. The same man Maggie had identified – the same man who'd done a runner from the hostel, though nobody else had mentioned his injuries so they were clearly recent. Was he the guy the bouncer had seen talking to Gadge outside the bar that night?

'What had happened to him?'

'Dunno, but he was covered in bruises and limping quite badly. A nasty scar on his chin too.'

It had to be the same guy. Maybe he was finally on to something.

'Any idea where I'd find him?'

Gandalf started to shake his head. It was second nature for him to keep his mouth shut. Jimmy would have been the same a few years back. Not my fight and all that.

'Gadge could get sent down for life, man, give me something.'

Gandalf stared at him, obviously not wanting to get involved but understanding how important it was that he did.

'You didn't hear it from me, right?'

Jimmy nodded.

'Check out Jesmond Old Cemetery. I've heard the creepy fucker likes to hang out there.'

35

Broken gravestones littered the cemetery. Even those that weren't broken were lying flat as if some weird domino-effect shit had gone down.

Jimmy glanced around. He reckoned at least a third of the headstones had been damaged in some way, and that wasn't even counting those on the ground. The mess added to the general feel of neglect that surrounded the place; ivy completely covered most of the graves and there were overgrown trees and brambles at both ends. Most of the pathways had disappeared so the only way to navigate your way through was to walk in amongst the tombstones. If you were going to remake *The Omen* in Newcastle this would be where you'd head to with your cameras.

He wandered through the graveyard, Dog at his heels, checking some of the names, lots of the city's most famous surnames featured prominently: Bainbridge, Fenwick, Dobson and Armstrong among them. But there were some surprises too, a few foreigners had crept in, he'd seen a couple of Russian names, some Chinese, an Eastern European professor of archaeology and even the long-deceased Jean Pierre, who it was claimed had been the first secretary in the French Embassy in the 1800s. What the poor man had done to deserve getting buried here Heaven only knew, you'd have to have got mixed up in some pretty depraved diplomatic scandal to end up in this godforsaken place.

And, if Gandalf was to be believed, this was the place Gary Jones liked to hang out. The man obviously had a taste for Gothic wastelands. Jimmy headed to the right, keeping his eyes peeled for signs of life, a likely sleep-spot or just a place to rest up and shelter for a while, gradually moving towards the north end of the cemetery which was a bit further away from the action and slightly overgrown, more hidden than the rest. He moved through the trees at the end, dragging his coat away from some sharp brambles, and sure enough there was an open space behind them but, aside from a discarded shoe and maybe small traces of a fire, there was nothing to write home about. No rolled-up sleeping bag tucked under the bushes, no cardboard piled up to provide protection. Nada.

He trekked to the other end with the same result. The only signs of life there, apart from a grey squirrel, which a still-tired Dog couldn't be arsed to chase, were some weathered planks under one of the trees, a couple of discarded wheelie bins and some wisps of smoke coming from the ground. Jimmy had heard tales of underground fires around the north-east, especially at those sites built on reclaimed land where old collieries used to stand. He had no idea whether this was one of those places, but it would explain the smoke, he supposed. Gadge would have known in a heartbeat.

As Jimmy headed for the exit, he noticed an old fella looking after a grave near the entrance who looked like he might be a regular. The man turned around and smiled at him.

'Nice dog,' he said.

'Thanks. That family?'

'Aye. The wife. Married sixty-odd years. Still talk every day.'

'Come here a lot then, do you?'

'Well I can't talk to her anywhere else,' the man said, laughing. 'That would be weird.'

'You haven't seen a homeless guy hanging around here, have you?'

The man looked at him a little more closely.

'Apart from you, you mean?'

Jimmy looked down at his clothes. So much for thinking he'd smartened up his act.

'Guy with a scar on his jaw. Bit of a limp.'

'Nope, sorry. And I'm here all the time.' He looked around and shook his head sadly. 'You don't get many people in here these days, as you can tell by the state of the place.'

It looked like Gandalf had sold him a pup. Jimmy smiled to himself, he should have guessed that the cemetery would turn out to be another dead end. Then he noticed the grave a few feet away. It could have been the fresh flowers that caught his eye but more likely it was the inscription.

DENNIS SWEENEY

1979–1997

A beloved son and brother taken too early

He turned back to the old man.

'Did you see who left these flowers here?'

The man shook his head.

'Sorry, no. They weren't here yesterday though.'

Jimmy nodded his thanks and headed towards the gates. It seemed a hell of a coincidence that a man who had been seen talking to Gadge just before all hell broke loose had also been seen at the cemetery where fresh flowers had been placed on Dennis Sweeney's grave. He had to find Gary Jones and he had to find him quickly.

36

A large flat-bed truck with its contents covered in a tarpaulin narrowly missed Jimmy as he entered the builders' merchant's yard. The clouds of dust following it enveloped him and Dog and for a moment he lost his bearings. Once the dust had settled, he saw a thick-set mountain of a man in dark overalls staring at him from the other side of the yard.

The man was standing next to an enormous pile of timber, but he was big enough that he didn't seem lost there, unlike Jimmy who was way out of his comfort zone. He had never been one of those DIY-type men when he was younger, rebelling at the rare moments his dad tried to teach him something, just to piss the old man off. And after he'd messed up his life he hadn't ever had cause to become one – not having anywhere to live made home improvement skills a bit pointless.

It was pretty clear the timber guy wasn't going to come to him so he ambled across the yard, trying to look like he knew what he was doing.

'Can I help you?' the man said when he got within a few yards.

'D'you work here?' Jimmy said.

'It's my yard.'

Jimmy reached into his pocket and pulled out the leaflet he'd found in Gary Jones's room. He unfolded it and handed it to the boss man.

'This one of yours?'

The man glanced at it without taking it.

'Looks like it. What of it?'

Jimmy could tell he'd got off on the wrong foot, the man was already being defensive. So he tried to soften his approach a little, moving Dog to the forefront in the hope that the man was an animal lover.

'Sorry,' he said, reaching into his other pocket and pulling out a business card. 'I should have introduced myself. I'm Jimmy, I'm looking for someone.'

This time the man took the card and studied it thoroughly.

'Private investigator, eh? Not sure I've ever met one of them before. How d'you get into that line of work?'

That was a good question, but not one he wanted to dwell on.

'I'm ex-military, started there really.'

The man laughed, looking him up and down.

'Seriously? I wouldn't have guessed that. Which service?'

'Navy.'

'Ah, right, that makes more sense.'

Bollocks. An ex-pongo, obviously. Jimmy chose not to

be insulted, hoping the ex-forces bond would trump the inter-service rivalry.

'I'm ex-army myself. Royal Engineers,' the man continued. 'Stan Walker,' he said, holding out his hand, which Jimmy shook as firmly as he could.

'Easy, sailor,' Stan said, laughing. 'I'm not into arm wrestling. What can I do you for, anyway? Missing person, you said, was it?'

'Aye. Lad by the name of Gary Jones. I found your leaflet in his room, wondered if he'd come by here, maybe looking for work or something.'

Stan blinked a couple of times, glanced slightly to his left and scratched his nose. Jimmy didn't fully buy into the theories that people's body language could indicate lying but you rarely got three of the supposed indicators in one moment. When the man then looked at his watch to buy some more time he was pretty sure that the next words out of his lips would be a lie.

'Sorry, mate, never heard of him,' he said.

'He might not have given you his real name. Mid-thirties, quite fit, though he might have been carrying an injury or two. I think he got badly beaten up quite recently.'

The man didn't even seem to be listening to him now, looking over his shoulder as if another customer had come in needing attention. Jimmy glanced around. There was no one there.

'Sound familiar at all? Possibly had a scar on his jaw.'

The man shook his head. 'Nope. Nothing. I don't take on part-timers much, especially those with a limp. It's pretty physical work and my full-time staff can cope with pretty much anything that gets thrown at them.'

'D'you think I could talk to them? See if any of them remember him. Maybe he popped in when you were out?'

'Sorry, mate, they're all out on deliveries at the moment.'

Over Stan's shoulder Jimmy thought he could see someone sitting in the office, but the window was so filthy he couldn't be sure.

'And we're just about to close up, if you don't mind,' the man added, putting his hand on Jimmy's shoulder and gently steering him towards the gate.

He considered resisting but allowed himself to be guided out. He'd be coming back later. Walker knew Gary Jones; Jimmy had never mentioned the limp.

It was just after midnight. The local pubs had kicked out their late drinkers and all was quiet. Deano glanced at the 'Guard Dog On The Premises' sign and laughed, pulling out his picks from his pocket.

'You don't need a sign if you've got a dog,' he said. 'It would already be barking its head off.'

Jimmy wasn't quite as sure so he stared through the gates. There was nothing to see. And if there'd been a dog there earlier, he would surely have reacted to Dog's presence. Unless he'd been in the office with the worker who the boss had insisted wasn't there, of course. He thought Deano was probably right but, having seen the sign earlier, he'd brought a couple of sachets of Dog's food with him just in case.

Deano had the padlock on the gate's chain open in less than a minute. The kid swore blind that he didn't use his lock-picking skills much these days, but he seemed suspiciously deft with them still. Maybe it was like riding a bike.

They entered the yard and pushed the gate closed behind them, slipping the chain back around it so it would look secure, and headed over to the office. If there was any evidence that Gary Jones had ever been there it would surely be inside that Portakabin.

'Think you can get that open?' Jimmy asked.

Deano checked out the flimsy-looking door and laughed. 'Does the pope shit in the woods?'

This lock delayed him a little longer. They were inside with the door closed behind them in ninety seconds. Jimmy clicked on the torch he'd borrowed from the hostel. The office furniture was sparse. One desk with a couple of drawers and two filing cabinets, the bog-standard, metal, upright four-drawer types. There was an ancient-looking computer on the desk.

'We're buggered if he keeps all his info on that thing,' Deano muttered.

It was unlikely. If Stan was anything like every other army veteran Jimmy had met, he'd be an old-school, belt-and-braces kind of guy, someone who made sure that everything was written down on paper just in case.

There were no locks on the desk drawers but the cabinets both had keyholes in the top right-hand corners. Jimmy tugged at one of the drawers and it rolled open. No need for Deano's skills on these.

While he examined the cabinet Deano pulled the window blind closed, turned his own torch on, and started checking the desk.

'Remember we're looking for any trace of Gary Jones,' Jimmy said. 'Maybe a wages book, or even an order book if he was a customer. I'm pretty sure there's a connection somewhere here.'

The first drawer Jimmy pulled open was full of orders and invoices, dating back at least a couple of years by the look of it. He flicked through them to work out what order they were in.

'Jimmy?' Deano whispered. Jimmy glanced over and saw that the kid was holding a ledger in his hand. 'Does this say "Wages"?' he asked, holding the book up to display the cover. Jimmy shone the torch on the book and nodded, laughing at Deano's broad smile. His reading was coming on a treat.

Jimmy turned back to the cabinet and quickly realised the papers were in alphabetical order of client's surnames. He flicked through H and I until he got to J. He pulled out the thick file but just as he did there was a scrape of metal outside.

'Torches,' Deano whispered, turning his own off. Jimmy followed suit, edging over to the window and glancing out around the edge of the blind.

They had a problem. A van was parked outside the now-opened gates, its headlights pointing into the yard. A uniformed security guard was standing just inside, holding the unlocked chain in his hand, surveying the scene. The bigger problem was the Dobermann on the end of his lead. Jimmy patted his pocket to make sure the food sachets were still there but had a horrible feeling that the dog might prefer to chew on an arm or leg.

Fortunately, it was a big yard with a lot of hidey-holes so he could see the guard hesitating as he glanced at the huge piles of timber off to one side and the equally large piles of bricks on the other. The man clearly had no idea if anyone was there, where they were or how many of them there might be. Jimmy wondered if he'd play safe, lock the gates back up and sod off – he was probably on minimum wage with no interest in getting the shit kicked out of him. Or maybe he'd radio for help.

Eventually the guard made his mind up. The dog could choose. He unleashed the Dobermann who immediately hared over towards the timber. A cat leapt out from behind the wood, jumping from one pile to the next as the dog stayed on the ground barking fiercely. The cat stopped at the top level and looked back as if mocking the snarling dog below. The guard whistled and the dog, slightly reluctantly it seemed, returned to his side. The cat settled down on the highest piece of timber to watch the show.

'We're screwed,' Deano whispered as the man started walking towards the office, the dog firmly in front of him, growling as it moved closer.

'Maybe not,' Jimmy said, grabbing the file and ledger and opening the door.

'What the f—' Deano exclaimed before following him as the slavering dog lurched towards them, straining at the lead. The guard held him back, for the moment, and stopped about six feet away.

'Fuck are you two clowns doing?' he shouted, reaching for his radio. 'Drop that shit now.'

'I'm working for Stevie Connors,' Jimmy shouted back. Even in the dim light from the van's distant headlights he saw the guard's body stiffen.

'Aye, right,' the man said hesitantly.

'You've heard of him then?'

'Who hasn't?'

Jimmy reached for his pocket.

'Steady,' the guard said, backing away. 'There's no need for that.' He clearly thought it was a gun.

'I'm just getting my phone,' Jimmy said. 'You can give Stevie a call, ask him yourself.' He held the phone out to the guard, who looked at it as if it was a hand grenade. He wasn't the only one in a state of shock. Deano was staring at Jimmy as if he'd grown a second head.

'You're bluffing,' the guard said.

'Fucking better be,' he heard Deano mutter quietly.

'Check out my contacts. He's on there. I'm sure he won't mind being woken up this late.' He nodded at the phone to encourage the guard to make the call.

The guard started to reach for the phone but then changed his mind. He glanced behind him then looked back at Jimmy.

'Get out of here. But you're not taking whatever it is you've nicked from the office. You can put that down now.'

He nodded at the file and ledger that Jimmy had tucked under his arm.

'No chance. Tell you what, I'll give Stevie a ring myself. What's your name? I'm sure he'd like to meet you.'

Jimmy made a big show of clicking through his contacts. He pressed the button and put the phone to his ear. And waited. He was pretty sure there wouldn't be an answer because he was ringing Gadge's phone. It didn't take long before the guard cracked.

'All right, fuck it, put your phone away and piss off. I never saw you and you never saw me, right?'

Deano was gone before Jimmy had a chance to move, giving the still-snarling dog a wide berth as he ran towards the gate. Jimmy nodded at the guard and followed the lad's path. He saw the kid dash across the road and dive through a small gate which led down to the river and chased after him. Deano was waiting on the path at the bottom of the steps sucking in some air.

'Are you really working for Stevie Connors?' he said, once he'd got his breath back.

'It's complicated,' Jimmy said.

'It's not, man, he's a psycho.'

'True enough but needs must. And I didn't see you come up with a plan to get us out of there!'

Deano laughed. 'What d'you mean us, old man? I had a plan. I was just gonna leg it. Pretty sure I can run faster than you so if the dog was gonna get one of us it wouldn't have been me.'

37

Andy Burns scratched his head. If stress had a human face this is what it would look like, Jimmy thought, as the cop pushed the file and the ledger back across the table to him.

'I'm not sure what you want me to do with this, Jimmy.'

'Stan Walker claimed he'd never heard of Gary Jones, but these show he was lying.'

Jimmy pulled out an invoice that he'd found with Jones's name on the top.

'Jones ordered all of these materials from Walker just a couple of months ago.'

'It's hardly a crime to forget a customer's name.'

'Jones wasn't just a customer though. If you look at the invoice there's no payment involved. He was given these materials in lieu of wages.'

Jimmy had hardly slept, spending hours poring over the file and ledger when he got back to his room which was a nightmare as he wasn't a numbers kind of guy. Eventually he realised there was a cross-reference on the invoice which led him to the wages ledger. Jones had worked for Walker for two weeks and had been paid in kind – timber, sand, cement and aggregates, whatever the fuck they were, some kind of gravel, Jimmy guessed. He'd eventually worked out that, apart from the timber, he was looking at the ingredients of concrete. Though what the hell a supposedly homeless man would want with that he couldn't begin to imagine – unless he planned to send someone to sleep with the fishes in concrete shoes.

Burns sighed. Jimmy had persuaded him to come to the hostel first thing for a chat, but Jimmy could tell that the man was ready to pull the plug on their relationship if he kept pressing him for help. He knew he was pushing his luck but Gadge's life was on the line so what choice did he have?

'There are so many things wrong with this it's hard to know where to start,' Burns said. 'Firstly, none of these things are a crime. A businessman is allowed to employ someone on a payment-in-kind basis. The employee is equally entitled to get recompense for his work in materials if that's what floats his boat.'

'Yes, but—'

Burns held his hand up to stop Jimmy in his tracks.

'Let me finish. Secondly, Mr Walker is under no obligation to tell you a damn thing. If he wants to keep his business private then he can. In fact, he's pretty much obliged to under the laws regarding customer confidentiality.

'Thirdly, and I don't know how many times I have to say this, Gadge's situation is unfortunate but *it's not my case*. I'm missing persons, remember. I can't just saunter up to another cop's desk and drop evidence on it. Particularly when it's not really evidence at all.'

Jimmy again went to speak but the cop hadn't finished. He picked up the file with his fingertips as if it was tainted. Which it obviously was.

'Finally, I'm not even going to ask you how you got your hands on this' – he dropped it back on the table – 'but it's obvious that Walker didn't give it to you and I very much doubt that any of his staff would have done so either. So I'm going to go out on a limb here and assume you've nicked it. In which case it would be worthless as evidence, even if it was evidence, which it isn't!'

He practically shouted the last three words, which seemed fair enough, he was right. Jimmy knew he was clutching at straws, but a drowning man has to clutch at something.

38

Dog pulled at his lead, desperately wanting to chase the seagull that was taunting him from its lofty position on the park gates. Jimmy could see that young Aaron was struggling to keep hold of him but didn't want to irritate him by taking over. The kid had a short fuse.

He didn't know how Dog's seagull feud had started but ever since they had got together the mongrel seemed to be on a mission to rid the world of the flying rats. Maybe that was what united them – they both liked to set themselves impossible tasks.

Jimmy knew his investigation was floundering; he was chasing ghosts while Gadge languished in his cell. The poor man had put his faith in Jimmy and like most faith it had been horribly misplaced. What was it they said about 'beware false gods'? He didn't blame Andy Burns. The cop was right. He had less than nothing to go on, just some vague theory and an invoice for building materials.

Somehow Aaron succeeded in pulling Dog away and the pair of them strolled towards the park gates. The kid had seen Jimmy heading out for a walk and asked if he could come with him – said he knew a good place to take him. Jimmy didn't really want the company, but he felt a little guilty about Aaron. He and Deano had persuaded him to return to the hostel, vowing to find a way for him to return home, and they'd done the square root of sod all about it since.

'Have you spoken to your mam again?' he said

'No. She won't answer my calls.' Aaron sighed. 'You promised to help me,' he mumbled. 'But you've done nowt so far.'

That's all he needed; another mind-reader. Though, fair play, he was right. Jimmy had been racking his brains to try and come up with some way to help the lad but so far he'd drawn a blank.

They stopped by a large area full of wild flowers, it was overgrown but pretty colourful. Aaron bowed his head and muttered something. It took Jimmy a moment to realise he was praying. After a minute or so the kid looked up again.

'What was that about?' Jimmy said.

Aaron nodded towards the back of the bed.

'That's where I buried Dizzy.'

'I thought you said your mum's boyfriend threw him in a wheelie bin?'

'He did. But after we'd had the fight he went to the pub and I pulled Dizzy out and gave her a proper burial at the back of that flower bed, near the fence. I put a stick in the ground so I'd know where to find her.'

Aaron pointed through a slight gap in the flowers. There

was a patch of loose soil with a short fence post sticking out with the letter D on it.

'I used some Tipp-ex to write on it,' the kid said proudly. Jimmy rubbed the lad's shoulder, but his hand was shrugged off.

'You shouldn't make promises you can't keep.'

Jimmy sighed. The kid was right. The sight of yet another overflowing rubbish bin by the gates gave him an idea though.

'I'm working on something,' he said.

The kid turned his back on him and kicked a stone off the path. He didn't believe him.

'Your mam's house, is it council?' Jimmy asked.

Aaron looked a bit puzzled at first but then nodded. 'I think so, aye, Mam's always complaining about the council not fixing stuff.'

'And it's in Byker, you said?'

'Aye, Molineux Court, just behind Shields Road.'

Jimmy smiled, a vague plan beginning to take shape in his head. It was like watching one of those street artists that you sometimes found by the Monument, just some disconnected lines that didn't fit together but would eventually make a complete picture. At least that's what he hoped it was.

As they left the park a large black car pulled to a halt just in front of them, causing Dog to leap away from the kerb – he hated cars even more than seagulls. The front passenger door opened and a large shaven-headed woman got out. She looked like the actress from that *Alien* film – tough, fit and deadly serious. He could hear classical music coming out of the car radio.

'You, get in,' she said, pointing at Jimmy and yanking open the rear door.

Dog growled at her and she took a step forward.

'Don't make me hurt him. Just get in.'

Jimmy took Dog's lead from Aaron.

'Get out of here, kid, this is nothing to do with you.'

Aaron looked at him, then at the woman.

'Do as he says, son, not your fight,' she said. 'Though if you want to get in the car, I'll introduce you to Alex. He likes boys your age.' Aaron didn't need telling twice. He turned and ran off as if his arse was on fire.

Jimmy glanced into the car. There were two rows of seats in the back. A burly skinhead, with a tattoo on the side of his neck – Alex, Jimmy guessed – sat on the far side of the middle row, beckoning him in. Stevie Connors was sitting in the back, smoking furiously.

'Keep me waiting one second longer and the dog goes in the boot,' he said.

Jimmy climbed in, dragging a whining Dog behind him. The shaven-headed woman climbed in behind him, forcing him into the middle. Dog reluctantly settled at his feet, still moaning. The driver, who Jimmy was pretty sure was the mechanic he'd seen at the taxi firm, turned the music down and adjusted the rear-view mirror so that Jimmy could see Connors without having to turn around.

'Shut the fucking mongrel up or I'll do it for you,' he said. Jimmy reached down and patted Dog until he quietened.

'You talking to the cops about me?' Connors said.

Jimmy shook his head. 'No. Absolutely not.'

'So has Alex here messed up again? That's why we don't let him out on his own any more, isn't it, Alex? Hope I don't have to move you even further down the chain of command.'

The tattooed man turned around to protest, but Connors held his hand up to stop him.

'I don't pay you to argue. Keep it shut.' He turned his attention back to Jimmy.

'According to Alex here you had breakfast with a certain Detective Sergeant Burns this morning. Are you saying that's not true?'

Fuck. They were watching him.

'That wasn't about you. Andy Burns is a friend of mine, I was hoping he could help me get some information.'

'That right? You've got a tame copper in your pocket? I was always told Burns was a straight arrow. I'm almost impressed.'

Jimmy kept schtum. Connors was on the edge and he didn't want to do anything to tip him over.

'And what about security guards? You been talking to them?'

Double fuck. He should have known using Connors' name would backfire.

Alex flung out a casual elbow that smashed into Jimmy's cheekbone.

'Answer the man,' he grunted as Jimmy stuck his head in his arms to avoid further punishment. When he was sure no more blows were coming, he looked up into the mirror again. There was a large red mark on his cheek. Connors was still glaring at him from the back.

'I was trying to find evidence for you, got caught in the act, panicked.'

'Fucking right you panicked,' Connors said, jabbing the burning cigarette towards Jimmy to make his point. 'I'm not your bogey man, understand?'

Jimmy nodded, keeping to his silent routine.

'Understand?' Connors screamed. Sweat trickled down Jimmy's back.

'Yes. I understand.'

'I'm not sure you do. But I can help you.'

Connors' two goons suddenly grabbed Jimmy from both sides, gripping his arms and pinning him to the seat. He jerked around frantically to try and shake them off, disturbing Dog who barked loudly and tried to wriggle out of the footwell to help him.

Jimmy could feel Connors' breath on his ear.

'Rule One, Jimmy: don't fuck with me.'

The driver turned the classical music up to full volume. The sound of soaring violins filled the car. Connors wrapped his left arm around Jimmy's head, pulled it back and stubbed the burning cigarette into his neck. Jimmy screamed in agony and tried to thrust his head forward but Connors' arm and the two heavies on either side of him held firm. Jimmy's eyes were streaming, and underneath the sound of the violins he heard Dog's furious barking. The shaven-headed woman kicked out at Dog who howled in response.

'Get me something solid by the end of the week or I'll try this on someone you love,' Connors muttered in his ear before pulling the cigarette away and letting go of Jimmy's head. 'Get rid of him.'

The car screeched to a halt. The tattooed thug threw his door open and dragged Jimmy out onto the pavement, scraping his hands along the ground and giving him a couple of kicks just for fun. Despite the searing pain in his neck, Jimmy tried to reach out for Dog but Connors shouted, 'Keep the mutt, Bonnie' and the shaven-headed woman yanked the lead away from him. He grabbed hold of the door frame instead but had to let go when the door was kicked shut, crushing his fingers. He tried to sit up but the tattooed man pulled the door open again, cracking Jimmy on the head, before climbing into the car and pulling it shut again. The car moved away. They'd taken Dog.

The number plate was clear. Connors could go fuck himself – you don't mess with a man's dog. He was going to call the cops and bollocks to the consequences. Jimmy reached for his phone but his pocket was empty – it must have fallen out when they threw him out of the car. He looked around and saw it in pieces, crushed under the wheel when the car sped away.

Another screech of tyres. He looked up and saw Connors' car pull up by the side of the road about a hundred yards away. The rear door opened and Bonnie got out, dragging Dog behind her. The pair of them walked slowly back towards Jimmy, who leapt up and ran over to them. As he got closer Bonnie let go of the lead and Dog sprinted to meet him, licking the blood off Jimmy's scraped hands as he bent down to stroke him.

'Filthy sod pissed on the seat,' Bonnie said. 'Good job for you I like dogs, the boss was ready to stamp the little sod to death. Don't let me see you again though, or me laddo there will be mince.'

'This will sting,' Carrie said, as she placed a disinfectant wipe to Jimmy's neck. She was right. He leapt out of the chair as if he'd been electrocuted.

'Jesus, Carrie, that hurt more than the burn,' Jimmy said.

'I did say,' she said, indignantly. 'Sit back down and don't be such a wuss. If that wound gets infected it will be a lot worse.'

'Maybe she should keep hurting you until you tell us what really happened,' Kate said from her ringside seat on the sofa next to a zonked-out Dog. Jimmy had headed straight there, hoping Carrie would be in to treat his wound.

'I told you, it was an accident.'

'Aye right, and that Nigerian prince who keeps e-mailing me is the genuine article. You do know I work as an Anti-Social Behaviour Officer, don't you, Dad? How many times do you think I've seen victims of domestic abuse? Believe me, I know what a cigarette burn looks like.'

There was no way he was telling Kate he was involved with Stevie Connors so outright bollocks was all he had left.

'I told you. There was a scuffle amongst some of the lads at the hostel and I tried to break it up. One of them caught me with his fag. By accident.'

'And punched you in the face?'

Jimmy automatically touched his bruised cheek.

'A stray elbow.'

'And then you somehow smashed your phone when you fell?'

'Exactly.'

'Sting the lying sod again, will you, Carrie. He deserves it.'

Jimmy sat back down on the chair, hoping Kate wouldn't press him any further, he really hated lying to her. Carrie picked up another wipe.

'Have you got one of those leather straps I can bite down on, cos I'll probably bite my tongue off if you do that again.'

'At least you won't be able to tell any more lies,' Kate said.

'Call a truce, guys, will you?' Carrie said. 'It's worse than Friday night in A and E.'

She pressed another antiseptic wipe onto Jimmy's neck. He flinched slightly but the worst was over as she wiped gently around the wound.

'I'll put some cream on this and dress it but you should get it checked out again in a couple of days' time to make sure it hasn't become infected. OK?'

'Course.'

'You can come back here if you don't want to go to the doctor,' she added.

'Aye, we wouldn't want you telling anyone else that pile of crap about how you got it, would we? Keep the lies in the family instead.'

Carrie threw a wet wipe at Kate to shut her up.

'Enough, love. He's probably got a good reason for talking shite. I'm sure he'll tell us when he's ready.'

'He'd better.'

Jimmy breathed a quiet sigh of relief. He was out of the firing line for a bit. A good moment for a change of subject.

'D'you still cover the Byker area?' he asked Kate.

'Aye, course. It's where all the action is.'

'Block of flats called Molineux Court?'

'I know it. Not a major trouble spot but, you know, stuff happens.'

'When you're back at work can you check on something for me? See if anyone's raised any alarms about the people in one of the flats there?'

'Is it anything to do with the burn?'

'No, honest.'

'OK, have you got a name for me?'

'Yes. The woman who lives there is called Debra Mason. Her son's name is Aaron.'

39

The clock ticked slowly round to eleven thirty. Jimmy had been waiting for half an hour and every extra minute tormented him. Sandy had always been a stickler for time, but her replacement obviously followed a different model – make the bastards sweat – and it worked.

Finally, the door to Sandy's old office opened and a young girl walked out, no older than eighteen, he guessed, her orange face streaked with tear tracks which she was trying to wipe away with a tissue. She didn't look at Jimmy, just went straight out the door. A moment later a man's head popped out of the doorway. He looked like a stick insect, only thinner.

'In you come, Mullen,' he said, before spotting Dog asleep under his chair. 'And leave the creature there. I'm allergic,' he added, before disappearing back inside.

Jimmy took a deep breath, gave Dog a quick pat, making sure his lead was hooked around the chair leg, and followed his new probation officer inside. The man had to fold himself almost in half to sit down, his long legs poking all the way through to Jimmy's side of the desk.

'Take a seat,' he said, nodding at a hard-backed wooden chair that had replaced the padded leather one that Sandy had provided. Jimmy was already getting a glimpse of how things had changed – he was clearly not going to be allowed to get comfortable.

'I'm Mr Harding, and I'll be standing in for Mrs Fowler for the foreseeable future, as I'm sure you've been told.' He cocked his head to one side to prompt Jimmy to speak.

Childishly, Jimmy said nothing. Harding waited for a moment, a small smile gradually crossing his lips.

'I see. You'll find, Mr Mullen, that playing games with me is not a good idea. In fact, it's a very bad idea, a very bad idea indeed.'

The man had the charisma of a speak-your-weight machine, but Jimmy had no doubts he could still do him some damage if he didn't play nicely.

'I wasn't playing games.'

'That's good. Because you're in enough trouble as it is.'

'Why would I be in trouble?'

'You're aware that the terms of your licence preclude you mixing with known criminals.'

'Of course.'

'And yet you've been mixing with Stevie Connors, the most infamous criminal in the city. You're clearly not very bright.'

'That's not true.'

'What, the "consorting with villains" bit or the "not very bright" bit?'

Jimmy ignored the insult. 'I don't know what you're talking about.'

'You were seen in Connors' car just yesterday. Having a long conversation with him in broad daylight. I wouldn't say that was particularly clever on your part, would you?'

Jimmy blinked. He expected this kind of thing from Sandy but, as far as he knew, this guy didn't have the contacts she did. Someone had stitched him up. Young Aaron? He was there when Connors' car pulled up. Surely not? Maybe he wasn't being paranoid when he'd had that sense of being followed by someone. If that someone had taken a photo he was screwed but Harding would surely have enjoyed throwing that at him straight away. Jimmy called his bluff.

'Who told you that shite?'

'I have my sources.'

'You should get better ones cos it's bollocks. I don't know the man.'

Harding stared at him for a long time but this time Jimmy held his gaze, knowing the man had nothing or he would have produced it by now. Eventually the new PO dropped his eyes to a folder on his desk, which he flicked open.

'You seem to have led a charmed life since you were released from prison, Mullen. Mrs Fowler must think the sun shines out of your arse. There are several things in here that I would have had you sent back down for. And I certainly wouldn't have approved you acting as a counsellor for young delinquents – not with your record. It's a bit too much blind-leading-the-blind for my tastes. I might have to have a word with Mrs Fisher at the hostel about that.'

Jimmy said nothing, not wanting to take part in a pissing competition. There'd only be one winner and it wouldn't be him. He knew that Harding would carry on anyway, the man clearly liked the sound of his own voice.

'I'm going to be watching you like a hawk, Mullen. If you so much as cross the road when the red man's showing, I'll be all over you like a rash. Clear?'

'Crystal.'

'Then we're done. Get the fuck out of my office. And next time leave that filthy creature of yours outside the building. The sign on the door says Probation Service not Animal Sanctuary.'

40

Seagulls peck at his head. Jimmy brushes them off. Screams from behind him as the fire rages on the flight deck.

He tries to keep his eyes fixed on the horizon, not wanting to see the burning bodies behind him but a movement to his left catches his eye. There's a man swimming, waving at him as he bobs up and down. What the fuck?

It can't be his friend, Red, he's dead. He peers closer. It's Gadge.

It's obvious he's imagining it, so he closes his eyes and opens them again to make sure and it works. The sea is still there but Gadge has gone. He breathes a sigh of relief, not mad then. But then his friend reappears, his head bobbing back above the waves, his arms windmilling frantically. And Jimmy realises. He's not waving, he's drowning.

'They've started up again. I thought they'd gone for good, but I should have known better.'

Jimmy hadn't been to the veterans' therapy group for way too long. He'd been a reluctant attendee at first, but the combined weight of Kate, Carrie and Aoife had persuaded him to keep going and to his surprise it had worked. After his ship was bombed in the Falklands, Jimmy had been plagued with nightmares, a form of PTSD, everyone reckoned, though he'd resisted the diagnosis for a long time – too long. Despite his doubts – and they were huge – talking about his problems with a group of ex-servicemen with similar issues had made things better. So much better that he'd stopped going, thinking he was cured. He was wrong. Which was why he was sitting in front of them, spilling his guts again. It wasn't the sole reason but if you only had one stone you may as well try and kill two birds with it.

'One of my friends is in trouble and I don't know what else I can do to help him. My ex-girlfriend used to reckon I've got a God complex and maybe she's right. We've all been trained to fix things – had it drummed into us that there's no problem we can't solve with a bit of determination and a shitload of effort. Maybe I need to learn that I can't solve everyone's problems, not even my own.'

Several of his audience were nodding. They were an untypical bunch for a therapy session: no experts, no doctors or psychologists, just a group of former squaddies, airmen and sailors, recruited by word of mouth, sharing their war stories, their nightmares, their personal hell-holes without fear of judgement. Jimmy had quickly learned that having someone else to help carry your baggage could take the weight off your shoulders. But now, after dropping out of the group for a while, the nightmares were back. Not as vivid and not as frequent but just as troubling.

'I know we've all been trained to cope with this shit but

sometimes it's not that easy, is it? Sometimes you need permission to fail. So if anyone wants to volunteer to do that I'm all ears. Or maybe you need to give yourself that permission? I'm rambling now but I can't talk it through with anyone else so you're just going to have to suck it up.'

That brought smiles from some familiar faces. Although the group was supposed to be kind of anonymous, first names only was one of their rules, a few of the older members knew a bit more about him than he would ideally have liked. The payback was that he'd got to know a couple of them too: Joe, an addict turned drugs counsellor, who'd given him a ton of information when he'd got tangled up with a gang of dealers a couple of years back, and Mac, a former sapper who'd trained with the Israeli Defence Force and was therefore more than handy with his fists.

Mac had bailed him out of trouble a couple of times in the past. And, though it had never been raised by either of them, he strongly suspected the man was Aoife's grandson. He saw the two men sitting in the back row conferring and wondered which one of them would offer to help him first. Though it wasn't either of them he really wanted to talk to.

'Anyway, I think my point is that nobody's perfect, I'm definitely not and I'm pretty sure none of you are either.'

More smiles.

'And if this group's taught me anything, it's that we're not alone. There's always help out there if you need it. Even if some of the potential helpers have been royal fuck-ups in the past, they still have something to offer. Even you, Joe.'

The rest of the group turned around to taunt a red-faced

Joe, so Jimmy took his chance to get off the speaking chair and rejoin the group. He'd planted a seed and just had to wait for it to start growing. He wouldn't have to wait long.

The post-session tea and biccy chats were always lively affairs though nobody spoke about their problems after the formal meeting was over. The soul-searching was done until the next time. Now it was manly chat and the usual chest-beating, normal order restored.

Football was nearly always the main subject which was problematic for Jimmy as he knew zero about it and cared even less.

'That was about as subtle as a headbutt,' a voice said behind him. Help had come even quicker than he'd expected.

'All right, Joe?' he said, without turning around.

'Sound, thanks. Long time no see. Been too busy for us?'

Jimmy turned around and dipped his head, acknowledging that he'd gone AWOL for a bit. One of the expectations of the group was regular attendance – even if you didn't need help there'd be others that did and you had to pay your dues.

'My bad. I got sidetracked.'

'You're not the first. Just don't make a habit of it. How can we help you?'

It was Joe who'd figured out that Jimmy was the man people had started calling 'Sherlock Homeless'. A name conjured up after word got around that the same man who'd pulled Andy Burns from a fire had also been responsible for helping to solve a murder. Turned out that Jimmy wasn't the only ex-serviceman who needed a purpose – there were others in the group like him and they were keen to offer their services.

'It was Sammy I was after but I can see he's not around.'

Sammy worked for a surveillance company. He had access to some pretty high-tech gear, spy cameras, tiny microphones, stuff that might come in handy when you were chasing down people who were never going to talk to the police.

Joe looked around to make sure no one else was listening.

'What do you need from him?'

'I could tell you but then I'd have to kill you. Strictly need to know basis.'

Joe smiled. Jimmy had passed the test.

'I'll get him to call you.'

Sammy looked like a cool Jesus, with his long dark hair and neatly trimmed beard offset by a black T-shirt and jeans combo and sleeve tattoos which contained umpteen religious symbols.

He was already sitting in the corner of Heaton Perk with his laptop open when Jimmy arrived, drinking a cappuccino and looking nothing like the ex-intelligence officer he'd been in his younger days. Jimmy had already told him what he was looking for on the phone – he'd splashed out on another cheap throwaway to replace his shattered mobile – so Sammy had turned up fully prepared and got straight to business.

'Before we do anything I need you to sign for the camera

just here,' he said, handing Jimmy a pen and pointing to a document he'd laid out on the table.

'Maybe I should see the camera first?' Jimmy said. 'It might not be what I'm looking for.'

'You've already got it,' Sammy said, laughing.

Jimmy looked more carefully at the pen. It was exactly like any other pen, with a press-button top to start writing. He pushed it and scribbled on the edge of the document to test it. Just like a normal pen.

'I feel like James Bond,' Jimmy said.

'Well you've got the right Christian name, all you need now is a hot girl and an Aston Martin.'

'D'you really want me to sign this?'

'Up to you. But that's an application form for the gym around the corner so unless you want to pay thirty quid a month to keep fit I wouldn't.'

Jimmy smiled. He hadn't even looked at what he'd been about to sign. Sammy grabbed the form from the table and screwed it up.

'No names, no pack drill. I don't want any record of this in case it goes tits up. Just don't fucking break anything. I'm not supposed to lend this stuff out like some kind of spy-tech librarian.'

Jimmy couldn't imagine anyone who looked less like a librarian. Sammy took the top off the pen to reveal a memory stick connection.

'You can upload any photos or film onto a laptop by just plugging that in. Have a go.'

Jimmy was a bit of a technophobe, but he'd learned a few

things from watching Gadge over the years and this was something even he could manage. He plugged the end of the pen into the laptop on the table and an 'Upload Video' link appeared on the screen. He clicked on it and the film of the document in front of him began, morphing into a close-up of Jimmy's face staring at the camera. He pressed the pause button on the screen.

'And you can send live film straight to a screen as well?'

'Course. It's not the 1990s. There's a wireless facility so someone can be sitting in a remote location with a laptop seeing everything the camera sees in real time.'

'What if I haven't got a laptop?'

Sammy closed the laptop on the table and handed it over to Jimmy.

'You have now.'

'Really?'

'We look after our own, Jimmy, you know that.'

Rumour had it that a much younger Sammy, posing as a journalist, had been captured by Saddam Hussein's Republican Guard just before the US invasion of Iraq and had the scars to prove it. But he wasn't one of those who gave up much when he spoke at the meetings and his silence on the matter would always be respected so Jimmy just nodded and took the pen-top back out of the laptop. He replaced it and clipped the pen onto his jacket pocket so that only the end where the camera was poked out.

'So it can film when you wear it like this?'

'Exactly. No one would ever know. What's it for anyway?'

Jimmy hesitated and Sammy burst out laughing.

'Excellent answer. Loose lips sink ships. We'll make a spy out of you yet. D'you want to try it out?'

Jimmy nodded. Sammy pointed to an icon on the screen. A man in a black hat.

'If you want to access the app you just click on that. It'll then give you an option to watch live streaming. I'll bugger off with the camera for a minute just to prove it works.'

He took the pen from Jimmy and put it in his own top pocket and walked towards the back of the café, out of Jimmy's sight. Jimmy gave it a moment and clicked on the icon and then 'Live Streaming'.

An image of a white-tiled wall came up on the screen immediately. The sound should have told Jimmy what was going to happen next, but he was a bit slow off the mark. Gradually the camera panned down until he got a full on close-up of Sammy's dick, pissing into a urinal. A woman sitting at the table behind Jimmy groaned in disgust and a cackle of laughter spilled out of the laptop.

'Now that's what I call live streaming,' Sammy said.

41

When Jimmy had been released from prison he'd vowed never to set foot inside one again – but he'd been back so many times recently that he was on first-name terms with two of the guards.

As he approached the visitors' entrance on his latest visit, he was surprised to see an elderly woman waving at him from a disabled bay in the small car park. He hoped she didn't have some kind of mechanical trouble she needed help with as he was the last man to ask about that. He needn't have worried.

'You're Jimmy, aren't you?' she said, as he approached her.

He stopped, puzzled, and looked at her a little more closely. She was tiny, less than five foot, and looked way too fragile to be standing around in a prison car park on her own. Her grey hair was so wispy it barely covered her scalp and she had that slightly bent over way of standing that made him think she had a back problem of some kind. There was, however, a brightness in her eyes that suggested she still had her wits about her. One thing was certain, he'd never seen her before.

'Who's asking?' he said, looking around to make sure she didn't have company. He'd walked into enough traps to be wary of innocent-looking strangers, no matter how frail they looked.

'I'm Lilian. Lucy's mother.'

It took him a second or two to join the dots. Lucy. Gadge's late wife. The elderly woman standing in front of him was Gadge's former mother-in-law.

'D'you mind if we sit down a moment?' she asked, pointing at a bench by the side of the road. 'I'm not quite as nimble as I used to be.'

Jimmy nodded. Lilian shuffled towards him and he instinctively put out his hand to help her.

'Thank you. He said you were a nice man.'

'You've seen him then?'

'Of course, Keith told me you were due soon. That's why I was waiting for you. To see if I could help.'

He supposed he'd get used to Gadge having a real name some time but it still sounded weird. It took a couple of minutes to reach the bench and neither of them spoke on the journey, which Jimmy was glad about as he didn't have a clue what she wanted from him.

'He didn't do it, you know,' she said, as soon as they were settled. 'I've known him since he was a young man. He wouldn't hurt a fly.'

Jimmy did his best not to smile. There were many things he was still discovering about his old friend, but he knew fine well that he was more than capable of hurting people if he believed they deserved it. He chose not to remove Lilian's rose-coloured glasses but wondered if this was going to be a waste of time.

'He was so good for Lucy. She was always a troubled girl, even when she was very young, but he calmed her down, made her happy.'

Jimmy sensed that Lilian wanted to talk about her daughter so he left her space to do just that.

'I'd never seen her quite as alive as when she found out she was pregnant. It was devastating for her to lose that baby boy. She never really got over it. The accident may have pushed her over the edge but she'd been on the precipice for a while before that.'

Lilian looked at Jimmy knowingly. It was clear that she knew Lucy had been driving the car that killed Dennis Sweeney.

'She never told us, not in so many words, but a mother knows when her child's in pain.' She glanced across to the prison. 'That man in there sacrificed his reputation to give us three more years with our daughter. But even he couldn't save her in the end, hard as he tried.'

For the first time Jimmy could see a small glimmer of hope for Gadge. It might not help with his number one problem but having this woman as a character referee would do him no harm at all. He put his hand on her arm.

'Would you be willing to speak on his behalf if it came to it?' he asked, gently. 'I know it's a big ask, and it might mean blaming your daughter for the accident, but Gadge needs all the help he can get at the moment.'

'Does that mean you think he's going to be convicted?'

She may have been getting on a bit but she was still on the ball. He shook his head.

'No. Just want to have my bases covered.' He wasn't sure she believed him. He wasn't sure he believed it himself. He knew she sensed his doubt but she let him off the hook anyway.

'Of course I'll help. Why do you think I was waiting for you?' she said. 'After Lucy's suicide I was pretty sure that Keith would soon try to join her. I'd never seen a man so low, and I include my late husband – who never really recovered – in that. I tried to get him to come and live with us so I could keep an eye on him but I knew he wouldn't. When he disappeared I didn't ever expect to see or hear of him again. And I didn't until I saw the story in the paper the other week.'

She pulled a tissue out of her sleeve, wiped a tear away from her cheek and blew her nose.

'Unfortunately, I can see he's not far off that state again.'

42

1997

Gadge is sitting on an upturned furniture crate in an otherwise empty front room nursing a bottle of beer. If Carlsberg did misery, he thinks to himself, and laughs. He sometimes believes his black sense of humour is the only thing keeping him alive.

He'd sold everything he owned to try and keep the business going – including the Jaguar and most of his furniture – but even that hadn't helped. And now the house has gone. He's hardly ever been there recently – spending all his time in the office, sleeping there most nights, to try and salvage something from the patent debacle, but now he's done. He's pretty sure that Lennon has been putting the squeeze on, making sure his contractors won't extend his credit; he's probably invested in one of Gadge's rivals. He's tried to tell people but they just laugh at him, call him a conspiracy nut. But none of it matters now, Lucy's gone, the business has gone and now he's lost his home too.

It's a clean slate, he supposes; pity he hasn't got two brass farthings to rub together. He'd remortgaged the house twice to keep things ticking over so the money has all gone to the bank. Lucy's mum has offered him a room in their house but Gadge knows she doesn't mean it really, she's already got one depressed man sitting around staring at the walls, the last thing she needs is another one. Nope, he's going to take to the road, be like Caine – the guy in the TV series *Kung Fu* that he loved back in the seventies – wandering around the world battling evil and helping strangers before moving on to a new town.

The bell rings and Gadge gets up, humming 'King of the Road'. He walks into the hallway, picks up the rucksack that contains all his worldly goods – a change of clothes, a washbag and a picture of him and Lucy snogging from their wedding – and heads for the door. He can see the silhouette of another lovely young couple, the ones who've bought the house, standing outside.

As he opens the door, he sees their two boys kicking a ball on the front lawn, squealing in excitement.

'I'll be Shearer and you be Pavel,' one of them shouts.

'Nah, man, I'll be Shearer and you be Pavel,' the smaller one yells back, mis-kicking a shot towards his brother who catches it in his stomach and falls over pretending to be in agony, rolling once, twice, three times.

'Keep it down, boys,' the dad says, smiling at Gadge. 'Sorry about your lawn.'

'It's your lawn now, bonny lad,' Gadge says, dropping the

house keys in the man's hand. 'Hope the place brings you more luck than me.'

'Have you left a forwarding address in case we get any mail for you?' the man asks as Gadge heads down the drive.

'I'll be at the Heartbreak Hotel,' Gadge says without turning around. 'It's down at the end of Lonely Street, I hear.'

43

'You look like shit.'

Gadge's complexion was greyer than it had ever been, his beard was all over the place and he'd got the shakes back big time.

'I know,' he said. 'They found the illegal still in the workshop store. My supply's been cut off.'

Whoever said alcohol was a killer should see an alcoholic who'd been deprived of it, Jimmy thought.

Gadge stood up and wandered over to the door. He looked like he was going to try the handle even though he knew it was locked. Desperation was leaking from his every pore.

'I need to get out of here,' he said.

'We're working on it.'

'Not fast enough.'

Jimmy stared down at his hands. He would have liked better news but there wasn't any.

'It's going to take time.'

Gadge's face dropped. 'Do I look like I've got time?'

The question didn't need an answer. He looked like a walking corpse.

'I can't ever switch off in here, Jimmy. There are people in here who'd shiv you for a packet of coffee. I can feel them watching me, waiting for their opportunity. My best chance of getting out is on a stretcher. Have you found out any more about Connors' involvement? He's got his fingers in the pie for sure. Half the people in this shithole are his eyes and ears.'

'I'm working on that as well.'

'You sound like a police spokesman.' Gadge put on his posh voice – the nearest thing he had to a posh voice. '"We're exploring several lines of enquiry."'

Jimmy laughed. His friend hadn't completely lost his sense of humour.

'D'you think I should hire a PR consultant to help me deal with the press?'

Gadge looked him up and down.

'A fashion consultant would be a better investment. You look like shite 'n' all.'

'Bit rich coming from you.'

'I'm serious. I'm surprised Dog will even be seen with you. How is the manky mutt anyway? Never thought I'd miss him. Recovered from his poisoning OK?'

'Aye, he's fine, the vet wanted him to rest up for a while which suits him down to the ground. Lazy sod's barely left my room.'

'You any idea who was responsible yet?'

'I've got a pretty good idea, yes.'

Gadge sighed. 'Aye, well, one out of two ain't bad.'

'Give me a chance, man. I'm seeing Dennis Sweeney's older sister this afternoon, to find out a bit more about where the family are now.'

Gadge sighed and sat back down again.

'If you flog that horse any more the poor thing's gonna drop down dead before I do.'

Jimmy couldn't keep the irritation from crossing his face and Gadge didn't miss the look.

'I'm sorry, I know you're doing your best, Jimmy, and I appreciate it, I really do, but I've had enough.'

'Don't do anything stupid.'

'Why not? It's pretty much a family tradition.'

That was dark, even for Gadge. He probably didn't mean it but Jimmy made a mental note to suggest to the friendly guard that they put his pal on suicide watch just in case.

'I'll get you out of here soon, I promise. I'm sure that the Sweeneys are involved in some way,' Jimmy said. 'You're just going to have to trust me on that one.'

'I don't have much choice, do I?' Gadge said. 'You're all I've got.'

44

The room looked like any other on the university campus, if you ignored the overall-clad body on the floor and the blood spatter running up the wall.

Jimmy reached out to touch the latter but felt a tug on his arm.

'You can look but don't touch,' Professor Sweeney said.

'Sorry, Professor.'

'Please, call me Leanne. Professor makes me feel ancient.'

'The blood looks real,' Jimmy said.

'It wouldn't be much use for training the students if it looked as if someone had just been throwing paint around like some Jackson Pollock wannabe, would it?'

Not wishing to show his ignorance Jimmy just laughed. He'd ask Gadge who Jackson Pollock was next time he visited him.

'That's what this building is for? Replicating murder scenes?'

'Yes. Setting up reconstructions in the Scene House is as close as we can get to the real thing. Sadly, the vice chancellor isn't keen on us actually killing people.' She had a deep, exuberant laugh that made him like her immediately, which was a shame as he was about to implicate her family in a murder. He'd been necessarily vague on the phone when he'd made the appointment.

'Now, let's sit over there out of the way, just in case you're tempted to tamper with my scene again,' she said, indicating a small table and chairs on the other side of the room.

He studied Leanne Sweeney closely; she was much smaller than he'd imagined, had short brown hair, cropped close to her face, clear green eyes and an open, welcoming look. A long time had passed since her brother died and if it wasn't for the name badge, he wouldn't have recognised her as Dennis Sweeney's twin from the photo Aoife had shown him in the newspaper.

When she'd told him that Professor Sweeney had recently taken up a job at Northumbria University, Jimmy had been immediately suspicious. A forensic scientist with a vengeance returning to the city just before Gadge's arrest – who better to construct a crime scene that would fool the experts? But Aoife was less convinced. She'd explained to him about the GRF, as the locals called it – the Geordie Retention Factor. Apparently, you could take the Geordie out of Newcastle but you'll never take Newcastle out of the Geordie and many of those who left the city to pursue some career ambition or other came back eventually. Aoife reckoned the city punched well above its weight in attracting highly qualified professionals back home and Leanne Sweeney was probably just another one who'd been unable to stay away.

'Now, you said on the phone that you were a private investigator looking into a murder,' she said. 'I'm intrigued, though I should warn you I haven't worked out in the real world for quite some time so I'm a bit rusty. And if you're looking for someone to give evidence in court then you're definitely barking up the wrong tree. It's been years since I last did that. I could refer you to someone else though?'

'It's more for background than anything else. You might have seen something about it in the local press?'

She shook her head.

'I've been away at a conference for a couple of weeks.'

He'd check that later. Could be she had an alibi.

'A man's been accused of murder,' he explained. 'There's a great deal of forensic evidence to suggest that, but his lawyer is convinced he's innocent and I'm helping her prepare her case.'

'OK, but how do you think I can help? Like I say, it's been a while and I don't have any local contacts with the police yet.'

'The man who's been accused of the murder is Keith Kane.'

The professor blinked a couple of times, like a computer processing new information. The calculations ended.

'The man who ran my brother down?'

'Well . . . that's one of the things I wanted to talk to you about.'

'I don't understand.'

She glanced at the door as if checking her escape route was clear before focusing back on him.

'Are you telling me that the man who killed my brother has now killed someone else?'

If Leanne Sweeney was feigning ignorance, she was a bloody good actress. She seemed genuinely bemused.

'That's the thing, you see, I don't think he's killed anyone.' *What about Becket?* the voice in his head murmured.

Her frown deepened. 'But he confessed to running Dennis down. I was there, in court.'

'He was protecting his wife. She'd been drinking. He swapped places with her.'

She frowned, taking a moment to absorb the news.

'So she escaped any kind of punishment!'

'Not really. She committed suicide a couple of years later. Couldn't live with the guilt.'

She put her hand to her throat in shock. This was all going way quicker than Jimmy had hoped – he needed to put the brakes on.

'I'm sorry to dump all this on you. I understand it's difficult to take in.'

Leanne Sweeney shook her head. He didn't blame her. She got up and went to a sink at the side of the room, poured herself a glass of water and took a huge gulp before looking back at Jimmy.

'Did Kane tell you all this? Surely the police would have done a little more digging if that was the case. I'm sorry for the woman, of course, but it seems convenient for him to blame her now when she can't speak for herself.'

'To be fair he didn't want to talk about it at all, I had to drag it out of him, but it's been corroborated by her elderly mum, so I'm inclined to believe it.'

She stared at him for several seconds before nodding, as if she'd made her mind up about something.

'Can we go outside?' she said.

As soon as they stepped out she pulled a packet of cigarettes from her pocket, lit up and took a deep drag before slowly blowing the smoke out. She pushed the packet towards him. He almost flinched, suddenly remembering Connors stubbing that cigarette out on his neck, but he managed to control it and just shook his head instead. He must have pulled a face as she tucked them away quickly.

'Sorry. Terrible habit, I know. Can't seem to shake it off though.'

She took one more long drag and then dropped the cigarette on the floor and stubbed it out with her foot. That was one way of cutting down. He'd seen Deano collecting dog-ends that big to smoke another time.

'The accident blew my family apart,' she said. 'Mum and Dad were devastated. Dad never really recovered.'

'I heard they moved to Australia.'

She looked at him curiously, clearly wondering how much more he knew about her family, which was, in fact, pretty much nothing. He thought she might challenge him but in the end she just nodded.

'That's right. I was just starting my studies so decided to stay on but the rest of them headed to Perth. I feel quite bad about that now.'

'Why?'

'I didn't see any of them again for years.'

'Why not?'

She hesitated and he didn't blame her. Why should she tell him? But maybe she'd never had a chance to get this out there before. He knew to his cost that sometimes there were things you had bottled up for so long that when you had the chance they just came spilling out.

'They kind of disowned me. My dad was, um, difficult, to say the least.'

'I know how that can be,' Jimmy said.

She smiled, weakly. 'I don't think anyone had stood up to him before. He couldn't understand how I could put a career before my family. Might have been different if I'd been a boy.'

'Did you win him round in the end?'

'Never really had a chance. He died in a fire a couple of years after they left.'

Jimmy shuddered. A memory of his friend Red getting caught in a firebomb in the Falklands flitting quickly through his head.

'I'm sorry to hear that.' It was callous but he mentally crossed a possible suspect off his list.

'My mum married again, pretty soon after, actually, and Gary, her new husband, wasn't exactly welcoming. They st—'

She noticed Jimmy's reaction to the name and stopped. 'What is it?'

'What's his surname, this Gary?'

'Jones.'

It was a pretty common name, but it seemed too big a coincidence. He'd been looking for a Gary Jones without any luck and another one pops up within days. But why would Leanne Sweeney's stepdad want revenge on Gadge? Dennis Sweeney was nothing to do with him really.

'How old is he?'

'I'm not sure. About sixty, I guess. Why?'

That was way too old for the man Jimmy was looking for. Maybe it was just a coincidence.

'It's not important. Carry on, you were telling me about your mum moving on?'

'Yes, her and Gary started another family and he wasn't really interested in her old one. I've got two young half-sisters that I've never met.'

'That must have been difficult, all that happening so far away.'

'It was. My mum called me occasionally but even that contact dwindled out eventually.'

'How about your little brother, Adam?'

She sighed. 'Not so little any more. He was so young when it happened he doesn't really remember any of the difficulties. He worshipped Dennis though, there was a real bond between them.'

Jimmy could tell there was something else there but didn't want to push her – all in good time. Sometimes you had to take a longer route to get to your destination.

'What about Dennis? What was he like?'

A small cloud passed over Professor Sweeney's face.

'Why do you want to know about all of this? I'm not seeing how any of it might be relevant – it was nearly thirty years ago. What precisely is it Kane has been accused of doing this time?'

'There have been a series of attacks on the homeless, some kind of vigilante group trying to clean up the streets. A man was found dead in an alley and Kane was found unconscious nearby, covered in blood with the murder weapon in his hand.'

'That sounds pretty comprehensive to me. So they're thinking that the vigilante attack went too far. I can easily picture Kane getting involved in something like that.'

'No, sorry, I should have been clearer. He's the homeless man in this story, has been for nearly twenty years.'

Professor Sweeney looked bemused.

'But he was one of those wannabe entrepreneurs back then, a real go-getter. I remember thinking it was one of the reasons the sentence was so light – some kind of old boy's network closing ranks. How did he end up living on the streets?'

Jimmy knew there wasn't one answer to that, there never was, but he sensed that she was starting to run down the clock.

'He's an alcoholic.'

A rueful smile crossed her lips.

'What?' Jimmy said.

'Nothing really, just the irony that he shares my family curse.' She waved the cigarette packet at him. 'We've all got the addiction gene. My dad spent nearly every night in the pub and Dennis was a chip off the old block. He . . .'

She hesitated, clearly wondering if she was saying too much.

'I know it's hard,' Jimmy said. 'It's personal for me too.'

'I could tell that. Is Kane a friend of yours?'

He nodded. 'I was on the streets myself for a while. He helped me out when I needed it. I owe him.'

Now it was her turn to nod.

'Dennis was hammered the night of the accident; he was most nights. The prosecution buried the evidence. I thought at the time that he probably did just walk out right in front of the car but obviously I didn't say anything in public. I tried to talk about it with my dad, but he just went ballistic, accused me of being on the wrong team. That was another reason I didn't go with them when they moved – we were already at each other's throats. And the alcoholism must be genetic because Adam's the same.'

'How do you know that? I thought you had lost touch with everyone.'

'I had. But he got in touch recently and suggested a reunion.'

'He wanted you to go to Australia?'

She looked at him as if he was mad.

'No, don't be silly. He's here . . . in Newcastle.'

Jimmy felt the ground shift. Dennis Sweeney's younger brother was in the city and someone had turned up at the Pit Stop using his stepfather's name. No way was that a coincidence.

Leanne Sweeney didn't register his shock as she continued.

'I mean, I think he's still here but, like I said, I've been away for a couple of weeks so I haven't spoken to him recently.'

'D'you know how I can contact him?' Jimmy could tell immediately that he'd jumped the gun. She looked puzzled initially and then angry.

'Wait a minute, you don't think Adam is involved in this somehow, do you? Some kind of belated revenge attack? It was thirty years ago, for God's sake.'

Jimmy held his palms up to try and placate her.

'I don't think anything at the moment, honestly. It looks like Gadge . . . Kane was set up and I'm just trying to track down everyone who might have had a grudge against him, and your family obviously ended up on my list.'

'So am I a suspect too?' she said, stepping forward, looking ready to slap the shit out of him if he said 'Yes'. 'I mean I'm well qualified to have staged the scene and I've only just come back to the city as well. Surely I fit the bill better than Adam.'

'No, but . . .'

She could clearly tell from Jimmy's expression that she'd hit the nail on the head.

'Oh my God, you actually do suspect me, don't you!'

Jimmy stepped back, out of arm's length, but to his surprise she burst out laughing.

'Well, I've been accused of many things in the past but never murder. I guess you're never too old to start on a new career path. Have you seen the size of me? D'you genuinely think I could overpower a grown man in an alley?'

'There were two of them, actually. One ran away and hasn't yet been found.'

'So I battered one to death and chased the other one off? Is that what you think?'

He shook his head. Now that he'd met her in person, he knew there wasn't a cat in hell's chance she'd been involved.

'I'm sorry, but it's a lead I had to follow up. You're a scientist, you know that you have to examine every possibility no matter how unlikely before you eliminate it.'

'You sound like Sherlock Holmes.'

'You're not the first one to say that, though they normally say Sherlock Homeless.'

She looked at him with fresh eyes.

'I wouldn't mind hearing your tale one day; I'm a sucker for a redemption story.' She reached up and fiddled with her necklace. It was a crucifix. The professor caught his glance.

'Don't be so alarmed. You can be a scientist and a Christian, you know, the two aren't mutually exclusive. Could be worse, I could be a Christian Scientist – now they are barking.'

Jimmy had no idea what she was on about, religion had always been a complete mystery to him and the idea that there was a god looking out for him wasn't reassuring at all. If there was such a creature, he must have fucking hated Jimmy, the amount of shit he'd put him through.

She glanced at her watch. 'Look, I've got to go. I've got a seminar in five minutes. I know I hadn't seen him for a long time but there's no way Adam could have done what you're thinking either. He's too fragile, mentally, not physically, scared of his own shadow these days and drinking too much as per.'

'I still wouldn't mind talking to him,' Jimmy said.

Leanne Sweeney hesitated for a long time, too long Jimmy thought. Something was bothering her.

'I'll see what I can do,' she said, eventually.

'Thank you,' he said. 'And I don't want to alarm you, but don't leave it too long. Even if he's not involved directly, I think he might know something about it. There are some vicious people linked to this, and I've got a horrible feeling that your brother might be in some kind of danger.'

45

Aaron's mum shuffled towards her tower block with two heavy bags of shopping, her head down as she wove between the skateboarders blocking the path. One of the kids seemed to say something to her and she turned back to glance at them. That was a mistake as she was greeted by the sight of two of their arses as they dropped their trackie bottoms to moon at her. Jimmy shook his head. He doubted the kids were even in their teens.

'Shouldn't you be stopping that kind of thing?' he said to Kate, who sat in the driver's seat next to him.

'No problem at all if you give me an army to do it. I've got a staff of four and an in-tray full of complaints, most of which are far more concerning than someone getting a glimpse of a spotty backside.'

Debra Mason didn't seem overly distressed by the sight either, turning back around and trudging towards the flats. The kids shouted something at her, but she didn't look back before opening the doors with her residents' card and disappearing into the entrance hall. Thankfully the kids didn't follow her, or he and Kate would have had to step in earlier than he wanted to.

Jimmy didn't like putting Gadge's investigation on hold, even for a day, but Kate was doing him a big favour getting him in to see Aaron's mum and it was the only time she was available. Aoife had played a blinder tracking down Dennis Sweeney's twin sister, and this time it was his daughter who'd been doing the legwork for him. What he'd do without the women in his life helping out he couldn't imagine, especially when they were stretching their job descriptions to the limit.

'You sure you're OK with this?' he asked Kate.

'Aye. There's more than one way to skin a cat. And if the reports are true then we'll be helping her out in the long run, won't we? And that is my job.'

Kate had been as good as her word and checked up on any complaints that had been made about the Masons' flat. And there were a few. Most were from neighbours complaining about shouting and screaming. Kate reckoned there were some classic tell-tale signs of domestic abuse.

'Young Aaron did say that this new boyfriend, Ned, has a temper. Though to be fair the kid's not exactly calm himself.'

'It's a pretty common scenario, sadly. Women take in a new partner and at first he's all sweetness and light, bringing gifts, getting on with the kids, the whole nine yards. Then gradually the gaslighting starts. He'll claim the kids are ungrateful – especially if they're teenage boys – or that the woman is being used, that things would be much better if it was just the two of them. Eventually he'll force the woman to choose between them but as soon as they've got rid of the kid the violence starts. It's textbook.'

Jimmy knew there were people who would blame Debra Mason. How could she be so stupid? Why did she put up with it? But he'd heard plenty of war stories from Julie. Her ex had liked to throw his weight around, and he knew how hard she had found it to tell people. And she was no push-over. Some people were just very skilled at making their victims feel like they deserved it.

'Talking of partners, did you give Mum a call yet?'

'What about?'

'Don't play that game with me, Dad. We want you two to play nice for the wedding – maybe even sit together – and you both need to build a few bridges for that to happen.'

Jimmy had picked up his phone to call Bev several times but each time he found a reason to put it off.

'She hasn't called me.'

Kate rolled her eyes. 'You're both as bad as each other. I should just un-invite the pair of you.'

Jimmy was going to point out that he hadn't actually received a proper invitation anyway when he was distracted by another woman stopping to talk to the kids, who were pointing down the road. Looking for directions, maybe? She was familiar though, something about her body language. After a brief chat in which she seemed to show the kids something and they shrugged, shaking their heads, she turned around, walking towards their car. As she passed Jimmy realised it was Susan Becket. He had hoped she'd given up trying to find out what happened to her brother and gone back to wherever she came from but obviously not. Fortunately, she didn't notice him in the car. Another problem for him to worry about.

'Who was that?' Kate asked.

'No one. Just someone I've seen at the Pit Stop.'

Kate looked doubtful but let it go. They got out of the car and wandered over to the tower block. Jimmy went to push the doors open but they were locked. Kate pulled a weird-looking key out of her bag and inserted it into a hole in the wall by the side of the doors which sprang open.

'Don't look so impressed,' she said. 'It's a Fireman Drop Key, we all get issued with one so we can get into the blocks when we need to.'

Jimmy was surprised how clean the place was. There were a couple of well-maintained plants in the lobby. Even the lift was working properly.

'It's not all condoms, needles and puddles of piss, you know,' Kate said, seeing the look on his face. 'The caretaker here is on the ball and most of the residents take pride in their surroundings. You can tell that from the number of calls we've had about Debra Mason. In some blocks people just ignore stuff like that, don't want to get involved.'

Once they found the right flat, on the fifth floor, Kate took the lead. Aaron's mum would probably respond better to a younger woman. She rang the bell – another thing that was working properly – and almost immediately it was pulled open, though only as far as the attached chain would allow.

'Yeh?' Debra Mason said, looking through the gap.

Kate held her ID badge up for the woman to check.

'I'm Kate, from the Anti-Social Behaviour Unit. We've had a few reports of a disturbance. I was hoping we could come in for a chat.'

'Who's he?' the woman said, staring at Jimmy.

'This is Jimmy, he works at a hostel for eighteen to twenty-fives. He'd like to talk to you about Aaron.'

The door was pushed shut but Jimmy heard the chain being undone and it swung open again.

'You can come in but I've only got five minutes. I've got some shopping to do.'

She saw Jimmy glance at the bags on the floor that she'd just come home with and reddened slightly.

'I forgot a couple of things for tea tonight.'

Debra Mason bustled them into the lounge which had a large picture window looking out over the city. There were doors on either side of it, bedrooms probably. The room itself was immaculately tidy but somehow cold, no pictures on the wall or ornaments on the shelves. And only one photo on the mantelpiece – of Debra Mason and a blond-haired man that looked like it had been taken in a photo booth and blown up. She pointed them to a small sofa but stayed standing herself.

'I'd offer you tea but I'm out of milk,' she said. Neither of them really believed her but they didn't say anything. 'What is it you want?'

Kate pulled a folder out of her bag, opened it up and glanced at the first page.

'Like I said, Mrs Mason, we've had a few reports of

disturbances, shouting and screaming coming from your flat, night of the twenty-fourth, I believe, and I wanted to make sure you were OK?'

'That'll be her in number fifty-three, I bet,' Mason said. 'She's a nebby bitch, right enough, thinks she's better than the rest of us.'

'I can't tell you who has made the reports, but I can say they're not from one person, three or four different people called us – so obviously we have to take that seriously. Do you want to tell us what happened?'

Debra Mason finally sat down, seemingly forgetting her pressing shopping trip. She tugged at the end of her long sleeves and Jimmy caught a glimpse of a bruise on her arm.

'How's Aaron?' she said, ignoring Kate's question and turning her attention to Jimmy. He wasn't sure if she was genuinely concerned or desperately trying to change the subject.

'Upset,' he said. 'He's OK health-wise but he doesn't understand why you've thrown him out of the house.'

'I didn't throw him out, he chose to leave.'

'That's not quite his story.'

'He's a teenage boy. You can't believe a word he says.'

'How old is he, Mrs Mason?'

'Nearly seventeen,' she mumbled.

Jimmy sighed. He had been pretty sure that Aaron had been lying about his age.

'Technically he's too young for a place in the hostel then.'

'What do you mean? You're not going to throw him out, are you?'

'It's a bit late to be concerned about his welfare,' he snapped.

Debra Mason flinched. Kate put her hand on Jimmy's arm and he knew he'd pushed a bit too hard.

'Where's your boyfriend, Mrs Mason?' Kate checked her notes. 'Ned, isn't it? I was hoping to have a word with him about the shouting. The reports indicated that he was threatening you. You know that we can do something about that, if that's what happened.'

'W-what do you mean?'

'If you're willing to make a statement we can get an exclusion order preventing him from entering the building.'

Debra Mason was already shaking her head.

'It was probably just the telly they heard, *EastEnders* or something. I'll make sure to turn the volume down next time.'

Kate's glare would have shamed a dodgy Catholic priest and Mason twitched a little before glancing at the door nervously as if someone was about to come into the flat.

'Like I said, it wasn't like that. I think I'd like you to leave now. Ned might be home soon.'

'Might be?' Jimmy asked. She hesitated.

'He's been away for a bit.'

'Aaron thinks he killed your dog,' Jimmy said, suddenly, and to Kate's obvious irritation. He knew she'd bawl him out later, but patience wasn't his strong suit.

'Like I said, teenagers don't always tell the truth. Dizzy hadn't been well for ages.' She sighed. 'The two of them don't get on and they both have a temper. Aaron is messy and Ned likes things just so.'

Jimmy wondered if the room had always been this tidy or whether that was one of the things that Ned liked 'just so'. And he wondered how he reacted when it wasn't.

Kate opened her bag and took out a card, handing it over to Debra Mason.

'If you ever feel threatened or scared call that number. We can issue a Section 21 Private Tenancy notice and have your boyfriend removed from your house, with an exclusion order, very quickly.'

Debra Mason stared at the card without taking it.

'It's not what you think,' she said.

46

Blisters were forming on Jimmy's hands as he dug away at the earth. He cursed the unusual dry spell that the city had been going through – the soil at the back of the garden was rock hard and the cheap spade he'd borrowed from the allotments felt like it was about to fall to pieces.

He heard a car coming slowly down the road and caught a glimpse of the headlights approaching. Another early riser. Even though it was still dark he ducked behind a tree just in case. Once it had passed the park gates he returned to his digging. Surely it couldn't be much deeper? He was three more half-shovelfuls in and going for a fourth when the spade caught on something, a plastic bag handle by the look of it.

Jimmy dropped the spade on the ground and knelt down, clearing the soil away from the plastic, to find a white bin-bag, still half-buried. Eventually he cleared enough soil away to pull the heavy bag out of the ground. As he lifted it up a paw flopped out of a hole in the thin plastic.

*

'I'm sorry, what?' Mr Green said. 'You dug it up?'

Jimmy nodded. He'd thought the vet would be pleased but it wasn't quite working out that way.

'Did no one ever tell you to let sleeping dogs lie?' the vet added, laughing. He placed the bag on the table and peeked inside. 'So which one are you? Burke or Hare?'

Jimmy had no idea what the man was on about.

'I must be out of my mind even considering it,' Mr Green said, pulling Dizzy's remains out gently onto the table, as if the poor animal could somehow still feel something.

'Like I said, she was poisoned. I thought you could do some tests to see if it was the same stuff that Dog ate.'

'Did you now? I'm not made of money, Jimmy. And I'm not generally inclined to encourage grave robbing. Not to mention that I need the permission of the owner to do a post-mortem.'

Jimmy thought of getting Aaron to OK it but wasn't sure how the kid would react to his pet being exhumed – maybe he'd be horrified? And maybe he'd be right to be. Best to leave him out of the loop for now.

'I think the owner is the one who poisoned her so that would kind of defeat the object,' Jimmy said.

The vet rolled his eyes. 'You wouldn't believe how many times people tell me they think their neighbours had poisoned their dogs. It's very rarely the case and they never have any evidence. Are you any different?'

Jimmy shook his head. 'No. Just a hunch . . . but he's definitely the sort who might have.'

Green opened Dizzy's mouth and used a small torch light to peer inside.

'Hmmm, definite signs of bleeding. Could be the same thing again. How long has . . . what was her name?'

'Dizzy.'

'How long has Dizzy been dead?'

'About a month.'

Jimmy could tell the vet was wavering.

'I just thought that, you know, if it's this guy who's poisoned the other dogs, we would probably be saving lives if we stopped him.'

The vet laughed. 'Not above a bit of moral blackmail then?'

Jimmy could feel a blush coming on but knew that Green was coming around to his way of thinking. He was having another good look at Dizzy's corpse.

'There's not going to be much in the way of blood or urine to test. I'd have to send a liver section to the lab. It's going to cost though. I'm willing to do pro bono work for you but actually paying to get stuff done is a step too far.'

'How much?'

'Well, I took samples of Dog's blood and urine when he was in here, just in case, so for that and poor Dizzy's liver we're probably talking the best part of four hundred quid.'

Jimmy thought about the small naval pension pot he'd put aside for Kate. That kind of sum would make a big dent in it, but he knew she wouldn't mind.

The vet sensed him stalling and assumed it was a negotiating strategy. 'You drive a hard bargain. How about we go halfers?'

'Works for me,' Jimmy said.

Green smiled. 'You never mentioned you had that kind of money when I was doing Dog's health checks for free! Maybe I should give you a bill for those.'

'I didn't, um, it wasn't—'

The vet burst out laughing. 'Just winding you up, man. Spilt milk and all that. Leave it with me. But don't expect miracles, it'll take a while to get test results back unless I give it some kind of priority.'

Jimmy was about to suggest that he should do exactly this but the vet was way ahead of him, holding a finger to his lips to indicate he should keep his gob shut.

'Don't push your luck,' he said.

47

When Jimmy left the vets he checked his phone. Three missed calls. All of them from Leanne Sweeney.

He hadn't expected to hear from her again quite so soon but maybe her brother had agreed to talk to him. He called her back.

'Professor Sweeney.'

'Hi, it's Jimmy Mullen. You tried to ring me.'

'Yes. Um, look, it's probably nothing but after what you said I thought I should talk to you.'

'What is it?'

'It's Adam. He's missing.'

It was pissing down. Fucking typical bad timing, Jimmy thought, twenty-four hours earlier and resurrecting Dizzy would have been a lot easier on his hands. He had arranged to meet Leanne Sweeney outside the Pit Stop but instead he was hanging around in the doorway waiting for her taxi to pull up. There was someone he wanted her to meet.

He checked his watch. If he got this sorted quickly there

was still a chance to catch Andy Burns before he clocked off. He knew he'd already gone to that particular well once and been turned away but this time he might have evidence that hadn't been freshly nicked. He glanced out and saw a black cab pulling up outside, skidding slightly in the pools of water that were rapidly expanding by the side of the road. He remembered a story from school about some guy putting his coat over a puddle for a lady to keep her feet dry and for a second imagined doing that for his guest – but he'd never really understood how that would work: surely the minute she stepped on the coat it would sink? Anyway, there was no need, the door opened and Leanne Sweeney stepped gingerly out, sidestepping the water easily. He guided her inside and she looked round in amazement. The place was rammed – it always was when the weather was bad.

'I didn't know this place existed,' she said.

'Not many do. Though you soon find out about it when you need help. They feed around a hundred people every night.' Sometimes more, he thought, glancing around the room. There was barely a spare seat to be had.

'The joys of austerity,' she muttered. 'Makes you proud to be British, eh?'

Jimmy didn't respond. He didn't have the time to worry about the big picture – he was more about doing what he could to fix the things happening on his doorstep. Like Gadge being in prison.

'Have you got the photo?'

She nodded. 'It's on my phone.'

Jimmy signalled to Maggie who he'd already briefed and she hustled over to join them.

'Leanne, this is Maggie, Maggie, Leanne.'

'Just get on with it, man,' Maggie said. 'I've barely had time to scratch my arse today.'

Leanne Sweeney already had her phone out and was scrolling through her photos. Eventually she found what she was looking for.

She turned the phone around and showed it to Maggie.

'This is a selfie I took with my brother the last time I saw him,' she said.

Maggie took a quick look and nodded immediately.

'Well he's looking a bit worse for wear than the last time I saw him,' she said. 'But yes, that's Gary Jones. Can I get back to work now?'

Jimmy nodded. As Maggie walked away he grabbed the phone from the professor's hand and glanced at the screen.

'Why didn't you tell me your brother had been in a fight? It would have saved a lot of time.'

She snatched the phone back.

'Because I knew what you'd think. But you're wrong. Adam wouldn't hurt a fly. Now are you going to help me find him or not?'

Andy Burns' expression made it very clear that Jimmy was drinking in the last-chance saloon. If Leanne Sweeney hadn't been with them, he would probably have thrown him out already. He made a point of ignoring Jimmy and addressing the professor directly.

'You're absolutely certain that your brother . . .' he looked at his notes, 'Adam, and Gary Jones are one and the same person.'

She nodded. 'No doubt about it.'

'Why do you think your brother is in danger, Professor Sweeney?' he said wearily.

'He'd been working at this local builder's yard and he thought there was something illegal going on there. I think he was going to blow the whistle on them. And last time I saw him he looked like he'd been beaten up.'

'And why are you telling me this?'

'Jimmy, um, Mr Mullen told me that you dealt with missing persons.'

'Did he now? And how long do you think that Adam has been missing?'

'I haven't heard from him in more than a month. Since just after he told me that he was planning to report it.'

Burns looked at Jimmy. They'd been here before and he knew that Jimmy knew how things operated with missing persons. Leanne Sweeney was hitting all the right notes in exactly the right order. Almost like she'd been coached, which she obviously had.

Leanne Sweeney had taken a great deal of persuasion to go along with Jimmy's plan but in the end her fear for her brother outweighed her need for honesty. Jimmy was certain that Stan Walker knew a lot more about where 'Gary Jones' was than he'd let on, but he needed the weight of the law to find out what that was.

Burns sighed. The man knew he was being played like a

cheap violin but there wasn't much he could do about it – there was a remote chance that Jimmy was onto something and he had to cover his back.

'OK, leave it with me, Professor Sweeney. I'll talk to Mr Walker.'

48

The builder's yard opened at the crack of dawn but Burns and Jimmy were already sitting just around the corner waiting for the gates to swing wide.

'I can't believe I'm doing this,' Burns said, opening his glove compartment and taking out a packet of fags. He pushed the cigarette lighter in with more force than necessary. Jimmy kept schtum. Don't poke the angry bear was a motto he'd always thought worth following.

'I know I've said this before, but this is absolutely your last Get Out of Jail Free card. Don't think for a second that I don't know you put that professor up to this. I owed you but our debt is settled, after this I'm done. Clear?'

Jimmy nodded.

'Now show me how this works again.'

Jimmy took the camera pen from his hand and pressed down on the top. Immediately the inside of the car came up on the laptop he held on his lap.

'Just turn it on like that and the rest takes care of itself.'

'And it doesn't make a noise or anything?'

'Can you hear it?'

Burns listened intently, practically putting his ear up against the pen. There was nothing.

'I must want my bumps feeling,' the cop said, grabbing the pen, turning it off and jamming it into his top pocket.

'I could always just come up with you like I suggested in the first place.'

'Aye, right, and I'll just hand back my badge and give up my pension now just to save time and money being spent on the disciplinary hearing when Walker puts a complaint in. Unless you've got a fucking invisibility cloak, of course?'

Burns waited for a response but Jimmy knew when to keep his gob shut. The cop finally lit his cigarette, threw open the car door and strode off without even shutting it. Jimmy stared at the screen, praying that Burns remembered to turn the camera back on.

A minute or so later the laptop screen burst to life. Burns was already through the gate and halfway to the office when Stan Walker came out to see what his early morning visitor wanted. Burns took his ID out and held it in front of him.

'DS Burns, Northumbria Police,' he said. 'I'm looking for Stan Walker.'

'That's me,' Walker said.

'I'd like to talk to you about one of your former employees.'

Walker held his ground for a moment, clearly weighing up his options.

'Always happy to help the police,' he said, eventually.

'I'm looking for a missing person, name of Adam Sweeney, I understand he worked for you.'

Walker looked relieved.

'Can't help you, not one of mine.'

'You might know him as Gary Jones.'

Jimmy watched on as Walker pretended to be thinking. Eventually the man shook his head.

'Sorry, never heard of him either.'

'Really? Because I have it on good authority that you have.'

'Not again. This wouldn't be from that so-called investigator who was round here the other day, would it? Reckoned he was ex-navy but I doubt that. I'm not sure he counts as "good authority". Not sure he counts as good anything, truth be told. I think we're done here.' He turned to walk back to his office.

'The information came from Jones's sister.'

Walker stopped moving and turned back slowly. He was too far away from the camera for Jimmy to see the expression on his face, but he guessed the man wasn't happy.

'His sister?'

Burns must have nodded.

'Then she's mistaken.'

'Can I take a look in your office?'

'You got a warrant?'

'No, but I could get one. I could also get the VAT men to come and have a look at your books if you'd like that too. Just to make sure you're on the straight and narrow, you understand?'

Burns had moved closer so this time Jimmy saw the look on Walker's face. Resignation. Burns had done him up like a kipper.

'Fine. Take a look. But you won't find anything. Quite literally. We had a break-in the other day, someone stole our wages ledger and our most recent invoices. Same day that dodgy investigator fella came sniffing round, coincidentally.'

'Really?' Burns said, moving even closer to the man. 'Have you got a crime number for that? I'll see if there's been any progress on chasing it up.'

Walker's face reddened. He looked at his feet as if hoping to find inspiration there.

'Um, no, I didn't, um, report it.'

'Why not?'

'There was no real damage and we have most of those records on computer anyway. Probably just kids messing about.'

'You won't mind me looking around then?'

'Like I say, nothing much to find but fill your boots. You can't check the computer though, my secretary's not in till later and she's the only one who knows how to work it.'

'Handy,' Burns said, sarcastically. Walker ignored the taunt, turned, and led the way back to the office, holding the door open for Burns to enter.

'Mind if I look in the drawers and cabinets?' Burns said.

'No bother. Nothing to hide. They're all unlocked.'

Burns went behind the desk and slid open the left-hand drawer. It was empty aside from some standard stationery equipment, a stapler, a hole punch and a couple of rolls of Sellotape. Burns closed it and opened the other desk drawer.

The wages ledger was sitting right on the top of a pile of papers. As Burns knew it would be. He pulled it out and though the camera stayed on the find, Walker's voice could still be heard.

'What the fuck?' he said. Burns must have stood up as the camera moved up to Walker's face and his surprise was obvious.

'I thought you said this was stolen,' Burns said.

'It was! I don't understand.'

His disbelief was clearly genuine. It wasn't often that a thief broke back into a place to return stolen goods but that was exactly what Jimmy had persuaded Deano to do the previous night. This time they'd waited until the security guard had completed his visit.

Burns started flicking through the pages looking for Gary Jones's name. It didn't take him long to find it as he'd seen it before, when Jimmy had brought it into the station. He pointed at an entry in the ledger and turned the book around so Walker could see it.

'I think you've been telling porky pies, Mr Walker,' he said. 'I'm going to have to ask you to come down to the station for a formal interview.'

'Look, I can explain,' Walker blustered.

'I'm not sure you appreciate how serious this is,' Burns said. 'Sweeney-slash-Jones hasn't been seen for several weeks – since roughly the date that you supposedly paid him, according to this entry.'

'It's not like that. Look, he did some work for me and I did pay him – in kind.'

'But now he's missing,' Burns said. 'And you may be the last person to have seen him.'

Walker sighed. 'He's not missing. He's hiding,' he said.

Inside the car the screen suddenly went black and the sound disappeared. Jimmy hit a couple of buttons but nothing happened so he gave it a bash. Again nothing. What was going on? Yet again Jimmy found himself wishing Gadge was around, he'd have known how to sort this.

He waited for a few minutes, his eyes fixed on the rear-view mirror hoping to see Andy Burns appear but got no joy. Eventually his patience snapped. He leapt out of the car and half-jogged towards the builders' yard but as he turned the corner he saw Burns heading back from the office towards the gates.

Stan Walker had been standing in the doorway watching Burns leave but Jimmy's sudden appearance on the scene caught his eye and he stared across the yard towards him, shaking his head.

Jimmy watched as the man took his phone out of his jacket and made a call.

49

Jesmond Old Cemetery still looked as if a typhoon had blown through it. Toppled graves and broken headstones covered the ground, a chaotic mess joined up by overgrown brambles and ivy.

Jimmy was pretty sure that Walker was sending them on a wild-goose chase. It was the same place that Gandalf had told him to look at, but he'd searched the place pretty thoroughly just a week ago and, apart from the flowers on the grave, there was no sign that Sweeney had ever been there. However, he couldn't work out what Walker had to gain by sending Burns there – he'd even drawn the cop a map.

Andy Burns led the way, keeping to the outside of the burial sites, skirting along the grass towards the southern end of the cemetery where there were a few more trees. Jimmy followed close behind, still dubious as he had covered all that area before and, aside from some planks and a couple of discarded wheelie bins, he'd found nothing there.

'Can you not give me a clue what he told you?'

The audio from the pen camera had cut out when Walker

began to tell Burns where he might find the missing man and Burns had enjoyed keeping Jimmy in suspense – a small measure of payback for putting him in this position, Jimmy reckoned.

'Patience, man, any moment now.' Burns entered the trees and was only yards away from the cemetery's surrounding wall when he held up his hand and stopped.

'It's around here somewhere,' he muttered, studying the hand-drawn map. Jimmy was mystified. He even looked up into the biggest oak, searching for a tree house.

Burns was looking down, though. He began scuffing around the ground, clearing away some dust to reveal an iron ring. He grabbed the ring and pulled a hatch upwards, opening up a large hole in the ground. What the hell was going on?

'Open sesame.' Burns leant inside and appeared to press something. Down under the ground a small light came on, illuminating the entrance. He looked back up to Jimmy.

'Fuck me. Walker was telling the truth.' The cop re-adjusted his body and descended underground. Jimmy watched in disbelief as the man disappeared from view.

'Come on, man,' Burns shouted from wherever he'd gone, his voice muffled by a ton of earth above him. Jimmy peered down and saw a small stepladder perched against the side of the hole. He followed Burns down. The man had moved away from the entrance into the rest of the bunker, which was a rectangular space, about twelve feet by ten and around five feet high. They both had to crouch slightly to move around on the concrete floor. Burns started pressing other switches and, as the place grew brighter, Jimmy could see a series of small push-button LED lights stuck to the timber walls with masking tape.

'You're shitting me!' Jimmy said as he gradually got a full view of the place.

There was a camp bed pushed up against one of the walls with an empty sleeping bag on top of it. In the opposite corner was a small gas stove and a box full of unopened soup tins. Jimmy suddenly remembered the smoke coming from the ground the last time he'd been there. He'd put it down to some kind of chemical reaction but clearly he'd been wrong.

An open bin bag sat in the other corner, half full of rubbish, including several empty beer bottles. There were a couple of hooks on the wall, one of which had a coat hanging from it, and a shelf with some books and a small alarm clock on it.

More significantly, leaning against the side of the bed was a baseball bat. There was no sign of Sweeney though.

'How the hell did Sweeney find this?' Jimmy said.

'He didn't find it,' Burns said. 'He built it – well, most of it anyway. He did pretty much all the digging himself, apparently. Walker claims he only helped him with the timber struts and walls and the concrete floor.'

'How did they get the concrete made? They sure as hell didn't drag a mixer into the cemetery, someone would have seen it,' Jimmy said.

'That's what the wheelie bins were for. They used one of them to collect rainwater and the other one to mix it in.

Then they just lowered the bin into the hole with a rope and poured it into sections. The whole thing only took about a month from start to finish.'

'But why?' Jimmy said, shaking his head. 'Bit fucking extreme, isn't it?'

'Sweeney told Walker that he was on the bones of his arse after coming back from Australia. He'd spent every penny he had getting back here, didn't qualify for social housing and couldn't afford even the cheapest rent around. He briefly had a hostel place but fell out with the manager there.'

Fucking George, no doubt. Maybe he should have slipped the old bastard a couple of quid for some information. Burns continued.

'He was living on the street but had seen something he shouldn't have, thought someone was after him, and was terrified of the attacks that were going on. He approached Walker about doing some work in exchange for materials. Apparently, the lad had worked in the building trade since he was a kid and he had a lot of useful skills so it was a good deal for both of them. They got on and Sweeney told him what he was planning.

'Walker thought it was bonkers, but it appealed to his engineering background – he told me he really missed some of the mad stuff he had to do in the army – so he helped him out.'

Jimmy laughed. 'When I was in the navy we used to call soldiers "pongos". It came from the name of an orang-utan that couldn't climb trees. Instead it used to dig holes and hide in them. I never realised how bang-on it was.'

'Walker reckoned they were almost finished when Sweeney's fears came true,' Burns added. 'He was badly beaten up over Byker way. Walker finished off the work for him while he was in hospital and as soon as he was released he moved in.'

'How long has he been living here?'

'Walker reckons they finished the work about a month ago.'

'Only one problem then,' Jimmy said.

'What's that?' Burns said.

'Where the fuck is he now?'

The full moon smiled down at Jimmy as he sat under the large oak tree waiting for Adam Sweeney to return to his makeshift home.

A council worker had turned up to lock the gates on both sides of the cemetery just after he'd settled down. He hadn't noticed Jimmy hiding behind the two wheelie bins and Jimmy had got a sense of how easy it had been for Adam to build his den without anyone noticing. The area was well hidden and a long way from the main entrances. And as soon as the gates had been locked it was literally as quiet as a graveyard.

He glanced at his phone. It was nine fifteen and he'd been sitting there alone since just before six aside from a brief appearance from a couple of large rats that had sniffed around his feet curiously before disappearing into the undergrowth. Andy Burns had made his excuses and gone home. A couple of years earlier his wife had read him the riot act about his constant absences and to his credit the man had prioritised his family ever since – even taking the post in Missing Persons to keep the overtime down. Jimmy admired him for that and wished he'd taken a leaf out of the cop's book when he could have all those years ago. If he had he wouldn't be sitting there now freezing his arse off. He pulled his bobble hat down around his ears, his coat tight, and leant back against the tree. It was going to be a long night.

He woke up at five a.m., freezing cold and on his own. Sweeney hadn't come back.

50

The photo showed a short, blond man entering a house with a black door. An address was scrawled underneath it – the number of the address matched the number on the door. Jimmy wasn't particularly superstitious, but he would have preferred something other than thirteen.

Caroline Fisher had handed him the envelope when he'd returned to the hostel. It had been amongst the morning post but there was no stamp or postmark and only Jimmy's name on it, written in block capitals.

He had no idea who might have sent it to him, or why. The man in the picture had his back to the camera. He was wearing a padded jacket, jeans and what looked like Doc Martens. He had a shaven head and a small hoop earring in one ear. Obviously, he'd been looking for a short man but who knew if this was him as Gadge had been unable to describe the man who'd helped drag him into the alley. In the picture he had something in his hand which could have been a balaclava – the only thing Gadge did remember about him – but could just as easily have been gloves or a bobble hat. There was only one way to find out.

The house was in the middle of a large housing estate in Scotswood, in the West End of Newcastle. Jimmy and Deano got the bus there, the kid dashing up to the upper deck to grab the seat at the front, just like Jimmy had when he'd been a kid. Sometimes it was easy to forget the lad was in his mid-twenties.

Just before their stop Jimmy saw a jogger running past on the other side of the road who looked familiar, but he was out of sight before he could get a better look. It was a fleeting glance and by the time they got off he was long gone. Probably nothing.

The area had been known as one of the more deprived a few years back but there were signs that it was picking up, neat lawns and decent-looking cars were scattered in amongst some less well-maintained properties with debris-strewn front yards. Number thirteen, however, was one of the latter. The front window was partially boarded up with plywood and there was an old fridge lying in the front garden. At least the door had been removed to prevent the neighbourhood kids shutting themselves in.

'What a shithole,' Deano said, as they surveyed the house from the other side of the road. 'Don't think you'll need me to get in there. The place looks like a squat. You could probs just walk in.'

There were no signs of life, so they crossed over and headed up the drive, avoiding a couple of rain-filled potholes.

A couple of wires stuck out of the wall where a doorbell used to be so Jimmy went to knock on the door instead. There was no need. It swung open.

'Told ya,' Deano muttered. 'We should get out of here, it's got "trap" written all ower it.'

Jimmy peered into the hallway. A pile of fast-food leaflets were scattered over the carpet. There was a coat hanging on the banister at the bottom of the stairs and a pair of Doc Martens on a mat.

'Looks like he might be in,' he said.

'If he's not I'm trying those on,' Deano said, nodding at the boots. 'They look as good as new.'

'Hello,' Jimmy shouted. No response. He stepped into the hallway and tried again. 'Hello.' Nothing.

Deano tugged his arm. 'This stinks, Jimmy, and I don't just mean the smell. Let's get away.'

The kid was right about the smell – a combination of BO, fried food and cheesy feet filled Jimmy's nostrils.

'Let's just have a look around, nowt to lose is there?'

'Not sure about that,' Deano muttered.

There were two doors leading off the hallway, one to his right which was open and led to the small front room and a second at the end which was closed, probably a kitchen, he thought. Before moving into the first room Jimmy sifted through the leaflets on the floor, picking up a brown envelope. It was a council tax bill addressed to a Mr S. Hawley. He stuffed it into his pocket and glanced into the room to his right. Seeing it was empty he stepped inside.

'Fuck's sake,' Deano cursed, following after him.

The room was relatively neat in comparison to everything they'd seen so far. A small two-seater sofa had been pushed against the back wall and an armchair sat in the corner, facing a big screen telly which was bracketed on the wall near the window.

'Place can't have been wide open for long or that would be long gone,' Deano said, nodding at the TV.

Jimmy moved back into the hallway and headed to the kitchen. As he went to open the door Deano pulled him back.

'Fingerprints,' he said, moving past Jimmy and putting his hand inside his sleeve before grabbing the door handle and pushing it open. He didn't get very far. A couple of inches in, the door hit something and wouldn't budge.

'Give us a hand, man,' he said, pushing his shoulder against the door. Jimmy moved alongside him, lending his weight to the shove. Gradually it opened far enough for them to edge past it into the room, Deano leading the way.

'Oh, fuck,' he muttered, as soon as he was inside the kitchen. Jimmy was on his shoulder and saw the body a couple of seconds later.

A man was lying face down on the floor, his feet against the back of the kitchen door. It reminded Jimmy of the dummy on the floor of the Scene House at the university. Except this body had the back of its head caved in.

Jimmy's on his knees. His sleeves are soaking wet and stained dark. The fire extinguisher is still in his hands, the bottom of it covered in blood and little flakes of white bone and brain matter.

Jimmy blinked. He hadn't had a flashback in ages. He

closed his eyes, trying to erase the distant memory of his attack on Wilkinson that had extended his long stay in prison. He'd saved a nurse's life but that wasn't the point. He'd killed a man – a monster, maybe, but still another human being. He blinked again. Back in the real world his heart was pumping through his shirt.

Deano was saying something, the kid's hand on his shoulder. Jimmy tuned back in.

'I said "You OK, man?" You zoned out on me for a sec there.'

Jimmy nodded. 'I'm fine I think, just give me a moment.'

He took a deep breath and then another. Calming down. As he refocused, he saw a blood-stained ratchet lying on the kitchen table in front of them. He reached over to pick it up.

'NO,' Deano shouted, knocking his arm away. 'How many times, man! Don't touch anything. I told you, this is a set-up.'

'D'you think?'

'For sure. Why d'you think they told you where to find this guy? I bet he was already dead when they posted that photo through the letter box.'

'What if the killer's still here? He could be upstairs.'

'They'll be long gone.'

Jimmy looked around the kitchen. The back door was wide open. Outside, the back garden hadn't seen a lawn mower in years. There was a path of sorts in the middle of the overgrown grass which stopped a couple of yards short of a wooden fence that surrounded the rest of the garden. It looked like a back alley ran behind it.

'Can we get out of here now?' Deano pleaded. 'Oh, for fuck's sake, what are you doing now?'

Jimmy had leant down to check the body, carefully keeping his feet away from the small pool of blood that surrounded the victim's smashed-in head. Every contact leaves a trace; he knew that from his naval days, it had been drummed into him by a very scary master-at-arms.

The man was obviously dead, there was no doubt about that, but he wanted to make sure it was the same guy in the photo. The shaven head was still just about recognisable amidst the gaping wound, and the hoop earring was there too. He glanced up and saw the grey balaclava on the kitchen worktop next to a camera – surely proof that this was the second guy from the alley.

A police siren shattered the silence of the kitchen. Deano was out of the back door and into the garden before it had stopped. Jimmy was slower off the mark, only moving when he heard car doors being slammed. Deano was way ahead of him, already hanging onto the top of the fence at the back and scrabbling his legs up to try and clamber over it. By the time Jimmy was halfway there the kid was sitting on the top and leaning down to offer him a hand.

'Here, man, I'll pull you up.'

Jimmy sprinted the last couple of yards and leapt up at the fence, almost trying to run up it, simultaneously grabbing Deano's hand.

'Oh, shit,' Deano said.

Jimmy looked up and saw the kid was staring back at the house but he couldn't turn his head to see what was up. He didn't need to. The cry of 'STOP, POLICE' and the sound of boots pounding through the kitchen told him all he needed to know.

As Deano yanked him up, Jimmy managed to get his other hand onto the top of the fence to add to his momentum but as he did someone grabbed him from behind and dragged him back down. He turned to try and knock the hand away, but his other hand slipped from Deano's grasp and he collapsed on top of the uniformed cop who had caught up with him.

A second cop pulled him away, forced him face down into the mud under the fence and cuffed him.

'You're nicked, son,' he said, pulling Jimmy to his feet.

When he looked back, Deano was nowhere to be seen.

51

All cells were pretty much the same in Jimmy's experience and he'd seen the inside of a few. Four bare walls, a door and some kind of solid, fixed bench to lie on. The bench was always too small for an adult human – even one as short as he was – just to make sure you couldn't get too comfortable. It didn't help that he was wearing a too-tight set of overalls and flimsy overshoes that the cops had provided when they'd taken his own clothes away for testing.

He'd been there for several hours, couldn't be arsed to do his normal pacing to pass the time. And anyway, this time was different to the rest. This time he had a proper lawyer.

Charlie Gascoigne had been pretty pissed off when he'd rung her from the station. She'd reminded him of the terms of their deal – if he was caught breaking the law he was on his own – and that being caught in someone else's house, especially someone who was lying dead on the floor, was way over that line. But in the end she'd caved as he knew she would.

The cell door opened and a uniform came in.

'Your brief's here. Straight down the corridor until you can't go any further, last door on the right. I'll be just behind you so don't piss about or you'll get my size ten boot up your backside.'

Charlie Gascoigne was already sitting at the table in the interview room when he got there. She glared at him through the glass window in the door, a glare that remained in place until he was sitting in front of her. Once the cop had left, she tore him a new one.

'What kind of idiot are you? I told you to steer clear of trouble. Which doesn't mean breaking and entering, tripping over bodies or resisting arrest.'

'I didn't—'

She held up a hand.

'You can have your turn later. Much later. We're a reputable firm, we can't have our investigators trailing blood through a suspect's house.'

'I wasn't—'

'Still not finished. My boss is incandescent that I didn't supervise you a bit more carefully. It's not just your skinny arse on the line, it's mine, so this is going to have to be some watertight shit-hot defence you're about to hand me. Have you ever seen the victim before?' She checked her notes. 'Benedict Hawley.'

Jimmy shook his head.

'What about his brother, Steven? It was his house.'

'Nope. Never heard of him either.'

'Well that's something at least. Now the police tell me

you had an accomplice who escaped down a back alley. Who was it?'

Jimmy kept his mouth shut. As he had when the cops quizzed him after throwing him in the back of their car. They'd probably work it out eventually, but he was fucked if he was throwing Deano under a bus. They had their rules and he had his.

The lawyer shook her head.

'This is how it works, Jimmy. I ask, you answer. Forget your omertà or honour amongst thieves or whatever other shit you think you're pulling. I'm not going into bat for you with one hand tied behind my back, so one last time or I walk. Who was with you?'

'Your ears only?'

She sighed. 'Of course it's my ears only. I'm not going to tell them anything they don't already know, am I? I didn't just tumble off the bus from lawyer school. Now spill.'

'It was Deano.'

'That'll be convicted housebreaker Dean Buckley, yes?'

Jimmy nodded.

'Pretty convenient that you rocked up at this house with your own burglar in tow. Someone more cynical than me might think you were planning to break in. Someone like the DCI in charge of this case, for instance.'

'He was there in case there was any bother.'

She snorted her disbelief. 'This is the Dean Buckley who's about eight stone wet through, yes?'

Jimmy tried to avoid her stare but she grabbed his face and made him look at her.

'I do my homework, Jimmy, or due diligence as we call it. I wouldn't take you on without knowing pretty much everything there is to know about you and your friends.'

Even Charlie Gascoigne couldn't talk bollocks without giving herself away. His connections to Deano were personal, there was nothing written down, no family links, no previous form that connected them. Someone had told her who it was likely to be. Someone who had recommended her to him in the first place.

'Andy Burns told you,' he said.

She couldn't hide her surprise.

'Son of a bitch,' Jimmy muttered.

'Give the man a break. He's only trying to help,' she said.

'Has he tipped his colleagues off too?'

She nodded. 'Of course. It's his job, Jimmy, what else could he do? You saved his life, it's common knowledge. You're friends. Everyone gets that. But that also means he knows who your known associates are. Stands to reason. You can hardly expect him to deny it.'

Fuck. The last thing he wanted to do was get the kid in trouble. Deano had turned things around in the last year or two, cleaned himself up, started learning to read. Even nailed down a part-time job. If any of that went up in smoke because he'd helped him out, Jimmy would never forgive himself.

'He didn't do anything either,' he said.

'He was there with you though.'

Jimmy nodded.

'They're bound to bring him in now Andy Burns has given them his name.'

'Will you represent him too?'

'I'll think about it,' she said. 'Now talk me through everything that happened from start to finish. And I mean everything.'

52

Jimmy was no stranger to police interviews – most recently it had been Andy Burns on the other side of the table – but he'd never had a lawyer he trusted before so was more relaxed than normal.

Charlie Gascoigne had told him not to say anything that they hadn't already agreed on and for a change he was planning to do as he was told. It was the first time he'd met the cops working on Gadge's case, Detective Sergeant Alison Brewster and Detective Constable Micky Fulton. Brewster was tall and slender with a solemn, considered manner while her DC was the opposite, a short, stocky, wise-cracking man who barely paused for breath.

After the usual rigmarole of introducing themselves 'for the tape' and reading Jimmy his rights the DC had been about to produce the photo they'd found in Jimmy's pocket of the short man outside the house when Charlie Gascoigne interrupted him.

'Before we start can you promise me that you will get my client some proper clothes when this is over, please? He looks like a painter and decorator at the moment. I nearly asked him if he was free to paper my walls next week.'

She was obviously trying to put them on the back-foot right at the start, though DS Brewster was unperturbed.

'I'll see what I can do,' she said and nodded to Fulton to carry on.

He took the photo and placed it in front of Jimmy.

'Can you tell us where you got this?'

'It was posted through the letter box of the hostel I work at this morning.'

'And can someone verify that?'

'Yes, my boss, Caroline Fisher, gave it to me when I got in.'

'When you got in? I thought you had a room at the hostel?'

'I do.'

'Why didn't you use it last night? Get lucky? Walk of shame this morning?'

Jimmy smiled, remembering how many of his shipmates used to wander up the gangplank in the morning with a big cheesy grin on their faces and a tell-tale pint of milk in their hands.

'Something funny?' Fulton added.

Jimmy shook his head.

'For the tape.'

'No comment.'

'So where were you?'

An alibi would have been useful but Jimmy couldn't see any way to explain the bunker without mentioning the builder's yard and then Andy Burns would be in deep shit.

'No comment,' he said again.

'Aye, right,' Fulton said. 'Pay for it, did you?'

Charlie Gascoigne sighed theatrically.

'Is this relevant? Everyone gets lucky some time, maybe even you, DC Fulton? It's not a criminal offence, is it?'

'Move on,' Brewster said. Fulton nodded and pointed at the photo again.

'Did you know who this man was?'

'No.'

'But you still went to the house?'

'Yes.'

'Why?'

Charlie had briefed him on how to deal with this, so he was happy to answer.

'As you know I'm working for Ms Gascoigne on the defence of Keith Kane. Witnesses have been clear that there was a short man involved in the attack on him and I thought there was a good chance this was that man.'

'Did you now? And who do you think gave you the photo?'

'I have no idea.'

'Why don't I believe you?'

Jimmy just stared at the cop who tried to move on but was interrupted by Charlie Gascoigne.

'While we're on the subject, can I assume you're going to drop the charges against Mr Kane now that the other man involved in the attack on him has been murdered while Kane is still in custody?'

Fulton gaped at her but Brewster barely blinked.

'That's pure conjecture. Please stick to the issue at hand, Ms Gascoigne, or I'll have you removed from the interview.'

'I'd like to see you try. Another man involved in harassing the homeless is beaten to death in a very similar way to his partner in crime and you don't think it's very likely to be the same murderer?'

'Don't push your luck. You've been warned.'

Charlie laughed as if this was the most ridiculous idea.

'For the record I will be appealing against the decision to lock Mr Kane up once we've finished this interview,' she added.

'Noted,' Brewster said. 'Now can we get back to the case in point.' She nodded to Fulton to continue.

'Let's go back to the start. Talk us through what happened when you got the photo again,' Fulton said.

'I told you. I thought I'd better check it out, so I went to the address written on there. When I got there the door was open, which seemed suspicious, so I went in to make sure everything was all right.'

Fulton snorted. 'What with you being a concerned citizen and that.'

Jimmy ignored him and pressed on.

'I found the body in the kitchen and was just about to ring the police when I heard someone coming into the house, so I ran.'

'What a load of jackanory,' Fulton said. He pushed the photo back in front of Jimmy. 'Trouble is, we've seen photos like this before.'

As Charlie had coached him, Jimmy waited for an actual question.

'When someone has been putting out a contract,' the cop added.

They hadn't seen that coming. Jimmy's calmness went out the window.

'I'm not a fucking hit—' Before Jimmy finished his sentence Charlie interrupted again.

'Are you seriously suggesting that my client is a hitman?'

'If the cap fits,' Fulton said.

'How about you, DS Brewster? Have you signed up to this flight of fancy too?'

Brewster kept a straight face. 'We have to explore every possibility. Your client was sent a photo of a man. That man was then murdered in his kitchen and your client was caught on the premises while the body was still warm.'

'Still warm? I heard that rigor mortis had started to set in.'

Suddenly Brewster looked uncomfortable. Charlie's guess had hit the spot.

'We're still waiting for the results of the post-mortem.'

Jimmy's solicitor was sensing blood now, he could feel her energy levels lifting.

'Do you have any evidence at all that he killed the man in question? Any DNA, fingerprints even?'

'We're also awaiting the results of several forensic tests,' Brewster said.

'That's a "no" then.'

'It's a "not yet",' interrupted Fulton. 'Let's go back to your book at bedtime story, Jimmy. If you're innocent, why did you attempt to flee the scene?'

'I thought the murderer had returned. I was scared for my life,' Jimmy said. He was tempted to wink at Fulton but he reined the impulse in.

'So you didn't hear the sirens?'

'I'm a little deaf.'

'Or the officers shouting "Stop, police".'

'No, I heard that, that's why I didn't jump over the fence. As soon as I realised it was the police I stopped and waited to talk to them.'

Even Brewster smiled at that one.

'Can you tell us why you haven't mentioned your accomplice?' Fulton checked his notes. 'Dean Buckley.'

'No comment.'

'Were you planning to break into the house? Wouldn't be the first time he'd been involved in something like that, would it?'

'No comment.'

'What if I told you he's in the next room being interviewed by my colleagues at this moment?'

He saw Jimmy's surprise.

'Kid walked in off the street half an hour ago. Said he wanted to make a statement. I hope you've got your stories straight?'

Jimmy could well believe that. Deano would have been mortified that he left Jimmy behind and would have wanted to make amends. He hoped he knew what he was doing but Charlie had that covered too.

'I hope he has legal representation?' she said.

Fulton hesitated.

'Well, he does now. I insist that you halt his interview now. I want to be there when you question him.'

Fulton glanced at Brewster who nodded. He got up and left the room.

'For the benefit of the tape DC Fulton has left the room,' Brewster said. 'Did you know Benedict Hawley?' she suddenly asked Jimmy.

'No,' he said.

'You certain?' she asked, taking out another photo from Fulton's folder and placing it on the desk. This time it was a front-on photo, full-face, like a mug shot.

Jimmy's surprise was obvious to the other two. He'd seen that face before. In a photo on the mantelpiece at Aaron's mum's home. Benedict Hawley was Debra Mason's boyfriend; otherwise known as Ned.

DS Brewster had been keeping her powder dry. She was clearly no slouch at reading facial expressions and was on Jimmy's case in a heartbeat.

'You do know this man, don't you?'

Jimmy was so shocked that he forgot to say, 'No comment.'

'I, um, he looks familiar. If it's who I think it is then I only know him by the name of Ned.'

Charlie Gascoigne put her hand on Jimmy's arm.

'I need a moment with my client.'

The cop hadn't been happy to pause the interview, but the lawyer had insisted. They'd turned off the recording equipment and left the pair of them in the room.

'Where do you know this guy from?'

Jimmy hesitated, knowing full well that he was going to be putting young Aaron in the frame.

'Don't piss about, Jimmy. Tell me everything.'

'There's a kid at the hostel, Aaron Mason, who's been thrown out by his mum, Debra, because he didn't get on with her new man. Hawley is . . . was, that new man.'

'And you know all this how?'

'I was trying to help the kid get back home, so I had a quiet word with his mum.'

He left out the part about Kate helping him. Some things he'd take to his grave. Charlie shook her head in frustration.

'You really do have a saviour complex, don't you?'

There seemed to be a consensus about this amongst the women in his life. He didn't bother answering.

'Have you ever met Hawley?' she continued.

'No. Never.'

'Did he know that you'd been to see his girlfriend?'

'I don't know. Don't think so.'

'OK. You have to tell the police about this.'

'But they'll go after the kid. The two of them were at each other's throats, apparently.'

'Not your problem, Jimmy. And to be frank, it won't do you, or your friend Deano, any harm if there's a better suspect than you. Anyway, if he didn't do it then there's nothing to worry about.'

That's the problem, Jimmy thought, knowing how much Aaron despised the man. There's every chance he did do it.

53

Jimmy and Deano walked out of the police station the next morning, released pending further investigation. Charlie Gascoigne had played a blinder, making sure their stories matched up. She was pretty certain that the cops had fast-tracked the fingerprints and when they hadn't found either Jimmy's or Deano's had decided to keep their powder dry. DS Brewster had made it pretty clear that they'd be keeping an eye on both of them though.

As they left the station, they saw Aaron and his mum being escorted in. He tried to hold her hand but she shook it off, angrily. She looked devastated, which wasn't surprising. Her boyfriend was dead and now it looked likely her son was the number one suspect; not only did he have a motive, but he was in pole position to leave that photo for Jimmy, though why he'd want to was another matter. Jimmy put that to one side for the moment – he had a much bigger problem coming up.

Someone had tipped off the probation office about his arrest and Jimmy had been called in for an urgent meeting with his new PO, Hardass Harding. Out of the frying pan into a fire that could badly burn him.

'D'you want me to come with this afternoon?' Deano said, when they got back to the hostel.

'No point. If Harding has his way, I'll be leaving in a Group 4 security van, heading off to join Gadge in Durham nick.'

'But you haven't done owt.'

'Not sure Harding cares about that. If I don't come back out, you're gonna have to be the grown-up around here.'

'Fuck off, I'm only twenty-five. And I don't look my age, not like you, old man.'

Jimmy tried to give him a clip but the kid was too quick for him.

'Seriously, man, there's no way I can do the investigating stuff that you do. You're Sherlock Homeless.'

'You'd be surprised what you can do if you have to. And it'll be up to you to look out for the young 'uns, like Aaron. He's going to need all the help he can get, whatever really happened with Hawley.'

'You don't think he killed him, do you?'

'Not really, but he sure had a motive. The guy had him thrown out of his own house and was probably beating his mum up.'

Deano nodded. 'I'd have killed the prick if it had been me. D'you reckon he was the fella who attacked Gadge in the alley as well?'

'Who knows? Maybe. Someone sent me that photo for a reason.'

'I told ya, it was to set you up. Almost worked 'n' all. Good job we made sure we never touched owt.'

'Aye. Might not be enough to keep me out of prison, though.'

'It's not right, man.'

'You'll be all right, you've managed without me before.'

Deano stared off into the distance, as if he could see the future and didn't much like it.

'Aye. But I had Gadge to bail me out then.'

54

2007

The bastard things are everywhere. On the metro and the buses. There's no escaping them. In every shop window and on every street corner. Even, here, on the park bench. Fucking iPods. That little rhythmic noise coming from the numpty with the headphones sat next to him is driving Gadge crackers. He reckons that someone is paying people to taunt him with them. Nathan Lennon most likely. Bet he didn't miss out – his investment portfolio was probably bulging with shares.

He takes out his hip flask. The best way to drown out the noise.

When the little gadgets first appeared in the shops, he tried his best to ignore them, pretended they were nothing like his vision and as long as he was pissed he could just about get away with that. But when he was sober they taunted him. Popping up when he least expected it – he'd even seen one of the friends at the Pit Stop using one – nicked, obviously, but that's not the point.

And of course, when he tries to tell people that they were his idea they just laugh at him. And ask him what else he's invented. Bluetooth? The flash drive? Fucking Facebook?

If only he'd stuck to his plan to get away from this place. If he'd done what he'd planned and roamed from town to town helping people, he'd probably be back on the straight and narrow by now – some kind of folk-hero even. Instead he got sidetracked by a bottle and has never strayed outside the city limits.

Gadge gets up, nudging the kid with the iPod as he does, just in case he's been sent to troll him, but the kid barely notices, lost in music. He heads out of Leazes Park down past St James' towards the Pit Stop. Doesn't know what he'd do without that place. Starve, for one thing.

When he gets there he grabs some bait – beef curry and rice – and sits down on his own as usual. He's one of the first there which suits him cos he doesn't much like company. Not even his own. He watches as the odd couple he's been puzzling over wander in. A skinny rat-faced man with cold eyes and a much younger lad who always seems to be off his face. They could be father and son, but he doesn't think so as the older one's a right ugly twat. He's seen him knocking the kid around a couple of times too, nothing extreme and not really proof that he's not his dad, but enough to piss Gadge off.

'Tragic, isn't it?' a voice says in his ear.

He turns sharply. It's Maggie, one of the volunteers. She's been there for ever. She's a nebby sod but sound enough.

'What is?' he mumbles, hoping she quickly gets bored and leaves him alone.

'That poor lad. Deano.'

'What about him?'

'The way he lets that man Becket take advantage of him just because he can get him drugs.'

'How d'you mean?'

'That loathsome creature makes him beg in the streets. They reckon young Deano gets a lot of money given to him because he looks so innocent. But Becket takes all his cash off him and makes sure he's wasted most of the time, so he doesn't have a clue what's going on.'

Gadge stares at the pair who are sitting next to each other, eating. Neither of them speaks to the other but he notices that when Becket moves his hand quickly to reach for the salt the kid flinches. Maybe it isn't too late to help someone in need after all.

Gadge asks around and enough people confirm Maggie's story to get him worried. He begins to follow the pair around town and quickly discovers the kid's situation is worse than even she imagined. They hang out in a squat in the West End, looks like they've got the place to themselves, sort of.

One night, Gadge watches as a succession of men turn up at the house every hour, on the hour. Could be drugs but he doesn't think so. They spend too long inside and they're a sleazy-looking bunch, all older men, mostly overweight and pig ugly. He sees one of them doing up his flies when he leaves.

The next day he comes back just before seven o'clock

and takes up a position at the side of the house where he can't be seen from the road. There's a broken fence running between the two houses and he grabs a snapped post that's lying on the ground. It's heavy and has a nice spike on the end for maximum effect. He hears the door open and one of Becket's customers comes out but, much as he'd like to teach the twat a lesson, it's not him Gadge is waiting for. It's the next one.

Ten minutes later a car pulls up across the road and a chubby, blond-haired man climbs out. He looks a bit like that posh wanker who they reckon is going to be the next Mayor of London. The man ambles across the road and is just about to open the door when Gadge moves out of the shadows, fence post in hand.

'Your appointment's cancelled,' he says.

The man backs away, his eyes fixed on the post.

'I don't want any trouble.'

'Piss off then.'

He turns and sprints back to his car, almost slipping and falling on his flabby arse in his haste to get away. Gadge waits until the car has disappeared before opening the door himself and entering the house. The room downstairs is an empty shit tip, so he trudges up the stairs.

'In here,' Becket shouts, 'first door on the left.'

Gadge walks in and the smell makes him gag. Deano's lying on a stained mattress, as near to unconscious as makes no difference. The squat is littered with rubbish. Soiled underwear, needles, condoms, chip wrappers, pizza boxes and small piles of shit, some of it human, he reckons. He shakes his head, bewildered by the level of depravity you'd need to reach to get off on this squalor.

Becket emerges from a darkened corner of the room.

'Who the fuck are you?' he says.

'I'm your worst nightmare,' Gadge says.

Becket moves towards him but then sees the fence post in his hand.

'What do you want?' he says, edging away. 'I haven't got any money.'

Gadge is distracted by one of the chip wrappers moving across the floor, watching, fascinated, until the rat trapped under it emerges sniffing at a stain on the floor that looks like blood. He turns his attention back to Becket, who has stepped closer, clearly hoping to catch him off guard. Gadge closes the gap even further.

'I'm taking the boy,' he says.

'Over my dead body,' Becket says, shaking his head. 'He's mine.'

'Not any more.' Gadge takes another step forward. Becket reaches into his jacket pocket and pulls out a big knife with a serrated edge, waving it in Gadge's face.

'Fuck off now, or I'll cut you,' he screams.

Gadge smashes the post into Becket's wrist, sending the knife flying across the room. Becket screams in agony, clutching at his wrist with his other hand. The next blow is to his left knee. Gadge feels the man's bones crumbling under the weight of the strike and Becket falls to the floor, rolling up into a ball, shrieking like a baby. Gadge kicks him in the head repeatedly until the noise stops and Becket is still.

He drops the post on the floor, walks over to the mattress and tries to pick Deano up. It's harder than he imagines as the boy is completely lifeless.

'Come on, son, let's get you out of here,' he says, shaking the kid to try and wake him, knowing that will make it easier to move him.

He's just about to give up when Deano opens his eyes and looks up. He blinks three or four times as if waking from a dream. Then, bizarrely, he smiles, as if Gadge is exactly what he was hoping to see.

'Who are you?' Deano asks.

'I'm Gadge,' he says.

55

Jimmy was clearly on the fast track back to prison. Harding called him into his office the moment he stepped into reception. He'd left Dog with Deano this time, not wanting to antagonise the man.

'I knew you'd be back before the ink was dry on my last report,' the probation officer said. 'I've got an eye for a screw-up.'

Jimmy had learned a lesson from his police interview that he'd forgotten recently. Silence is golden. Don't give them any ammunition. Instead he stared at the plastic lunchbox nestled perfectly on the corner of Harding's desk – its bland neatness somehow summed up everything he hated about the man.

'Nothing to say? Any reason at all I shouldn't have you returned to custody?'

'I haven't done anything.'

Harding laughed. 'The fact that you consider being arrested at a crime scene as "not doing anything" speaks volumes. You're a habitual criminal who should clearly still be behind bars. I hope you've got someone prepared to look after that mutt of yours?'

'I could do it at a push.'

The voice came from behind Jimmy. He swivelled round to see Sandy standing in the doorway.

'What are you doing here?' Harding said, climbing to his feet.

'False alarm,' she said. 'Benign polyps – apparently I talk too much, who'da thunk it.' Jimmy grinned at the news, but Harding looked like someone had stolen his packed lunch. 'I'm feeling much better, thanks for asking,' Sandy added. Her stand-in at least had the grace to blush.

'Obviously that's great but shouldn't you be resting?' he said.

'I was but then I heard a rumour you were going to shaft one of my offenders, so I thought I'd rested enough. Justice never sleeps and all that.'

'I think you'll find he's my offender now.'

Harding was becoming very red in the face and had leant over the desk aggressively. It was like watching a tennis match, Jimmy's head turning this way and that as he became absorbed in the contest going on around him.

'You don't have "offenders", Hardass. You have scapegoats. I hate to be the one to break it to you but being a dick will never compensate for actually not having a dick. Not one that anyone can see without a magnifying glass, that is.'

For a moment Jimmy thought that Harding was going to go for her, but he held back and straightened himself up, pulling his cuffs down as he did.

'I'm just following the rules,' he said, moving over to the window.

'You know what they say about rules – they're for the obedience of fools and the guidance of wise men. Although I think it was Douglas Bader who came up with that and he lost both his legs so, you know, go figure.'

Sandy finally moved away from the doorway, strolled past Jimmy and dumped herself in her old seat behind the desk, making a big show of lowering the chair to reclaim ownership of it. When she'd finished, she looked up to see Harding glaring at her.

'You still here?'

'You—'

'Haven't heard the last of this? Too predictable, Hardass. Off you pop.'

She gave him a send-off, flicking her hand continuously towards the door until the exasperated man was back in the reception area.

'D'you mind?' she said to Jimmy, nodding towards the doorway. He took the hint, got up, shut the door and returned to his seat.

'Are you really going to be OK?' he said.

'Apparently so, though I've got to pack in the vaping and talk a lot less.'

He wondered which one she'd find the easiest, thought it was probably the vaping.

'That's fantastic news.'

'Thank you,' she said. 'Now tell me this . . . why shouldn't *I* send you back to prison?'

56

The soup was so hot that Jimmy couldn't tell what flavour it was. It hit the spot though, as the Pit Stop food always did.

Sandy had read him the riot act but he could handle that. Harding had been ready to fire a bullet with his name engraved on it, and he'd somehow dodged it. He also knew that while he was a free man, he would still do whatever he could to help Gadge.

His phone buzzed in his pocket. Mr Green, the vet, had left a voicemail.

'I've had the results back from the lab. They say it's definitely rat poison. Both Dog and Dizzy, that is. It's not conclusive but there are some markers that indicate that they could both have ingested the same brand. Give me a call if you need to know more. Like I say, not conclusive, but suspicious nonetheless.'

Jimmy shook his head, more confused than ever. Was it just random chance? He couldn't think of a single reason why Ned Hawley would have poisoned Dog as well as Dizzy?

A plate of bangers and mash was slammed down on the

table in front of him and he glanced up into the face of Susan Becket. She didn't look happy. All he needed.

'D'you think it's funny to piss people about?' she hissed.

Over her shoulder he saw Deano in the queue for food. The kid hadn't seen her yet and Jimmy tried to get his attention to warn him but it was no use. He'd got his eyes on the prize behind the counter.

'I'm talking to you, Sherlock,' Becket said.

She'd obviously been doing her homework. Jimmy put his spoon down.

'Can I help you?' he said.

'Yes, you can. And you could have last time I spoke to you but you didn't. You pretended you didn't know my brother.'

He nodded. No point denying it.

'I'm sorry. I could have been more helpful. I'm careful about who I trust. And your brother was a prick.'

She went to say something else but then paused, seeming to weigh up what he'd said. Jimmy took the opportunity to pick up his spoon again, not wanting to let his soup get cold.

'You're probably right, but he was still family. And now I'm trying to find someone who knows what happened to him and I'm told you're the man who can help me do that. I'll pay you, obviously.'

'Let's eat first, I'm starving,' he said. He knew from experience that pounding the streets trying to get people to talk to you usually meant missing a few meals and wasn't surprised when she nodded in agreement and speared a sausage. Jimmy took the opportunity to catch Deano's eye and steered him to another table where the kid sat watching them. He really hoped she wasn't talking about finding Gadge. Not that she'd be able to get to him in prison anyway, at least not personally. There were other ways though; people already inside who'd do real damage for a carton of cigarettes and a couple of porn mags.

'So can you? Find people, that is?' she said between mouthfuls. Patience clearly wasn't her thing.

He sighed and put his spoon down again.

'Depends who it is you're looking for. And why.'

She took a piece of paper out of her pocket.

'I've been doing some digging and I've tracked down the witness who spoke at the inquest – the one who said my brother was off his face on spice. I want to speak to him but I can't get anyone to help me – they all lose their tongue when I mention his name. Look, I found this.'

She pushed a copy of an *Evening Chronicle* article over the desk towards him. He glanced up at the date. It was from a couple of years earlier.

'His name's Alex Bolton. That's a photo of him leaving the inquest.'

The name didn't mean anything to him but the face did. He tried hard not to react but it wasn't easy. It was the tattooed guy who he'd last seen in the back of Stevie Connors' car. No way was that a coincidence. No wonder no one would talk to her. Becket saw his shock. He clearly needed to work on keeping a straight face; two days in a row that he'd failed to hide his shock at seeing a familiar face in a photo.

'You know him, don't you?'

'Not really, no.'

'But you know who he is? And where to find him?'

She was going to get herself into some serious bother if she kept poking her nose into this. Her brother may have been an evil twat but his sister shouldn't have to pay the price for that. He handed her back the clipping.

'I'm not sure you want to get involved with this guy.'

'You're not the first person to tell me that.'

'He's connected to some very unpleasant people.'

'I know that much. And I know my brother was dealing drugs. No surprise there. No one would tell me anything specific but there were a couple of whispers that he was treading on some toes that he shouldn't have been. Undercutting the wrong people.'

If that was true, then maybe Gadge did the man a favour. Connors would have delivered the same end result but much more slowly and with a world of pain. Over her shoulder Jimmy could see Deano sitting on his own in the corner staring at the pair of them, his food uneaten in front of him.

'I really think you should leave it alone.'

'I'm not sure I can. I don't think his death was an accident. He may have been a bad man but he was my brother.'

There was a glint of obsession in her eyes, he'd seen it in the mirror often enough. Some people just had to know the truth.

'Bad wasn't the half of it.'

'If it's a question of money . . .'

She wasn't going to be put off easily. He glanced across at Deano, who still wasn't eating, his eyes fixed firmly on the woman across the table. The kid wasn't going to like this, but he could only see one way to stop her.

'I think there's someone you should talk to,' Jimmy said.

They sat in a small seating area just inside the main entrance where no one would overhear them.

Understandably, Deano was reluctant to talk to the woman. Jimmy knew he found it agonising to talk about it at all, but he convinced him it was the right thing to do and for all his problems the kid still had some kind of moral compass. The info she'd found might be useful in helping their friend and if they could prevent her blundering around and alerting Stevie Connors and his cronies then it was a win-win situation for Team Gadge.

'I'm not sure I want to hear this,' Susan Becket said. Jimmy was pretty sure she'd already heard rumours about her brother and had an idea what was coming.

'Your brother pimped me out,' Deano said. 'To anyone with a couple of quid in their pockets.'

She kept her eyes down, seemingly afraid to confront the pain in Deano's.

'How old were you?' she asked.

'Sixteen when it started.'

Finally she looked up at him.

'I'm so sorry.'

'Not your fault,' Deano said.

'How long did it go on for?'

'Couple of years. Until a friend rescued me and sent him packing.'

'But then he came back.'

Deano hesitated, glancing at Jimmy, who nodded for him to keep going.

'Aye, couple of years ago. He hadn't changed.'

'D-did he try to do it again?'

'He might have if my friends hadn't got in the way. He probably had his eye on some of the younger ones instead though, fresh meat, ya knaa, to make more money from the pervs. There'd be no shortage of kids out there who wouldn't see what was coming until they had a twenty-stone pervert hanging out of their arse.'

Susan Becket's face was ashen. She put her hand to her mouth, stood up and turned to go.

'You really should let it go,' Jimmy said. 'He's not worth you getting hurt.' She stopped but didn't turn back, her shoulders slumping as she headed to the door and left. Deano put his head on the table and Jimmy put his arm round the lad's shoulders.

'You did good, kid,' he said. 'Hopefully, that's one less thing we have to worry about now.'

57

Debra Mason was waiting for Jimmy when he and Deano got back to the hostel – he'd completely forgotten about her and her son being marched into the cop shop.

'Your daughter told me where to find you,' she said, as the pair of them sat down next to her at one of the common room tables, though not before Jimmy had gone to get Dog out of his room.

'Where's Aaron?' he said.

'They're keeping him in for further questioning.'

Jimmy wondered whether Charlie Gascoigne would help the kid. Maybe he should give her a call.

'Has he got a lawyer?'

'Just the duty solicitor. Waste of time anyway, he's not that clever, probably left evidence all over the place.'

Jimmy thought he'd misheard for a minute but could tell by her face that he hadn't.

'You don't think he did it, do you?'

Her hesitation spoke volumes. If the kid's mother wasn't sure, then Aaron really was in bother.

'Jesus,' Jimmy said.

'He's not the angel you seem to think he is,' she said.

Jimmy waited for her to expand, sensing she had something to get off her chest.

'The police searched his room this morning, looking for evidence.'

'Did they find anything?'

'Not really. At least nothing *they* were looking for.'

Again, he waited. She must be there for a reason, and she was obviously building up to it. She reached into a holdall by her feet and pulled out a bag full of blue pellets that she placed on the table in front of him.

'They found this at the back of his wardrobe.'

Jimmy examined the bag. It was rat poison. What the hell? He remembered the message from Dr Green confirming that was almost certainly what had been used on Dizzy. And Dog. Was Aaron involved?

'You think he poisoned his own dog?'

'I tried to tell you about him,' Debra Mason said, nodding. 'He's not the victim here.'

Jimmy remembered her telling them that they'd got it wrong when he and Kate were in her flat, but he'd put it down to her protecting her dodgy boyfriend. Now he saw a slightly different picture emerging. She'd been protecting her child.

'The fight that people heard, that wasn't you and Ned, was it?'

She shook her head.

'Ned could be a dick but he never hit me. And anyway,

he was already lying low at his brother's house then, in some kind of trouble that he didn't want to bring into my flat – though he reckoned he had a way out of it that was going to solve all our problems. He wasn't clever but he was a dreamer, I liked that about him.'

'And Aaron came round?'

'Aye. He only ever came back when he knew Ned wouldn't be there. He's always stroppy but that time he was manic. I think he might have taken something. I tried to calm him down, but he was yelling and screaming, grabbing my arms, shaking me.'

Jimmy remembered the kid kicking off in the hostel that time and the fight with the security guard outside the library. Flashes of a quick temper. Maybe a pattern.

'That wasn't the first time he'd assaulted you?'

She hesitated, her eyes watering, then shook her head.

'It was one of the reasons that he and Ned were always at each other's throats. Ned knew there was history – though Aaron didn't dare act up when he was around.'

He nodded at the bag on the table.

'And you think he poisoned his own dog to try and blame your boyfriend?'

'Dizzy was on her last legs, didn't have long left anyway, maybe he thought he was doing her a favour, but yes, I'm sure that's what he was thinking. It's partially my fault, I'd read about someone leaving poisoned meat in the park and warned Aaron to keep an eye out when he walked the dog. That's probably where he got the idea from.'

The vet's message had said similar poisons were used on Dizzy and Dog though. Had Aaron poisoned Dog as well? Why the hell would he do that?

'My dog was poisoned too,' he said.

Mason looked bemused.

'And you think Aaron did it?'

Jimmy didn't tell her about the vet's verdict. It would have meant mentioning the fact that he'd dug Dizzy's body up. That was way too weird.

'Maybe,' he said.

'I don't understand. Why would he do that?'

'I have no idea.'

'Could be down to me,' Deano said, quietly.

Jimmy waited for him to explain; the kid looked nervous, embarrassed.

'I might have told him a few stories about you,' he said, glancing up at Jimmy. 'Ya knaa, when he first got here, some of the Sherlock Homeless stuff. Sorry, I was just showing off, really.'

'I still don't get it,' Jimmy said.

'Maybes he did it to attract your attention. He might have thought that if he got you to look into the dog poisoning that's been going on and pointed you towards Hawley, you'd cause problems for the man, maybe get him locked up, or at least chucked out.'

'I guess it's possible,' Jimmy said.

'I should have kept it shut.' Deano mimed zipping his mouth closed. He looked mortified, reaching down to stroke Dog as if that would make things right. Jimmy sighed. The kid was a gobshite but he'd never knowingly do anything to harm Dog.

'You weren't to know,' he said, turning back to Aaron's mum. 'D'you mind if I keep this?' He picked up the rat poison.

She shook her head. 'Least of my worries.'

She stood up to go.

'Why did you bring this to me?' Jimmy said.

She sighed. 'I know that Ned wasn't a good man. I know that. And he probably tried to hurt your friend – he spent way too much time trailing around with that fuckwit Tommy Benson. But he was good to me. I loved him. I want to know what happened to him. I was told you wanted to know that too.'

'I do.'

'I told Ned about Aaron coming round. He said he'd sort it. It's my fault.'

The tears had crept out of her eyes now. She pulled a tissue from her sleeve and tried to wipe them. It looked like she'd been doing a lot of crying lately.

'You don't really think it was Aaron that killed him though, do you?' Jimmy asked for the second time.

'Nothing that Aaron does would surprise me,' she said.

58

It was Saturday night and Archie's was rocking, the punters singing along loudly to the karaoke chorus of *Mr Brightside*.

Jimmy was sitting on the bench opposite the bar – the same one that Gadge had been dragged from by two vigilantes just a few weeks ago. Two vigilantes who were now dead while Gadge remained stuck in prison. As investigations went this one was sinking like a giant stone with chains on. Jimmy was about as far removed from being Mr Fucking Brightside as was possible.

He was hoping to speak to Che Kennedy again, the bouncer, who was perhaps the only witness to some of the events that took place that night but the man was busy, keeping a close eye on the weekend partygoers queueing to get into the bar. There were always two bouncers on the door but he was obviously the man in charge and, unlike the others, never got a moment's rest.

Crowds of revellers streamed past Jimmy, many of them stopping to stroke Dog, who was loving the attention. One or two tried to press some money into his hands but he soon put them right. There were others who needed it more than he did, including one sorry-looking youngster sleeping in the doorway of an empty, boarded-up restaurant on the other side of the Bigg Market. He made a mental note to point the kid in the direction of the Pit Stop before he left.

Eventually the flow of drinkers started to slow and the queue was down to manageable proportions. Jimmy saw the bouncer say something to his counterpart and step away from the door to the front of the alley where he lit a cigarette, still keeping his eye on the people being allowed in but no longer engaging with them. Jimmy headed over to join him, Dog trailing at his heel.

'No rest for the wicked, eh?' the bouncer said as he saw Jimmy heading towards him. 'Didn't expect to see you again.'

'Why not?'

The bouncer hesitated and for a second his customary smile slipped.

'No reason, really, just seemed like an open and shut case. I was told your man was caught red-handed.'

'I'm surprised the son of an old Marxist believes everything he's told.'

'Touché! Go ahead then, you've got until the end of this fag to get your interrogation over with.'

'Interrogation? So you won't mind if I shine my torch in your eyes?'

The bouncer burst out laughing. 'That's not a bad idea, pal. I might try that on the punters when I ask them if they've got any drugs on them.'

'Feel free. But that means you definitely owe me more than a minute or two for the idea.'

'Go on then, shoot. But make it quick, rumour has it the boss is paying a rare visit tonight and he gets a bit fractious if there's no one on the door.'

'Archie Simons is coming in?'

'Aye, Archie, right,' Kennedy said, laughing. 'Come on, get a move on, you've already lost thirty seconds.'

Jimmy reached into his pocket and pulled out a print of the selfie Leanne Sweeney had taken with her brother Adam. Andy Burns had printed some out when he'd added the man to his mispers list. He handed it to the bouncer.

'Is this the guy you saw sitting on the bench with my client on the night of the murder here?' He glanced down the alley, an image of Gadge sitting there covered in blood flashing through his mind.

Kennedy took the photo and examined it closely, taking another drag from his cigarette as if it was a concentration aid.

'Aye,' he said. 'That's him. D'you think he might have been involved somehow? Like I said before, he did look pretty handy.'

Jimmy was still thinking about that when an entourage swept out of a black limousine that had pulled up in front of the bar.

'Shit,' Kennedy said, dropping his cigarette, and moving swiftly to his usual place by the door.

Jimmy stepped back into the shadows of the alley, pulling Dog with him, and stared at the unmistakable sight of Stevie

Connors and his crew sweeping past the regular punters queueing up outside and piling into Archie's Bar unchallenged. It took a moment for the penny to drop and even when it did, he wasn't sure what to make of it. One thing he was now sure of after seeing Che Kennedy's reaction to their arrival: Archie Simons wasn't the real boss around here, Stevie Connors was.

59

Jimmy was getting too old for this shit. He glanced up at the cemetery gates and shook his head, wishing he'd asked Deano for some climbing tips. Or even just sent the kid to check the place out and grabbed a good night's sleep instead. But Deano was still feeling a little raw after the confrontation with Susan Becket and he was giving the lad a bit of space to get his mojo back.

He glanced around, checking for nosy neighbours. There was an annoying streetlight across the road which seemed focused on him but most of the houses there were in darkness and, apart from the occasional passing car, there was no one around. He grabbed the bars of the gate and began to climb. It was easier than he expected, the footholds weren't great, but there was a sign with the opening times on it attached to the gate which proved useful. He quickly reached the top and pulled himself up, one leg on either side of the gate, ready to ease himself over and drop down to the other side.

'Are you a ghost?' a loud voice said from below. He

glanced down. A teenage girl was standing on the pavement holding a bag of chips and swaying from side to side. In the streetlight he could see she had more piercings than a pin cushion.

'I've always wanted to see a ghost,' she slurred, smiling up at him. 'Me nan had the gift and she always reckoned I'd inherited it but she's dead now, in there,' she nodded, 'second row on the left. She's never, like, come to visit us since she passed, mind, which has been a bit disappointing, truth be told, so maybe she was wrong?'

The girl was clearly hammered and probably wouldn't remember any of this in the morning, but Jimmy needed her to go away before she attracted attention. He glanced across at the houses to make sure there were no lights going on but so far he'd been lucky. He was also in danger of getting some serious ball-ache, perched precariously on top of the gate, one leg on either side with a row of spikes ready to impale him if he slipped. He thought about doing some ghostly impressions to try to scare her off but she looked like she'd drunk her own bodyweight in alcohol so she wouldn't scare easily and he could never carry it off without cracking up.

'I'm not a ghost,' he said, eventually.

'Just my luck,' she said. 'Nothing exciting ever happens to me. D'you wanna chip then?' She held the bag up towards him, half the contents spilling out of the newspaper on to the ground beside her.

'No thanks,' he said. 'I've just eaten.'

'Ah, OK. Goodnight then, love,' she said, turning and

stumbling off towards the Coast Road, one pace sideways, one pace forwards. Jimmy sighed with relief and lowered himself down the other side of the gate until he was able to drop to the ground. He moved away from the gate quickly before any other passing drunks stopped for a chat, hoping that the girl's loud voice hadn't alerted Adam Sweeney to his presence.

He made his way around the edge of the cemetery until he reached the bunker's location. The ring to pull the hatch up was clearly visible this time, which was a good sign. It was impossible to cover it up once you were in the bunker so it was a fair bet that his target was inside.

Maybe he should have brought a weapon of some kind? From what Che Kennedy had said, Sweeney could take care of himself and if it was him who killed the man in the alley, he was pretty ruthless, to boot. And last time he'd looked the man had a baseball bat in there with him.

He knelt and listened hard for any sound coming from down below but couldn't hear a thing. Jimmy hadn't really thought through what to do at this point. It's not like he could ring a bell, and banging on the hatch lid would just give time for Sweeney to arm himself. Surprise was the sole advantage he had.

He snatched up the hatch lid and dropped down the hole as quickly as he could, only flicking on one of the many light switches when he hit the ground so Sweeney had no time to react. It didn't matter. The bunker was empty. Not completely empty, the camp bed was still there and the bin bag sat in the corner of the room but that was it. The stove and the cans of soup had gone, as had the books, and the coat-hooks were now empty. The baseball bat was gone too. More significant was the absence of the alarm clock and sleeping bag. Sweeney had fled the nest and Jimmy was back to square one.

60

Jimmy woke up coughing; the bunker full of smoke. Couldn't see his hand in front of his face. He rolled off the camp bed, banging his head on the concrete floor. Getting to his feet he groped for the wall, gradually edging towards where the steps should be, eventually banging his knee on them. He climbed up too quickly, slipping twice when he missed his footing. At the top he pushed the hatch but it was stuck, like someone had put a heavy weight on top of it. He moved higher and put his shoulder against it but it was hopeless. He tried once more but the stepladder tilted and he crashed to the ground, cracking his head again. As he drifted into unconsciousness he could feel the smoke filling his lungs.

Jimmy woke up coughing but the smoke had gone. He looked around. He was in his own bed. Thank fuck for that. He stumbled up to crack open the door, somehow desperate for some air, even though it was only another nightmare. 'Only' wasn't really the word – after a long spell where he thought they'd gone away the frequency of his nightmares seemed to be increasing. He knew he was long overdue another therapy group meeting, which always helped, but he also knew that the best way to stop them would be to keep his head down and drop all the investigating shit.

When he opened the door he had a surprise waiting for him. Andy Burns was sitting on his doorstep looking like he'd been dragged there.

'About fucking time,' the cop said. 'Thought you'd never get up.' A waft of alcohol hit Jimmy full in the face.

'What are you doing here?' Jimmy said. 'You smell like you've been on the piss all night.'

'I have,' Burns said.

'Got something to celebrate, have you?'

'Aye, you could say that. I've been suspended.'

The vending machine coffee wasn't great but Burns was in no state to complain. Jimmy manoeuvred the cop to a table in the corner of the common room and went to get them both a cup. While he waited for the machine to work its magic, Burns rubbed at an imaginary stain on his jacket, still half pissed by the look of it.

By the time the coffee was ready the cop had slumped down in his seat, his head resting on the table.

'Drink this,' Jimmy said. 'Then I might get some sense out of you.'

Burns pulled himself up and took a sip of the dark liquid, wincing as he did.

'That's not coffee,' he said.

'It's the barista's day off,' Jimmy said. 'You gonna tell me what this is all about? What have you done?'

'Not me. You.'

Jimmy wasn't surprised the blame was landing on him. Why else would Burns have ended up at his door?

'Stan Walker made an official complaint about me. Said I threatened him.'

'Why would they care what he said?'

Burns stared into space.

'Andy?'

'They don't really. Bastard DCI's been looking for an excuse. And that wasn't all. Someone told him I'd been passing on information.'

'Who to?'

Burns looked down at the table.

'Me?' Jimmy guessed.

The cop looked back up and nodded. 'Aye, the chief suspect in the murder of Ned Hawley, apparently.'

'The *chief* suspect! They can't be looking that hard. What about his partner's kid, Aaron, I thought he was in the frame?'

'They've released him for the time being. Not enough evidence. He's gone back to his mum's.'

Jimmy was surprised after what Debra Mason had said at the hostel, but then had an image of her getting back to her silent, empty flat and realising that Aaron was all she had left. Better the devil you know had never seemed more apt.

'It's not just that, mind. They also reckon you're working for Stevie Connors,' Burns added.

Jimmy took a gulp of his drink. Burns was right, no coffee beans were involved.

'That's bollocks,' he said.

'Doesn't matter, really, damage is done.'

'I'm sorry. I know how much the job means to you.'

'Used to. Not the same since I moved back to mispers. Too quiet.'

'Aye, but it gives you more time to spend with your family.'

'Does now, that's for sure.' Burns gave up pretending the coffee was drinkable and pushed the cup to one side. 'Sometimes I think they'd rather I wasn't around so much.'

'I'm sure that's not true.'

Burns yawned and stretched out his arms before focusing back on Jimmy.

'So are you?' Burns said.

'Am I what?'

'Working for Connors.'

'Course not.'

'You've been seen with him. More than once, I hear.'

Jimmy sighed. The least he owed the man in front of him was some honesty.

'The guy who Gadge is accused of killing was one of his boys. Like me, Connors doesn't think you've got the right man. If I find out who did it, he wants to know.'

'You do know that if you give him a name then whoever it is will probably never be seen again.'

'Aye.'

'So, if you do work it out, will you tell him?'

'Doubt it.'

'He won't like that.'

'Aye, I know that too.'

61

The radio was blaring out some hideous earworm about cheeky boys and cheeky girls. Jimmy tried to make his presence known but the only man in the garage, a blue-overalled mechanic standing underneath a ramped-up black cab, couldn't hear him.

'Excuse me!' Jimmy shouted. No response. He wandered over to a nearby workbench and turned the radio off. The mechanic turned around immediately. It was the same guy he'd seen the last time he'd been to Stevie Connors' taxi firm, the one who'd been driving Connors' car when they'd picked him up on the street.

'What are you doing here?' the man said, pointing a screwdriver at him.

'I'm here to see Stevie.'

'Mister Connors to you, dickhead.'

'Whatever. He's expecting me.'

Jimmy had rung Connors to set up a meeting as soon as Andy Burns had headed home. It was time to fight back a little. Get some insurance. He'd been told to be at the garage by 10 a.m. but thought he might catch them off guard if he turned up early.

'Office at the top of the stairs,' the mechanic said, pointing to a spiral staircase in the corner of the garage. 'Leave the mutt down here. And turn the fucking radio back on.'

Jimmy had brought Dog along as even though Connors' henchwoman had made it clear she didn't want to see him again, the main man did seem to have a soft spot for dogs and he needed all the help he could get. He was happy to leave him down in the garage, though, as the poor thing was getting a bit too old to be climbing up the steep staircase. He tied his lead around the leg of the workbench, turned the radio back on and headed up to the large office where he found Connors sitting behind a desk, his two goons, Bonnie and Alex, on chairs to one side.

'You're early, son. Piss the bed, did you?' Connors said. The two goons pretended he was hilarious.

Jimmy thought about saying something about early birds catching worms but there was no need to antagonise the man, probably too subtle for the present company anyway. Behind him, above the sound of the radio, he heard Dog whining at the bottom of the stairs, as if complaining about the shit music.

'I'd offer you a seat but you're not staying. What was so important that you couldn't tell me over the phone?' Connors said.

'I wanted to talk to you about a man called Becket,' Jimmy said.

Connors looked at him curiously.

'Never heard of him.'

Jimmy looked directly at Alex, who seemed agitated by the mention of Becket's name.

'I was told that Alex here knew him.'

'Were you now?' Connors said. 'And why do you think I'd give a fuck about what you were told? Though I would like to know who's telling tales about my staff.'

Down below, Dog's whining was getting worse. Connors looked at Bonnie.

'Take your pal down there for a quick stroll, will you, can't hear myself think. And try not to get bitten this time.'

Bonnie frowned but did as she was told.

'Now. Where was I?' Connors continued. 'Oh yeah, not giving a fuck about what you want to know about some toerag who bit off more than he could chew.'

So much for never having heard of Becket. Jimmy bit his tongue, he didn't want to press Connors' buttons any more than he had just yet, the man was in a talkative mood. And Jimmy wanted him to keep going – which he did.

'More importantly, let's talk about what you're supposed to be doing for me. I was told you knew what you were doing but while you've been wasting time hanging around one of my bars, I've lost another man.'

Jimmy had been hoping to push the gangster into admitting that the two men who attacked Gadge had been working for him, but it looked like he wouldn't need to push at all.

'So the other man in that alley was Ned Hawley! They were both your men?' Jimmy asked. Connors looked at him suspiciously but didn't say anything, turning instead to his tattooed muscleman, Alex.

'Did you bring that bit of kit along that I asked you to?'

'Aye. It's in my jacket.'

'No use in there, is it. Get the thing switched on and give Jimmy here the once-over. He seems to have a bug up his arse this morning.'

'I'm not checking up there,' Alex said, laughing. He stood up and reached into his jacket, which was hanging on a hook on the wall behind his chair. He pulled out a gadget that looked like a radio transmitter.

Sweat ran down Jimmy's back. He knew exactly what he was looking at. Sammy had warned him about this. It was an Anti-Spy detector for tracking down listening devices. He quickly clicked the pen in his top pocket off. He had no idea whether that would prevent it being detected but it was all he had.

Alex switched the detector on and it emitted a steady beat. He turned around to move towards Jimmy and as soon as he did the gadget let out a continuous high-pitched noise.

Shit! He was a dead man. Jimmy glanced down the stairs. The mechanic was now in an inspection pit, working on a second cab. Maybe if he sprinted down there he'd be out before they could do anything about it. But he doubted he could outrun the much younger tattooed thug in front of him. And anyway, he couldn't leave Dog behind and he didn't know where Bonnie had taken him. He turned back. Alex hadn't moved any nearer and was staring at the device, a puzzled look on his face.

'What's going on?' Connors said.

'Not sure,' Alex said. He moved the device back and the noise stopped. He moved it forward again, towards a second jacket on the hook behind the chairs and the continuous beep started again. The closer he moved it to the jacket the louder it got.

'Well?' Connors said.

'There's a bug here all right, but it's not this idiot who's got it – according to the machine it's in Bonnie's jacket.' He pulled the jacket off the hook and felt around. 'It's here, look. There's a small hole in the front.' Alex tore open the lining to reveal a miniature camera taped inside. He ripped it away, dropped it on the floor and stamped the shit out of it.

Connors looked confused for a second but then the penny dropped.

'Get the bitch,' he yelled, leaping to his feet and running towards the stairs, closely followed by the lumbering Alex.

Jimmy tried to control his breathing, slowing his heart rate, to stop it bursting out of his chest. Trying to stay calm he walked out to the top of the stairs just in time to see the pair run out of the back. He heard shouting, followed by a loud scream and a few seconds later Dog came running into the garage, his lead trailing behind him. Jimmy didn't know what the hell was going down but he knew he had to get out of there PDQ.

Down below, the mechanic was still in the inspection pit, facing the other way. He'd moved the radio to the side of the pit and didn't seem to have a clue what was happening around him. Jimmy slid silently down the stairs on the handrails. The man didn't hear a thing.

He hit the ground running, remembering there was a door into the office underneath the spiral staircase. From there he could get outside without getting involved with whatever was happening at the back entrance. He grabbed Dog's lead and headed towards the door. The mechanic still hadn't moved so Jimmy slowed down, walked calmly into the office, nodded to the old man behind the desk, who was absorbed in the morning paper, and went straight out of the front door.

As soon as he was out of sight he started to sprint, expecting to hear shouts behind him at any moment. Dog ran alongside him, struggling to keep up. Jimmy headed straight across the main road, dragging Dog behind him, ignoring the traffic and causing a bus to jam its brakes on, only stopping when he'd taken several turns to make sure no one was following him. When he finally caught his breath there was only one thought in his mind. Was Bonnie an undercover cop?

62

Jimmy stared at the CCTV images on the small computer screen in Charlie Gascoigne's office.

She'd called him as he made his way back into town and he'd gone straight there, thinking it was as good a place to lie low as any. Even Stevie Connors wouldn't barge his way into a solicitor's office. Would he?

The CCTV camera must have been positioned at the front of Archie's pointing down the Bigg Market as it covered the entrance to both the bar and the alleyway but not the bench on the other side of the street. You could tell it was a weekday evening as the crowds were much smaller than when he'd sat watching the bar a few nights earlier. At times the place looked deserted. Che Kennedy was in his usual place, out front, sometimes accompanied, mostly on his own. Nothing was happening.

'And this is the interesting bit?' he asked the lawyer.

'Be patient,' she said.

Suddenly, out of the left side of the screen, Jimmy saw what she'd been talking about. Three men appeared, arms around each other's shoulders, a bit like the front row of a rugby scrum preparing to confront their opposite numbers. He moved closer to the screen just to be sure but there was no doubt, in the middle of the three men was Gadge. He appeared to be dragging his feet, and it didn't take a genius to realise that he was out of it, the two men on the outside carrying him towards the alley.

'And the police gave you this?' he said. Charlie nodded.

'They have to. It's the law.'

'But surely it proves that Gadge was in no state to defend himself.'

'You'd think that, wouldn't you? Anyway, even that's not the interesting part. Keep watching.'

Jimmy kept his eyes glued to the screen as the three men disappeared into the depths of the alley. He waited for the next piece of action but, aside from the picture flickering briefly a couple of times nothing interesting happened. A variety of punters strolled across the screen, one or two entering Archie's but that was it.

'I don't get it,' he said. 'What am I supposed to have seen?'

Charlie rewound the video until the point when the three men disappeared into the alley.

'Watch the time code in the corner,' she said.

Jimmy stared at the numbers changing in the corner, the seconds changing rapidly, the minutes more slowly until . . .

'What the fuck?' he said. The timecode had suddenly changed from 22.33 to 23.06.

'Told you it was interesting.'

'What does it mean?'

'What it means, Jimmy, is that someone turned off the CCTV camera for thirty minutes. I've watched the rest of the tape, admittedly I fast-forwarded it a lot, but no one comes out of or goes into that alley again until the two cops in the middle of the night.'

'Can you show me it again?' Jimmy asked.

'Sure.'

She rewound the tape back to the start and hit play. The same images played out before Jimmy until the men disappeared, something nagging away at the back of his mind.

'One more time,' he said, when the timecode jumped. Charlie repeated the procedure again and this time he realised what it was. It wasn't something he could see that was bugging him, it was something that was missing.

He was thinking about what that meant when Charlie Gascoigne's phone buzzed. She tried to ignore it but it buzzed again and she pressed a button on the intercom.

'I'm busy.'

'Sorry to bother you, Charlie, but they insisted,' the secretary said.

'Who insisted?'

'The police. A Detective Sergeant Brewster.'

'Put her through.'

Charlie switched the phone from her intercom so Jimmy could no longer hear the conversation, but he was pretty sure what the subject was – the altercation at Stevie Connors' cab firm. If he was right about Bonnie he knew he'd get a tap on the shoulder at some point and this was obviously it. Maybe he should be grateful that the police had found him before Connors had.

It appeared that DS Brewster had a lot to say about the subject. Charlie Gascoigne was doing a lot of nodding, then her eyes went big – in surprise, probably – and then she went back to nodding.

'I understand,' she said, eventually. 'And thanks for letting me know.' She put the phone down and stared at Jimmy for a moment. He could see that she was struggling to take in what she'd just been told and he was wondering how to justify his involvement with Connors.

'I can explain,' he started to say but she held up her hand to stop him.

'It wasn't about you,' she said. 'It's Gadge.'

No. Please no. His friend had looked like shit when he'd last seen him and he'd imagined getting this call several times. He bowed his head and steeled himself for the bad news.

'They're withdrawing the charges,' she said. 'He's getting out.'

63

When Bev opened the door it was obvious that she'd made an effort. Even Jimmy could see she was wearing discreet make-up and had put a dress on that she would never normally wear to swan about the house in. They stared at each other for a second too long before he gave her a quick peck on the cheek and entered the house.

He'd been there once before – though not inside – some three years earlier, just after he'd moved back to the city. He'd stood across the road and watched from behind a wall as she and her new husband – new to Jimmy anyway – had moved into the place. He wasn't being all stalkerish, but he hoped that seeing her again would let him move on with his life again. It didn't really work.

The place was very different to the small, terraced house that he and Bev had shared in another lifetime, moving in just after they'd got married. Graham had clearly been an upgrade for her – though it was all a bit sterile for his tastes. It reminded him a little of Debra Mason's place – not much in the way of family photos or ornaments scattered around.

Bev used to like clutter so he couldn't help wondering if Graham had been like Ned Hawley, another one of those men who liked things 'just so'.

'Nice house,' he said.

'You don't have to be polite,' she said. 'I think we're a long way past that.'

'Fair enough.'

'So you don't like it then?' Bev made a pouty face which made Jimmy laugh and broke the ice. 'I've got some beer in the fridge if you want a cold one,' she added.

'I don't drink. Haven't had a drop in twenty-odd years.'

She frowned. His drinking had been one of the final straws for their marriage and had ultimately played a part in his first prison sentence.

'How did I not know that?'

'To be fair, we haven't been going to the same parties for a while.'

'We had dinner with Kate and Carrie just a few weeks ago. I could have sworn you were drinking then.'

'Alcohol-free beer. Stops people asking questions.'

They were more relaxed now, some of the rhythm that they used to have coming back, an effortless banter that had kicked in the minute they first met and lasted until that bomb in the Falklands blew the shit out of it.

'Cup of tea then?'

'Lovely.'

'Come and sit in the kitchen while I make it.'

The kitchen was bigger than Jimmy's entire hostel room. A large central worktop dominated the space. There were a few stools scattered around it and Jimmy plonked himself on one as Bev put the kettle on.

'Milk, two sugars? Or have you changed that as well? I've got some almond milk in the fridge.'

'No, you're fine, though I've dropped the sugar these days.'

'Sweet enough,' she said and then obviously regretted it – the early awkwardness kicking back in. She kept herself busy instead, taking two cups from a mug tree and wiping them clean.

'How are you?' he said, blandly, not wanting to add, *now that you've kicked your husband out.*

Bev stopped what she was doing, clearly wondering how much detail to give him. Jimmy suspected it would be a while before they shared too much information, that they'd be stuck in neutral for the foreseeable future. But maybe he was wrong.

'It's been too quiet. So I'm looking for a job,' she said.

'That's brilliant,' he said.

'Graham didn't like me working, always said he earned more than enough for the both of us – which was true – but I need to be self-sufficient now. I've got an interview this afternoon, doctor's receptionist.'

Something must have shown on his face as she looked at him curiously and glanced down at her dress.

'Oh, Jimmy, you didn't think this was for you, did you?'

He could feel himself blushing. Was it that obvious? He tried to change the subject.

'Course not. I mean, you don't even want to sit next to me at the wedding, do you?'

'Who told you that?'

'Kate said I had to talk to you about seating arrangements.'

'Yes, well, annoyingly our daughter has opinions.'

'Must get that from you,' he said. 'I don't really have any myself.'

She gave him a look but the kettle started to boil so she moved away and poured the hot water into a teapot, putting a fluffy tea cosy on it to keep the warmth in – one habit she hadn't changed since the old days.

'If it's what she wants I'd be happy for us to sit together,' she said, not quite catching his eye. Maybe she was worried that he'd decline the offer. Maybe he should. She noticed his hesitation. 'Isn't that why you came here? To sort that out?'

Jimmy shook his head. He'd barely had time to think about it since their meal out together.

'To be honest, I thought you might not want me there at all.'

'Why would you think that?' she said.

Jimmy shrugged. 'I know you think I'm bad ju-ju, a trouble magnet.'

She laughed. 'Aren't you?'

She had a point.

'Anyway, it's what Kate wants and it's her wedding,' Bev added.

'Great.'

'Don't get your hopes up, mind, I'm not trying to restart anything here. That ship sailed a long time ago. I just think it will piss Graham off.'

He held back a sigh of relief but his face was really letting him down at the moment.

'You might try to look a little bit disappointed.'

'Sorry,' he said.

'Anyway, if you didn't come here to talk about that, why did you come?'

He looked out of the kitchen window. The garden was bigger than he'd imagined, there was so much room in the place.

'I was wondering if you fancied a lodger?' he said.

Her face dropped. 'You can't move in, Jimmy, no way. Think about how it would look. Anyway, I thought you had a live-in job at the hostel.'

'I do. I wasn't asking for me. I was asking for my friend, Gadge. The police have withdrawn the charges and he's going to be released but he needs somewhere safe to stay. He can't live on the streets any more. He's not well.'

That was true, but it wasn't the whole truth. Jimmy was worried about the man's safety. Someone had stitched him up for murder but he wasn't a murderer, he was a witness, and that same someone might be after him now. He'd be an easy target on the street whereas no one would think of looking for him here. To his surprise she didn't say 'no' straight away. In fact, she didn't say anything, just stared down at her tea.

'It wouldn't be for long,' he added. 'Just until we can sort out something longer term for him.'

She finally looked up. 'And you're sure he had nothing to do with that man's death?'

She'd never met Gadge but he and Kate had spoken a little about his plight at the meal so Bev knew the broad brushstrokes.

'Absolutely certain.'

'But he's an alcoholic, right?'

No point lying. It wouldn't take much time in the man's company to see that.

'Yes, but high-functioning.'

She still hadn't ruled it out so he pushed a little harder.

'You said it was quiet – it won't be with Gadge around.'

She smiled. 'I'm sure. But that's not why I'm considering it.'

'Why then?'

'Because it'll piss Graham off even more than the seating arrangements at the wedding.'

64

Deano was bouncing around like the Duracell bunny on speed. He reminded Jimmy of a kid on Christmas Eve waiting for Santa to turn up, which wasn't that far from the truth.

'Where is he, man? What's keeping him? They were quick enough to lock him up. Bastards are dragging their heels now they've got to let him go.'

He was right. The wheels of justice turned slowly when it came to releasing people. To be fair, the police had no choice but to get a magistrate to approve the withdrawal of the charges, but he knew from bitter experience that if it was a search warrant they'd wanted they'd have been knocking on the man's door in the middle of the night to get the required signature.

Still, the kid didn't need any encouragement to get his dander up.

'Cool your heels, man, you got an urgent appointment or something? You're wearing a hole in the pavement with your leaping about.'

Just as Deano was about to sit down next to Jimmy on the

bench, a door in the wall opened and Gadge stepped out, wearing a black hoodie with the words 'Thug Life' on the chest and carrying a small rucksack. Deano went tearing across the car park and nearly knocked the old man over as he launched himself into a full-on hug.

'Take it easy, son,' Gadge said. 'There's no need for that, I've only been away a few weeks.' He may have been playing it down but over Deano's shoulder, Gadge was grinning at Jimmy and he'd returned Deano's hug with interest, almost lifting the kid off his feet.

'I knew Jimmy would get you off, man, I just knew it,' Deano exclaimed overexcitedly.

Jimmy had explained to Deano several times that Gadge wasn't out of the woods yet but the kid didn't really do subtlety. It was true that the police had withdrawn the charges due to lack of evidence but they hadn't *dropped* the charges which was a different thing entirely. They could re-charge him any time. Ned Hawley's death hadn't helped the cops' cause. Jimmy guessed they'd been hoping he'd identify Gadge as the assailant, so it was a tactical move on their part – living to fight another day. They still clearly thought he was guilty and that it was just a matter of finding another witness or more proof elsewhere.

Gadge didn't correct the kid either, just raised his eyebrows at Jimmy, acknowledging that Deano was never going to understand so there was no point trying. The kid finally let go of him and pulled out his car keys.

'Come on then, man, car's around the corner,' Deano said, 'just by the law courts.'

'I was thinking I'd get the train back,' Gadge said.

'But I borrowed it specially,' Deano said. 'I thought it would be nice for you to get chauffeured.' The kid looked distraught. He didn't know anything about Gadge's car phobia, there wasn't any reason he should. Gadge glanced at Jimmy knowingly and yawned, ruffling Deano's hair at the same time.

'Thank you, my friend,' he said. 'That's very kind of you. But I'll probably be asleep before you hit second gear. I haven't slept since Jimmy told me I was getting out. Too excited about seeing your little chubby cheeks.'

He squeezed Deano's face until the kid squirmed away from him.

'Get off us, man.'

Gadge backed away and pointed at the Thug Life hoodie.

'What d'you think of this?' he said. 'One of the guards dug it out of the unclaimed property for us. How do I look?'

'I thought it was Tupac for a minute,' Deano said, and started giggling like a naughty kid, which set them all off, even though Jimmy suspected that, like him, Gadge didn't have a clue who Tupac was.

'It's all this witty banter that I've missed,' Gadge said once they'd calmed down. 'And some good bait, obviously. I hope you've got a nice restaurant booked somewhere?'

'How about the Pit Stop?' Jimmy said.

'That'll do nicely.'

Gadge settled in the back of the car as they set off towards Newcastle.

'Bit weird you shacking up with Jimmy's missus,' Deano said, before they'd even got out of the car park.

Jimmy was tempted to slap him round the head but Gadge was quick to jump in.

'For starters, I'm not "shacking up" with her, she's letting me stay in her spare room, and secondly, she hasn't been Jimmy's missus for some time now.' He paused for comic effect. 'Even though he still holds a candle for her.'

'Bollocks,' Jimmy said, glaring at Gadge in the rear-view mirror. 'That's not true.'

'Howay, man, every time you talk about her your voice gans all gushy.'

Jimmy knew his friend was just winding him up but it bothered him that there might be a grain of truth in what he was saying. He leant back again to think about that, which was like pouring oil on the fire.

'See, told ya,' Gadge said. 'No comeback. The man's still smitten.'

Jimmy kept schtum; Gadge could be incorrigible if he thought he'd get a bite. Even Deano was quiet for a while as they headed towards Chester le Street, seemingly happy that the three street musketeers had been reunited. The next time Jimmy glanced behind, Gadge was fast asleep, lying along the back seat, snoring gently.

They were almost on to the A1 when Jimmy caught a glimpse of the car behind them. He'd seen that car before. It belonged to Stevie Connors.

'Don't look round but we're being followed,' he said.

He saw Deano glance at the mirror.

'Black car, tinted windows?' the kid asked.

Jimmy nodded.

'Leave it with me.'

Deano had been taught how to nick cars when he was just a bairn, way before he was even old enough to drive. The kid wasn't particularly proud of that but he was proud of the advanced driving skills he'd picked up escaping his pursuers. The car slowly picked up speed.

'You know who it is, don't you,' Deano said, glancing across to Jimmy.

'It's Stevie Connors' car. Not sure who's in it though.'

When Jimmy had rung Gadge to explain his plan to house him at Bev's temporarily, the old man had been reluctant, but he'd persuaded him that he needed to lie low. As far as he knew, Stevie Connors was still keen to find out what had happened in that alley and even though he didn't seem to believe that Gadge had attacked his men, Jimmy knew he wouldn't hesitate to lean on the man for answers as soon as he had the chance. And he'd probably heard about the impending release before any of them – the man had eyes and ears everywhere.

As they turned on to the A1, Deano upped the speed considerably. Before they'd even come off the slip-road the speedo was showing ninety-plus and the car was beginning to judder. Jimmy glanced behind him, worried that Gadge would be freaked out but he was still fast asleep. The black car was still there though, it had dropped back a little but the driver seemed to have realised what was happening and had moved into the outside lane to try and close the gap. Deano put his foot down further, veering in and out of the lanes to overtake anything in front of him. Up ahead Jimmy could see a sign – one mile to the next exit. Traffic was beginning to build up on the car's inside and Deano was now stuck behind a lorry in the outside lane. He flashed his lights but was ignored. The exit was only a hundred yards ahead now so Deano clearly had other plans.

'Brace yourself,' Deano said, suddenly hitting the accelerator, whipping the wheel left and veering straight across the path of the cars inside of him. Horns blared and brakes squealed as the other drivers swerved out of the way. The kid timed it perfectly, keeping his eyes on the prize as he tore up the slip road. Jimmy turned around and saw Connors' car go sailing past the exit, still stuck in the outside lane, the inside lanes blocked with cars that had ground to a halt to avoid hitting each other. He turned to Deano in disbelief but the kid just winked at him and laughed.

'Skillz, eh!'

At the top of the ramp, Deano swept around the right turn and sped on until hitting another roundabout where he turned left. Almost immediately he swung left again, into a Premier Inn car park, pulling up on the other side of a large van so they couldn't be seen from the roadside. He killed the engine. In the distance they heard the sound of sirens.

'What's going on?' Gadge said, suddenly. Jimmy and Deano turned around, the old man was sitting up again, yawning but awake.

'Lewis Hamilton here had to take evasive action. We were being followed.'

'Who by?'

'Connors, I think.'

'We should ditch the car,' Deano said. 'Someone might have got the registration.'

'I thought it was your mate's car,' Jimmy said. 'You can't just dump it.' He caught Deano's eye in the mirror. The kid looked guilty.

'Fuck me,' he said. 'You nicked it, didn't you?'

'Twat let me down last minute, said he had to take his girlfriend shopping. If people are stupid enough to leave their spare keys in a magnetic box underneath the bumper what do you expect me to do?'

'You picked me up from Durham prison in a stolen car?' Gadge said. 'You trying to get us all locked up together?'

The pair of them gave Deano the evil eye. Deano started to get agitated, he hated getting in their bad books.

'I didn't want to let you down, man, I didn't think . . . I mean, I thought . . .'

Neither of them could hold the stare and they both cracked at the same time, howling with laughter at the kid's face.

'Ungrateful pricks,' Deano muttered.

Charlie Gascoigne picked them up from the Premier Inn, not even pretending to believe their story that their car had broken down. She had more important things on her mind – the cops had invited her and Jimmy in for a 'friendly chat'.

65

Jimmy sat back on his chair. He'd been here before. And in pretty identical circumstances. Charlie Gascoigne on his side of the table and DS Brewster and DC Fulton on the other side. It wasn't déjà vu if it was actually happening, was it?

The exception was another older, male cop who hadn't been introduced. He stood just inside the door, seemingly distancing himself from his two colleagues to make it less of a 'them and us' situation.

The other change from his previous visit was that nobody had read him his rights and they hadn't switched the tape machines on. Whatever was happening it was definitely unofficial. Brewster did, however, have another photo to show him, just like last time. She pushed it across the table to him.

'D'you know this woman?' she said. He didn't need to look that hard. It was Bonnie, Connors' henchwoman. Only she looked a little different. It was probably the uniform she was wearing. Fucking knew it, Jimmy thought.

'She's a cop? Undercover?' he asked, glancing at Brewster, who nodded in confirmation. Jimmy's suspicions were bang on; it was either that or she was working for one of Connors' rivals, but he'd have put good money on the former.

'A Level One operator. One of our best,' the older cop said, from over by the door.

'Sorry, but who are you again?' Jimmy said.

'I'm Superintendent Hanrahan, I was overseeing her operation.'

'Well "one of your best" held me down while Connors stuck a cigarette in my neck.'

'Shit happens,' Hanrahan said. 'Sometimes you have to bend the law a little to keep under the radar.'

'It was my fucking arm she was bending, not the law.'

Hanrahan nodded. 'I'm sure if she could have avoided it then she would have. At the moment I'm a bit more concerned that she has had her cover blown out of the water.'

'What's that got to do with me?'

Hanrahan gave him one of those 'I know what happened' looks but Jimmy ignored him.

'She's the one who got caught with a wire in her coat.'

'Only because you blundered in there asking stupid questions.'

Jimmy resented both 'blundered' and 'stupid' but he had a more pressing grievance.

'Was it you who told my probation officer that I was talking to Connors?'

'You were getting in our way, we just wanted you shunted to one side.'

'You nearly had me shunted back to prison.'

The cop shrugged. 'Not really my problem.'

'And Bonnie's not mine. So unless you get to the point I think we're done here,' Jimmy said.

'My client's right, I think it's time for you to shit or get off the pot,' Charlie Gascoigne added, earning more brownie points from Jimmy. He loved that saying.

'We know that you've been working for Connors,' Hanrahan said.

'Not really.'

'We think he's got something big on the horizon and we want to know what it is and when. But he's gone to ground since Bonnie got away.'

'She got away?'

'Aye, otherwise you and I would be having a very different conversation. They tried to beat the shit out of her but she was too quick for them. Managed to leg it before they could do too much damage.'

'So what do you want from me?'

Hanrahan hesitated.

'I think we've heard enough,' Charlie said, picking up her papers.

'Hold your horses,' the cop said. 'We need your help.'

'You want me to go back in there miked up.'

'I was told you were smart.'

Jimmy could see an opportunity.

'Flattery will get you nowhere. The problem is I don't trust any of you.'

'You don't know me,' Hanrahan said.

'OK, then, how about you scratch my back first to prove I can trust you.'

'I don't think you're in any position to be making demands.'

'No problem,' Jimmy said, standing up. 'See you around.'

Charlie Gascoigne pushed her chair back from the desk but stayed sitting.

'Your move I think, Superintendent,' she said.

Hanrahan pushed himself off the wall and moved towards the desk with his serious face on.

'What is it you want?'

'I want you to drop the charges against Gadge completely.'

'No chance,' Brewster said.

Jimmy had known that was going to be the answer but it was an old gambler's move, start big, back down and then go smaller for the win.

'You see,' he said to Hanrahan. 'It's one-way traffic with you guys.'

'That's not fair. You're asking too much.'

'OK then, I'll only help you if DS Burns is involved.'

'I'm sure that can be arranged,' Hanrahan said.

'DS Burns has been suspended, boss,' Brewster said.

'Well maybe he should be unsuspended,' Jimmy suggested.

Brewster looked across at Superintendent Hanrahan, who nodded.

'I'll see what I can do,' she said.

66

Gadge was bored shitless. How long could you play solitaire for without wanting to poke a rusty fork in your eye? For one thing it was too easy. He'd nailed it five times in a row now. Obviously he'd cheated a bit but everyone did that, didn't they?

He stared out at the garden. Since he'd moved into Bev's he'd spent both afternoons snoozing in a hammock she'd tied between two trees – it was chilly but being outside felt like freedom after being locked up so he'd wrapped up warm and loved every second. He remembered his mam always used to say 'Ne'er cast a clout till May is out' and she was bang on, especially if you lived in Newcastle. But it was pissing down this afternoon so that was a non-starter.

The fridge was making a buzzing noise. The beer was calling him. He liked Bev and if he was ten years younger, a few stone lighter and a lot more handsome he might have laid on the old Gadge charm to see where it would go. But those days were long gone and Jimmy would rip his balls off just for thinking about it. How the man had pulled her back in the day was a mystery; he'd definitely been punching.

However, the woman had issues. It was nice of her to let him stay there – and Gadge knew that he had to keep out of Stevie Connors' way – but her terms and conditions left a lot to be desired. He could live with the daily shower and the bed-making, even with the cleaning duties she'd delegated to him – but restricting a man's beer intake was cruel. He'd tried to invoke his human rights but apparently it was non-negotiable so, reluctantly, he'd agreed. Seven cans a week it was.

Gadge opened the fridge. Two cans left. And it was only day three. He was good at maths but he didn't like the answer that came up when he divided two by five. Man cannot live on coffee and water alone. At least she didn't mind feeding him up. He'd lost weight in prison and he didn't look well on it. Some men needed a bit of flesh on their bones to look their best. She was a bit too fond of salad though, the drawers in the fridge were chocka with lettuce, tomatoes and cucumber. He sighed. Maybe he should humour her and eat some of it?

As he thought about it, he heard the front door close. She was home early. Now was his chance to impress her. If he showed he was willing to go down the healthy eating route she might up his beer allowance. He smiled to himself, he knew a cunning plan when he heard one. He removed the salad drawer with one hand and closed the fridge door with the other.

A sharply dressed man was staring at him from the

doorway. Jimmy had warned him that Connors' men might pay him a visit but Gadge had laughed it off. How had he found him so quickly? And how had he got in? The staring contest didn't last long, the other man lunged towards him but Gadge was ready. He hurled the salad drawer at him and ran towards the glass doors that led to the garden.

'No, you don't,' the man said, chasing after him.

Gadge quickly realised he'd be trapped if he went into the garden, so he changed course and veered down the other side of the island, closely pursued by the intruder. He tried to grab a knife from the block on the counter but was moving too quickly and missed his chance. The other guy saw his move and stopped, reaching for the knives himself. Gadge knew he had to stop him, if the invader got the knife he was as good as dead. He looked around for a different weapon but there was nothing. Well, not nothing, but . . . fuck it, beggars can't be choosers. He grabbed the cucumber, which had fallen onto the counter when he'd thrown the salad drawer across the room, and twatted the man around the head.

It was surprisingly effective. The man yelled and put his hands up to block the blows, so he switched the attack and rammed it into his crotch. He groaned and sank to his knees so Gadge whacked him around the head twice more for good measure. The cucumber was falling apart in his hand but the knives were in reach now, so he dropped it and pulled the biggest one out of the block. The man had rolled into a ball, covering his head, but when the blows stopped, he glanced up and saw the knife.

'No, please, don't hurt me. You can take whatever you want.'

Gadge hesitated. What was he on about? Did he think he was going to steal his wallet, or his watch maybe? That didn't make any sense.

'What are you after?' he yelled.

The man looked equally puzzled. 'What . . . what do you mean?'

Gadge raised the knife threateningly. 'I'll only ask you one more time. What are you doing here?'

The man edged back, trying to get out of reach of the knife, but his back soon hit the wall. He looked back up at Gadge.

'It's my house,' he said.

Jimmy looked around the kitchen. There was cucumber everywhere: on the door, on the counter, on the floor and the ceiling, but mostly on Graham's suit.

Bev's husband – or did he count as another ex-husband now? – was sitting in a chair with an ice pack held against his reddened face, miserable as sin. Gadge was sitting in the opposite corner nursing a beer, looking pale but a bit too pleased with himself. He'd called Jimmy fifteen minutes earlier and told him that he'd got a bit of a problem. A master of understatement, obviously.

'I might have known this barbarian would be something to do with you,' Graham muttered, moving the ice pack to the other side of his face. 'Man's a lunatic.'

'You started it,' Gadge said. 'I just finished it.'

'I thought you were a burglar!'

'Stealing the fucking salad drawer, was I?'

Jimmy sighed. This was going to be hard enough without these two having a dick-swinging competition.

'What's your excuse?' he asked Gadge.

'I thought he was Stevie Connors' man. How was I supposed to know what Bev's ex looked like?'

'Can we please stop saying "ex",' Graham muttered. 'Surely there are still some pictures of me on the walls?'

Gadge shook his head. 'Don't think so.'

Graham's head dropped a little. Jimmy almost felt sorry for the man – he knew what it was like to lose Bev. The man would have regrets for the rest of his life.

'Does she know about this?' he said.

'Not yet, but she will just as soon as she checks her phone messages,' Graham said. 'She's got a lot to answer for. I've only been gone a few weeks and she's already moved another man in here.'

Jimmy laughed. 'You don't think . . .' he stopped when he saw Gadge's expression.

'Go on,' the old man said. 'Finish what you were saying. He doesn't think what?'

Graham watched with obvious interest as Jimmy rewound a little.

'It's not like that,' he said, eventually, which seemed to appease Gadge a little. 'Gadge is a friend of mine and he needed a place to stay for a while. Bev kindly agreed to let him use her spare room.'

'Our spare room,' Graham muttered.

'I thought you'd moved out,' Gadge said.

'Temporarily,' Graham said. 'Just until she comes to her senses.'

'Well maybe until that happens we should clean this place up a bit,' Jimmy said.

'I'll be doing no such thing,' Graham said. 'He's the one who made the mess.' He glared at Gadge who faked a lunge towards him just to watch him flinch but then winced in pain, holding his arm, which undermined the fun he was obviously having. Jimmy made a mental note to get the guy checked out properly – he probably hadn't seen a doctor since his last heart attack.

'Touch me again and I'll call the police,' Graham said, but only after he'd seen Gadge was in pain.

'And tell them what?' Gadge muttered. 'That you were attacked by a salad-wielding pensioner? I'm sure they'll send a SWAT team in.'

'If anyone's going to call the police, it'll be me,' a woman's voice said.

All three men turned around sharply. Bev was standing in the kitchen doorway, a couple of Sainsbury's carrier bags at her feet. She looked around the kitchen, paying particular attention to the ceiling.

'Is that cucumber?' she said.

Jimmy nodded.

'Would somebody like to tell me what the fuck has been going on?' she said.

In the end Bev saw the funny side. She even let Deano bring round a couple more cans for Gadge 'to ease his nerves'. The man sure knew how to milk a situation, Jimmy thought.

The same couldn't be said for Graham who left the house in a huff, muttering veiled threats of legal action which no one took remotely seriously, especially Jimmy. He had far bigger things to worry about.

Once they'd cleaned up the kitchen she left the boys to get on with it while she caught up with the latest soaps.

'Did you really beat up her ex with a cucumber?' Deano said, as he settled on a stool.

'Guilty,' Gadge said. 'I tried to use a lettuce but it wasn't enough.'

'Really?' the kid said, grinning.

'Aye, but maybe that was because it was only the tip of the iceberg.'

Jimmy and Gadge snorted with laughter but Deano didn't have a clue what they were laughing about.

'I don't get it.'

'Never mind, son, we'll explain it when you're out of nappies,' Gadge said.

'Tossers,' Deano muttered, which set them both off again, as the kid looked on, completely bemused. Jimmy doubted he'd ever made a salad in his life.

'Stevie Connors spoke to me last night,' Deano said, which brought the laughter to an abrupt end. 'Thought that would shut you up.'

'How d'you mean?' Jimmy asked.

'Just came over to me at the dog track while I was cleaning

up the greyhound shit and asked me how I was getting on. Said he'd heard a lot about me.'

'If you lie down with dogs you catch fleas,' Gadge said, giving Jimmy a told-you-so look.

'Did he say anything else?' Jimmy pressed.

'Nah, just that he'd be keeping an eye on me, that he was always on the lookout for new talent.'

'You should keep away from him.'

'Aye, I knaa that, bit hard when he owns the place I work at though. Anyway, listen who's talking, you're the one who's been working for him. Dick's move, that was.'

Gadge nodded. 'The kid's not often right, but maybe this reading lark is making his brain a bit bigger. You need to take your own advice. It's no good hiding me away when you're out there in plain sight with a target on your back.'

Jimmy kept his gob shut. There was no way he was telling these two what he was planning to do next. They'd have locked him in Bev's attic for his own safety.

'Hey, it's not me who got us into this mess.'

Gadge put his hand to his chest, got up, and staggered over to Deano like an old man, winking at the kid as he did.

'What kind of friend would give a man with a dodgy heart, who was just trying to do a good thing, a hard time, eh, Deano?' He took the opportunity to grab another can from the fridge.

Deano shook his head in sympathy as if he couldn't believe such cruelty would exist, happy to be in on the joke this time.

'Maybe we should take that beer off you and rush you

over to casualty, get you checked out,' Jimmy said, knowing how much Gadge hated hospitals. 'You've had a lot of excitement for an old man.'

Gadge put his hand round the kid's shoulder, comrades in arms against a common enemy, and pointed an accusing finger at Jimmy.

'See, my young friend, I knew this one was a heartless twat the minute I set eyes on him.'

67

2012

Gadge doesn't notice the new guy at first, maybe because the shepherd's pie is delicious. It's been a while since he's been this hungry and he's enjoying every meaty mouthful. It's only when Deano laughs like a nut-job that he looks up.

'What's up?' Gadge says.

The kid nods at the door. Gadge glances over to the Pit Stop's entrance where the man is talking to Maggie, one of the volunteers.

He's bog-standard homeless, short, scruffy, shaven-headed and too skinny for his own good. He's no idea why Deano thinks it's funny and hopes he isn't back on that spice shit again. He'll fucking batter him if he is. The kid has been clean for a good while now and Gadge was hoping he'd finally cracked it.

Not that he can point the finger. Deano's done his best to talk him into cutting down on the booze – it was the kid who saved him last time, dragging him to the hospital when his heart stopped doing its job properly – and he knows fine well what the doctors said after they'd brought him round. But what else has he got? The pub's his spiritual home, it's where his tribe hangs out and he's too old to change his ways now. He does worry about what will happen to the kid if he should cark it suddenly, though.

Forgetting about the newcomer for a moment, he notices Deano's not eating again which pisses him off. It's free food and it's fucking great so it shouldn't go to waste. And the lad's all skin and bones so he has to eat.

Deano sees him watching and picks up a spoon but Gadge isn't fooled. He's just moving the rice pudding around the bowl a bit. He nudges Deano's arm.

'You need to eat, bonny lad,' he says.

'Not hungry.'

The new guy has got his food now and is sitting down on the same table as them, a few feet away. He's keeping himself to himself but Gadge glowers at him anyway. He doesn't like strangers getting too close to him when he's eating, not natural, is it?

The man ignores him but Gadge maintains his stare, willing him to look up and understand he's in the wrong place. He can tell he's an ex-con. It's not just the not-long-out-of-prison look but the way he's shielding his food, like he's afraid someone's going to steal it. There's no danger of that here, especially whilst Gadge is there but the new boy doesn't know that so that's OK. Gadge hopes he's not going to be a problem though, some of the ex-cons think they can play the Big-I-Am when they first get out but they soon get sorted.

Deano's still pissing about with his food so Gadge takes the spoon out of his hand and loads it up with rice pudding.

'Open up,' he says, shoving the spoon towards Deano's mouth.

The kid keeps his lips closed tight and moves his head out of the way like a baby, nearly causing his ridiculous Cossack hat to fall off. The sooner he grows tired of wearing that shit the better as far as Gadge is concerned. Either that or the little bastard can walk a few yards behind him so no one thinks they're together. He tries with the spoon again but Deano resists, pulling his head right back.

'Piss off, I'm not twelve,' he says, laughing.

If he's going to be a baby about it Gadge doesn't mind treating him like one. He starts moving the spoon around and making aeroplane noises.

'Nyooooooooooooooooooom!' He does loop-the-loops with the spoon, almost dropping the rice at one point but he manages to keep it upright. He remembers how good he used to be at the egg-and-spoon race when he was a kid, how disappointed he was when his mam told him it wasn't a proper sport, his dreams of one day winning an Olympic medal disappearing in an instant.

Deano's laughing like a drain which means his guard is down so Gadge goes in for the kill.

'Here comes the aeroplane, coming into land,' he says, bringing the spoon back towards Deano's mouth.

'Open up, now. Nyooooooooooooooooooom!' This time

Deano does as he's told – laughing too much to resist. He opens wide and accepts the food, swallowing it in one go.

'That's better,' Gadge says, handing the spoon over. 'Now eat the rest properly or I'll lamp ya.'

That's when the new guy makes a strange noise, and it takes Gadge a moment to realise that he's laughing. Another thing Gadge doesn't like is people watching him and it's obvious that's what's been going on.

'Think it's funny, do ya?' Gadge says.

Most people would move away at this point, but the new guy doesn't. He just keeps laughing, if that's what that noise really is. He doesn't seem at all fazed by Gadge either, despite the fact that he outweighs the newcomer by at least five stone. Maybe he needs to be taught an early lesson. Gadge is about to upend the table when Deano pats him on the arm.

'Chill out,' he says, quietly. Gadge stares at him for a moment, sees that the kid doesn't want to make a fuss. Maybe he's right. He should give the guy a chance. It's not like he's flush with friends. And he does need someone to step in and look after Deano if his dodgy ticker should run out of batteries. He nods and turns back to laughing boy.

'Aye, fair play to you,' he says. 'It must've looked pretty stupid.' He shuffles along the bench so that he's in front of him. 'New boy, eh?'

The man nods. Gadge points his thumb towards Deano. 'The Twat in the Hat calls himself Deano.' He sticks his hand across the table, waiting for a shake. 'I'm Gadge.'

The new guy stares at him. He'd better not fucking blank

me, Gadge thinks, not after I've offered him an olive branch. He can tell Deano's worried by the way he's holding his breath.

Eventually the man takes his hand and shakes it. He hears Deano exhale. Peace is restored.

'I'm Jimmy,' the man says.

68

Jimmy had done enough digging recently for one lifetime but Dog was happy to pick up the slack. There were no bodies to find this time, just carrots. A growing mound of them standing at the side of the allotment.

'D'you mind him doing that?' Jimmy asked, looking up at Andy Burns, who was leaning on his spade, soaking up a rare burst of sunshine. He looked glad of the rest.

'Not at all, saves me the bother.'

'I never took you for the gardening type,' Jimmy said.

'I'm not, normally, don't even like carrots. The missus does most of this, but with me having a bit of time on me hands lately she's put me to work.'

'She'll be a bit pissed off with me for getting you back in, then?'

'Aye, she was quite enjoying having someone do the hard graft for her.'

Burns sat down on the bench next to Jimmy.

'You don't have to do this, you know,' he said. 'You could tell them to stick it. They'd have brought me back in a couple of weeks anyway. It was just a slap on the wrist, really.'

'I have to be honest – I was expecting a bit more gratitude.'

'Fuck off, man, I am grateful, though I seem to owe you one again which pisses me off no end.' Burns sighed. 'I just think it's going to be dangerous and I don't want to feel responsible if anything happens to you.'

'It was my fault in the first place, so it was only right that I sorted it.'

'You could get hurt.'

'Wouldn't be the first time. Getting hurt is one of my few areas of expertise. I'll put Carrie on standby.'

The cop laughed. 'Handy that you can go private.'

'Cheaper than BUPA as well.'

They sat in silence for a moment watching Dog slowly exhaust himself until he finally gave up and sat at Jimmy's feet.

'Did Hanrahan tell you what it was all about?' Burns asked.

'No. I said I'd only talk to you.'

'I bet he loved that.'

'Not exactly but he had to lump it, didn't he?'

'Connors has moved into trafficking. They think he's bringing in more girls from Eastern Europe any day now and they're hoping to catch him in the act. Trouble is, they don't know when and they don't know where. He runs a tight ship. Bonnie was inside the tent for three months and didn't get a sniff of what was going on. And she's one of the best we've got.'

'Can't really see why I'll succeed where she failed.'

'Nor can I, and Hanrahan knows it's a long shot, but with Bonnie exposed you're all we've got.'

'I'll do what I can. Good job I've got my pen camera handy.'

'You can't use that man; they'll have a fit if they think you've got your own spy equipment. Anyway, I've had a much better idea. Listen up.'

69

Connors' car pulled into a parking bay on the edge of Paddy Freeman's park.

Alex, the tattooed thug, climbed out and saw Jimmy watching from one of the kids' swings. He beckoned him over to the car. Jimmy wondered if they'd replaced Bonnie yet, but, as he approached, he couldn't see anyone else inside the car besides Connors and whoever was driving – the grease monkey from the garage again, no doubt.

Before getting in he looked around the park and sighed. The warmer May weather had brought out the crowds so the chances of someone seeing him with Connors had gone up tenfold. He had no doubts that Sandy would hear about this; she had spies everywhere.

'Get in, the boss wants a word,' Alex grunted.

Jimmy reluctantly moved towards the car but felt a hand on his shoulder.

'Just you. I'll take the mutt for a stroll.'

'You're all right, no need for that,' Jimmy said, pulling

Dog out of the man's reach. Connors was probably worried he'd piss in his car again.

'It wasn't a request. I had to get the interior shampooed the last time the little sod was in there.' The man's grip tightened and shifted onto Jimmy's collarbone, pressing into the nerves there and causing him to sink down on one knee. Alex took the lead out of his hand.

'Just get in, there's a good lad.'

'But—'

'Now.'

Jimmy held his hands up in defeat and Alex let go, moving out of reach just in case Jimmy was mad enough to try and retaliate. He wasn't, though that didn't mean he was happy about leaving Dog behind – far from it.

'Come on, walkies,' Alex said, heading into the main park area.

With little choice, Jimmy climbed into the car. Connors was sitting in his usual place in the rear and, as expected, the mechanic was in the driver's seat.

'You've lost one of your team then,' Jimmy said.

'She's been terminated,' Connors said.

Jimmy almost panicked but then realised it was a rare moment of humour from the gangster, who smiled and added, 'Her employment that is, obviously. Not that I'd tell you if it was the other thing. Otherwise I'd have to terminate you too.'

The driver sniggered.

'Where did you disappear to the other day?' Connors continued.

'I didn't think you'd want me around when it all kicked off.'

'Aye, you were probably right. Leave a note next time, though, eh. I don't like surprises. You said you had some information for me.'

Jimmy had left Connors a phone message earlier, tempting him to come out from whichever rock he'd been hiding under.

'She's a cop. Bonnie, that is.'

'D'you think?' Connors said, with the maximum of sarcasm. 'Never fucking occurred to me. How come you're so well-informed?'

'I told you I was mates with DS Burns, he told me.' He and Burns had cooked up the idea over a drink or two in the Bluebell, a pub just around the corner from the allotment they'd met in. They hoped that telling some truths might gain Jimmy a little bit of trust, even if it was something the man already knew.

'You'll not be mates for much longer if I do decide to top the cow.'

The mechanic snorted again. Jimmy wondered if Connors thought he was actually funny or whether he realised that his crew were too scared of him not to laugh at his shit jokes. Probably the latter – the man may have been a psycho but he wasn't stupid. Jimmy glanced out of the window and, frustratingly, saw Alex talking on his phone while Dog sat patiently, waiting for his promised walk.

'I heard your friend has been released from the nick,' Connors said. 'I'd like to talk to him.' Jimmy waited for him to mention the car chase but he either wasn't there and his men had been afraid to tell him about it or he was pretending it didn't happen to save face. Jimmy didn't care either way. It suited him not to have to explain why they'd taken evasive action.

'Aye, the cops have finally come to their senses. It was obvious he wasn't involved in whatever happened to your man.'

'Men! I've lost two now remember. Three if you count that fucking cuckoo in the nest.'

'Maybe you should put me on the payroll,' Jimmy said. 'I'm available and cheap.'

'But why should I when you're doing so well for nothing? It's like having an intern.' Another snort from the front. It was like a nervous tic. Jimmy was going to slap him if he kept this up.

'So what about this friend of yours? When can I see him?'

Jimmy played for time.

'I'm not sure that's wise. The cops have got him under surveillance. I think they're hoping he'll do something incriminating now he's got a bit of freedom.'

He could see that Connors was trying to decide if he was taking the piss.

'You got anything else for me?' Connors added. 'I heard you were dragged into the cop shop again the other day.' The man obviously had spies everywhere. Another bent copper taking a backhander. Jimmy hoped it wasn't anyone who knew that he was now a double agent.

'I've seen the CCTV footage from the alley. Your men

dragged my friend in there to beat him up. Did you know that's what they were up to?'

'What do you think?' Connors said. 'My men don't brush their teeth unless I say so. Isn't that right, Sloth?'

'Abso-fucking-lutely,' the driver muttered, glancing back. Jimmy was perfectly prepared to believe the man hadn't brushed his teeth in years. Most of the friends in the Pit Stop had better gnashers.

'Was that "clean the streets" campaign your doing then? Was it really scaring customers away from your business?'

Connors laughed. 'What is this, fucking twenty questions? Course it wasn't, not really. One of those homeless twats saw something he shouldn't have – caught us moving some, um, merchandise around. He managed to leg it before we could catch him.'

'So the fake homeless thing was cover for something else?'

'It's not just politicians who can spin a good line, you know – Archie Simons had been whinging for ages about the homeless hanging around outside the bar so I just put the two things together. The nosy bastard had gone to ground so I thought it might help flush him out. That's why they were taking photos – I hoped one of my men might recognise the guy so we could help him forget what he'd seen. Not that they ever did, useless twats. So, aye, the campaign was good cover for them – I mean, some of the lads might have got a little over-zealous but it's not my fault that some other wankers jumped on the bandwagon, started beating people up just because they could.'

'Which was exactly what your two men were doing with Gadge.'

Connors gave him a glare which clearly said, *Don't push your luck.*

'It's like fucking Humpty Dumpty, dipstick. You can't make an omelette without breaking some twat's head open. Some of the boys maybe enjoyed the whole hunt a bit too much. Or maybe they thought it actually was your mate we were looking for and they wanted to ask him a few questions.'

'With a baseball bat?'

'As I understand it the baseball bat was his.'

'I don't think so. Anyway, Gadge never shuts up. If he'd seen something dodgy I'd know about it. It wasn't him you were after.'

'Doesn't really matter now anyway.'

'Why not?'

Connors looked at him suspiciously.

'You got that gadget, Sloth.' He turned back to Jimmy. 'No offence but when you've been bitten once you get a bit iffy about people who ask too many questions.'

The driver reached into the glove compartment and pulled out the tracker that had found Bonnie's device back in the office. He switched it on and thrust it towards Jimmy's chest. Nothing happened. He moved it down towards his crotch. Still nothing.

'You sure that thing's working?' Connors said.

The man had a quick glance at it. 'Aye, pretty sure, light's on. He's clean.'

Connors looked disappointed. 'Could have sworn you were a snitch. I can smell the deceitful fuckers a mile away and you stink of lies.'

'Maybe you've lost your sense of smell, I've heard something's been going around. Maybe that's why you didn't spot Bonnie was a wrong 'un?'

'Don't mention that rat bitch's name to me.'

'Isn't it sinking ships that rats desert?'

'Oh, I'm not sinking, son – in fact you might say I've got some new blood coming in any day now.'

Jimmy hesitated. Was Connors talking about the trafficking? He just needed one more nudge.

'Word on the street is that you're bringing girls in.'

Connors face gave him nothing. The man was probably a mean poker player.

'You shouldn't believe everything you hear. Lot of gobshites out there.'

'Is that why you said it doesn't matter now? That it's too late to stop it?'

Connors laughed. 'Nice try but I'm bored now. Go and do what I'm not paying you for.'

Connors nodded towards the door.

'But—'

'Just fuck off,' the gangster added, giving him a send-off with his hand and pulling out a packet of fags from his pocket. Jimmy took the hint, his neck didn't need any more burns. The conversation was over. He'd got close, but crashed and burned on the final bend.

He looked out of the window and saw that Alex and Dog

hadn't moved. The man was still talking on his phone. Connors didn't look impressed. Jimmy hoped the call was something to do with arrangements for the trafficking because that would mean that Burns' idea to put the bug on Dog, which he thought had misfired, might pay off after all. It was a long shot but maybe, as Burns had joked, they would still get 'a collar from a collar'.

70

Jimmy was getting out of the car when he heard a familiar bark and a lot of shouting. Over by the swings Alex Bolton was being pushed in the chest by a woman. He was trying to stand his ground but she kept on coming at him and he stumbled backwards, hitting his back on the nearby climbing frame. He'd let go of Dog and the animal was doing his usual thing of running around like a headless chicken when things got a little crazy.

Jimmy ran over towards the argument. As he got closer, he realised the woman was Susan Becket. She was relentless. He'd really thought she'd give up her search after she learned the truth about her brother. Had she followed him to the park? He wouldn't put it past her.

Bolton was trying to grab her arms but she shook him off and aimed a boot at his balls. The big man had clearly had enough. He drew back his giant fist and punched her in the face. She dropped like a stone. Jimmy got there just as she hit the ground, out cold.

Bolton was shaking his hand.

'I think I might have broken it,' he said.

'Like her nose,' Jimmy said, crouching down and moving the poor woman into the recovery position. Dog wandered over to study the prone body, licking her face but getting no response.

Behind them, tyres screeched and Jimmy glanced around as Connors' car disappeared down the road. So much for Team Connors. Bolton was on his own.

'Are you going to call an ambulance or what?'

Bolton looked at the phone, which was still in his hand, then shook his head.

'No chance. She'll grass me up to the cops.'

'Couldn't you have been a little gentler?'

'Did you see her? She was mental, kicking and screaming at me. Wouldn't let me get a word in. Accused me of killing her brother. I haven't killed anyone. Don't even know who her brother is.'

'It's Becket. Her brother's Becket.'

'The sleazy twat who tried to sell cheap shit on our territory? The one who walked in front of a bus?'

'Aye.'

'I never touched him.'

'She saw that you'd given evidence at the inquest. Put two and two together.'

'And made six.'

'You can hardly blame her. You just happened to be hanging about, did you?'

Bolton looked a little sheepish. He glanced around to make sure no one was listening.

'The boss just asked me to lean on him.'

'Sounds like you leant on him a bit too heavily.'

'Nah, he was wasted. I was just keeping an eye on him. Unfortunately, there were a couple of cops nearby who realised I'd witnessed the whole thing and took my details down. Had to give evidence. The boss wasn't impressed. Been in his bad books ever since, more or less.'

Susan Becket moaned quietly, beginning to stir.

'Not sure this is going to get you back in his good ones,' Jimmy said. 'You might want to think about getting another job.'

'Already was. He blames me for Bonnie as well. Reckons I should have known. How could I have? We weren't friends, she thought it was funny to tell people that I'm a paedo. And I'm fucking not. And he's the one who hired her.' He looked around again as if worried that Connors could hear him.

'I bet Mr Connors isn't keen on people leaving his "employment".'

'You could say that.'

In the distance a siren blared. Jimmy looked around and saw a small group of parents, keeping their kids away and pointing at Susan Becket.

'I think you'd better make yourself scarce,' he said, guessing that Bolton had no idea there was a hospital just across the road – the man hadn't mentioned it when he suggested calling an ambulance. 'I think they've called the police.'

Bolton looked at the small crowd gathering. The siren was getting louder. He nodded, turned around, and legged it across the field towards Jesmond Dene. As he did an ambulance flashed along the road and turned away from the park and into the hospital entrance.

Susan Becket's eyes were flickering. He was pretty sure she'd be all right. Maybe he should get away too. The blood pouring from her nose was worrying him though. He sighed. Why did these things always happen to him? Luckily, she was all skin and bones. He bent down and picked her up, manoeuvring her over his shoulder and set off towards the hospital across the road, Dog at his heels.

As he moved through the hospital car park people were keeping well out of his way. A man carrying a woman covered in blood didn't look great, he knew that, but he couldn't just leave her lying there.

He went through the main entrance, Dog still close behind, and headed to the empty reception desk, leaving a trail of Susan Becket's blood behind him. She still hadn't come round.

'This woman needs treatment,' he shouted. A receptionist poked her head out of the back office and gaped at the scene in front of her.

'What happened to her?'

'She was punched in the face.'

The woman shied away from him.

'Not by me,' Jimmy added. 'Can you get her some treatment or not?'

'There's no A and E here.'

'There are doctors though, aren't there? Why don't you get one here before she bleeds to death on your desk?'

The woman stared at him for a moment before picking up the phone. She turned her back so he couldn't hear what she was saying. For all he knew she was calling security. He thought about leaving but then had a better idea. He laid Susan Becket down carefully on some nearby seats and called Carrie, hoping she was working. He was in luck.

'To what do I owe this pleasure?' she said.

'I'm at reception with a woman who needs help, can you get down here?'

'On my way.' Carrie never pissed about. It was one of the things that had helped to drag him out of the slump he was in when he met her. She was the living version of actions speak louder than words.

'Is she going to be all right?'

Jimmy turned around. One of the young mothers from the park had followed him over, probably to make sure he wasn't abducting the injured woman.

'I think so.' He raised his voice. 'Provided they can find a fucking doctor in this hospital.'

The receptionist finished her call.

'Did you see what happened?' she asked the young mum.

'Yes. She got into a fight with a big man who punched her in the face and looked like he might do even more damage until this man intervened. The other man then ran off so he' – she pointed at Jimmy – 'picked her up and brought her all the way over here.'

'So he's not the one who hit her?'

'No. Definitely not. If anything he saved her from a beating.'

'Like I told you in the first place. So you can cancel security,' Jimmy said. By the look on her face, he knew he'd guessed right. Behind him the lift doors opened and he turned around to see Carrie walking swiftly towards him.

'What happened to her?' she said.

'A big bad guy punched her in the face, very hard, knocked her out cold. She's been bleeding heavily ever since.'

Carrie turned to the receptionist.

'Page Dr Knights now.'

The receptionist hesitated.

'NOW!' Carrie shouted.

The receptionist flinched but this time she did what she was told. Carrie brushed past Jimmy and knelt down to take a closer look at the injured woman. He moved away to make room.

'You need to get that dog out of here,' the receptionist said. 'It's unhygienic.'

'No bother,' Jimmy said grabbing Dog and taking him outside. He didn't go back.

71

Superintendent Hanrahan had a face like a wet weekend.

Jimmy had been called into the station to hear what they'd got from Dog's undercover mission but it didn't look promising.

'You didn't get anything?' he said.

The senior cop shook his head.

'Nothing. Even though Bolton had his mobile on speakerphone. I thought that was good news for us, particularly after we'd got our techy to tidy up the sound, but then I had to sit through ten minutes of Bolton grovelling while his girlfriend kicked his arse from pillar to post.'

Clearly it didn't matter how big or tough you were, if your girlfriend wasn't happy you got your arse kicked.

'I wouldn't say it was nothing, boss,' Andy Burns said. 'I think we can use it with Jimmy's help.'

'I don't see how.'

'Have a listen, Jimmy, this is the important bit – see what you think.'

Burns hit a switch on the laptop in front of him and Bolton's voice burst out of the speaker.

'I told you I'm busy.'

'I don't care. You're supposed to be taking me to the clinic for my three-month check-up.'

'It's just routine, isn't it? Can't you get the bus?'

'I'm pregnant. I shouldn't be walking about.'

'The boss needs me.'

There was a long silence. Jimmy could almost hear the anger coming down the phone from Bolton's girlfriend.

'Have you told him yet?'

There was a pause. Then the girlfriend spoke again.

'You haven't, have you?'

'Not yet. He's had a, um, difficult few days. It's not a good time.'

'You promised me, Alex. You swore on the life of our unborn child.'

Bolton sighed.

'I have to handle it carefully. The boss has a very short fuse. You can't just hand your notice in. It's not that kind of job, Meg. You know that.'

'You're frightened of him.'

'Everyone's frightened of him. Give me another couple of days and then I'll sort something out.'

'And how many crimes is he going to ask you to commit in those two days? I don't want to bring up my daughter on my own. Or to have to tell her that her daddy's in prison.'

'I'm not going to prison.'

'If you do, I won't be there for you when you come out.'

There was a click as the woman ended the conversation. Bolton was caught between a rock and a hard place, probably why he'd taken out his frustration on poor Susan Becket. Jimmy understood exactly how the man felt. He'd been there many years before and would have chopped his arm off to have been given the opportunity to escape the situation that was coming Bolton's way. Burns was looking at him eagerly. Jimmy nodded.

'We can definitely use this.'

'D'you think Susan Becket will want to press charges?'

'That depends on how far you're willing to stretch the truth,' Jimmy said.

Susan Becket's face was a mess, sporting two black eyes and a large sticking plaster across the bridge of her nose. Jimmy had expected that. The surprise was her smile.

'My hero,' she said, as soon as he got near enough for her to recognise him.

'I wouldn't say that,' he said.

She shook her head, way more animated than he'd seen her before.

'One of the nurses here told me you were the talk of the wards, that you carried me from the park to the hospital to get me some treatment and then demanded they find a doctor when they tried to fob you off.'

Jimmy suspected Carrie's hand in this. If so, she'd really done him a favour, considering what they were about to ask the patient to do.

'It's only across the road.'

'You saved me from some nasty complications. I had a blood clot, a septal haematoma they called it, which was causing me breathing problems. The doctor said if I hadn't had it drained quickly some of the cartilage would have been permanently damaged. So thank you for that.'

She finally noticed Andy Burns standing just behind Jimmy.

'Who's your friend?'

'Detective Sergeant Andy Burns,' the cop said, moving forward. 'I'd like to talk to you about what happened in the park. And what we're going to do about it.'

'I want him prosecuted for assault,' she said, trying to sit up but stopping when the pain got too much.

'Of course,' Burns said. 'But there are other options.'

'How about attempted murder?'

Burns laughed. 'Might be tricky. How about we bring down the man who's probably responsible for your brother's death instead?'

Now Susan Becket did sit up, despite her obvious pain.

'You serious?'

'As a punch in the face,' Burns said. Becket frowned and Jimmy thought she was going to lose it for a moment but then she grinned.

'I like your friend,' she said to Jimmy. 'He can stay.'

Jimmy and Burns had both got the same vibe from Alex Bolton's conversation with his girlfriend. The man would do pretty much anything to avoid going to prison, including, hopefully, spilling the beans on Stevie Connors' trafficking operations. But they'd need leverage. Holding an assault charge over him might do the trick but they had to persuade Susan Becket that Bolton could be promised immunity, or their idea was worthless. They knew he wouldn't say anything without that guarantee.

Jimmy had explained Susan Becket's theory about her brother's death to Burns, leaving out Gadge's involvement and instead inserting the idea that Connors had plied him with dodgy drugs as a punishment for treading on his toes. He once again felt guilty about tricking his friend, but the ends justified the means, didn't they?

'So, will you help me?' Burns asked her.

Susan Becket looked to Jimmy for advice. Carrie must have laid that 'hero' shit on real thick as she seemed to have forgotten that he was the one who led her to Bolton's fists in the first place.

'Can I trust this guy?' she said, nodding at Burns.

'With your life,' Jimmy said.

Jimmy left Burns taking a full statement. His work was done and the police could take it from there. Alex Bolton had already been taken into custody and once they'd got Susan Becket's statement, which would be enough to send him down, Jimmy was convinced the man would fold.

With Gadge out of prison and Connors hopefully on his way in, Jimmy was feeling unusually positive as he made his way out of the hospital. As soon as he was outside his phone bleeped several times: Bev had been trying to reach him. He called her back immediately.

'What's up?' he said, as soon as she answered.

'I need you here,' Bev said.

'What? Why?'

'Just do it, will you.'

'Has something happened to Gadge? Have Connors' men found you? Is there someone in the house?' He imagined someone holding a gun to her head.

'Just get here quickly, please,' she said.

Then the line went dead.

72

Gadge was stretched out on the bed in Bev's spare room. Deano and Jimmy stood on either side, staring at their dead friend.

'I keep expecting him to start snoring,' Deano said, wiping tears from his face.

Bev had found Gadge lying unconscious on the floor in the bathroom and called 999. An ambulance had turned up within minutes, but the paramedics had declared him dead on the spot, a massive heart attack, they reckoned. She hadn't wanted to tell either of them on the phone.

There was a tap on the door. Bev poked her head around.

'The funeral directors are here,' she said.

'Just give us another minute or two,' Jimmy said. She nodded and disappeared again.

'I don't want them to take him,' Deano said.

'I know.'

'What are we going to do without him?'

Jimmy shook his head. 'I have no clue.'

Whoever said three's a crowd had been talking bollocks – it

was the perfect number for them. Nobody talked about the *two* musketeers, did they? Three was the magic number. Two was shit.

'It's good that you got him out of prison before this happened though, isn't it, Jimmy? Imagine if this had happened in there. He'd have been so alone.'

The kid was right, but it was a small mercy.

'I'd be dead if he hadn't saved me from Becket,' Deano said. 'I should have tried harder to help him, shouldn't I? Kept him off the ale.'

Deano looked at Jimmy beseechingly, begging him for some kind of reprieve, which he was happy to provide.

'No one could stop Gadge drinking, not even you, you know that.'

Deano nodded. Of course he did, they'd both tried, but they'd also both known it was like pissing in the wind. The man was a drinker to his boots and always would be. Had been.

Jimmy remembered teasing his friend about taking him to casualty the last time they'd spoken. If only he'd followed through on the idea. He'd had a lifetime of regrets but this one was right up there.

Deano seemed to sense what he was thinking and put his hand on Jimmy's shoulder.

'It's not your fault either, Jimmy,' he said.

There was another tap on the door, it was time to say goodbye.

73

The van doors opened and around a dozen policemen piled out, racing up the garden path towards the house. Jimmy watched them line up on either side of the front door as two of their colleagues approached with a red battering ram.

The door was smashed down within moments and the officers charged into the house. Jimmy wound down the window and heard shouts coming from inside, some from the cops but others undoubtedly from the occupants.

'This shouldn't take long,' Andy Burns said. They'd allowed Jimmy to come on the early-morning raid on the non-negotiable condition that he stayed in the car. The responsibility for making sure he did as he was told was forced on his friend, who was a bit pissed off to have been placed on 'baby-sitting duties'.

'You can join them if you want,' Jimmy said. 'I'll stay right here, I promise.'

'More than my job's worth,' Burns said, nodding towards the pavement, where Superintendent Hanrahan stood watching the house. 'He's not my biggest fan anyway, big mates with the DCI, they'd both love it if I fucked up again.'

Jimmy watched as a small group of women were helped out of the house towards a second van. There were four or five of them, looking shell-shocked and desperately under-dressed except for the coats which had been draped over their shoulders to help keep them warm. The shouting had died down now and once the women were safely driven off the police began to remove the other occupants, some of whom had clearly been dragged out of their beds, seemingly too stunned to put up much of a fight.

The exception was Stevie Connors himself. That was a result none of them had really expected, even though Bolton had told them that Connors sometimes 'tried out the new merchandise himself'. The man obviously didn't take kindly to being firmly held between two heavy-set cops, as they dragged him towards a third van. Despite having his hands cuffed behind his back he was putting up a fight and the two men were struggling to keep hold of him.

Somehow, he managed to trip one of the cops, catching the second cop with a headbutt as the first fell, and immediately sprinting down the street straight towards Jimmy and Burns with one of the cops in hot pursuit. Jimmy saw the cop pull out a Taser and shout a warning, causing Connors to look back. As he did, Jimmy flung open the car door and Connors crashed into it, yelling in pain and careering over a small garden wall onto his back.

As Jimmy got out of the car, the chasing cop pulled up,

holding the Taser in front of him, unsure what he was seeing.

'It's all right,' Burns said, stepping out of the car. 'He's with me.'

Jimmy glanced over the wall to see a mud-covered Connors struggling to get back on his feet. The gangster caught sight of him and did a double take.

'Is this down to you?' he yelled, scrabbling up onto his knees.

Jimmy nodded.

'You're a fucking dead man,' Connors screamed, clambering to his feet and leaping over the small wall. He was about a yard away from Jimmy when the chasing cop tasered the shit out of him and he collapsed in a heap, cracking his head on the wall as he fell.

Jimmy leant down beside the quivering wreck to make sure he could hear him.

'That's for Gadge,' he said.

74

POLICE RAID THWARTS TRAFFICKING GANG

Police have raided three properties in Newcastle as part of an operation to crack down on human trafficking.

Officers from Northumbria police smashed their way into the houses, arresting eight men, including the notorious north-east gangland boss Stevie Connors. The gang are believed to have trafficked slaves from Eastern Europe for sexual exploitation. The police rescued a number of victims who it is suspected were being held captive in the properties.

Superintendent Cormac Hanrahan, who led the operation, said: 'Today's enforcement action was the result of some excellent police work by my team. The investigation isn't over yet, however, but today's action should send a very clear message: trafficking won't be tolerated in the north-east. We will continue to work with partners, nationally and internationally, to identify those involved in slavery and exploitation and to bring them to justice.'

Jimmy put the newspaper down on the library table and stared off into space. It was almost over. Hopefully the attacks on the homeless community would stop now. Stevie Connors' men may not have been responsible for all of them, but they'd cut the head off the beast – the rest of the body would collapse pretty soon.

'Penny for them,' Aoife said. As usual she'd crept up on him unnoticed. She'd make a better investigator than him – though to be fair anyone could have done a better job this time. He was supposed to have cleared Gadge's name, but no one had been charged with the murders of Tommy Benson and Ned Hawley and the man he'd been tasked with clearing, his best friend, was dead.

'You don't want to hear what's in my head at the moment,' he said.

The librarian sat down next to him on the leather sofa and patted his hand.

'I'll miss your friend,' she said.

'You banned him from here twice.'

'I know. And he deserved it. It's a library, you're supposed to be quiet, not go around trying to fart the National Anthem on the Queen's birthday.' She smiled. 'But he didn't half liven things up around here.'

'He livened things up in most places.' It was true. The Pit Stop was a quieter place without Gadge and he'd wager that several of the local drinking dens were more sombre too.

'If it's any consolation no one round here thinks he had anything to do with that man's death in the alley,' she said.

'He didn't.'

'Do you know who did yet?'

Jimmy shook his head. He'd let his friend down big time. Aoife squeezed his hand.

'I'm sure you'll work it out eventually. Did you ever go and see that Professor Sweeney I tracked down?' she said. 'Was she any use?'

'I did, thanks, she was very helpful.'

Or at least she had been. Since Gadge's death Jimmy had been in a slump. He'd barely talked to anyone, despite the best efforts of Kate and Carrie to lift his spirits. But they were getting increasingly excited about their forthcoming wedding and he didn't want to dampen their enthusiasm so was keeping his distance.

Deano was the only one he could bear to spend any time with and that was mainly because the kid didn't want to talk either. Misery loves company, especially if that company is silent. But, now that Aoife had mentioned it, Leanne Sweeney had been silent as well, hadn't she? One minute she'd been desperate to track down her brother, the next not a dicky bird. Even though he'd apparently disappeared off the face of the earth. Jimmy had meant to follow that up but with everything that had happened it had slipped his mind. Or maybe it was just that, with Gadge dead, it had hardly seemed to matter any more that they still didn't know who'd killed those two hired thugs.

Jimmy took a deep breath as the realisation hit home: it still mattered to him.

75

Jimmy was back in his comfort zone: following someone. As always, his naval training kicked in, he knew exactly how to maintain the right distance to enable him to keep the target in his sight without being seen himself. Leanne Sweeney didn't stand a chance of spotting him.

It had taken way too long for the penny to drop. She'd been avoiding him. One minute she's worried about her brother going missing and then, when Adam Sweeney flees from his hidey-hole, she goes quiet. She was either a classic absent-minded professor or she didn't need to talk to Jimmy because she knew fine well where Adam was. Most likely because she was now the one hiding him.

He'd waited outside the university and followed her home – a nice semi in Benton, an unusually leafy area on the edge of the city, not far from her place of work. Once she'd gone inside the house, he realised that the location was a problem. With its wide-open streets, zero hiding places and nobody loitering on the pavements, it was a difficult place to keep tabs on someone without being obvious.

Instead he took a more direct approach, heading through a gate at the side of the house into the back garden. He glanced through the kitchen window and saw her hanging up her coat before heading upstairs. He moved a few yards to his left and stared through the French doors at the back. There was no sign of anyone in the living room either. Maybe he'd got this all wrong. Maybe Adam Sweeney had simply found another place to hide and his sister had just been snowed under at work.

There was a large, wheeled recycling bin to one side and Jimmy thought about climbing on top of it to see if he could get a look through the upstairs window, but it was the kind of place where the neighbours' curtains would twitch and he didn't want anyone to think he was a peeping Tom. The neighbourhood watch would be onto the police in an instant. Instead he hatched a different plan, headed back to the front door and rang the bell.

She opened it immediately.

'Oh, it's you.'

'Thought you'd want to know what I've found out about your brother. You know, the one you reported missing.'

She frowned.

'How did you find out where I live?'

'Didn't I tell you I was an investigator?'

That raised a pale imitation of a smile. 'I'm a bit busy at the moment.'

Jimmy did his usual thing of not replying, knowing she would fill the space. Most people felt uncomfortable with silence.

'I forgot to tell you that he'd, um, contacted me. Said he was OK but had to go away for a bit. Sorry I didn't pass that on.'

'That's great,' Jimmy said. 'I'm delighted he's OK. I guess my work is done.' He turned as if to go but then turned back. 'Any chance I could use your toilet before I head off?'

She hesitated, glancing behind her into the hallway, before stepping outside and pulling the door behind her so he couldn't see into the house.

'I'm sorry, it's a bit embarrassing but I've got someone with me. You know, a man.'

I know that, Jimmy thought, that's why I'm here. A sudden clanking sound interrupted his thoughts. To Leanne Sweeney's surprise he turned and legged it through her side gate again, into the back garden. A man was halfway out of the French doors, no doubt wondering which idiot had put the recycling bin right in front of them.

'Hello, Adam,' Jimmy said.

Adam Sweeney leapt up in the air like he'd been electrocuted and before Jimmy could say anything else, he was brushed aside as Sweeney ran past him towards the side gate. The suddenness of it all took Jimmy by surprise and by the time he'd reacted Sweeney was almost away and gone. The man wasn't quick though, a slight limp hampering him as he ran, no doubt a product of the beating he'd received. By the time Sweeney reached the gate Jimmy was only a yard behind him and when the man stopped to push the gate open Jimmy grabbed his coat and pulled him back.

'Get off me,' Sweeney shouted, throwing his arm back to try and loosen Jimmy's grip.

'Pack it in, man,' Jimmy said. 'I'm here to help you.'

Sweeney continued to struggle, kicking back at Jimmy's ankles, cursing and swearing as he did. Behind him the gate opened. Leanne Sweeney stared at the pair of them as if they were a couple of her badly behaved students.

'Calm down, Adam, he's not one of them, I know him, he's OK.'

Sweeney slowly stopped struggling and Jimmy loosened his grip on the man as they glared at each other, getting their breath back.

'Maybe I should make a brew while you two have a chat,' Leanne Sweeney said.

Jimmy sat opposite Adam Sweeney in the front room while his sister made the tea. The scar that the bouncer at Archie's had mentioned was still visible along the man's jawline.

'That looks nasty,' Jimmy said, indicating Adam's face.

Sweeney ignored him, as stiff as a block of ice, staring towards the door, clearly angry with his sister for insisting that he talk to Jimmy.

'Who did that to you?'

'What's it to you? Who the fuck are you?'

'I'm Jimmy, I'm the guy who tried to help your sister find you.'

'You're that wanker's mate? The man who killed my brother.'

'Except he didn't.'

'Whatever. Are you the one who came to the bunker?'

Jimmy nodded. 'Your friend Stan Walker told me where to find you.'

'I know. Some dodgy copper forced him to, but he tipped me off as soon as he'd told him.'

'I'd guessed that. It was the only thing that explained you not coming back that night and then clearing the place out. I understand why he did it, though. He told me about you getting jumped. Stevie Connors' men, was it? Because of something you saw.'

Sweeney looked surprised. 'How did you know that?'

'Lucky guess, although the fact that you were desperate enough to build an underground bunker helped. You weren't the only one they attacked but I think you might've been the one they went looking for initially. Trouble is, some of his men got a taste for it and started going after anyone on the streets, and then others followed. I've been investigating the attacks.'

Sweeney looked dubious. 'Leanne said that's what you did. You don't look much like an investigator.'

'That's my superpower,' Jimmy said. 'I pretend to be an arsehole. Fools them every time.'

Sweeney laughed, maybe he was thawing out a little. Jimmy applied a bit more heat.

'You did see something, didn't you? Something to do with Connors.'

Sweeney nodded. 'I was living on the streets. I'd spent everything I had getting back over here from Australia. Thought I could just pick up some work when I got here but it was more difficult than I'd expected. I couldn't stay with Leanne because she might have guessed what I'd come back to do. I wanted to keep her out of it.'

'You came back to get some kind of revenge on my friend.'

'He fucked up my life. My family was never the same again. My brother was dead, my sister estranged and my dad never recovered. I knew Leanne would try and talk me out of it.'

'What stopped you?'

'I couldn't find him at first. Keith Kane seemed to have disappeared off the face of the earth. Then one night, when I was crashed out in the garden shed of an empty house, I heard a woman scream. I came out and saw these men unloading some girls from a van in the back lane and dragging them into a house. One of them saw me watching but they had their hands full with the girls so I managed to get away before they could do anything.'

'And you didn't tell the police?'

Sweeney looked a little shamefaced.

'I was scared. And I didn't think anyone would believe me.'

Jimmy could only nod. It was easy to judge but he remembered when he'd tried to tell the police he'd seen a crime a few years previously. It was like repeatedly headbutting a brick wall.

'I don't think you need to be afraid any more.'

'Easy for you to say.'

'Both of the men I think attacked you are dead.'

'Really? What happened to the second one?'

Jimmy knew he was on the right track, Sweeney didn't ask about the first guy; he already knew how Tommy Benson had met his fate.

'He was found dead in his house a few days back. Beaten to death with a wrench.'

'Serves him right. Vicious bastard.'

'And Stevie Connors has been arrested.'

'Who's he?'

'The guy behind the trafficking. The one who set his attack dogs on you.'

'He's locked up?'

'Don't you read the news?'

Sweeney shook his head. 'Why would I? I don't much care what's going on in the outside world.'

'You care about justice though, don't you? That's why you came halfway across the world, wasn't it? To try and get justice for your brother.'

Leanne Sweeney walked into the room with a tray of tea, clearly hearing the last bit of the conversation. She put the tray on the table and sat down, turning to Jimmy.

'I told Adam what you told me about your friend's wife driving the car.'

'Was that the truth?' her brother said.

'Gospel.'

'But you're his friend, aren't you? Why should I believe you?'

Jimmy bowed his head for a moment then looked back up at Sweeney.

'You don't have to. But it won't make any difference to him. Sadly, he's dead as well.'

Both brother and sister looked shocked to hear that.

'Was he murdered too?' Adam Sweeney said.

'No. Heart attack.'

'I'm sorry to hear that,' Leanne Sweeney said. Adam frowned but didn't say anything.

'Thank you. I know what you think, Adam, and Gadge was no angel, but I'm as confident as I can be that he wasn't driving the car that hit your brother. I understand that's difficult to accept when you've dwelt on it for so long, but the truth is important, don't you think?'

Eventually Sweeney nodded, and he looked up at his sister.

'You believe him, don't you?'

Leanne Sweeney nodded. 'He's always been honest with me.'

Adam Sweeney turned his attention to Jimmy. 'It wasn't me who killed that guy in the alley.'

'I know that.'

'But it wasn't your friend either. I don't know what to believe about Dennis's death, but I do know the truth about that.'

Jimmy exhaled heavily. Although he'd always known it to be true it was something else to hear it said out loud by someone he was convinced had been there.

'Don't get me wrong, I'd imagined hurting them. They really worked me over. After I got out of hospital and was more or less recovered, I started watching them from a distance – they didn't exactly hide away – planning another ridiculous revenge attack. Truth be told, they'd probably have kicked the shit out of me again. I followed them to that pub on the night it all kicked off when I saw your friend asleep on the bench outside the bar. I recognised him immediately from the pictures in the press that my mum kept, even though he'd changed so much. I guess when you've obsessed about someone for so long his image is imprinted on your brain.'

'Did you speak to him?'

'No, not really. I knew he wouldn't have a clue who I was, so I went and sat next to him, hoping to strike up a conversation, but he was comatose, completely shit-faced. I realised I'd built him up into some kind of devil figure and he wasn't, just a bit of a saddo, really, another man hiding behind the drink, just like me. I went into the bar for a quick half but it was crowded and there was no sign of those two wankers so I left. I was just walking away when I saw the pair of them grab your friend from the bench. He was still out of it. There's no chance he got the better of those two.'

'But you know who did?'

'I think so, yes.'

The silence that followed seemed endless. But it wasn't.

76

The house was covered in streamers and balloons, one of which was a large number five. There was a paddling pool and a small, semi-inflated bouncy castle on the lawn. Near the front door a little girl was sitting on her daddy's shoulders with her hands over his eyes.

'Forward,' she said. The man did as he was told.

'Stop. Turn right.' Again, he obeyed.

'Forward again.'

The man followed his orders to the letter, stopping just in front of the paddling pool. The girl sniggered.

'One more step.'

'I hope you're not making me do something silly,' the man said.

The girl shook her head but couldn't control the snorts of laughter without removing her hands from her dad's eyes and she clearly didn't want to do that.

Suddenly she stopped laughing. She'd seen Jimmy standing at the small garden gate, next to the For Sale sign, watching them.

'Daddy?'

'What is it, Rosa?'

'There's a man with a doggy.'

The father pulled his daughter's hands away from his eyes, saw Jimmy standing there and slowly crouched down so she could get off his shoulders.

'Just pop inside a minute, would you, love, see if your mum needs a hand with the party food.'

'OK,' the girl said happily, running around the back of the house and out of sight.

'She's a sweetheart,' Jimmy said.

'I know,' Che Kennedy said. 'Well mostly, anyway.'

'You just got the one?'

The man shook his head. 'Little boy as well, just turned two. D'you want to sit down?' he added, nodding towards two camping chairs set up near the bouncy castle.

'Why not?' Jimmy said, moving across the lawn.

The man was surprisingly calm, as if he'd been preparing for this moment.

'I could probably find a beer somewhere.'

'Don't drink,' Jimmy said as they both sat down, Dog immediately settling under his chair. Kennedy looked surprised about the drinking but didn't pursue it.

'You come to make a citizen's arrest?'

Jimmy shook his head, though he wasn't sure why he'd come. Why he hadn't just told Andy Burns what he knew. To join the dots, maybe? He'd always liked answers.

'Pretty sure that's not a thing.'

'Thought you were an investigator? Shouldn't you know the law?'

'Part-time. Different rules apply.'

Kennedy smiled. 'You just made that up, didn't you?'

'Story of my life,' Jimmy said. 'I've been making it up as I go along for years.'

'You and me both.'

Jimmy had warmed to the man on their first meeting and, if he was being honest, he hadn't really changed his mind, despite what Adam Sweeney had told him. Maybe because he'd just lost a friend, he was searching for another one. It wasn't like he was over-blessed in that department. Under the circumstances it wasn't going to happen but a man could dream.

'Why did you do it?' he said.

Kennedy's expression changed, more resignation than fear.

'Would you believe me if I said it was an accident?' Jimmy waited him out, knowing from experience that the man would continue. Everyone has a story to tell eventually.

'I knew what those two clowns had been doing,' he said. 'You hear stuff, working on the doors. And they weren't exactly subtle about it. What can I say? I've never liked bullies.'

'You saw them drag Gadge into the alley?'

'Yes. Poor man was out of it. I knew he was going to get the shit kicked out of him. There was no way he could defend himself.'

'So you intervened?'

'Aye. Thought I could just stop them but that stupid prick Benson went for me. It was a piece of piss getting the bat off of him. If he'd just legged it everything would have been fine but he tried to play Bertie Big Bollocks instead. Didn't mean to hit him so hard. Man may have been thick but his skull wasn't.'

'And Hawley?'

'He had the good sense to run off. It was only later he got stupid.'

'So you thought you'd make my friend a scapegoat.'

Kennedy put his head in his hands.

'Bit of a spur of the moment thing. Benson fell on to your mate, covered him in blood. Seemed the obvious move.'

'Blame the drunken homeless guy.'

'Not my finest moment but I was desperate.'

'You know he's dead now?'

'Your friend from the alley?'

Jimmy nodded.

'I didn't. I'm sorry. I guess that means it was all a waste of time. I could have just let them get on with it.' Kennedy shook his head and sighed. 'I'm not cut out for this shit. How did you work it out, anyway?'

Jimmy had decided not to mention Adam Sweeney by name. He was pretty sure that Kennedy wouldn't go after him but – aside from petty revenge for Sweeney not speaking up about what he'd seen – there was no point painting a target on the man's back. And he had something else up his sleeve that had been nagging away at him since he'd watched the tapes in Charlie Gascoigne's office.

'The CCTV.'

'There was no CCTV. I turned it off before I confronted them. Didn't want anything on the record. Connors wouldn't have been happy with me fighting his boys. I only turned it back on when it was all over.'

'Aye, that was the problem. You weren't on the screen. Every time I saw you at work you never left the door. When I watched the CCTV back you weren't there when it cut off or when it came back on again. I reckoned you must have been the one who was playing about with it.'

'See, you're not bad at the investigating thing.'

'I have my moments. Plus there was a witness.'

'Other than Hawley? Care to name him?'

'I don't think so. I saw what you did to Hawley.'

Kennedy looked puzzled.

'That was nothing to do with me.'

He looked sincere but Jimmy had another card he hadn't yet played.

'I saw you, running away from his house after he was killed. I was on a bus and I didn't register it fully at the time but now I'm pretty sure it was you.'

Kennedy held his hands up but shook his head at the same time.

'You're right, but you're wrong as well. I assumed Hawley would go straight to Connors when he legged it that night. I sent the family away to the in-laws and was getting ready to do a runner, even put the house up for sale. But Hawley wanted out as well, so he decided to try and blackmail me instead; to get some running-away money, money that I don't have. And even if I did, I wouldn't have given it to that toerag.'

'Sounds like a motive for murder to me.'

'Don't think it didn't occur to me. I tried everything to reason with him, but he wouldn't let it go, said he'd go to the cops instead. I've got two young kids. I didn't want them to grow up with a lifer for a dad.'

Jimmy winced. Been there, done that. Alex Bolton had said almost exactly the same thing recently.

'In the end I decided to pay him something, just a small amount to see if he'd leave it, but when I got to the house I found him dead and legged it.'

'Pretty convenient for you.'

'I know how it sounds but why would I lie about that and admit the first one?'

It was a fair point and Jimmy saw nothing that made him think the man was lying. But if it wasn't Kennedy who killed Hawley then he was all out of suspects. Young Aaron had been released and there was no one else in the frame.

The bouncer shook his head and got to his feet. 'Believe me or don't, not much I can do about it, but Rosa's pals are going to be here soon; I have to finish pumping this castle up. Probably best if you're not here when they arrive.'

'No problem,' Jimmy said. 'I've got a funeral to go to this afternoon.'

'And then what?' Kennedy said.

Jimmy was about to answer when the little girl, Rosa, reappeared, walking very carefully, carrying a plate with two iced buns on it. Dog raised his head, sensing food in the offing, but she headed over to her dad first.

'Mum thought your friend might be hungry.'

'Why don't you ask him?' Kennedy said.

She glanced at Jimmy and then back at her dad.

'He won't bite.'

The girl looked back at Jimmy who gnashed his teeth together which made her jump.

'He might!' she said, giggling.

77

Jimmy headed back to the hostel to get changed for Gadge's funeral feeling like he'd finished a jigsaw only to discover one of the most important pieces was missing.

He was halfway there when Kate rang.

'I'm just heading over to Debra Mason's place,' she said. 'Apparently, it's all kicking off there, we've had several calls from the neighbours about a screaming match. Thought you might want to join me?'

Jimmy checked the time. He had about an hour to spare and it wasn't that far away.

'I'll see you there,' he said.

The main door of the flats was being held open by the caretaker.

'Are you Kate's dad?' he said. 'She's trying to get into the flat now. The police are on their way.'

Jimmy didn't stop to ask questions and ignored the lift, running straight for the stairs and haring up to the fifth floor where he could hear his daughter shouting and knocking on the door.

'What's happened?' he said, as he reached her side. He could hear something banging inside the flat.

'The neighbours heard a lot of shouting and a crash, like something heavy had been thrown against the wall. The woman next door said Debra Mason screamed at someone to stop. She thinks her son is in there. Reckoned he'd moved back in recently.'

'Shall I try and talk to him?' he said.

'May as well. I'm getting nowhere.'

Jimmy banged loudly on the door.

'Aaron! It's Jimmy, from the hostel, let me in, will you?'

No answer but the noises inside the flat stopped.

He tried again. 'Can I speak to your mum, Aaron? Just to make sure she's all right.'

'Fuck off and leave us alone!' the kid screamed.

'We'll do that if you let us speak to your mum?'

'She's asleep.'

'Can you go and wake her up then?'

The banging inside started up again. Jimmy heard something splinter, a door maybe? He turned to Kate.

'I think we should go in.'

She looked alarmed.

'The police are on their way. Maybe we should leave it to them?'

'What if Debra Mason's injured? I saw Ned Hawley's body. It wasn't pretty. If Aaron did that then . . .' He let the thought hang in the air, stepping back to examine the front door more closely. It looked similar to the one he'd kicked down in the other hostel, when he broke into Adam Sweeney's old room.

Kate read his intentions and put her hand on his arm.

'There's no need for that. I've got a master key from the caretaker.'

Jimmy held his hand out.

'No chance,' she said. 'If you're going in, I'm coming with you.'

Jimmy closed his eyes. Bev was going to kill him when she heard about this.

They went in.

There was a trail of broken glass in the entrance but no sign of Aaron or his mother. While Kate checked the small kitchen on the left, Jimmy went into the lounge. It was empty though a small table was lying on its side and a lamp was in bits in the corner of the room – a large dent in the wall above it told its own story. The door to the main bedroom was closed but badly damaged. There were boot prints all over it and two large holes in the top half. A dining chair was on the floor with one of its legs snapped off. Jimmy had no doubt that someone had tried to use the chair to smash through into the bedroom.

He tried the door but it was locked.

'Debra, are you in there? It's Jimmy, from the hostel.'

No answer.

'Are you OK?'

Kate came into the room, gasping at the damage.

'Jesus!'

Suddenly a noise from behind the bedroom door, then a voice. 'Have you . . . what . . . where's Aaron?' Debra Mason sounded broken, her words forced out.

'I don't know, but you're safe now,' Jimmy said.

She mumbled something that he couldn't quite make out. Or at least he hoped he hadn't. He leaned in closer.

'Say again.'

'He killed Ned,' she whispered.

A door opened somewhere. Jimmy turned around. The noise came from the other room leading off from the lounge. Aaron's bedroom? He nodded to Kate to talk to Debra Mason while he checked it out. He tried the door, not locked but something heavy behind it. Jimmy put his shoulder against the door and pushed, it shifted a fraction. He doubled his effort and it moved further, the chest of drawers behind it edging back enough for him to squeeze into the room.

Aaron was standing on a small balcony leaning back against the rail.

'Stay there,' the kid shouted.

Jimmy held his hands up.

'No problem, I won't move.'

Behind him he could hear Kate making soothing noises through the other bedroom door. At least she had some training for this kind of situation; he was flying by the seat of his pants and hoping no one got hurt. If he could keep the kid talking until the police came maybe they could sort it.

'What's going on, Aaron?' he said.

The kid glanced behind him. Jimmy didn't need to look.

It was a long way down. He took the chance to edge a few inches nearer. Aaron didn't seem to notice.

'Why don't you come back inside the room?' Jimmy said. 'We can talk. Maybe I can help.'

'Aye right. You promised to help me before, remember. Too fucking late now.'

'It's never too late.'

'What would you know?'

'I've been there. I killed someone once.'

Aaron looked puzzled. Jimmy was surprised Deano hadn't mentioned it but maybe the kid knew how to keep a secret after all. He took the chance to edge closer to the balcony.

'You're lying.'

'You don't lie about stuff like that.'

'Did he deserve it?'

It was a question Jimmy had asked himself many times since then. He still didn't know the answer. In the distance he could hear a siren getting closer.

'Not really my call to make.'

'Whose then? God's?' The kid looked behind again, and again Jimmy shuffled forward.

'I don't think either of us believes that.'

'Mam does. She thinks I'm evil.'

'I doubt that.'

'She said so.'

'We all say stuff we don't mean.'

'She meant it all right,' the kid said. Behind him a police car turned into the car park and skidded to a halt. Two cops jumped out of the car and ran towards the block.

Aaron put one leg over the balcony rail. Jimmy moved forward but the kid screamed at him.

'Keep away or I'll jump!'

'Looks like you're going to jump anyway.'

The kid glanced down again. 'Best for everyone, probably.'

'Why did you do it?' Jimmy asked.

The kid shrugged. 'Why not? It was me or him, I reckon.'

Jimmy heard a door open behind him and glanced back through the doorway. Kate had talked Debra Mason into coming out. The woman had a cut on her forehead and was holding her arm close to her side as if it was broken. She caught Jimmy staring at her and hobbled across towards him.

When Jimmy turned back, Aaron had put his other leg over the rail and was now standing on the drop side. He looked scared but determined.

Debra Mason made her way slowly into the room. She let out a sob when she saw Aaron.

'Don't,' she said quietly.

'I'm sorry, Mum,' the kid said and let go of the rail. Debra Mason screamed.

Jimmy leapt forward, grabbing for Aaron's arm. He missed but managed to get a hold on the kid's leather jacket, nearly wrenching his shoulder from its socket as he did. His stomach hit the balcony rail, his chest and shoulders pitching over the edge but he held on to Aaron, who now dangled in mid-air, some sixty feet above the ground. It was unlikely he'd survive the drop and even if he did he'd probably be crippled for life. Jimmy managed to grab the kid's arm with his other hand. Debra Mason and Kate were now holding on to Jimmy, making sure he didn't get dragged over the balcony himself.

Aaron stared at him, begging for release.

'Let me go,' he shouted.

'No!' his mum screamed.

'I poisoned Dog,' the kid yelled, flailing at Jimmy's arms to break his hold. 'And set you up with that photo,' he screamed, desperately trying to press Jimmy's buttons.

It would be so easy to just open his hand, Jimmy thought. It was starting to cramp up anyway, the pain surging through his palm into his fingers. No one would blame him if he let go. The kid clearly wanted to die. Why not let him? Would anyone really care?

The answer came to him quickly. He would. He firmed up his grip.

Behind him Jimmy heard loud footsteps charging through the flat. A hefty uniformed cop suddenly appeared on his right, managing to grab Aaron's armpit, then a second appeared on the other side and did the same. The kid was kicking and screaming but it was no use. Between the three of them they dragged him back up and over the rail onto the balcony. The second he hit the ground all the fight went out of him and the first cop snapped on some handcuffs without resistance.

It was over.

78

Jimmy and Kate made it to Gadge's funeral by the skin of their teeth. The cops had insisted on them giving statements so neither had time to get changed. Jimmy knew Gadge wouldn't give a fuck what they were wearing. His best friend was dead and no smart suit would change that.

Deano had chosen 'You'll Never Walk Alone' to end the service. The kid reckoned that, despite his generally pessimistic outlook, their friend always had 'hope in his heart'. As the coffin disappeared, Jimmy imagined Gadge banging on the inside of the lid, shouting, 'I'm not a fucking Scouser.'

The celebrant did a good job, managing to steer as far away from religion as she could, which Jimmy had told her was a deal-breaker. Gadge was more a 'burn the churches to the ground' kind of guy than an atheist. Instead she praised his team spirit, talking about how he always looked after the younger kids on the street, how he used his computer skills to help people out with their benefit claims. How he'd saved Deano.

It was a great turnout for someone who lived on the margins, around forty people, Jimmy reckoned. Bev and Carrie were there, and Andy Burns sat next to Aoife from the library, who Jimmy knew had a soft spot for his friend. She'd deny it, obviously, but you could always tell. Loads of the volunteers from the Pit Stop had turned up as well and quite a few of the 'friends'. As the celebrant had said, Gadge had helped a lot of them out, so it was the least they could do.

The three musketeers had been to a Public Health funeral – one where the council had to pay for it – for Deano's brother a couple of years earlier which had been so depressing that Jimmy had vowed not to let that happen to any of his friends. It had cost him a few bob and meant that his contribution to Kate and Carrie's wedding – only a few weeks away now – was pretty much non-existent but they didn't mind. They'd told him in no uncertain terms that they didn't want his money anyway – something about not taking handouts from the patriarchy. Whoever they were, Jimmy was pretty sure they wouldn't want him as a member.

They went back to Rosie's Bar afterwards, it was Gadge's favourite watering hole, probably because it was the nearest pub to the Pit Stop so it saved him wasting valuable drinking time on other things, like walking.

Jimmy could tell that Burns wanted a word with him, but

he did his best to avoid the conversation as he was pretty sure he knew what his friend wanted to talk about. However, it was a small bar and it was inevitable that he'd get cornered at some point.

'Quick word,' Burns said, pulling him over to an empty spot around the back of the bar. 'I heard about what happened with the Mason kid. Sounds like we got there just in time?'

Jimmy just nodded. He was too tired to offer much of an explanation. Burns would find out the details soon enough.

'They were coming out to get him anyway, you know. His DNA was all over Ned Hawley's body and the ratchet. It's pretty much a slam-dunk case.'

Another wasted life. There had been so many, including his, he thought. But then he heard Kate laughing in the background and realised that was bollocks. Despite everything, he was doing OK. Unlike poor Gadge.

'What about Tommy Benson?' he said. 'Have they got any closer to solving that?'

'It's not great news, I'm afraid,' the cop said. 'They're closing the case.'

'So they still think Gadge did it?'

'I guess,' Burns said. 'Or at least they don't have any other suspects.'

But Jimmy did. He closed his eyes. It was the moment of truth. Was he happy that his friend's name was tarnished by this? No, obviously not. On the other hand, he didn't give a fuck about Benson's death. The man was a vicious bastard with a long history of violence who took pleasure in beating up the homeless. So was he willing to tear a family apart just for his friend to get a posthumous pardon? He hadn't really had a decent mantra since 'Not My Fight' went past its sell-by date but he'd developed a new one for moral problems like this that he suspected he'd be using for the rest of his life: *What would Gadge do*?'

'Of course, if you've got any information that you haven't coughed up yet, things might be different,' Burns said, giving him a knowing glance.

Now or never. A series of images flashed through Jimmy's head. His attempt to stop a man beating up his girlfriend which ended with Jimmy kicking the shit out of him. A subsequent prison fight where he stopped a psychopath from killing a prison nurse and ended up with more jail time. He'd spent way too much of his life in a cell and he wouldn't wish that on anyone. It was said that no good deed goes unpunished but maybe that didn't always have to be true.

'Well?' Burns said.

Jimmy shook his head. 'I've got nothing.'

Burns laughed. 'So much for the much-vaunted Sherlock Homeless! Does this mean you're going to hang up your deerstalker and magnifying glass? That you're never going to get in my hair again?'

Jimmy glanced across at the people who had come back to the pub after the funeral. Some of the hostel staff had now joined them. It was the kind of thing he'd imagined for years but never thought would happen. He had friends, family and a job. A kind of normality. Maybe it could stay that way now? Then he remembered one of Gadge's favourite mottos: Shit Happens. He turned back to Burns.

'Never say never,' Jimmy said.

Newport Community
Learning & Libraries

ACKNOWLEDGEMENTS

Three – that's the magic number according to De La Soul. And Jimmy clearly agrees with them. As he has mentioned once or twice, nobody talks about the two musketeers!

After being convinced, back in the day, that *The Man on the Street* wasn't a standalone I eventually worked out a way to make it a trilogy. After learning of Jimmy's back story in *The Man on the Street*, we would find out more about Deano's life in *One Way Street* and learn of Gadge's torrid history in this book, eventually titled *Dead End Street* (or it was when I wrote this – check the cover, it may have been changed due to some last-minute sales dictum!).

Partly inspired by *Fawlty Towers* and *The Office* I'm holding to the notion that it's better to leave people wanting more than to outstay your welcome (yes, I'm talking to the creators of *Lost* here) so in the words of Porky Pig from Looney Tunes 'That's All Folks.'

I thought that my wonderful editor Jane Wood might push me for a fourth Jimmy book, but, as always, she has allowed me to go with my instincts and supported me all the way – even waiving the need to see a synopsis for my new standalone. (For the record a synopsis is the work of the devil and anyone who says different is wrong.) The rest of the Quercus team, in particular Ella Patel, Lipfon Tang and Florence Hare have always had my back too. Thanks also to my copy editor Liz Hatherell, who yet again had a much better grasp of dates and ages than I did, and to Joe Mills for the superb cover design.

Another shout out to my brilliant agent, Oli Munson, who kept the faith from the beginning when others wilted. Everything that has happened since is down to him (though I'm keeping the trophies.)

The Man on the Street was developed on the Crime Fiction MA at UEA where I had a huge amount of help from my tutors and fellow students. Thankfully, two of the latter have remained on hand for *Dead End Street*, offering reading, feedback and a kick up the arse when needed, so, yet again, massive thanks to Harriet Tyce and Kate Simants, brilliant writers but far more importantly, great friends.

There are so many others who have continued to help. My small but select Newcastle writing group, who offer considered, constructive criticism on my latest offerings have kept me going when the Muse has deserted me. Many thanks to Simon Van der Velde, John Hickman, Karon Alderman and Ben Appleby-Dean. I must also mention my fellow Northern Crime Syndicate writers, Robert Scragg, Rob Parker, Judith O'Reilly, Adam Peacock, and Chris McGeorge. Oh yes, and Fiona Erskine (gotcha!), whose late arrival on the scene meant she was omitted from the original acknowledgements of *One Way Street* and has never let me forget it.

Yet more support has come from my fellow Debut 20 authors. Originally a Facebook Group, that posse of virtual lockdown friends from every genre have inevitably become real-life pals. Our first actual meet-up, appropriately at Harrogate Crime Festival, was a delight.

A huge cheer too for all the readers, bloggers, reviewers and friends who have supported the books to date. The word of mouth has been fantastic for this series and a big factor in its success. I owe you all a pint.

I mustn't forget the experts that contributed so much to *Dead End Street*. My great friend and fellow Mallards CC cricketer Gareth Taylor freely passed on his knowledge and somewhat scathing views of investment bankers, complete with the obvious rhyming slang.

Nick Edwards, from the Veterinary Poisons Information Service gave up his time to answer all of my inane questions about animal poisoning, its effects and the processes that can be followed to investigate it.

I did have some inside information about the work of an Anti-Social Behaviour Unit but have been sworn to secrecy by my source. However, that knowledge was built upon by reading the quite brilliant *Anti-Social* by Nick Pettigrew, a hilarious, disturbing and deeply political book that I urge you to read. If you liked *This Is Going To Hurt* then you'll love it.

I have been ordered to say another thank you to my drinking buddy, former Detective Superintendent Tony

Hutchinson for his advice on all police matters. And I always do what he tells me. As per, any mistakes are mine, any deviations from the norm in service of the story.

Two elements of *Dead End Street* were inspired by real life. Adam Sweeney's hidey-hole was loosely based on the incredible story of Dominic Van Allen which I first read about in this terrific, old-school piece of journalism from Tom Lamont in the Guardian https://www.theguardian.com/news/2020/mar/05/invisible-city-how-homeless-man-built-life-underground-bunker-hampstead-heath and Gadge's iPod backstory and real name is a nod to the early, visionary work of Kane Kramer, which I first discovered in this article from Wired https://www.wired.com/2008/09/briton-invented/.

I'm also incredibly grateful to the uber-talented Louisa Roach, from She Drew The Gun for giving me permission to quote some lines from her wonderful song 'Poem' for the epigraph of this book. If you haven't seen the band then do whatever it takes to change that – they're the best new band I've seen in years and I've seen a lot.

A big shout out also to Phill Johnson, my IT guru, who tolerates my total ignorance of how things work and fixes all my problems in a heartbeat, thus saving me an immense amount of wasted time (at very reasonable rates).

Two charities to mention. I invented my friendly vet, who looks after homeless pets for free, but subsequently discovered the existence of Street Paws, a charity that does this for real. If you're looking for a cause to support then look no further: www.streetpaws.co.uk/north-east. I must also again mention the inspiration for the fictional Pit Stop.

The People's Kitchen in Newcastle is a fantastic organisation which provides essential comfort to the homeless and disadvantaged. Entirely funded by donations, its unpaid staff provide food, clothes and support to hundreds of people every day. I am honoured to volunteer there for an afternoon a week. If you have the means to help them, whether financially or with your time please try to. For more information see www.peopleskitchen.co.uk.

Last, but obviously best, my everlasting gratitude to my wonderful family, Pam, Becca and the furry boys Dexter and Leo who all combine to keep me sane. Ok, saner.